ALSO BY KAREN RUSSELL

St. Lucy's Home for Girls Raised by Wolves

SWAMPLANDIA!

KAREN RUSSELL

SWAMPLANDIA!

ALFRED A. KNOPF
NEW YORK

THIS IS A BORZOI BOOK
PUBLISHED BY ALFRED A. KNOPF

Knopf, Borzoi Books, and the colophon are registered trademarks of
Random House, Inc.

A portion of this work was originally published in *The New Yorker.*

ISBN 978-1-61129-944-6

Jacket image by Luther Daniels Bradley © Blue Lantern Studio / Corbis
Jacket design by Carol Devine Carson

Manufactured in the United States of America

For my family

"I see nobody on the road," said Alice.

"I only wish that *I* had such eyes," the King remarked in a fretful tone. "To be able to see Nobody! And at that distance too! Why, it's as much as *I* can do to see real people, by this light!"

—Lewis Carroll, *Through the Looking-Glass*

SWAMPLANDIA!

CHAPTER ONE

The Beginning of the End

O ur mother performed in starlight. Whose innovation this was I never discovered. Probably it was Chief Bigtree's idea, and it was a good one—to blank the follow spot and let a sharp moon cut across the sky, unchaperoned; to kill the microphone; to leave the stage lights' tin eyelids scrolled and give the tourists in the stands a chance to enjoy the darkness of our island; to encourage the whole stadium to gulp air along with Swamplandia!'s star performer, the world-famous alligator wrestler Hilola Bigtree. Four times a week, our mother climbed the ladder above the Gator Pit in a green two-piece bathing suit and stood on the edge of the diving board, breathing. If it was windy, her long hair flew around her face, but the rest of her stayed motionless. Nights in the swamp were dark and star-lepered—our island was thirty-odd miles off the grid of mainland lights—and although your naked eye could easily find the ball of Venus and the sapphire hairs of the Pleiades, our mother's body was just lines, a smudge against the palm trees.

Somewhere directly below Hilola Bigtree, dozens of alligators pushed their icicle overbites and the awesome diamonds of their heads through over three hundred thousand gallons of filtered water. The deep end—the black cone where Mom dove—was twenty-seven feet; at its shallowest point, the water tapered to four inches of muck that lapped at coppery sand. A small spoil island rose out of the center of the Pit, a quarter acre of dredged limestone; during the day, thirty gators at a time crawled into a living mountain on the rocks to sun themselves.

The stadium that housed the Gator Pit seated 265 tourists. Eight tiered rows ringed the watery pen; a seat near the front put you at eye level with our gators. My older sister, Osceola, and I watched our mother's show from the stands. When Ossie leaned forward, I leaned with her.

At the entrance to the Gator Pit, our father—the Chief—had nailed up a crate-board sign: YOU WATCHERS IN THE FIRST FOUR ROWS <u>GUARANTEED</u> TO GET WET! Just below this, our mother had added, in her small, livid lettering: ANY BODY <u>COULD</u> GET HURT.

The tourists moved springily from buttock to buttock in the stands, slapping at the ubiquitous mosquitoes, unsticking their khaki shorts and their printed department-store skirts from their sweating thighs. They shushed and crushed against and cursed at one another; couples curled their pale legs together like eels, beer spilled, and kids wept. At last, the Chief cued up the music. Trumpets tooted from our big, old-fashioned speakers, and the huge unseeing eye of the follow spot twisted through the palm fronds until it found Hilola. Just like that she ceased to be our mother. Fame settled on her like a film— "Hilola Bigtree, ladies and gentlemen!" my dad shouted into the microphone. Her shoulder blades pinched back like wings before she dove.

The lake was planked with great gray and black bodies. Hilola Bigtree had to hit the water with perfect precision, making incremental adjustments midair to avoid the gators. The Chief's follow spot cast a light like a rime of ice onto the murk, and Mom swam inside this circle across the entire length of the lake. People screamed and pointed whenever an alligator swam into the spotlight with her, a plump and switching tail cutting suddenly into its margarine wavelengths, the spade of a monster's face jawing up at her side. Our mother swam blissfully on, brushing at the spotlight's perimeter as if she were testing the gate of a floating corral.

Like black silk, the water bunched and wrinkled. Her arms rowed hard; you could hear her breaststrokes ripping at the water, her gasps for air. Now and then a pair of coal-red eyes snagged at the white net of the spotlight as the Chief rolled it over the Pit. Three long minutes passed, then four, and at last she gasped mightily and grasped the ladder rails on the eastern side of the stage. We all exhaled with her. Our stage wasn't much, just a simple cypress board on six-foot stilts, suspended over the Gator Pit. She climbed out of the lake. Her trembling arms folded over the dimple of her belly button; she spat water, gave a little wave.

The crowd went crazy.

When the light found her a second time, Hilola Bigtree—the famous woman from the posters, the "Swamp Centaur"—was gone. Our mother was herself again: smiling, brown-skinned, muscular. A little thicker through the waist and hips than she appeared on those early posters, she liked to joke, since she'd had her three kids.

"Mom!" Ossie and I would squeal, racing around the wire fence and over the wet cement that ringed the Gator Pit to get to her before the autograph seekers elbowed us out. "You won!"

My family, the Bigtree tribe of the Ten Thousand Islands, once lived on a hundred-acre island off the coast of southwest Florida, on the Gulf side of the Great Swamp. For many years, Swamplandia! was the Number One Gator-Themed Park and Swamp Café in the area. We leased an expensive billboard on the interstate, just south of Cape Coral: COME SEE "SETH," FANGSOME SEA SERPENT AND ANCIENT LIZARD OF DEATH!!! We called all our alligators Seth. ("Tradition is as important, kids," Chief Bigtree liked to say, "as promotional materials are expensive.") The billboard featured a ten-foot alligator, one of the Seths, hissing soundlessly. Its jaws gape to reveal the rosebud pink of a queen conch shell; its scales are a wet-looking black. We Bigtrees are kneeling around the primordial monster in reverse order of height: my father, the Chief; my grandfather, Sawtooth; my mother, Hilola; my older brother, Kiwi; my sister, Osceola; and finally, me. We are wearing Indian costumes on loan from our Bigtree Gift Shop: buckskin vests, cloth headbands, great blue heron feathers, great white heron feathers, chubby beads hanging off our foreheads and our hair in braids, gator "fang" necklaces.

Although there was not a drop of Seminole or Miccosukee blood in us, the Chief always costumed us in tribal apparel for the photographs he took. He said we were "our own Indians." Our mother had a toast-brown complexion that a tourist could maybe squint and call Indian—and Kiwi, Grandpa Sawtooth, and I could hold our sun. But my sister,

Osceola, was born snowy—not a weak chamomile blond but pure frost, with eyes that vibrated somewhere between maroon and violet. Her face was like our mother's face cast forward onto cloudy water. Before we posed for the picture on that billboard, our mother colored her in with drugstore blusher. The Chief made sure she was covered by the shadow of a tree. Kiwi liked to joke that she looked like the doomed sibling you see in those Wild West daguerreotypes, the one who makes you think, *Oh God, take the picture quick; that kid is not long for this world.*

Our park housed ninety-eight captive alligators in the Gator Pit. We also had a Reptile Walk, a two-mile-long boardwalk through the paurotis palms and saw grass that my grandfather and father designed and built. There you could see caimans, gharials, Burmese and African pythons, every variety of tree frog, a burrow hole of red-bellied turtles and lachrymose morning glories, and a rare Cuban crocodile, Methuselah—a croc that was such an expert mimic of a log that it had moved only once in my presence, when its white jaw fell open like a suitcase.

We had one mammal, Judy Garland, a small, balding Florida brown bear who had been rescued as a cub by my grandparents, back when bears still roamed the pinewoods of the northern swamp. Judy Garland's fur looked like a scorched rug—my brother said she had ursine alopecia. She could do a trick, sort of: the Chief had trained her to nod along to "Somewhere Over the Rainbow." Everybody, without exception, hated this trick. Her Oz-nods terrified small children and shocked their parents. "Somebody, help! This bear is having a seizure!" the park guests would cry—the bear had bad rhythm—but we had to keep her, said the Chief. The bear was *family.*

Our park had an advertising campaign that was on par with the best of the aqua-slide attractions and the miniature golf courses; we had the cheapest beer in a three-county radius; and we had wrestling shows 365 days a year, rain or shine, no federal holidays, no Christian or pagan interruptions. We Bigtrees had our problems, too, of course, like anybody—Swamplandia! had been under siege from several enemy forces, natural and corporate, for most of my short lifetime. We islanders worried about the menace of the melaleuca woods—the melaleuca, or paperbark tree, was an exotic invasive species that was draining huge tracts of our swamp to the northeast. And everybody had one eye on the sly encroachment of the suburbs and Big Sugar in the south. But it always seemed to me like my family was winning. We had never been defeated by the Seths. Every Saturday evening (and most weeknights!) of our childhoods, our mom performed the Swimming with the Seths act and she always won. For a thousand shows, we watched our mother sink into black water, rise. For a thousand nights, we watched the green diving board quaking in air, in the bright wake of her.

And then our mom got sick, sicker than a person should ever be allowed to get. I was twelve when she got her diagnosis and I was furious. *There is no justice and no logic,* the cancer doctors cooed around me; I don't remember the exact words they used, but I could not decode a note of hope. One of the nurses brought me chocolate duds from the vending machine that stuck in my throat. These doctors were always stooping to talk to us, or so it seemed to me, like every doctor on her ward was a giant, seven or eight feet tall. Mom fell through the last stages of her cancer at a frightening speed. She no longer resembled our mother. Her head got soft and bald like a baby's head. We had to watch her sink into her own face. One night she dove and she didn't come back. Air cloaked the hole that she left and it didn't once tremble, no bubbles, it seemed she really wasn't going to surface. Hilola Jane Bigtree, world-class alligator wrestler, terrible cook, mother of three, died in a dryland hospital bed in West Davey on an overcast Wednesday, March 10, at 3:12 p.m.

The Beginning of the End can feel a lot like the middle when you are living in it. When I was a kid I couldn't see any of these ridges. It was only after Swamplandia!'s fall that time folded into a story with a beginning, a middle, and an ending. If you're short on time, that would be the two-word version of our story: *we fell.*

I was thirteen years old when the end of Swamplandia! began in earnest, although at first I was oblivious of the dangers we now faced—Mom was dead, so I thought the worst had already happened to us. I didn't realize that one tragedy can beget another, and another—bright-eyed disasters flooding out of a death hole like bats out of a cave. Nine months had gone by since Mom's passing. The Chief had not done anything to alert the tourists, beyond a small obituary that ran in the *Loomis Register*. Her name was still listed in every Florida guidebook, her face was on our billboards and gift store merchandise, her Swimming with the Seths act was just about synonymous with Swamplandia! itself. Hilola Bigtree was the lodestar that pulled our visored, sweaty visitors across the water. So then I had to break some pretty bad news:

"We lost our headliner," I told them, gesturing vaguely, as if Hilola Bigtree were of no specific relation to me. But not to worry, I was quick to assure them—"I'm Ava Bigtree, I'm her understudy, so you'll still get to see a world-class alligator-wrestling show . . ."

The tourists would frown down at me, or briefly touch my shoulders.

"That man over there, in the feathers? He said the wrestler was your mother?"

I held very still. I shut my eyes as whole shuddering flocks of hands descended. Wings brushed the damp hair off my cheeks. When some other kid's mother asked me how I was doing, I'd say, "Well, ma'am, the show must go on." I'd overheard Kiwi saying this to a group of mainland teenagers in a tone like flicked ash. If a tourist knelt to hug me, I'd try to smile. "Be kind to the kind people, Ava," the Chief said. "They are going to want to talk to you about her."

But you know what? No one really did. Not after I told them what had killed her. I think they were hoping to hear that Hilola Bigtree had been attacked by her gators. They were after a hot little stir—bones crushed, fangs closed around a throat, and an unlucky vent of blood. It was interesting to watch the tourists' reactions when I said the words "ovarian cancer." Cancer was banal enough that they were forced to adjust their response.

"Cancer? How awful! How old was she?"

"Thirty-six."

The tourist ladies said, "Oh!" or "I'm *sorry,*" and squeezed me harder. Most of the husbands drew back a few steps: cancer, I could tell, did not impress these guys in the least.

Most tourists sat through the show after we announced Hilola Bigtree's death, but a few asked for their money back. Those who had traveled the shortest distances always seemed for some reason to be the angriest, the Loomis bingo and jai alai set—these ladies behaved as if our mother's death had somehow cheated *them.* "This was our Tuesday outing!" these blue-haired women whined. They had paid good money to see Hilola Bigtree do her Swimming with the Seths act; they didn't take a forty-minute ferry ride to eat corn dogs with some big lizards and some extremely sorry-looking children!

Death was just another kind of weather to these ancients, the Chief explained to me and my sister. As ordinary as a rain delay. "If they make a big stink, girls, you comp their Gator Tots."

I came to hate the complainers, with their dry and crumbly lipsticks and their wrinkled rage and their stupid, flaccid, old-people sun hats with brims the breadth of Saturn's rings. I whispered to Ossie that I wanted to see the register for Death's aeroplane. Who was boarding the plane in such a stupid order?

The Chief made up a "shut-your-crone-face" conciliation package that we were supposed to give the outraged senior people seeking refunds. The conciliation package contained: a foam alligator hat designed to look like it was eating your head, a crystal flamingo necklace, fifty green and amber Seth toothpicks in a collector case, and a souvenir flip book of our mother. If you turned the pages quickly enough, Mom moved like a primitive cartoon: first she dove, then her body tore a green seam down the center of the artificial lake. But my sister and I figured out that if you flipped in the opposite direction, just as fast, our mom zipped backward. Then the Pit bubbles flooded inward to form a smooth and undisturbed lake, and Mom landed on the diving board, her high dive reversing itself in a shimmering arc. She flew like a rock unbreaking a window. Glass fused, and then you were at the little book's beginning again. Who could complain after watching that?

For some reason the tourists seemed depressed by this trick. More than one Hilola Bigtree flip book ended up in the park's mesh trash cans. Within a month of her funeral, people were calling the Chief to cancel their annual passes, and many more of Swamplandia!'s regular visitors simply stopped coming.

Mom wasn't the only Bigtree wrestler we were missing. Grandpa Sawtooth had vanished that year, too. He was still alive, but the Chief had exiled him to the mainland about a month before Mom died. The Chief had installed Grandpa Sawtooth in an assisted-living facility called the Out to Sea Retirement Community—a temporary thing, the

Chief had assured us kids. Just until we "tied up some loose ends" on our island. We missed Grandpa but he didn't miss us. During his last days on the island he had more than once gotten lost inside our house. He still knew our names, sometimes, but he could not match them to our faces; his memory winked on and off with the weird, erratic energy of a lightbulb in a torment. We had seen Grandpa Sawtooth exactly once since his move: a few weeks after he got "settled in," we spent twenty-two minutes in his cabin at the Out to Sea facility. Through Grandpa's porthole you could see the abridged ocean, lassoed in glass, and a low stone seawall. Inside the retirement boat, no music played, no living lizards curled tails along the walls, and the lights were halogen. The Chief kept promising us another trip to Loomis to visit him: "As soon as I muck out the Gator Pit, kids . . ." "As soon as I get a cage and rigging done on that airboat . . ." By December, we'd stopped asking.

I remember clearly the first time I saw the face of our enemy—it was on a Thursday in January, ten months and two weeks after Mom's death. A huge thunderstorm had rolled over the islands that afternoon, and the living room was unusually dark. I had been lulled into a half-awake state by an *I Love Lucy* marathon on channel 6. Grandpa's rabbit-eared TV was crackling like water, and I kept dozing off on the couch and getting my senses all tangled, dreaming that the storm had moved inside. Then the TV screen went entirely black, and a baritone voice intoned: "The World of Darkness comes to Loomis!" I was glued to the set: plaid-vested schoolchildren lined up to enter the gaping doors of what appeared to be a giant amusement park. The camera followed them down a narrow walkway—the "Tongue of the Leviathan!" an announcer called it. The Tongue appeared to be a sort of thirty-foot electric-traction escalating slide, covered in sponge and pink mesh, visibly slick; it gulped whole grades of kids into the park. The camera zoomed forward to give a teaser glimpse of the interior of the Leviathan: a scale model of a whale's belly, lit up by a series of green lights on a timer, so that it looked to my untrained eye like some kind of alien cafeteria. Then the TV flashed to a keyhole peek of riders disappearing down the Tongue. For a few seconds the screen went black again and the TV speakers burbled with "cetaceous noises of digestion." Then schoolkids screaming "We love the World!" on somebody's cue disappeared down a neon tube.

"Christ Jesus," said the Chief, "how much do you think this piece-of-shit commercial cost?" Swamplandia! had never done a TV spot.

The World of Darkness was located in southwest Loomis County, just off the highway ramp. The camera pulled back to reveal imbricating parking lots, a whole spooling solar system of parking lots. On its western edge, the Leviathan touched a green checkerboard of suburban lawns. A moat of lava lapped at the carports, the houses at the World's perimeter looking small and vexed. The World of Darkness offered things that Swamplandia! could not: escalator tours of the rings of Hell, bloodred swimming pools, boiling colas. Easy access to the mainland roads.

"Can the World of Darkness really do that, Chief?" I asked my dad. "Move right into the middle of a city?"

The Chief had stopped watching. He was draining a Gulch brandy and cola in the deep crease of our couch. "Don't let me catch you falling for that bullcrap, Ava. Who is going to pay a day's wage to slide down a damn *tongue*? That's about the stupidest thing I ever heard of. You go touch your Seth's belly scales and remind yourself who's got the *real* leviathans . . ."

One Tuesday in late January, just a week or two after the World of Darkness's grand opening, the morning ferry failed to show. On an ordinary weekday, the double-decker ferry departed from the Loomis County Ferry Port at 9:05 and arrived at our park's landing a few minutes after ten o'clock. This orange boat linked Swamplandia! to the mainland; we had no bridge system and no road access. So the ferry was our lifeline, the only way for tourists to get to our park. The twenty-six-mile trip took forty minutes in good weather, and could take as much as an hour and a half in rough water. The service was a vestige from the frontier days, when it connected a handful of drifters and homesteaders scattered throughout the Ten Thousand Islands to the mainland. The majority of the Ten Thousand Islands were still uninhabited, and there were just four stops on the original thirty-five-mile loop: Swamplandia!, Gallinule Key, Carpenter Key, and the Red Eagle

Key Fishing Camp. Our nearest neighbors, Mr. and Mrs. Gianetti, had an avocado farm on Gallinule Key, a fifteen-minute airboat ride to the south.

The Chief was on all fours when I found him. He was in the empty stadium, making some adjustment to the Pit pump. He was wearing a mainland T-shirt that said ALABAMA CARDINALS—this was from his "civilian" wardrobe. Without his radiant ropes and beads and feathers, you could see his pale scalp through a scrim of scant black hair. Color had ripened in twin spots on his stubbled cheeks, which made him look a little like a haggard Shirley Temple.

The Chief had to drain and clean the Pit every ten days because the Seths were undainty eaters; we fed them a commercial diet, which we ordered from Louisiana breeders, mostly chicken and fish but occasionally more whimsical proteins: frozen nutria, muskrat, beaver, horse. The Seths regurgitated bones and feathers. Once, after a hurricane, we pulled the bars of a tiny rib cage out of the leafy deep end—they were a crumbly, dark-honey color. Forensic arguments erupted over green peas and meat loaf at our own table:

"A Key deer, Sammy!" shouted Grandpa.

"Na-uh, Pops," the Chief disagreed. "My guess, those bones belong to a dog. Some poor mutt went for a swim . . . pass the gravy, honey?"

On Live Chicken Thursdays, a very popular and macabre attraction, the Seths jumped five feet out of the Pit to snatch the cloud-white hens suspended above them, tied by their talons to a clothesline. The Seths drowned and ate these chickens in an underwater cyclone called the Death Roll while tourists snapped photographs. Live Chicken Thursday was a Bigtree tradition dating back to 1942. The ritual was Grandpa Sawtooth's brainchild. I think my family traumatized generations of children and old women. And we girls must have inherited our forebears' immunity to gore, because Ossie and I could eat PB&J sandwiches during a Death Roll, no problemo.

"There now." The Chief gave a satisfied grunt as clear bubbles shot forth again, some clicky mechanism having reset itself. He knelt over the edge of the Pit. A few Seths swam calmly around the underwater platform that the Chief just had been standing on; his tool belt was still jerked up beneath his soaked armpits.

"Chief!" I said, bounding over. "Dad, the ferry never showed . . ."

He looked up with a blind, irritated glare—the sun was behind me but I was too short to block it. His arms were gloved in filth up to the elbows.

"Ava, you can't see I'm busy? Gus Waddell called from the docks. The ferry isn't coming today because Gus Waddell didn't have any passengers."

"Do you want me to go check the TV, to see if something bad happened on the mainland?"

"Ava Bigtree," he said. "You are making me truly crazy. You can watch TV if you want."

After cleaning the pit, the Chief disappeared into the Isolation Tank to do some work with a recalcitrant bull gator, a one-eyed, indiscriminately nasty fellow that kept biting not only the other alligators but also any driftwood or pond lily that floated up against his blind spot, attacks which were scary but somehow also very embarrassing to watch. I hung around inside the empty stadium. It was a hot day, and the Seths slid through periphyton, a brownish-orange algae that reproduced explosively in the Florida heat and could draw its pumpkin lace across the entire Pit overnight. Everything else was pretty still.

"The gators are not your pets, Ava," the Chief was always reminding me. "That creature is pure appetite in a leather case. A Seth can't love you back."

But I loved *them,* the dark tapering mass of them; I feared them, too, their alien eyes and sudden bursts of speed. Chief Bigtree hung wooden memos bragging on them all over our park, many of them accurate:

ALLIGATORS CAN RUN FASTER THAN ARABIAN HORSES ON LAND!

THE ALLIGATOR IS AN ANACHRONISM THAT CAN EAT YOU!

A SETH IS A 180 MILLION YEAR VETERAN OF OUR PLANET!

"There's no show today, you dummies," I told the alligators over the railing. I rained out a bag of marbles and watched the planetary spin of them off the Seths' black shoulders. The Chief said I could do this because the Seths used these marbles as *gastroliths*—they used them to grind up prey in their gizzards the way chickens use grit. And gastroliths allow crocodilians to float better—to settle their weight in the water. Our gators were born knowing exactly how much weight to swallow to find and keep their balance.

I checked my watch: on an ordinary day, we would be five minutes into our show by now. My dad would have waded into the Pit water, carrying a gator harness that he made out of old airplane cables. He would have selected a sparring partner, "a big respectable sucker," and slid the rusty harness over the Seth's snout. The Seth, dripping and black, would fight like a fish inside that harness while the other gators continued switching through the sludgy Pit, slow and pitiless inside their Seth-oblivion.

Once the Chief hauled his Seth onto the stage, the real fight began. The Seth would immediately lurch forward, yanking the Chief back into the water. The Chief would pull him out again, and this tug-of-war would continue for a foamy length of time while the crowd whooped and wahooed, cheering for our species. To officially win an alligator wresling match, you have to close both your hands around the gator's jaws. That was the hard part, getting your Seth's mouth to shut. Mom said that we girls were at a natural disadvantage because our hands were small—they could barely span a piano octave.

But one curious fact about Seth physiognomy is this: while a Seth can *close* its jaws with 2,125 pounds per square inch of force, the force of a guillotine, the musculature that opens those same jaws is extremely weak. This is the secret a wrestler exploits to beat her adversaries—if you can get your Seth's jaws shut up in your fist, it is next to impossible for the creature to open them again. A girl's Goody ribbon can tie off the jaws of a four-hundred-pound bull gator.

But we didn't just tape up the Seth's jaws and declare ourselves the victors—our Bigtree show was special because we did tricks, too, and practiced some of the more dangerous holds. Before she died, Mom was in the middle of teaching me her advanced moves. The Chin Thrust, for example, a Bigtree standard. To do the Chin Thrust, you make a latch out of your chin against the purselike U of a Seth's jaws, tucking its broad snout against your throat like a botched kiss. Another good one was the Silent Night, where you covered the alligator's eyes with your hands, fastened its snout with the tape, and then enlisted the help of Mom or the Chief or Grandpa to flip it onto its back. This was a sorcery that "put the alligator to sleep." Years later, I would learn that we were disrupting the alligators' otoliths, tiny sacs that connect the inner ear with the brain. We blacked them out.

If you are an animal lover, I can tell you what the Chief told us: that it was never a fair fight; that even taped and flipped, even "sleeping," its legs churning toward an ultimate befuddlement and stillness, the alligator had all the real advantages; that an alligator can hoard its violence for millions and millions of years. A Seth could trick you into thinking it had died with a days-long freeze, a mortuary pose on a rock, and then do a lickety-split lunge and snatch an unwary turtle or a tiny ibis. The Seths had a ferocity that no wrestler could snuff for very long. The first and last time I'd tried to do a Silent Night, the alligator managed to right itself and bruised my entire right side with its thrashing tail, and Mom told the Chief that I was still too young to perform the trick. I felt older now, though. Looking out at all the vacant stands, I felt like I had better become ready.

What the tourists paid to watch, the Chief always said, was an unequal fight. A little seesaw action: death/life. The Chief had long ago taught me a Bigtree strategy called "peacocking weakness." All the best Seminole wrestlers used this strategy, too. The true champions handicapped themselves, the Chief said, blindfolding their eyes or binding their dominant hand. *Weakness* was the feather with which you tickled your tourists; it was your *weakness* that pinned the tourists to their seats. They saw the puny size of you versus your alligator. They saw that you could *lose.* If you exploited this fact, you could float the outcome of your battle into the air over the stadium, like a balloon. During the really *scary* family shows, the electric, something-goes-awry times, I would picture it up there just like the Chief had said, our fate, a translucent black balloon wombling between the palm trees.

"You got to remind the mainlanders that your alligator is a no-shit dinosaur, Ava," the Chief used to lecture me. "Those bored, dead dry-landers. They act like they think they're watching robots up here!" He'd shake his head. "Prove to them that you can lose, so you can surprise people, honey, and *win.*"

Now I wondered: Would we ever do a show like that again? What if yesterday had been my last-ever chance to wrestle? To surprise the mainland people? I leaned over the railing to the Gator Pit. The little bag felt weightless and I realized that I was almost out of marbles. *Oh for heaven's sake, Ava Bigtree, don't be so melodramatic! Of course you will wrestle again. Today is a fluke; of course the tourists will be back!* I tried to give myself a lecture in my mother's stern voice. Then I used her same voice on the gators, who were blinking up at me so stupidly from the Pit:

"Eat up, you fools, because no one is coming," I hissed. Blue and gray marbles caught in their scales like stubborn bubbles. The big yellow shooter rolled around one Seth's scaly shoulders like a dollhouse sun. They all sank into the water and turned into gastroliths.

"Ava? What are you doing?" Ossie's voice erupted through the speaker hooked up to the ticketing booth. "Ha-ha—did you lose your marbles?"

Two weeks passed. The Chief discovered that we couldn't even sell out the once-a-day wrestling show. We started performing for whoever showed up, whenever they came (we were still getting a few confused Europeans, clutching these expired travel guides with hydrangea-pink spines and greeting my father with ¿*Qué?* and *Quoi?*). The Chief and I cut twenty minutes from the show, but you could feel the tourists' pity first and then their distraction, their attention wandering the skies of the open stadium like kites. Without Mom and Grandpa Sawtooth the whole show felt horribly incomplete to me. "The tourists can't tell," the Chief assured us, but it seemed like even the expressionless Seths had to know that something was missing. One Thursday when the Chief was in a black mood and caught a tourist yawning during his wrestling demonstration, he groaned loudly and released the Seth back into the water with a slap: "Ta-da," he growled, standing up. "That's all, folks."

We were still calling this thing the Bigtree Wrestler Spectacular.

I started to miss the same tourists I'd always claimed to despise: the translucent seniors from Michigan. The ice-blond foreign couples yoked into thick black camera straps like teams of oxen. The fathers, sweating everywhere, with their trembling dew mustaches. The young mothers humping up and down the elevated walkway to the Swamp Café, holding their babies aloft like blaring radios.

Where had all the families gone? The families were gone. All at once, it felt like. Families had been our keystone species of tourists on Swamplandia! and now they were rarer than panthers. Red-eyed men with no kids in tow started showing up at the Saturday shows. Solitaries. Sometimes they debarked the ferry with perfumed breath, already drunk. Sometimes they motored over from the Flamingo Marina in Loomis County on their own junker boats, and always they seemed far more interested in the cheap beer and the woodsmoke black racks of the fried frog legs than our tramway tours or our alligator wrestling—somehow Swamplandia! seemed to have earned a truck-stop reputation as a good place to "get obliterated" on a weekend night. One guy I found urinating on the side of our gift shop—the actual wall, even though the public bathrooms with the vault toilets were just a five-minute walk down the trail! I hated them. When we had a crowd of these red-eyes, the Chief would not let me wrestle and performed the whole show himself. The Chief liked most every tourist with a wallet but he cooled on these guys. He blamed the World of Darkness for them, too.

"We'll get the families back," the Chief promised us one night after a particularly scary set of individuals had mobbed up to see our show. These guys drank so much beer that Gus and Kiwi had to help them back onto the ferry; I'd caught one of them throwing up into the bushes behind the musuem. Another one had cozied up to the ticket booth window and whispered strange jokes to my sister, leaning into his elbows like a grasshopper, so that from where I was standing it looked like he was trying to kiss her through the glass. The Chief had started screaming at these men on the ferry dock, but now that we were home he seemed angry with us: "What's wrong with you girls? You need to calm down." He patted Ossie stiffly. "Those clowns are gone. Those fools are just paying our rent until we get the *families* back. This is like bad weather, you understand? It's gonna blow over."

But I couldn't sleep—because what horizon did we think the sun was dropping into? If the World of Darkness stayed open and Mom stayed in her grave, how, exactly, were we supposed to get the families back? We ate our dinners beneath a reticent crescent moon. The Chief picked at his molars with a yellow toothpick, Kiwi read, Ossie kept her head down and ate off everybody's plates. She ate with her fingers, peeling colorless grains of rice off Mom's blue tablecloth. But I couldn't stop imagining our fate up there, the black balloon. A thin globe of air clearly visible behind the toothy palms. I could see that balloon and the moon shining through it but I couldn't begin to imagine what was going to happen to us.

CHAPTER TWO

The Advent of the World of Darkness

Incredibly, Mom stayed dead but the sky changed. Rains fell. Alligators dug and tenanted new lakes. It became (how?) early April. We were doing four or five shows a week, at most, for pitiful numbers of people. Some audiences were in the single digits. I read my comics and memorized the speech bubbles of heroes. I dusted our Seth clock, a gruesome and fantastic timepiece the Chief had made: just an ordinary dishlike kitchen clock set inside a real alligator's pale stomach. The clock hung from a hook next to the blackboard menu in our Swamp Café. TIME TO EAT! somebody—probably Grandpa—had scratched into the boards above it. Water overflowed the sloughs and combed the black mudflats. Mangroves hugged soil and vegetation into pond-lily islands; gales tore the infant matter apart along the Gulf. Our swamp got blown to green bits and reassembled, daily, hourly. The wet season was a series of land-versus-water skirmishes: marl turned to chowder and shunted the baby-green cocoplums into the sea; tides maniacally revised the coastlines. Whole islands caught fire from lightning strikes, and you could sometimes watch deer and marsh rabbits leaping into the sea of saw grass on gasps of smoke.

Some days Gus Waddell—our fat angel at the ferry's helm—was our only visitor. Of course, we couldn't tally Gus as a Swamplandia! tourist because he didn't pay money to see us. Gus Waddell was the ferryboat captain, as per his monogrammed life vest and his little captain's hat and his squishy-foam I'M THE CAPTAIN drink cozy. Uncle Gus brought us mainland provisions: bagged butcher-shop meats and various zoo supplies and gallons of whole milk, big sandbags of rice. Several boxes of our favorite mainland cereal, Peanut Butter Boos. For the Chief, a rubber-banded roll of emerald Win This Lotto! tickets and the "Ziggurat"-size carton of Sir Puffsters cigarettes.

Back when Mom was healthy, we'd see the flash of orange paint behind the mangroves that meant the ferry had arrived and go scrambling for our staff positions, like mainland kids who hear a school bell. And then all day my siblings and I would barely see each other—we'd be too busy busing tables in the Swamp Café or selling tickets or giving a tram tour. Sometimes the first minute that we spent together didn't come until 3:30 p.m., when we met onstage for the Bigtree Wrestler Spectacular. But now Kiwi and Ossie and I were always lumping up in the Gator Pit, trying to figure out: what are we supposed to do? When Gus showed up with supplies and no people he gave us an uneasy gift: time. Free time. Many blank, untouristed hours of it. That's how my sister's metamorphosis started to happen, I think—inside that white cocoon.

We started spending the no-tourist days on the Library Boat—even Ossie, who had never been what you would call a bookworm. We boarded an airboat and motored over to the long bottleneck cove of a nameless pine island about a quarter mile west of Swamplandia! A coppery green twenty-foot schooner was at permanent anchor there, listing in the rocks. This was the Library Boat. Like Gus's ferry, the Library Boat was another link to the mainland, although this boat never moved. It held a cargo of books. In the thirties and forties, Harrel M. Crow, a fisherman and bibliophile, had piloted the schooner around our part of the swamp delivering books to the scattered islanders. Then Harrel M. Crow died and I guess that was it for the door-to-door service. But his Library Boat, miraculously, had survived on the rocky island, unscavenged and undestroyed by hurricanes. It was an open secret, utilized by all our neighbors. You could row over to the site of the wreck, descend into H. M. Crow's hold, return with an armload of semidamp reading material. People contributed newer books, too—the bottom shelves had filled with trashy romance novels, mysteries, somebody's underlined Bible, a mostly filled-in book of jumble puzzles, the plays of Shakespeare. So the collection was always evolving.

I can't remember when I first saw *The Spiritist's Telegraph* lying around the house, but once I'd noticed the book it seemed to be every-where—in our kitchen, facedown in the café. Ossie was never without it. I was surprised she'd found it out there. *The Spiritist's Telegraph* looked old, ancient, centuries older than Harrel M. Crow. It was a spell book, Gideon-thick. We didn't think it was from our country, even though the writing was English. Inside the print was so tiny—in places it was almost impossible to read—and Ossie said this was because each chapter had been written as a whisper to the reader.

"Well? So what the heck kind of machine is the Spiritist Telegraph?"

"I think," Osceola said wonderingly, turning a page, "that it's sup-posed to be *your body?*"

There were dozens of drawings in the appendix. Ossie showed me an old anatomical sketch of a woman floating with her arms akimbo, her private parts inked in. Her eyes were pupilless, serene, like the Egyp-tian sculptures I had recently discovered in a kid's World Wonders book of my own. THE SPIRITIST RECEIVES A MESSAGE, read an ornate scroll of Bookman type that furred her collarbone.

"Can I read it?"

"You're too little." She saw my face and relented. "You can flip through it. You can flip through it *once,* and *fast.*"

Together we spun through a hundred chapters: foxed pages, strange drawings, an appendix of gibberish. All these witchy psalms about a place called the underworld, which was neither the heaven nor the hell that I had learned about from Little Rabbit cartoons and Bandits of the West comics and the Bible. It sounded instead like a vague blue woods:

> In the Underworld, all suns and lanterns are unwelcome. The transfer of light is an unforgivable breach from Acheron to Lethe. One matchstick, one fingersnap of light, can feast on those shadows and blaze into a conflagration. Young Spiritists: you must gag your vision.
>
> Do not even say the word "sun" here, Aspiring Spiritists, or the trees of the Underworld will punish you for it: to do so would be like telling kindling the epic of fire, or whispering *lamp* to the dark.

—from *The Spiritist's Telegraph,* pages ix–x

"There's no such place, honey," said my father when I asked him about this underworld. His voice was like a shell with something oozing and alive inside it. "There's no such thing as heaven, no hell. That's a Christian fantasy. That's a very old fairy tale that your sister is reading."

"It's a book for witches, Dad. And the underworld isn't heaven or hell, it's like a whole separate country. Like a, a Germany under the world." I frowned; this description was nothing like the painting in my mind, which was like a woods but also in some uncommunicable way not like a woods at all. I defaulted to: "Like a woods, Dad. You can visit dead people there. It's always nighttime and the trees get angry if you bring flashlights or candles . . ."

"You girls want an underworld?" The Chief's booming laugh was directed at our sofa; there were no other adults in the house to echo it back to him. Our parents used to find each other this way, via laughs and gasps, an echolocation of incredulity and horror. "How deep do you want to go? You tell Osceola this: we are already underwater. Okay? Tell her that we live below sea level."

"Da-ad. That's not what the *underworld* is. The book says . . ."

"Ava Bigtree, why not let your sister have her hobby, huh?" His voice was wry and ordinary, but he looked at me with real pleading: "You and I, we've got the Seths, we've got the whole park to run, right?"

One picture in *The Spiritist's Telegraph* I stared at for hours, until I could see it fork behind my eyelids: a river cut a lightning shape through jagged, enormous boulders. Strange creatures lived in the margins of the mountains. The artist's brushstrokes had added shapes into the clouds: snouts and wings and eyes, a long whiplike tail. Obsidian flakes snowed over the entire range. This painting was titled *Winter on the River Styx.*

About this time, Ossie and I started playing Ouija every afternoon. We made the board ourselves. It had a blue painted alphabet and little suns and moons modeled on a picture from *The Spiritist's Telegraph.*

" 'The language of the living rains down on the dead,' " Ossie read to me from *The Spiritist's Telegraph,* " 'and often our communications can overwhelm them. The hailstorm of our words can be too intense for them to bear . . .' "

SO GET AN UMBRELLA, MOM, I wrote to her a little angrily.

Weeks passed and we didn't hear back. Sometimes to make me feel better Ossie would pretend to be our mother—I LUV U, DOTER, she'd write, or U ARE PREITY, AVA. I MIS U.

This is a true fact: my brother gave himself report cards. He modeled them after a Rocklands Middle School report card, which he had purchased from his obese mainland associate, Cubby Wallach. Cubby Wallach was complected like a bowl of oatmeal and yet carried himself as if he were wearing a top hat and spats. He had the bellicose dignity of a kid who refuses to excuse or even to acknowledge his own extreme ugliness. I admired this trait. It reminded me of the Seths, with their scarred, alien faces and their beautiful oblivion. Like a Seth, Cubby Wallach would let you stare at his face without apologizing for it. No red cheeks or downcast eyes, just a cool, invulnerable stare. In this way his ugliness got transmuted into a powerful hypnosis. Ossie used to have a bad crush on him, and I pretended to hate him. "What an asshole," I'd say, but it came out as sort of a giggle.

Whenever he came to Swamplandia!, Cubby Wallach brought a gigantic shopping bag filled with other kids' colorful graded homework and purloined protractors and sold this haul to Kiwi at an incredible markup.

Kiwi insisted that he was our homeschool's valedictorian. I was the salutatorian. Ossie mostly read magazines. Years ago, Mom enrolled us in Teach Your Child . . . in the Wild!, a vestigial statewide initiative from the early days of white settlement—we got a whole "substitute curriculum" for free in the mail. Every month some functionary at the Loomis County Public Schools sent us stapled booklets with titles like *Your Federal Government Is a Tree with Three Branches* and *Mighty Fungi: The* Third *Kingdom.* Several times a year we mailed back a stack of tests and completed worksheets, I guess to prove that we were learning *something.*

This stuff was too easy for my brother. He said that he was going to leapfrog over the LCPS high school requirements and go directly to college. He was studying for the Scholastic Aptitude Test—the SAT. If you put the fan on high in his bedroom these little powder blue cards

with funny words on them flew everywhere: FATIDIC [adj], OPPRO-
BRIUM [n]. My brother always had a pack of study cards with him. He
would rather conjugate Latin than do any of the chores the park
required of him. He was in charge of concessions. When the park was
open, Kiwi would sit next to the trapped snowfall inside the popcorn
machine at the top of the stadium steps, waving mechanically, his face
making a funny pucker beneath the paper cone of his hat. Cubby Wallach had sold him these dark-rinse jeans, and they fit him like a puddle.

Now Kiwi was free to spend most of every day mossed inside the
Library Boat, where the portholes gave his face a Frankenstein gleam.
He got this aura of expectancy about him that confused me. It wasn't
dread, not exactly, but you could not call it hope.

"What little test are you studying for?" I asked him once, and he
looked up with clouds for eyes and said, "My future."

I think that Kiwi resented my sister's new scholarly ways a little,
because up until this point he had always been the bookworm, the
captain of the Library Boat. But Ossie applied herself to *The Spiritist's
Telegraph* with the same diligence with which Kiwi studied science and
philosophy—she wouldn't meet our eyes anymore, she was lost in her
book.

On April 29, we threw Osceola a sweet sixteen party. Without Mom
and Grandpa the party felt dazed and sad. The guest list was us. The
Chief and I thawed out an ancient cake from the Swamp Café freezer
("Let's hope this doesn't kill us, Chief!" I said, the absolute wrong joke
to make). Our presents for her that year, not to put too fine a point on
it, really sucked. The Chief walked over to the Bigtree Family Museum
and returned with a pair of tawny moccasins. I had to remind him that
the moccasins didn't fit Osceola anymore; that's why we'd moved them
to the museum in the first place.

"Well, it's the thought that counts, Ava," he told me in an almost-
shout.

The Bigtree Family Museum, next door to the gift shop, contained
all kinds of crap from our house that the Chief had relabeled as BIGTREE
ARTIFACTS. The entryway to the palmetto-thatched museum burned
green in daylight: WELCOME TO THE "LOUVRE" OF THE SWAMP

ISLANDS! Sometimes you'd find a disoriented tourist in there, sucking a Fine Lime through a straw and looking mournfully for a bathroom. Ladies liked to change their babies' diapers on our glass cases. On one wall, the Chief had framed the flyers that had lured Grandpa Sawtooth away from Ohio in 1932. He named this exhibit Antique Promises. Each flyer featured an artist's sketch of the Florida islands "post-drainage": our swamp as farmland, complete with milk cows, orange groves, a heaven of clover "where the sea beasts once roamed."

Grandpa, who was born Ernest Schedrach, the white son of a white coal miner in Ohio, bought the land after losing his job at the Archer Road Pulp Mill, which was just as well because he was tired of the pitiful wages, tired of his ears ringing like Sunday church bells all shift and of his bleached vision caused by blinking into the chemicals. He changed his name to outwit his old boss. It turned out he owed a sizable amount of money to the mill foreman. He picked "Sawtooth" in homage to the sedge that surrounded his island; "Bigtree," because he liked its root-strong sound.

The farmland he'd bought, sight unseen, at the Bowles and Beaver Co. Land Lottery in Martins Ferry, Ohio, turned out to be covered by six feet of crystal water. Stalks of nine-foot saw grass glittered in the wind, in every direction, the drowned sentinels of an eternal slough. The only real habitable "property" in sight was the island he later named Swamplandia!: a hundred-acre waste. What the cheerful northern realtors were calling—with a greed that aspired to poetry—the American Eden.

Grandpa Sawtooth and Grandma Risa took the train from Ohio to Florida and then traveled by glade skiff to their new home. When they first docked on the lee side of the island, my grandparents' feet sank a few inches before touching the limestone bedrock. Sawtooth cursed the realtors for the length of an aria. A tiny crab scuttled over Risa's high buttoned shoe—"and when she didn't scream," Sawtooth liked to say, "that's when I knew we were staying."

According to Bigtree legend, it was that same day that Grandma Risa got her first-ever glimpse of a Florida alligator, the Seth of Seths, lolling in a gator hole near the cove where they had stowed their boat—and she later swore that as soon as they locked eyes, they *recognized* each other. That monster's surge, said our grandfather, sent up a tidal wave of black water that soaked Grandma Risa's dress. The prim china-dots on her skirt got erased in one instant, what we called in our museum Risa's Chameleon Baptism.

Alongside this bit of Bigtree history, the Chief kept an ever-changing carousel of objects from our lives, accompanied by little explanatory cards that he typed up and framed himself. Often the deck of our past got reshuffled overnight. He took down Grandpa's old army medallions, which did not fit with his image of our free and ancient swamp tribe. And nowhere did his posted descriptions of Hilola Bigtree's many accomplishments mention her maiden name—Owens—or her mainland birthplace. Certain artifacts appeared or vanished, dates changed and old events appeared in fresh blue ink on new cards beneath the dusty exhibits, and you couldn't say one word about these changes in the morning. You had to pretend like the Bigtree story had always read that way.

So it was with precedent that the Chief vandalized the Bigtree Family Museum, looting from my sister's past to find her a birthday present. Kiwi and I just grabbed some stuff from the clearance bin in the Bigtree Gift Shop: a variety pack of hats and this XXL version of a puffy-logo Seth sweatshirt that she already owned and hated. This is what the sweatshirt said: STOP IN THE NAME OF SETH, BEFORE HE EATS YOUR HEART. The Chief had ordered dozens of these. So far as I knew, nobody in the history of our gift store transactions had ever exchanged legal tender for one.

"Thanks, guys," Osceola said drily.

The Chief unwrapped Osceola's old shoes for her, hog-tied together in our mom's red ribbon.

"Remember how much you liked these moccasins?"

Ossie did not really remember, no.

"Do you want to do a birthday show, honey?" The Chief was smiling and smiling at her, pop-eyed with the strain, a smile that looked almost frightening in the dim Swamp Café. "Do you want to . . . what do you want? More cake?"

My sister shook her white head very slowly behind the tiny fence of birthday candles.

Ossie was polite, licking icing off the twisty candle stripes, pretending this was exactly the sixteenth birthday party she'd wanted. But I knew better—I thought she must be pretty lonely. I'd seen her on the ferry docks, trying to talk to the small knots of mainland teenagers. The only boys her age we'd ever met were tourists. Sometimes, to impress them, Os would corner a posse of older boys and play them her favorite songs in the blue iceberg glow of our jukebox. Yet this jukebox had not been updated since Dwight D. Eisenhower ruled the land.

"Cooool." The boys would drone, catting their eyes at one another. "Who sings that one? The, ah, the Scroobie Brothers, huh? Never heard of them . . ."

In fact, those Scroobie Brothers were playing right now, song after song off their only album, *Scroobing the Tub,* Ossie's jukebox pick. I think Ossie liked them because they sang about things that were exotic to us, like corn and car accidents. Between bites of cake I caught her mouthing along the words, but even these hokey songs weren't cheering her much. After the presents were opened nobody could think of what to say, so the Chief cut us second helpings of the rock-hard cake.

"What, you don't like your presents?" the Chief asked out of the blue, his voice alive and crackling. "Is that it? You don't think that sweatshirt is going to fit you?"

We all looked up. The thin whine of the jukebox seeped into the crater his voice had dug into the café dining room.

"No, Chief. It's great."

Ossie stretched the shirt between them like a fence.

"Try it on."

"Dad?"

"You're right, it looks too small to me. Kiwi, go get your sister the next size up."

Osceola stood. "Dad, I'll be back in a little while," she said. She tightened the ends of her long white braids. She'd smoothed three different shades of Mom's powder onto her eyelids. My sister, I realized with a funny dip in my gut, looked very beautiful. I think the Chief must have noticed this, too, because his face did something funny.

"What are you talking about?" He glanced down at his watch. "It's nine o'clock."

"I know. I'm going on a walk."

"Now? Baby, sit down. As long as we're all together I thought we could have a tribal meeting. We've got some important business to discuss . . ."

But Ossie took a step toward the door, where a fat green anole was clinging to the metal hinge and silently watching everything.

"I want to. Walk." She paused. "It's my birthday."

Ossie made it across the room. When her hand closed around the doorknob he finally spoke.

"Well, you're going to miss some really good news, Osceola."

"Okay. Ava can catch me up." She smiled at him sweetly. Her sweatshirt, all her birthday stuff, was still on the table. "Good night, guys. Thanks for a good party."

And then the door closed, and somehow we were not allowed to ask: *where is she going?* The Chief turned his attention back to us.

"As you may have noticed," he said, in his booming chieftain's voice, "we Bigtrees have a serious enemy. We have a new battle to win."

"Oh my God," said Kiwi. "Dad. This isn't a show. We are all sitting in the same room."

My brother had tugged the brim of his Swamplandia! hat as far down as it would go, practically to the freckles on his nose, which meant that we had to stare at our own cartoon images to talk to him. I think he did this on purpose, to mock us. (I really hated that particular hat—there had been a mistake at the factory and the whole family came out looking hydrocephalic and evil. Tourists would regularly mistake the bump-eyed alligator on the brim for me. They would tap at the grinning alligator on the hat and say, "And who could *that* one be, young lady?" like they were giving me an excellent present.)

"Don't you take that tone with me, son," the Chief bellowed again.

"Don't be an asshole, Kiwi," I said.

The Chief nodded at me, pleased. "Ava? You want to contribute?"

I shook my head. I had been working on my plan to save Swamplandia! but I didn't want to talk about it yet; I worried that I would jinx it, or that my brother would kill it dead with one joke. It had to stay in my head for now.

"What's everybody so damn glum about?" the Chief mumbled. He swallowed his humongous second serving of cake in three bites, and then he quickly finished the half piece that Ossie had left on her plate, his shoulders glugging up and down like an anhinga swallowing a fish. Then he left the dining room and returned with the little blackboard that rested on a tripod outside the Swamp Café. He wiped it clean and stared to write:

Island tameness is the tendency of many populations and species of animals living on isolated islands to lose their wariness of potential predators.

"We Bigtrees are an island species," he told us. "I've been reading your brother's textbook here." He hoisted an antiquarian-looking book with the faded coin of a Library Boat sticker on its spine. "Turns out we islanders are very special. A bunch of new and wonderful crap can evolve here because we're off to ourselves. But there are also trade-offs. Island species get complacent."

NEW PREDATOR: WORLD OF DARKNESS

he wrote, and beneath this:

OUR EVOLUTION: CARNIVAL DARWINISM

Kiwi chuckled. He could manufacture laughter as joyless as flat cola. "How are we going to adapt, exactly?" he asked the Chief from inside the cave of his hat. "Are we going to hike prices again? 'Cause if we only have two tourists in the stands, Dad, it doesn't matter how much we charge them. We'll never break even . . ."

The Chief continued to write:

REVENUE FOR MARCH: $1,230
OUTSTANDING DEBT: $52,560*

When the Chief put an asterisk next to something, it meant that he was only telling you the best part of the truth. He wasn't being dishonest, he explained—he was only letting us know that our debt was "evolving." Just like everything else in this universe. The asterisk, the Chief taught us, was the special punctuation that God gave us for neutralizing lies. One recent example would be "Your mother's cancer is getting better.*"

"What about the county taxes?" Kiwi asked, very quiet now. "What about Mom's medical bills?"

"Son, you need to quit on that. You think you're some kind of detective?"

"What about Mom's *funeral* bills?"

"We don't need to tally those. Those are being taken care of."

"Dad? I've been running some numbers myself . . . Admittedly, I'm not privy to all your records here . . ." Kiwi's voice was as monotonous as a sleepwalk. "For starters, you need to sell some of the equipment. Maintenance costs are going to crush us without tourists. The follow spot, the Seths' incubators . . ." Kiwi blinked, as if he'd woken from his sleepwalk on a cliff. "Think big. You could sell the whole park."

The Chief set his chalk on the little ledge. He stared at our brother.

"Think of what you could get for the airboats," Kiwi said. "And there are those alligator farms in central Florida, they would buy the Seths I bet. We can finish out school at Rocklands High, I'll get a job to help out, we can all enroll for the fall . . ."

Rocklands High. Ossie would be, what, in mainland nomenclature? A high school junior. I would be a freshman, assuming they didn't put me in some duncey catch-up school. I tried to picture myself in a Rocklands classroom: the place rapidly filled with swamp water, all its desks and books floating away until it became our Gator Pit. We were the Bigtree Wrestling Dynasty. Kiwi wanted to give up our whole future for—what? A sack of cafeteria fries? A school locker?

The Chief echoed my thoughts:

"That's what you want? To sell your mother's home? To let some damn Cajun factory farmers butcher our Seths for fifty bucks a head? What's that? Oh! Less! Have you been doing a little research? To live in *the city,*" he snarled. "To *go to school* . . ."

While they fought, I frowned and studied the blackboard. The eraser had left a ghostly square on the front of the Chief's Dijon-golden vest, which was unfortunate because nobody was really doing laundry anymore. Balls of socks and underwear banked like snow around the corners of our bedrooms.

I don't know what Kiwi was doing for clean clothing during that period; for months my sister and I had been spraying our undershirts and shorts with Mom's perfume. A strong rose scent. It was in a heart-shaped bottle beveled in tiny gold and pink hexagons with a black rubber pump. It was the fanciest thing in our house by a big margin—tinted and glamorous, foreign enough to feel a little sinister. (We thought of it as an ancient formula; it was a scent called Fox, discontinued in the early 1970s.) Ossie and I had worked out a rationing system:

two pumps, per sister, per day. We were using Mom up, I worried, and for some reason that fear made me want to spray on more and more. The perfume worked like a liquid clock for us: half a bottle drained to a quarter, that was winter.

Both my parents had denied that my mother's illness was serious, not just our father. They claimed that she was getting better right up until the moment that she left for the hospice. Dr. Gautman, her oncologist, was the first to show my brother and sister and me "the chart," to say "T3c" to us, and to translate this alphanumeric code into the frightening coda of "your mother's final days." Dr. Gautman gave us plastic glasses of water with lemon from the nurses' station before he broke the news to us: "The Malig-Nancy has spread beyond her, ah, her ovaries, I'm afraid . . ."

And into your mother's liver, and to the pleural fluid of her lungs. As a kid I heard the word malignancy as "Malig-Nancy," like an evil woman's name, no matter how many times Kiwi and the Chief and Dr. Gautman himself corrected me. Our mother had mistaken her first symptoms for a pregnancy, and so I still pictured the Malig-Nancy as a baby, a tiny, eyeless fist of a sister, killing her.

"Nobody is going to a *Loomis school*. We are not abandoning your mother's dream here, do you understand that? We are the Bigtree Tribe, son, and we have a business to run . . ."

Meanwhile the list beneath Carnival Darwinism kept growing:

ADAPTATION 1: INVEST IN SALTWATER CROCS
ADAPTATION 2: WE BECOME AMPHIBIOUS—NEW WET-SUIT
 COSTUMES FOR THE GIRLS? SCUBA WITH THE SETHS?
ADAPTATION 3: MODERNIZE THE GATOR PIT—ILLUMINATED
 DIVING BOARD, BUBBLE JETS

The Chief pulled out a booklet of photographs of the saltwater crocs he was interested in acquiring: horned and sad-looking, these crocs did not seem like gods of the Nile. They resembled partially deflated tires. The seller was a retired breeder in Myrtle City, South Carolina, who wanted twenty-five thousand dollars for them. Kiwi flipped the booklet over without looking at it.

*   *   *

That night Osceola never came home from her walk. When I woke up at midnight her bed was neatly made. Nothing like this had ever happened before; Ossie didn't even like to go to the tree house alone. I lay awake waiting for her return until 3:22 a.m. When you are waiting for somebody for that long, your ceiling fan can whip ordinary air into a torture. I must have finally nodded off, because when I woke again there was Ossie, snoring lightly in her black cotton dress. She had collapsed facedown on the pillow. Her puffy white arms were flung in a T over the mattress. Wet mangrove leaves clung to every clothed and unclothed inch of her, even her fingers, even the line of her scalp. Where had she been? In a gator hole? Crawling around a tunnel? Osceola was smiling, some good dream rippling over her.

The next day Ossie stalked downstairs without apology, as self-possessed as a cat, and slid the obituaries section out of the Chief's paper. She spooned eggs out of the frying pan, opened the obituaries on the countertop like this was all very normal. She still had on screwy lipstick and was wearing a pair of Mom's fishnet stockings, her legs pale and unshaven.

Your legs look like Sasquatches in nets, I considered saying. *They look nothing like our mother's.* I kept waiting for the Chief to make a comment.

Kiwi came downstairs and did a double take.

"Well, you look weird. New pajamas? Did somebody exhume you last night?"

Kiwi looked exhausted, too, with his baggy eyes and his dirty hair, the top half of his red scalp greased to a wet-looking brown, as if somebody had tried to put out a fire on Kiwi's head with a rag. He sat down and gaped at Ossie.

"You're the one who's been wearing that same shirt since, like, Christmas," Ossie mumbled. She left her toast and her runny eggs untouched and shoved past him, the stockings making an itchy noise as she opened and shut the door. Outside it was a beautiful sunny morning. For a second the sky yawned blue at us, then disappeared. The Chief looked blankly up from the newspaper. An ad on the front page read: WORLD OF DARKNESS TO HOST INFERNAL LIGHT SHOW. It was a hologram ad. If you let your eyes unfocus, a laser shot out of a whale's blowhole and fractaled into columns of fire.

"Well?" Our dad shuffled Kiwi's hair. "What's your problem today, son?"

"Ossie is talking to the *dead people* again, Chief," I told him.

My father was sipping at a third cup of black coffee. He glanced up at us with the dreamy look of a mutt leashed to a tree.

"It's a stage, Ava. We've been over this. You want me to talk to her?"

"Cancer happens in stages," my brother grunted, "and guess what the last one is?"

I stirred crumbs into a puddle of ketchup. Sometimes the word "cancer" was like a hinge we could swing onto a conversation about Mom, but not that day. Out of the corner of my eye I noticed something crawling along the bottom of the Chief's newspaper. Just the advertisement again, lifting fizzily away from the paper.

Lasers! We didn't have anything close to a *laser*. I felt queasy with a new kind of embarrassment. Until 1977, Swamplandia! had used crank generators. The caimans had eaten or destroyed most of the eraser-size bulbs in their terrarium. The poor bear was eating her fish heads under strings of five-and-dime Christmas lights.

"I need to go change some things, you guys," I mumbled.

Outside our porch had become a cauldron of pale brown moths and the bigger ivory moths with sapphire-tipped wings, a sky-flood of them. They entered a large rip in our screen. They had fixed wings like sharp little bones, these moths, and it was astonishingly sad when you accidentally killed one.

"Ossie!" I called. "Ossie, wait for me!"

CHAPTER THREE

Osceola K. Bigtree in Love

Shortly after Ossie's strange birthday, our Ouija "séances" began to change focus. Our sessions at the board became a game of spectral Telephone: Ossie would get me to anchor my side of the pointer while she cruised through the alphabet, summoning "boyfriends." It made her too sad, she explained, to get "a dial tone" when we tried to ring Mom; now we were going to practice conversing with other ghosts, the ones whom she could make contact with. At first I refused to play; I felt as though we were giving up on our mother. Getting Mom on the board was the whole point of the game, as I'd understood it. But pretty soon I started to sort of enjoy reading my sister's conversations with these ghosts—it was a very special kind of eavesdropping. Your eyes had to dart around the board and add up the words as fast as her pointer flew. We sat on the bedroom planks and spelled things to ourselves like I LOVE YOU, GORJUS. Wally Pipp was my sister's first "date." Wally looked like a living dimple, just this chubby footnote to sports history that she'd found in a book called *Baseball: An American Passion*. It was not for me to criticize my sister's tastes, but why not try for Jackie Robinson, Babe Ruth? I asked her. Or even Lefty Gomez? Why not Lefty?

"Too famous," Ossie told me, concentrating. "We've got to be realistic here, Ava."

Then the rules changed again, and Ossie told me that I was not allowed to play anymore. I was "too young to understand" her Spiritist communications. Ouija was no longer "our toy"; it was now a private rotary. She'd sit with her delicate hands vaulted over the pointer for an hour, like a concert pianist waiting for her score to appear.

Now that I couldn't play the game with her anymore, I was happy to ally myself with my brother. We'd tag-team tease her:

"Hey, Ossie, what do baby ghosts eat for breakfast? *Dreaded wheat!*"

"What do you call a ghost's mother? *Trans-parent!*"

In addition to his many academic aptitudes, Kiwi had a genius for embarrassing our sister—he could make her plump, serene face crumple into tears of rage in under a minute, and I encouraged him. If she got angry, then I knew she was listening to us. Frequently now she was within earshot of us but zonked, out of it. When she was doing a séance her pupils blew wide and her violet eyes became as hard and shiny as bottle caps. You could yell her name at her and she wouldn't look up. During the day it was easy to roll your eyes at Ossie's love spells. At night everything changed. Then something shifted in our house's atmosphere, and I felt outnumbered. Ghosts silked into our bedroom like cold water. Ossie sucked in her breath and twisted in the yellow sheets, just like my fantasy picture of a hurricane being born. Sometimes she called out strange names. Then a ghost would enter her. I knew it, because I could see my sister disappearing, could feel the body next to me emptying of my Ossie and leaving me alone in the room. The ghost went moving through her, rolling into her hips, making Ossie do a jerky puppet dance under her blankets.

Get out of here, ghost, I'd think very loudly across the chasm between our two beds. *Get back in your grave! You leave my sister alone!*

Ossie told me that when she left our room at night she was going on "dates" to meet these ghosts in the woods. She made me swear I wouldn't tell the Chief. "You have to cover for me, Ava, okay?" I nodded queasily, hoping that Kiwi was right, that the séances were just silly pageantry, an excuse Osceola made up to wear her homemade purple turban with the gold felt star. By noon her terrifying "possessions" became as unrecollectable to me as a dream and the whole problem seemed goofy. So what if she went on these "dates"? Probably it was just a new permutation of the game, and at least this way I got to play it with her again, albeit in the sidekick position of secret-keeper.

One Friday I found *The Spiritist's Telegraph* open on my bed. It wasn't anything I could read: the letters were printed in a runic alphabet that looked to me like flattened bugs. I'd had enough of this spooky crap, feeling scared in my own house—I carried the huge book to our bathtub, thinking that I would turn the faucet on it. When I set it down, a skinny velvet bookmark dropped out like a tongue. I screamed and threw a washcloth over it.

"Ava?" my sister called suspiciously later that evening. "Do you think one of the ghosts flew my book into the bathtub?"

"Yes. I do." In my comic book another radioactive superhero had just saved the planet Earth. Why couldn't Ossie read cheerful stuff like this? "Probably it was an ex-boyfriend of yours."

I developed a weedy crop of superstitions regarding *The Spiritist's Telegraph.* If accidentally I glimpsed one of the ink drawings of the Victorian Spiritists in their lizard-frilled dresses, or of one of the purple "daemons" built like pugilists, I had to knock twice on something real to ease a bad feeling inside of me. *Not-real,* I'd recite. *One-two.* I knocked on wood, food, the wavy black soap dish with melted pink soap flakes, even Tokay, our house gecko.

"Ava? Ahh, chickee, why are you knocking on your *sneakers*?" Ossie was standing in the door frame. "You are such a weirdo."

"That's not what I was doing." I pretended to do a sit-up. "See? I was exercising."

My sister wrinkled her nose at me, amused. For a second I was happy, because it looked like my stupidity had knocked her back into being regular old Ossie again.

"Hey, Ossie? Have you heard from Mom yet?"

"No, Ava. I haven't heard anything." She smiled an old, brave smile at me. "I'm looking."

Somehow I had worked it out in my mind to where I could believe in our mother without having to believe in ghosts exactly. In fact, I was discovering all sorts of beliefs and skepticisms turning like opposite gears inside me, and little drawers of hopes and fears I had forgotten to clean out. Sometimes while wandering around the park I'd still catch myself praying in an automatic way, like a sneeze, that my dead mom's blood test results would come back okay.

*   *   *

After the Chief unrolled his Carnival Darwinism scheme, I tried to speed my own evolution into a world-acclaimed wrestler. The Chief did rehearsals with me, and I got him to let me try Mom's old routines, which I ran so repetitively that I felt like my muscles were becoming hers. I held the tape loop under my right arm, like she did; I timed myself against Mom's best times. Once, with only a minimum of help from my dad, I got a Seth's jaws taped shut in four minutes and twenty-two seconds. (Hilola Bigtree could win a match in thirty seconds flat.) The Chief wouldn't let me climb up her diving board—he said I wasn't a strong enough swimmer yet—but I kept pleading my case. Pretty soon, if my plan succeeded, I'd be performing the Silent Night and possibly even Swimming with the Seths for a lot of people.

One morning on my way home from wrestling practice in the Pit, I saw my sister sitting at one of the picnic tables outside the Swamp Café. Her hair was a weird and glittery beacon viewed through the dense brush at the end of the wood-chip trail. I stared across the outdoor seating area: a sea of empty tables, several studded with blackbirds nibbling around for crumbs. Ossie was slumped over with her head on the table, eyes closed, the heavy clouds pushing seaward above her.

"Ossie," I hissed through my teeth. "Ossie, wake up! Nobody thinks that's funny but you."

Two tables over a cormorant was pecking at a dessicated potato chip, its head as glossy as a seal's; then it hopped onto Ossie's pile of books and began to stab its beak serenely near my sister's frozen face. I screamed. Ossie's nose twitched but her eyes stayed shut. I screamed but I couldn't get her eyes to open, I couldn't even startle the cormorant; it cocked its head at me impassively and then continued to nick at the table.

"OSSIE, WAKE UP!"

Ossie opened her eyes, three strands of pale hair striping her face. The bird flew off. My sister looked truly surprised to see me, and maybe a little scared.

"Ava? How long have I been out here? I was holding a séance . . ."

"Don't be stupid," I said happily. "You were just playing a trick on me."

"Sure. Gotcha." She smiled back at me but her eyes looked clouded, like agitated water after a Seth's roll. Ossie had been doing some serious reading, I saw. The black spell book was quilled with crimson bookmarks.

That night, Osceola didn't come home at all. I woke up and saw her comforter doubled under the pillow. Guilt made my logic run backward: I decided that I had to find my sister before I could tell anybody she was missing. At sunrise I tiptoed downstairs to look for her; by dumb luck I decided to check the Gator Pit first. Ossie was asleep in the middle bleachers in her dirty beige pajamas. Little strings of brown blood marked where she had been scratching bug bites in her sleep.

"She needs medicine," Kiwi said grimly when I told him where I'd found her. "She's not well . . ." He tapped his skull with his pencil. "She needs a mainland psychiatrist. Maybe she's sleepwalking."

"Nah, Kiwi. She's okay." I wished now that I'd kept Ossie's activities to myself. "She's just playing." But, so far as I could tell, it hadn't been a game for months. What sort of game made you blind and quiet?

Kiwi and I found the Chief in the kitchen, drawing his fork through an aluminum tin of melted cheese. Tiny broccoli florets floated in the gluey cheese like a forest consumed by lava.

"Chief, you need to help Ossie. She's experiencing delusions. Hallucinations. Ava says she was pretending, at first, but now she thinks she has real powers. She's reading this thing—" Kiwi dropped that book onto the table and stepped back, as if expecting a bomb to go off.

"Goddamn, what is this?"

The Chief's brows plummeted. He'd found the pictures in the appendix. Over his shoulder I saw a scary one: a devil squatted on the apron of a Spiritist's dress, wrinkling puddles into her skirt with its little hooves. It looked both lamblike and lascivious. The devil smiled shyly out at us. Spikes of hair covered its body.

"She doesn't date those things," I said hurriedly. "Only ghosts."

The Chief removed his reading glasses, shut the book.

"Kiwi, son, you two can't find something else for her to read on that Library Boat? Something that's not total bullcrap?"

My heart quickened in triumph—he *saw*. "We told you so! You have to stop her now, okay?"

"Christ, Ava, what do you want me to do?" The Chief looked up at me with a terrible blank expression. "She's going through something. She needs a distraction. We used to have a word for your sister: boy-crazy. It could be worse: at least she's not dating some mainland jackass with a motorcycle, huh?" He laughed his onstage laugh, ha-ha-har, the big seal bark in triplicate for an audience. "Some loser with an earring!"

"Could it not perhaps be better, Dad?" asked Kiwi. "That's the bright side here, that the dead man does not have a piercing?"

The Chief blinked and blinked, as if he had momentarily blinded himself with his own silver lining. There was no coffee left in his mug but he kept touching the chipped green rim to his lips. "Hell, who knows? Do you know, son? Ava? I guess I'm no longer the expert on Better versus Worse."

You could hear the serious effort of his laughter. I pictured my dad trapped inside Ossie's painting of the underworld, chipping away at the enormous rocks. His little Dule screwdriver producing sparks, flakes . . .

"Dad, I just . . ."

"Listen: your sis has a bad case of lovesickness. For a girl her age, that's like the common cold. A case of the sniffles." As if to prove his point, he made a gulping noise in his own throat. I noticed that our dad wasn't looking at us. "It'll pass."

"Lovesickness?" Now it was my turn to gape at him.

"Sure," the Chief said. "Puppy love. You're both readers, eh? Study up on Romeo. You can't forbid love to anybody. Forbidding is just stoking the flames. You can't boss love, kids."

The Chief pushed away from the table; I think he was trying his best not to yell at us. He put his fiery heron headdress on the countertop, next to the blue box of corn cereal; he opened the two faucets. Then he dropped to his knees under the twin gushers to fix the kitchen plumbing. We stayed to watch. Just a bad leak, he grunted. When the cabinet doors opened, we could actually smell the rank, strawberry-colored puddles of water. We could see around the Chief's head to tiny cairns of mouse turds.

"How's that look up there, Ava?"

Some of the pipes had turned iron red and his voice sounded hollow in that cavity. Kiwi gave it a last shot:

"Chief? Did you hear us, Dad? These guys she's dating—they're dead."

"Yes," the Chief sighed. "Yes, I'll admit, that is a little peculiar."

*   *   *

The Chief's efforts at normalcy began to make me feel many inexplicable things, like anger and sorrow and a peculiar self-loathing. Shame on me, I mean really on top of me, as slick and endless as a sweat. This shame was a weird alloy, but after a while I didn't even mind it—it was like a sword I'd made, glinting and strong. If I didn't hate myself, I had a feeling that I'd start hating him, my dad. Whenever I came across the Chief mucking out the Gator Pit, holding the little accordion trunk of the submersible pump above the algae, all alone, without Grandpa or Mom or help of any kind, my whole belly tightened.

Once I asked my father, "Chief, why are you hosing the stage when the stadium is empty? Why bother getting dressed at all, for nobody?"

"Well, my kids are hardly 'nobodies,' Ava," he'd chuckled, like we were this great comedy team. "My kids are not some mainland twerps—they are the finest wrestlers in America!" It was a scary comedy. Sometimes we'd try to clown around in the old way and I'd get a feeling like invisible pies dripping down both our faces.

Some team! The Chief was doing so many jobs alone. I'd fix on the Chief's raw, rope-burned palms or all the gray hairs collected in his sink, and I'd suffer this terrible side pain that Kiwi said was probably an ulcer and Ossie diagnosed as lovesickness. Or rather a nausea produced by the "black fruit" of love—a terror that sprouted out of your love for someone like rotting oranges on a tree branch. Osceola knew all about this black fruit, she said, because she'd grown it for our mother, our father, Grandpa Sawtooth, even me and Kiwi. Loving a ghost was different, she explained—that kind of love was a bare branch. I pictured this branch curving inside my sister: something leafless and complete, elephantine, like a white tusk. No rot, she was saying, no fruit. You couldn't lose a ghost to death.

She showed me a diagram in *The Spiritist's Telegraph,* part of a chapter entitled "The Corporeal Orchard." I've never forgotten it. It had a punctilious, surgical level of detail, like one of Leonardo da Vinci's anatomical sketches—only in this drawing the aortas and ventricles of a human heart burst into flowering trees.

"Gross, Os. You think there's a rotten fruit stuck inside me?" I touched a rib, horrified but also filling with a sort of dark self-regard.

"Not exactly. You're scared. See? You're angry because you think the Chief is going to die, too."

"Huh? No I don't!"

"You're angry at him but it's too early, Ava."

"Never mind." I frowned. Ossie thought she was so smart now that she'd read one book. Black fruit, how stupid can you get! "You know what, I think Kiwi is right." I lifted the dirty stripes of my Swamplandia! T-shirt and scowled at my belly. "It feels more like an ulcer."

But I couldn't shake the image, crates and crates of sunken black oranges. My heart gone wormy and rotten with fear. I thought of the corporeal orchard whenever I saw the Chief's face.

It was around this time that I developed a weird fascination with the tiny cockroaches that had overtaken our café. I'd see them marching around the perimeter and I'd feel a little twinge; I imagined a weird kinship between us. Their skeletons were flipped outward into hard mirrors, but inside, all jelly. They tapped and tapped at each other's backs. I'd get unaccountably sad some nights, just watching this little blind ballet go tickling up the walls. Kiwi noticed my creepy new interest and tried to encourage it with a book he'd found on the Library Boat called *Why Insects Amaze Us.*

On Saturdays the Chief continued to hold rehearsals for the two of us. This was a gift from my father to me, probably one of the most magnificent I will ever receive in this lifetime, although when I was thirteen I just thought of it as "a morning." Very extraordinarily ordinary.

"Wake up, Ava," he'd say into my dim room, beautiful words.

Ossie, meanwhile, continued to break curfew with impunity, to date the dead, to wear very unflattering homemade turbans. If the Chief couldn't fix Ossie, he still tried to stay active. He banished not ghost men but material things: six-pack plastics, empty tubs of Delacroix gator chow, paper plates, rotten eggs, dock flotsam—whatever trash we could produce in a day. Each night he burned our garbage in a ditch behind the coop. This was one of the last Bigtree routines to go. Columns of thick smoke rose behind the red wall at dusk, and frantic clucks rose from the chicken coop like rainfall reversing itself, spraying up into the cumulus puffs in the night sky. From the kitchen window, I would watch the Chief build his midweek pyre: leftovers and little bones and milk cartons, eggshells and newspapers, a grab bag of detritus. Whatever we couldn't use or sell before nightfall, our chieftain struck a match against and sent to the stars.

CHAPTER FOUR

Ava the Champion

One Monday in early May I sailed into the kitchen and snatched an envelope out of the Chief's blunt fingers—he held on to it for an extra beat out of a wrestler's instinct, his square nails raking scum across the envelope. He chewed his breakfast cigarette and regarded me with deadened amusement.

"Somebody has a pen pal?"

The Chief had put on his humongous bifocals to go through our mailbag, specs which made him look a little like Elvis Presley or an erudite bear. They were tinted dark yellow on the bottom. He hated to wear these glasses in front of us and he never wore them in front of our tourists. They were part of his accounting costume—glasses and red pens for sorting our bills.

"No, Chief. It's not a pen pal I'm writing to."

"No?"

"Nope. It's like a contest? For money? A lot of money, Chief." Lying to the Chief like this felt like freezing a lake into ice and skating quickly over it. "I probably won't win, but if I do I am going to donate it all to your Carnival Darwinism."

"Well. That's . . ." The Chief stared at me in a peculiar way, as if he were about to sneeze, and then the muscles in his face relaxed again. His voice sounded offstage, tired: "Just don't send these guys any of your own money, Ava. Don't get scammed." He patted my back.

"You know the real contests happen in the Pit with your Seth, right, champ?"

I nodded. The fan was blowing at the Chief's headdress, flattening every feather so that they waved in place, like a school of fishes needling into a strong current. Something lunged in me then, receded. A giggle or a sob. A noise. I thought: *You look very stupid, Dad.*

"You'd better not let me catch you writing to any grown assholes in jail, kid. Or dead guys." The smile crumpled on his face. "Please."

My still-secret plan was to enter and win the same national championship that Miss Hilola Bigtree swept before she was a mother or even a newlywed, when she was eighteen years old and had first started dating my father. I loved staring at the bend of my own shadowy features in Mom's trophies, and this was the largest one: NATIONAL CHAMPION, 1971. AMERICAN ASSOCIATION OF ALLIGATOR WRESTLERS. This trophy even looked a little like my mom to me: a busty golden lady with skinny arms and fists on hips.

"How come you never got to be the national champion again?" I asked my mother once when I was nine or ten. She'd won the other trophies here, on our island—the Chief had given them to her. This was still impressive to me. But I wondered: why didn't she want to beat the Seminole wrestlers, to show the Miccosukee alligator handlers what we Bigtrees were made of? We were pinning up laundry on the clothesline near the dandelion wash, and she'd laughed at me from behind a wailing wall of bedsheets. Only a square of forehead and her dark eyes were visible:

"Because I am your mother now, Ava. Because I have important things to do right here, on our island. Honey, did I leave that box of clothespins over by you? This wind!"

That day a category 2 hurricane was coming; truly, it was a strange time to try to pin up laundry, with the swamp wind whipping our hair at each other across the clothesline like a weird game of tennis. We had the same kind of hair, a black coffee shade with ruddy glinting, thick and ursine like Judy the bear's fur—a big point of pride for me.

Our mother, in several beautiful ways, may have been a little crazy. For example: who dries their clothing with a hurricane coming? Like Ossie, Mom got distracted easily. It was seventy-thirty odds whether she would remember a conversation with you. Her moods could do sudden plummets, and she'd have to "take a rest" in the house, but she'd always emerge from these spells with a smile for us. Until she got sick, I can't remember our mother ever missing a show.

"Honestly, can you imagine me without your father!" She used to say this all the time. With a sort of vacant, sticky violence, she'd kiss the forehead of whichever of her children was nearest.

Even as a kid I understood that she was kissing us to answer some question that she was putting to herself. Was she happy? we wondered. Were we the right answer? My mother married the Chief and gave birth to Kiwi at age nineteen; she started her career as an alligator wrestler that same year.

"She married him too young," Kiwi told me once in a sad, knowing voice. But when I told Mom what he'd said, she laughed herself dizzy. Then she repeated it to the Chief and they both roared.

"Listen: your brother is an unkissed thirteen, Ava," she told me. "He is just a boy. His judgments are like green fruit. He doesn't have any idea about that stuff."

"What stuff?"

"Well, love!" she said, exasperated but not with me, I didn't think. "Your father and I were sweethearts, you tell me what's too 'too' about that! Without Sam I'd still be on the mainland!"

But one night, the eve of their tenth wedding anniversary, she woke my sister and I and made us come out to the museum. It was very late at night—she'd been drinking rum and soda with the Chief and some of our neighbors. Nobody looked up from the porch as we crossed the lawn. Her palms were damp and she was a little wobbly on her feet, giggling like a girl herself as she let us guide her through the wet grass. We entered the main room of the museum holding hands. "Shh," she said. "No lights. We don't want your father coming out here, this is *just girls.*" I held the flashlight and let the light settle on one of her posters. In it, she wore her shrug of a smile and her dark hair in a bun. Half her body was submerged in the lake; behind her you could see the orange sun on the Seths' back plates.

"Turn the light off please, Ava," she whispered, and I remember her breath hot and rummy on our cheeks. To this day I think of rum as a marine smell; the scent of it on an adult's breath turned the big world as small and dark as a boat hold. Our mother took each of us by the hand and we shuffled awkwardly forward. Then she did a strange thing. She led us to the exhibit my father had made of their wedding day. Her dress, a long, simple gown in a mollusk shade of old lace, was behind glass. Her orchid headpiece, too, a ring of tiny, silvery blooms that looked like a halo with all the light crushed out of it. She made my sister and me put our palms on the glass, and then she made us each promise to wait until we were thirty years old to marry, *if* we married . . . We had both nodded very somberly. Mom was twenty-nine that year. In seven years she would be dead. We were six and nine at the time. I used to think the promise would make more sense when I got older, but I was thirteen now and that night in the museum seemed even more mysterious to me with each passing year, a memory too baffling to even broach with my sister. If we ever did succeed at locating Mom on the Ouija board, I thought, I had a list of important questions for her.

Where was the contest held? How did you enter? I didn't know. When I asked Grandpa Sawtooth about it, he'd raised an eyebrow at my father and squinted down at me for a long minute; then he snorted and told me that the contest was held in a top-secret location, where the judges threw you into seven feet of water, and you had thirty seconds to pull your alligator ashore and tape her jaws up. Bleeding too much disqualified you. Plenty of contestants died every year. A pipsqueak like me shouldn't enter, he said; I'd be gone in two bites.

I researched the Kentucky Derby on the Library Boat—the purse was one million dollars! And those leprechauns were only riding horses. Obviously my mother had not been a millionaire. My heroic logic was as follows: if I was the champion, like her, our fame would be a perennial draw.

You had to be eighteen to compete—that's what my mother told me at nine when I begged to be a contender. So in a typewritten letter that took me three drafts to compose, I asked the commission to make an exception and allow me to wrestle at age thirteen. I explained about my mother's cancer and Swamplandia!'s many troubles. My own feats with the Seths I tried to describe modestly but candidly. I didn't brag exactly, but I made sure the commissioners understood that I was the real deal; I wasn't some unserious church girl from Nebraska who had only ever handled pet-store geckos, or some inlander, "Rebecca" or

"Mary," a pigtailed zoo volunteer. The kind of girl who liked to do those drugstore paint-by-number watercolors of horses. Shetland ponies. *Palominos.* I bet the Marys were really excellent at that.

"I am a Bigtree wrestler" was the first line of my letter, and as insurance I'd enclosed a famous key-chain picture of my mother. It sold for $4.99 in the gift shop, and you could also get it on a cozy or a magnet. My mother looks a little older than Osceola, maybe eighteen or nineteen, her hair is shining like mahogany; she's sort of studious-looking in thick eyeglasses (contact lenses and chaste emerald bathing suits came later, as a concession to our modern tourists); she's got an eight-foot alligator's jaws in her bare hands. HILOLA BIGTREE AND HER SETH I wrote carefully on the bottom, and added in parentheses (MY MOTHER).

My best guess was that these individuals were based in America's capital, Washington, D.C., but I hadn't yet been able to locate an exact street address. Gus Waddell claimed never to have heard of them. Well, Gus was really more of a nautical man, a very nice man but not exactly what you'd call educated when it came to herpetological sports.

I wasn't going to risk a no by involving the Chief and Kiwi prematurely. I wasn't going to tell my sister, either—Ossie was like an aquarium when it came to other people's secrets. I sent this letter to the Smithsonian, the state universities, the Florida Wildlife and Gaming Commission, along with a flap note: "Sir or madam, please do me the great favor of forwarding this letter to the correct bureau(s). Thank you!!!"

If they accepted me, I figured that I would be the youngest person, boy or girl, ever to compete at the national level. Five years younger than my mother, even.

That same month, a remarkable thing happened on our island: a miracle, a freak rainstorm of luck during a time of cash and tourist droughts. I got to watch this miracle unfold inside a glass case—not in our museum but in one of the reptile incubators. On Swamplandia! we hatched baby alligators under heat lamps, dozens a year, using incubators that the Chief got on the cheap from a bankrupt chicken-farming family in Ocala. We restocked the Pit with the largest and the hardiest of the alligators, and the rest we sold to St. Augustine reptile farms in north Florida or released. Thermostats controlled the gender of the future alligators in their eggs, and the incubator I was polishing was set to 84 degrees Fahrenheit—a female brood. I breathed a tiny porthole onto the incubator glass and peered in.

This was *excellent* timing: as I watched, a tiny caruncle punctured the eggshell. Baby alligators are born with these, the "egg tooth," a tusk on the tip of their snout that allows them to punch through the membrane of their eggshells. A Seth's eggs are oblong and leathery, narrower than the eggs a hen lays. Next I heard the telltale squeal, a sound that came from inside the eggs—the alligators were pipping! The fetal gators coordinate their jailbreak by making a squeaky noise at a frequency that can be heard inside the shell; now the noise had begun, and the thirty-two hatchlings in this incubator were butting and rocking against the shell membrane.

The first alligator to hatch caused me to frown and lean in, because there was something unusual about her—the alligator's hide appeared to be red. A tiny, fiery Seth. Her skull was the exact shape and shining hue of a large halved strawberry. At first I thought her pigmentation was a trick of the light and I was afraid even to touch her. The red on her skin seemed like a disease I could contract through my fingertips or a spell I could break, a color so pure and unreal that I thought it might rub off.

I put her on the kitchen scale we kept next to the extra lamps. She weighed seventy grams. She was nine inches from snout to tail.

Her claws scrabbled at the air when I picked her up. The door to the shed stood open, and her skin brightened like an ember. I half-expected her temperature to flare up, too. To burn and sizzle. But her scales were cool and damp. She curled flat against my palms, reminding me of the inlay of a dragon I'd seen once on Mrs. Gianetti's fancy black Oriental dinette set. Her pupils were compass needles, thin and wobbly. Her camelia-pink eyes blinked and blinked, and I wondered if she was surprised to find a world outside her egg. Like any hatchling gator, her snout tapered into a look of flutey suspicion. A yawn revealed the paler watermelon chinks on her tongue, and I suppressed a laugh.

The Chief is going to turn a backflip! I thought. *This alligator could save our park!* But when I thought about telling my family about her, my mouth turned to sand. I felt very certain that she was going to die. That nothing born this color could live for long in the open air. We'd hatched hundreds of broods on Swamplandia! and they grew very slowly, a foot a year. Few hatchlings made it to adulthood, even in captivity. (I still don't know what melanistic fluke or mutation accounted for her. Her sisters were born the usual straw-yellow-banded black; they died later that same week, all thirty-one of them, of yolk sac infections.)

We had an old forty-gallon aquarium in storage and I dragged this out and swabbed it clean for her; I hid the tank in the fenced-in shrubbery behind the shed. All day I'd invent excuses to go back there. *Keep breathing,* I'd command her through the glass. The rise and fall of the Seth's belly scales could hypnotize me for an hour at a stretch.

When a week passed and the red Seth was still crawling around in her tank, I felt a terrible hope begin to grow inside me, at pace with the alligator. *Two more weeks, and then I'll tell,* I thought. *Three . . . If you tell him now, she will die.* What a dumb superstition! I knew that. When Mom was sick, I went around knocking on everything for luck, not just wood. I avoided black and even dark brown cats, I skirted the Chief's ladder, I carried around Grandpa's creepy, ostensibly lucky marsh rabbit's foot, and did any of this make a difference? My mom died. But my new superstition didn't care to hear about the earlier failure. It told me, *If you tell anyone about the red alligator, she will die or disappear.*

At first I thought this fear might be like a gut cramp that would pass. Then my throat would relax in a day or two and then I would be able to share the miracle of the red alligator with the other Bigtrees. I tried to bargain with the fear: *Four more weeks,* I told it. *If this alligator lives another month, then it's settled. I will definitely tell them.* If I could get her to nine months, she'd be eighteen inches long and out of the danger zone of predation. I figured I just had to keep her alive for long enough to prove my fear wrong.

So as the World of Darkness usurped our place in the rankings, I became a hunter of minnows. I looked for life that my pet Seth could gulp: tadpoles loitering in the cattails, green anoles, clear slugs that I peeled from the trees. Later I had to raise the baby rats she ate, and why I thought one creature was my beloved pet while the other creatures were food is still a mystery to me. That was my first clue that love can warp a hierarchy; the whole pyramid got flipped on its head. My pet, because she was mine, was at the top of the chain. I cared for the squirmy swamp rats in the most perfunctory way, with none of the love I felt for my red Seth. The rats and fish ate the small golden crickets, and the crickets seemed to live on air and chirpy fear, surviving for weeks on the pickleweed at the bottom of their cages, so that there was a whole food chain happening in the forty-gallon tank that culminated in my alligator, my lovely ruby girl.

Three weeks after my red monster was born, on a warm and limpid Sunday afternoon, the Chief finally made good on his promise and took us on the ferryboat to the mainland to visit our grandfather. On the ferry ride over, I stayed on deck. I stood mute as a heron on the stern, rubbing seawater across my rashy left shin with the toe of one sneaker to create a sort of pleasant burn and staring backward at Swamplandia!, where I'd left the red Seth in her hiding spot. To even think "the red Seth" was like staring into a radiance I'd swallowed, a sun. *Maybe I will tell Grandpa Sawtooth about her, just as a kind of practice.* Grandpa Sawtooth would be a safe husk for that sun, a good secret-keeper, because right away the secret would go dark again. Right away he would forget her. *Listen, a red alligator and I are going to save your real home, Grandpa,* I wanted to promise him, but I bet that Grandpa wouldn't even know my name this time. And Kiwi said that as soon as we stepped off the retirement boat Grandpa would lose the faces that had been talking to him.

There had been a dramatic buildup to Grandpa Sawtooth's eviction from Swamplandia!

First he'd gotten confused during a tram tour and driven the whole train of eight cars in tight doughnuts around the stilted foundation of the Bigtree Swamp Café, his tramload of twelve strawberry blond Utah tourists waving at everybody in polite despair to *please come help them?*

Eight days later, Grandpa bit a man. On his face and neck, mostly. Just hanging there from the screaming man's cheek like a grinning eel until the Chief wrestled him loose. "Oh shit!" shouted the Chief. "Ossie, babe, get some napkins!"

The bitten guy turned out to be a soupy-eyed lawyer from Arkansas. Now as a punishment for his forgetfulness Grandpa had to live at the

Out to Sea Retirement Community, in a peeling umber cabin, on this refurbished and possibly haunted houseboat that he shared with a bunch of pissed-off septuagenarians. Grandpa's bunkmate, Harold Clink, was ninety-two years old and almost entirely deaf and yet he would talk to you only in song, songs without rhythms, songs that he made up; we Bigtrees had all worried (some of us hoped!) that Grandpa would kill this person in the night. The houseboat was retired, too, at permanent anchor in the marina. The seniors got issued these pastel pajamas that made them look like Easter eggs in wheelchairs. If you went to visit, that's what you saw: Easter eggs in these adult cribs, Easter eggs on toilets with guardrails. Black curtains closed the portholes.

We all sat down in unison on the crinkly sofa. Flat red flowers crept up the wall. A nurse was mixing medicines in the galley, humming some jaunty tune—I could see her big brown arm stirring orange powder through a carafe. Grandpa called this woman Robina, although that didn't necessarily mean this was her name. We liked possibly-Robina because she brought us orange juice with flexistraws and teased Grandpa with a humor that he tolerated well.

"These your grandkids! No! *You* produced these beauties, Mr. Bigtree?" Robina's laughter rose like the bubbles in the aquarium of coffee behind her, rich and automatic. "They must take after their grandmother, eh?"

Ossie and I touched our crazy hair, flattered. Without consulting one another, we'd both worn our dresses. We smelled churchy, like Mom's bottled roses. Kiwi did most of the talking; the Chief grew small-mouthed and uneasy on the undulating boat. It was like he'd caught Grandpa Sawtooth's sickness—those two kept staring at each other as if they'd never before met. On our last visit to Out to Sea, the Chief hung the Seth of Seths skull on the wall, next to the steel clock, a gift that Grandpa failed to appreciate or even understand.

"It was your first Seth, Dad!" The Chief didn't start yelling until the second hour of our visit; you could almost watch his anger rising stealthily, like sweat stiffening on fur. "The Seth of Seths! The first alligator that you and Mama ever kept on the island. You're going to tell me you don't remember *that*?"

Possibly-Robina was waiting for us at the cabin door. She had wrapped the Seth of Seths skull in two Hefty trash bags, the twist tie done up like a bow, like this monster was her gift to *us* now. Robina ordered us to take the skull back home because all of a sudden it frightened Grandpa; he'd point at it and mewl, his eyes wet.

"It's his own damn alligator, ma'am," the Chief sighed, accepting the trash bag. "I don't know what's gotten into him."

Nobody had told Grandpa Sawtooth that our mother was dead. I could feel the secret rolling between the four of us like an egg in a towel. We never talked about why we kept this a secret from him—the secret just happened. *Somebody should tell him before* he *dies,* I frowned. I pictured Grandpa meeting my mom at a red-lit intersection in the afterlife, his cry of sad surprise.

"Why don't you kids go wait outside?" the Chief asked. "Head over to the bus stop. I need to talk to your grandfather."

Kiwi raised his eyebrows at me and Ossie. He stood and pulled his ball cap down, sharked around our father, and Ossie and I scrambled after him. Sunlight burst into the gently rocking room and dazzled my pupils. We exited on the aft side of the vessel. I was happy to leave the perfume of medication and bedpans that filled the cabin. We debarked and sat on the pier, watching the ripples of our sneakers on the oily water. I was prepared for a long wait, but then fifteen minutes later we watched the Chief burst out of Sawtooth's cabin door. He waved us toward the bus stop, looking flushed and upset.

I didn't try to talk to him until an hour later, when we'd boarded the ferry.

"Chief Bigtree?" I used Dad's formal title, hoping to make up a little bit for the indignity of his having to carry the Seth of Seths in a Hefty bag. "Gross," Ossie had whispered on the long city bus ride to the ferry dock. "Poor Dad." It did not even look like Robina had given us a fresh bag.

"Ava Bigtree?" The Chief stared down at me. It was a long time before he could smile.

"What did you want to ask Grandpa for?"

"For money, dummy," snickered Kiwi. "Where's the treasure buried, Dad?"

"For advice," the Chief snarled, in a nastier voice than he ever used on family.

Kiwi was still laughing softly to himself, but with these big alarmed eyes, as if only the lower half of his face were getting the joke. Then the ferryboat hit a bumpy stretch of water that splashed everybody's faces; on the starboard side, a few little kids swallowed up to the knees by their humongous orange life vests screamed in joyful terror; when Kiwi looked over at me his eyes were bulging, his cheeks wet. Over the groan of the ferry's engine I could hear him laughing and laughing. The entire time he had not stopped laughing.

"Dad," he mimicked, "I need to buy these saltwater crocodiles, see, it's for my quack business model called Carnival Darwinism . . ."

The Chief leaned in and grabbed the scruff of Kiwi's T-shirt, spoke low and close: "Don't mouth off again, son. That's my fatherly advice to you." Kiwi's mouth opened like a doll's, exposing a white paste of chewed gum. Ossie crammed a fist into her own mouth and craned around to find me. The moment passed.

The rest of our ferry ride home was a silent one. I remember it now as a turning point, one of our last "normal" days as a family together, and maybe *the* last time that we assembled as a tribe on Swamplandia!, although at the time I just wanted to get home to pee and watch TV. Ossie hid behind the trunk of children's life vests and ate fistfuls of these golden dietetic candies that she'd stolen from the nurse's bowl at Out to Sea. Kiwi and I played cards, Go Fish and Walla-Walla, and he let me win every game. The Chief held the black bag on his lap. As soon as we left the harbor, he lifted the Seth of Seths out of the Hefty bag, cradling the skull with an air of sorrowful apology. The Chief loved that Seth—it wasn't part of any act.

Two passengers from Loomis County kept staring over and whispering. The Chief was wearing his faded yellow "visiting" shirt, which was older than Kiwi, buttoned up to his collar (*Why, Dad?*); he had his big hands folded on the Seth of Seth's squamosal bone. It sat on his lap like a briefcase. These Loomis men were wealthy, or wealthy to me: they wore belts with shiny buckles, and their khakied laps held fancy red double-decker tackle boxes. They were most likely on their way to play Injun for a weekend at the Red Eagle Key Fishing Camp; they didn't know my father was a Bigtree, and you could see the sneer in their eyes.

These mainland men debarked at Red Eagle. The Seth of Seths grinned over at us from our father's lap. The Chief sat like that, starfish-lipped, until the sky paled—and then we were home.

CHAPTER FIVE

Prodigal Kiwi

When we got back to the island, Ossie and the Chief headed toward the house to get some grub, but I padded alongside Kiwi and grabbed ahold of his elbow. His arms surprised me with their thinness. Nobody was really eating right, and Kiwi wasn't wrestling. I would never have guessed that the cessation of our alligator wrestling would make the least difference to him, to his body. But it had *mattered* to Kiwi; the changes on our island had robbed my brother of actual matter, had changed him in a way that I could touch. Skin bagged under his biceps. When I gripped his arm, I could feel how much we'd both weakened. Instead of feeling sad about this, I was for some reason teetering inside a wash of total joy. I squeezed down on the arm again, hard, to make sure that I was right, that we had both lost mass in the same place.

"Ow, Ava! You think that's funny? No? What are you smiling for, then?"

It was a strange vise to be in, that feeling. I let go of Kiwi's shrunken biceps and closed my left hand around my right arm. *Too skinny!* I thought, but this only stoked the joy in me. It didn't matter. We'd go back to regular rehearsals. We'd be a team, me and Kiwi—we'd do it for Carnival Darwinism. We'd get strong again, build up together. Maybe we could even choreograph a brother-and-sister show, once Kiwi got back into the swing of things . . .

"Come with me to the museum," I said sternly. "I want to show you something."

We stepped off the wood-chip trail that led away from the touristed park to our house and walked to the museum. The Chief had forgotten to lock up again. Shapes nuzzled toward us. It took a few seconds of blinking before your memory filled each like paint—that rectangle to my left was Grandma Risa's bedside table, that long and skinny geometry on the wall was Grandpa Sawtooth's .22 Winchester rifle. Extinct and taxidermied objects to us kids. A small bat shot through the door; moonlight pricked at the strings of hanging sleeves.

Somebody—who else but Ossie?—had stolen our mom's wedding dress. I'd discovered this theft while cleaning out the museum earlier in the day. I pointed my flashlight at Mom's empty case to show Kiwi: there was a raisiny blot on the wall that yesterday had contained a froth of lace. The hook that used to hold her orchid headpiece was naked metal. It bounced light back at us, a frantic signal: *something used to be here.*

Kiwi sighed. "Okay, Ava. That's what you brought me here to see."

"Look at that! I think Ossie took it."

"You think, Sherlock?"

"Should we tell on her? What do you think she stole it for? If she's wearing Mom's dress out there in the mud . . . Oh my gosh, Kiwi? If she *ruins* it . . ."

"I thought you hated that thing," Kiwi mumbled.

"I do!" I said angrily. "That's not the point, though . . ."

But my brother seemed distracted.

"I am finished with that man . . ." Kiwi was mumbling to himself.

"Who?" I let out a shocked laugh. "What man? *Dad?*"

"Do you know how much debt we're actually in, Ava? Play Go Fish with the bills on our table. Go ahead. Open any letter addressed to Dad. Do you know how much money it would take to buy even one of the items for his Carnival Darwinism project? He really thinks we can compete with the World of Darkness . . ."

I wanted to say: *Of course we can!* I'd been practicing holds that only the Chief and the best Seminole wrestlers performed.

"Why do you talk like that, Kiwi? Only a traitor talks that way."

"Why do you want to stay here so badly?"

I kicked a rock. Why save your own life?

"Because it's our home, dummy."

"But everybody moves, Ava. Mainlanders do it all the time. We could find a decent place on the Atlantic side of the city, I bet. I don't think you'd hate it there. I mean, you could still come visit Swamplandia! It's not like the island would just vanish without you. The alligators, you could still . . ."

He trailed off.

"I could still what? Take the ferry out to look at them, our Seths?"

"Ava," my brother said in a careful tone, "if we get you into a Loomis high school, I bet you could go to college, too . . ."

"But I don't *want* to leave." I hated how small my voice sounded. *A-va,* my mom used to say when I cried tears after flubbing a move onstage, *now you tell me, is that the octave of a Bigtree wrestler?*

"But you will. You will want to. You don't want to turn seventeen on this island, Ava, believe me."

I would vanish on the mainland, dry up in that crush of cars and strangers, of flesh hidden inside metallic colors, the salt white of the sky over the interstate highway, the strange pink-and-white apartment complexes where mainlanders lived like cutlery in drawers. Well, Kiwi pointed out, but we had survived the tourists, hadn't we? Hundreds of strangers at a time! But tourists' faces were like these flumes of bubbles: they jetted over our island and disappeared. *We* stayed on the island past dusk; *we* waited until the moon rode up over the swamp and the only faces in the windows were our own. That's what "home" and "family" meant, I thought: our four faces, our walls. If we left Swamplandia! for the mainland, what would happen? It was too strange to think about. In Loomis County my family would be the tourists, the bubbles.

"Ossie doesn't want to go. She's just one year younger than you and she wants to stay."

"Ossie found a way to get out of here without leaving her bedroom." Kiwi pushed at the bridge of his nose. "It's pretty genius, actually."

"Mom would *hate* it. Mom would feel responsible if we left; she would never forgive us. She would never get over it."

"Huh. How do you figure, Ava? Because Mom's dead."

Kiwi kicked the rock at me and I whammed my right foot into it, not aiming at him exactly but also not aiming *not* to hit him, not 100 percent opposed to the possibility of hitting him; the rock flew high and wide of his left shoulder and pinged off the case of Grandma Risa's gator-skinning knives.

"Jesus, watch it! Don't do that indoors. Look, you can't think like that, okay? Ava? Pay attention—you are using that pronoun erroneously. Because there is no 'she' anymore."

Frogs were chorusing thickly, invisibly, somewhere under the dock. I heard a hunter's splash and wondered what the Seth was after.

"Oh, God, Kiwi, I *know* that. I know she's dead. I'm not like *Ossie*."

But in fact I was like Ossie, in this one regard: I was consumed by a helpless, often furious love for a ghost. Every rock on the island, every swaying tree branch or dirty dish in our house was like a word in a sentence that I could read about my mother. All objects and events on our island, every single thing that you could see with your eyes, were like clues that I could use to reinvent her: would our mom love this thing, would she hate it? For a second I luxuriated in a real hatred of my brother.

"I hate him," said Kiwi.

"Yup. I mean, I don't." I frowned. "But I can see how you—"

"He's going to ruin everything. He thinks he's being optimistic or something but it's sick, Ava, what he's doing. We won't even have enough money to move."

I found a knot to work out on my left sneaker. The light from my flashlight was drawing long fingers of pittering moths to us. They twittered on the museum screens. Their wing beats spooked me—so stupid, I knew, since moths are just a flying paper.

"Do you ever think that Ossie's ghosts might be real, Kiwi?" I asked. Kiwi groaned.

"But Ossie does have powers," I blurted out. Hearing myself say this to my brother, I wondered if that was what I believed. Because Kiwi was shaking his head at me, I kept going: "Really, I swear it's true, Kiwi—you haven't seen her possessions. You don't know about how bad they can be, like nightmares . . ."

I wasn't sure how to explain what I meant to him; of course you can't see anybody else's actual dreams. But after my sister's séances, when she rocked into her "love possessions"? I'd roll onto the edge of my bed and watch her face flicker open and shut. Who knows what was being shown to her? It was weird detective work, like trying to guess the plot of a movie from the twitching of a smile in the audience.

"Sometimes when the ghost shows up she starts . . . moving the bed and she moans, Kiwi, it sounds funny but it's a little scary, too? That part's supposed to be a secret. She told me she can't stop it from happening . . ."

"She *moans?*" Kiwi said, making a face. "Jesus, Ossie . . ."

I bit my lip, as embarrassed as if I had just made the sound myself. "Kiwi? Do you think, when she has the bad dreams or the possessions, you could come and wake her up?"

"I'll tell you a secret, Ava. When she's tossing and turning that way? You are probably watching a *good* dream."

I nodded, pantomiming understanding. The orange spot from my flashlight looked like a little dog sniffing along the floor. Through the museum window I could see a shattering of light that would become our house if we walked toward it.

"Let's get out of here, Ava," my brother said, pausing just before we reached the wooden archway of the SWAMPLANDIA! sign.

"Okay." I hoped Ossie was back in our bedroom, reading a regular book or cloth-eyed in sleep and dreaming nothing. "Where do you want to go? The café?"

"Let's get off of this stupid island."

I nodded more warily. I had thought that my brother and I were communicating from more or less the same neighborhood of feelings, but I'd been wrong.

In the morning, and not totally surprisingly, the Chief had nothing to say about Kiwi's absence. He looked right through the slats of his son's empty chair, and then got up to pour another gloomy-looking glass of pond-apple juice. If you've ever tried this pee-colored stuff, you know of its vileness. Eve and Adam would have spit this stuff out and waited millennia until they could get a soda from the café. Pond apples taste like turpentine—we fed them to the Seths—and the Chief and old Sawtooth were the only humans I knew who could hold that stuff down. Kiwi said it was because the men in our family were "competitive masochists" [n]. He held that we kids were absolved from ever having to drink the poison inside a pond apple by Florida law and medical science.

"So, Kiwi is gone," I said after a long silence, giving the words a little Kitty Hawk test run on the air. "Kiwi ran away or something. That's pretty dumb, right?"

We had all seen the note on the refrigerator that morning, underneath the round Swamplandia! magnet of our own smiling faces, as if we Bigtrees and Seths were overjoyed to wish Kiwi a bon voyage. Kiwi had labeled the note for us: the VALEDICTORY NOTE—like he really believed we might otherwise mistake it for a dollar bill or a horoscope.

The VALEDICTORY NOTE informed us in Kiwi's pretty lousy handwriting of his "insuperable horror at the mismanagement of Swamplandia! and the poverty of our island education."

It explained: "I am relocating to Loomis County to raise funds to preclude what will otherwise result in a fiscal cataclysm for our family and certain penury and insolvency."

About eight or nine synonyms for bankruptcy followed. It closed: "P.S. I will send cash to you guys as soon as I can. Please don't come looking for me. I will be fine. Ava & Ossie, remind Dad that I'm almost eighteen."

Osceola ate three bowls of corn cereal and pounded sugar like a horse. She said in a small voice that she thought he would be back later this week.

"Your brother stole from us," the Chief said, his head busy in the refrigerator. He emerged with a mesh sack of oranges and kept talking to us in the same cheerful drawl. "Three hundred dollars missing from my wallet. Kid took the change, too. Took the goddamn nickels. Really. Go on, girls, have a look."

Ossie made gentle waves in her cereal milk.

"Your brother thinks he's going to help this family?" the Chief said in a smiling, genial voice that scared me. "Three hundred dollars. What a hero, huh? Stealing from his father while he's asleep . . ."

"Who took him there, Dad?"

"Gus did. This morning. Motored him over on a private ride. Says he got a call from Kiwi late last night about some important errand that I needed your brother to run." The Chief snorted. "Goes, 'I wondered why the kid had two duffels with him.' I guess he thought I might be sending him over to the pawnshop!"

The Chief made a noise that was not laughter. Something was ticking inside the Chief's face. His jawbone thrust forward, and when he chewed he tensed his whole forehead. His brown eyes squeezed shut; his skull in profile took on the sharky definition of the Seth fossils.

"Kiwi is so stupid. He'll be back tonight," Ossie whispered to me.

"Sure. I'm not worried about it." Had he been trying to invite me to go with him, that night by the cannon?

"I am. I'm worried about Dad," she said.

"Shh, Ossie. He's taking this news okay." But at one point I looked up at him and saw a shock of orange. My father had put a whole small orange in his mouth, peel and all, and he was chewing it like a zombie. This was so horrible that I almost laughed out loud.

Oh, why aren't you trying? I thought in his direction. *Why aren't you doing anything? Try. Pay attention. Be the Chief again.*

Later that night, I hugged my knees on the bunchy sofa and I did not think about what Kiwi might be doing and I watched a TV program about Queen Elizabeth II while the Chief cursed and did a truly pathetic job of ironing his own slacks. Ironing had been a Mom job. He kept pausing to consult the crimson horseshoe ring around the iron's edges, as if the appliance itself might offer him some advice on how to beat the wrinkles.

The TV documentary I was watching was so boring that it felt like taking medicine, a thick syrup of information, a good antidote to thoughts.

So that I did not think: where was Kiwi sleeping tonight?

I did not worry: what was Kiwi eating tonight?

It did not occur to me to wonder: How much money did he have left? Was he safe? Was he lost?

Without looking up from the ironing board, my dad began to talk to me. His voice was so low that at first I didn't realize we were having a conversation over the drone of the television. He had some urgent business on the mainland, he said, that was going to require a jaunt to Loomis County. That was how he always put it to us when he left on business, "a jaunt." When Mom was well these trips could last a month or more. His eyes looked watery and small behind the iron's steam.

"You'll be okay?"

"Sure. You do these trips all the time." Which was true—the Chief went on three or four "jaunts" a year—although this would be the first time he'd left since Mom died.

"Gus Waddell is going to help you with the Seths, I got him on the horn today . . . think you can manage? Two weeks this time, I'm thinking, maybe three . . ."

I nodded. Inside the TV screen Elizabeth II was putting the millionth pin into her hair. DRAMATIC RE-CREATION! flashed across the bottom; truly I had never seen anything less dramatic in my life.

"Ossie is sixteen now, Chief. We're not babies."

The Chief didn't go into much detail about his upcoming mainland trip, but I understood that it had something to do with raising more capital for his Carnival Darwinism ideas. He was seeking investors. New partners. Men with the foresight to invest in our family's evolution!

"We don't have generations to wait around, try things out, see: Does it work? Is it a good adaptation? None of that bullshit, Ava. We want to get this thing done *soon*."

"Okay, Dad. Sounds good."

He was going to buy us adaptations: wings and goggled eyes, skin suits, new tridents for hooking Seths. The crocs in the Carolinas could be shipped to us by Christmas. Soon the indigenous Bigtrees would be able to compete with our niche competitor, that exotic invasive species of business, the World of Darkness.

I mentioned that he might run into Kiwi on the streets of downtown Loomis, and he looked up at me through a fog.

"What's that now, Ava?" he bellowed across the carpet. Steam came dreaming up from the little ark of the iron.

"Who?"

The last tourist we ever had that summer came on a Friday in June, four days after Kiwi left our island. It was raining, and I barely remember what she looked like. I remember her running up the boardwalk, screaming, had we seen her hat? She was worried about missing the ferry back.

Some things you know right away to be final—when you lose your last baby tooth, or when you go to sleep for the ultimate time as a twelve-year-old on the night before your thirteenth birthday. Other times, you have to work out the milestone later via subtraction, a math you do to assign significance, like when I figured out that I'd just blown through my last-ever Wednesday with Mom on the day after she died. "We do not have your hat, ma'am," the Chief apologized to this tourist, and she was very upset. She jogged back toward the ferry dock in a huff and I remember that as being one of the few times after the End had begun that I was glad to see a tourist go. Later we did find the hat, a crinkly pink-and-white-striped visor, mall-fancy from some chain haberdashery, and the Chief put it up for sale in our Bigtree Gift Shop for sixteen dollars, similarly ignorant of the fact that we were not going to have any more customers. We must've had a last customer make a last purchase in the gift shop and completely missed that milestone, too.

Nobody came the following day, or the day after, and a week later the Chief would "temporarily suspend" all Swamplandia! shows and activities in preparation for his business trip to Loomis County.

CHAPTER SIX

Kiwi's Exile in the World of Darkness

Forty miles south and west of Swamplandia! as the crow flies, beyond the grid of Army Corps levees and drainage canals, across a triangle of new highways that slide over and under one another like snakes in a warren, was the parking lot of the Loomis World of Darkness, where Kiwi Bigtree sat on the burning hood of a powder blue Datsun and watched with an anthropologist's prudish fascination as his new friend Vijay packed and smoked a bong. "Bong" was on a list of twenty-three new mainland vocabulary words that Kiwi had acquired just that week. "Dude, do you blaze?" asked dreamy-eyed Vijay. "You want a *hit?*"

Kiwi shook his head. He did not. He did not think that he did. He watched Vijay's work shirt contract, Vijay smiling with his eyes shut.

"Come on, Margaret Mead, get over here and do a hit with me! Seriously, bro, it trips me out when you just watch like that."

"No thanks . . . Listen, please don't call me that."

He was trying very hard not to respond to Margaret, although since this was the only name by which his colleagues in the World of Darkness knew him, Kiwi worried that he might come across as a little aloof. Somebody, probably Vijay, had discovered a copy of *Coming of Age in Samoa* in Kiwi's work locker and introduced the book as a break room conversation piece. It was Yvans, his Trinidadian coworker, who'd turned to the picture of a scowling Margaret Mead in her grass skirt and palm-leaf hood, kneeling between two Samoan girls with her field notes in hand, and had rechristened him as Margaret. Now everybody in the World knew him as Margaret or Margie Mead, although recently some of the girls had shortened this to M&M, a trend that Kiwi was trying to encourage. M&M was an improvement; M&M could stand for all kinds of mysterious things, much less emasculating things. Macho Macho? Maybe that was a little too on the nose, Kiwi conceded . . . The important thing here was that the abbreviation "M&M" didn't automatically equate Kiwi Bigtree with the encyclopedia photograph that Yvans had taped above Kiwi's locker of a middle-aged woman covering her breasts with jungle foliage.

Vijay was inhaling deeply and rhythmically; he was becoming a conscious participant in his own respiratory process, he said.

"Say what you will about our shitty jobs, Margine," Vijay said, exhaling, "but at least the World's got *air-conditioning* . . ."

The World of Darkness got shortened to "the World"—as in: "Hey, Kiwi, hook me up! Clock me out of the World, yeah?" and "What do you fools want to do when we get out of *the World*?" Everybody did this, Kiwi included, although to Kiwi the abbreviation felt dangerous; there was something insidious about it, the way it crept into your speech and replaced the older, vaster meanings. "The World" now signified a labyrinth of depressing stucco buildings that fed into a freezing airplane hangar. Neon tubing and the vaulted roof of the Leviathan made the place feel modern, but when the lights came on after hours, Kiwi had the same melancholy feeling that used to strike him when he waded ankle-deep into the pulpy napkins and Styrofoam cups that littered the stadium floor on Swamplandia! The owners of this franchise of the World of Darkness had filled the hangar with evil rides, evil water fountains, smoke machines, and unconvincing robots. Kiwi got paid $5.75 an hour to work as part of an army of teenage janitors. Park greeters, security officers, customer service reps, costumers, janitors: all of them pimpled gum chewers, deodorized for war. There were plenty of adults, too, but the worst work seemed to be reserved for the youngest summertime employees.

That morning Kiwi had aced his first test, the New Employee Quiz. You could use your employee manual to look up an answer if you forgot it, said the proctor, his manager, Carl. Kiwi was disconcerted to find that many of these questions were worded like unfunny knock-knock jokes:

63

Q: What do you call a guest to the World of Darkness?
A: A "Lost Soul."

Q: What maneuver should you perform during a Choking Incident?
A: The Heimlich Maneuver.

The other choices had been "A Naval Maneuver," "The Hoover Maneuver," or "No Maneuver."

Kiwi had been pushing brooms in the World for weeks now, and the only other employee besides Vijay with whom he'd become friendly was Yvans Parmasad, a Trinidadian man with Tabasco-red veins in his eyes and so many young children that he often got their names confused. ("Bum me some money, Kiwi, today it is . . . *Tam's* birthday.") Their friendship commenced when Yvans pointed out to Kiwi a particular Lost Soul—a stunning woman on crutches in a red sundress, Kiwi's age—and then very casually proceeded to detail the things he would like to do to her in bed, in a Jacuzzi, after a lobster dinner, on his Camaro's hood . . .

"Wouldn't that be extremely hot, Yvans?" Kiwi was thinking about the thermal conductivity of metal, the insulation of her crutches . . .

"Yes!" Yvans clapped his hands, the first person on the mainland to acknowledge Kiwi's genius. "Hot, that it would be! Kiwi, I'm saying it but you're thinking it, am I right?!"

"N-h-h." Kiwi made a clicky sound in the back of his throat. (Growing up with the Chief, Kiwi had become the master of the lukewarm assent.)

On their first day on duty together, Yvans announced that he would handle "the hard stuff"—tasks rated as difficult by Yvans included counting the cash drawer and "improving the retail experience" of the female customers. Kiwi could do "the easy stuff," defined by Yvans as plunging the toilets and running the gleaming armadillo-beveled nozzle of a futuristic vacuum over the carpeted walkway that constituted the Tongue of the Leviathan. *Yeah,* thought Kiwi, tugging at a fat knot in the vacuum cord with his incisors, *the easy stuff, real simple . . .*

Kiwi looked over with a spurt of envy to the Devil's Oven, the baked-goods stand where Yvans worked, ostensibly selling baked goods, although at this particular moment Yvans appeared to be making some kind of lewd visual analogy for a female customer using a container of pretzels and hot cheese. *How has he not been fired?* Kiwi wondered, but then the short Italian woman Yvans was talking to began giggling and scribbling something on a paper fished out of her purse. She let Yvans feed her a pretzel. Kiwi resisted the urge to document this baffling progression on his notepad—his note-taking seemed to make his fellow workers uncomfortable, and Carla García-Founier, a black girl with a smattering of beautiful acne on her nose, had asked Kiwi very seriously if he was some kind of serial killer.

Inside the World of Darkness, Time happened in a circle. Shifts were nine hours, and the hours contracted or accordioned outward depending on several variables that Kiwi had cataloged: difficulty of task, boredom of task, degree to which task humiliates me personally. For a while all Kiwi had to do was vacuum in the anonymous many-peopled solitude of the front hall, but then he screwed up that sweet gig. Kiwi made wide orbits with the industrial vacuum cleaner, which trembled and belched in repose like a rodeo bull; on the first day of his third week he ran over his own shoelaces with it and broke it in a way that he couldn't ignore, hide, or repair. *Fuck-fuck-fuck,* Kiwi thought—his fluency in mainland expletives had made huge leaps in just two weeks. Kiwi glanced around the World and considered ditching the vacuum in a different hallway to distance himself from the truly alarming sound it was making, a *g-r-r-r* like the prelude to fire or explosion. A group of Catholic schoolgirls in mauve-and-navy-blue checkerboard skirts froze in front of the Vesuvius Blast Off, just outside the mock-up of a charred Italian village; they began to scream, one after the other like bells tolling, their braids and faces bright spots of fever among the waxy Pompeian mannequins.

"Sorry, children!" Kiwi Bigtree waved at them from inside a cloud of smoke. "It's my first day!" He'd used this "first day" excuse at least three times hourly since his actual start date two and a half weeks before.

Vijay didn't know how to fix the vacuum either. He knelt and touched the vacuum cleaner's bag sorrowfully, as if it were the belly of a crippled horse, and Kiwi felt that in a different epoch he and Vijay could have been El Paso ranch hands together: *Vijay shoots the horse and romances all the saloon prostitutes, and I am the wussy sidekick. Yes—in the*

*movie I am the ranch hand slated for death in a midnight raid; I jump into a
barrel of rattlesnakes or small cactuses or something, trying to escape, a bullet
makes a hole in my hat, the crowd loves it . . .*

"Hey, did you hear me, Margie?" Vijay was staring up at him. "I said,
just tell Carl. He's not going to fire you."

Kiwi's manager was a baby-faced young man named Carl Jenks. Carl
Jenks was thirty-seven years old, his oldest sister taught astronomy to
undergraduates at Dartmouth College, he himself had a master's degree
in some undisclosed discipline—he'd offer these facts to anyone who
approached him, like a caterer with a tray of bitter hors d'oeuvres. He
was always reading fantasy books with orcs and orc princesses on the
cover. (Why did these orc princesses have breasts like human women?
Kiwi wanted to ask someone. Was that really likely?) In short, Carl was
the sort of mainland nerd with whom even Kiwi, with a rare social
intuition, knew better than to ally himself. Carl listened to Kiwi's
apologies with an expression of mild distaste; one thick finger was
folded in his paperback book. He was wearing his high school ring, a
Florida ring, an ugly garnet stone with a turd shape engraved on it—a
manatee, the high school mascot—which caused Kiwi to look down at
his own naked, knucklesome fingers in alarm. *That's the kind of wedding
I want,* Kiwi thought: *to a* school. *No, to a mainland* academy.

"Has anybody ever told you, you have a beautiful smile?" Carl
Jenks's tone made Kiwi think of iridescent acids. "What's so funny?
You think it's hilarious to break World equipment that costs more than
your weekly salary?"

"No, I'm sorry. I was just thinking of something."

"How exciting. Let's hear it."

"I was thinking that I'd like to enroll in high school here. To go to
college."

"School. Right. How old are you, fifteen? Sixteen?"

Kiwi straightened to his full height of six one. "I'll be eighteen on
September fifth, sir."

"Ah. You're a dropout and we hired you?"

Kiwi shook his head. "Homeschooled. But not really officially . . . I
mean, we didn't keep in the best touch with the LCPS Board. I assume
I will have to take some, you know, some tests before they let me
sign up . . ."

Kiwi was really hoping that Carl Jenks might clue him in as to who "they" might be.

"Well, gosh, I never would have guessed. You seem like an absolutely brilliant scholar. You speak like an orator. Look at that hair. I thought you were a professor emeritus. Ohkaaay, so let's review—you broke the vacuum. What is this, your first week? Your *third* week. Terrific. Keep up the good work, Bigtree."

Kiwi could feel his intelligence leap like an anchored flame inside him. His whole body ached at the terrible gulf between what he knew himself to be capable of (neuroscience, complicated ophthalmological surgeries, air-traffic control) and what he was actually doing.

"Why don't you take a crack at the family bathroom, Bigtree. It's disgusting."

At the World of Darkness, there was a dignity gulf between staff and management. Carl Jenks, for example, got to wear a plain black polo shirt, which made him seem like a pope compared with everybody else. Kiwi had gotten off relatively easy—at least his janitor's uniform had cap sleeves and a zipper fly. He'd seen a tall kid walking around in a red spandex jumpsuit and death hood. And this in Florida, in deep summer!

Kiwi's penance was to work overtime picking up the wetter, less decipherable pieces of trash with his gloved hands. The World's lasers moved in green helixes all around him, a lonely geometry that traveled up and down the entrance to the Whale's Gullet. Cleaning the family toilet was, by his inexact estimate, one million times more degrading than any of his Bigtree duties on Swamplandia! Worse than putting out popcorn fires, worse even than the buckskin costumes and the jewelry. He was trying to flip the clown-nose plunger inside out with his shoe.

"Gah!" he cried, successful.

Success, in this instance, meant an outpouring of terrible yellow bile from the plunger cap.

The good news: Kiwi had a place to live. Employees at the World of Darkness could apply to live in a block of staff dormitories in the basement of the complex. Originally these were built to house foreign workers, but the recruitment program had been suspended owing to some "legal snag," a bit of "red tape with Immigration." All the Turkish and Bulgarian teenage guest workers had been sent home, and now any employee could pay to live here. Kiwi's dorm, a linoleum cave, came furnished. His room had a bunk, a metal chair, and a desk bolted to the ground, and a dresser with a single, enigmatic tube sock in it— the only evidence of his foreign predecessor. A wonky mirror over the dresser gave his features a funhouse wave. The room was a single occupancy. "A luxury!" he was told by several different women in HR, none of whom lived in these dorms. It was just wide enough for Kiwi to turn a full circle without touching anything, and the windowless fluorescence made him feel like a submariner. Kiwi had figured out that the dorms were located two levels below the central room of the Leviathan, and sometimes he had nightmares of being crushed to death in his bunk. After shifts he'd stare at the ceiling and take a gloomy pleasure in imagining the Chief reading his obituary in the *Loomis Register.* EMPLOYEE BURIED IN AVALANCHE OF TOURISTS! Ossie would spot it. She'd try to locate Kiwi's ghost with her "powers" . . . Kiwi groaned and pushed his cheek against the metal coils inside his mattress, waited for the thought to float away. "Really, it's unproductive to ruminate on that particular problem of our sister's," he'd told Ava on the night before he left home, by which he'd meant "It hurts." Ossie's need was like a fire that ate all the oxygen in a room. Her "lovesickness."

Regarding fire and oxygen: whatever minor administrative deity in the World of Darkness's pantheon controlled the central AC, he or she liked to keep this basement at a freezing temperature. You could hear the whir of the air conditioner deep in your sleep. Kiwi had dreams in which he crawled along the World's hallways and subterranean pipelines until he discovered a CONTROL PANEL, labeled in buzzing gold letters; each night he reached out for it and shut off the air to the dormitory vents. Then he'd wake up under four blankets with a sense of relief, thinking that he'd switched off the indoor winter.

This is not forever, Kiwi would think as he held his breath and plunged one of the World of Darkness latrines with the clown-nose suction cup. *You are still a genius. You are just a temporary worker.* That was the rank that Kiwi had been hired at—full-time staffers all had their high school diplomas. The HR lady had flicked her dry eyeballs over Kiwi's body and shouted (Why so loud, madam?), "Women's size medium!" into an intercom. "And get me a temporary ID badge." Temporary workers, as opposed to staffers, got paid a dollar less and clocked out to take their lunch hour. Temporary workers were uninsured. This meant that if something fell on you, a flaming pretzel or one of the tinted panes from the Leviathan's intestinal slides, you were shit out of luck.

"Why do I have to be a peon in this system?" Kiwi grumbled.

"Aww, when you get your high school diploma they'll make you staff, Margine," Vijay said, trying to cheer him.

"Please do not call me that." Why were other dudes his age so averse to calling him M&M? "When I get my high school diploma I'm going to Harvard."

"Ooh, sorry, Mrs. Mead. Goddamn. Bring me back a sweatshirt."

But in the staff cafeteria, Kiwi's colleagues taught him that it was unwise to self-describe as a genius here in the World. It was unwise to mention colleges, or hopes. Telling your fellow workers that you were going to Harvard was a request to have your testicles compared to honey-roasted peanuts and your status as a virgin confirmed, your virginity suddenly as radiant and evident to all as a wad of toilet paper that was stuck to your shoe, something embarrassing that you trailed through the World. The other guys went after him with such vim (another pointless word from Kiwi's SAT box) that afterward he never mentioned college to anyone besides Vijay and Carl Jenks, whom he figured he'd need later as a reference. *Three* people had to recommend you, apparently. Yvans had already offered to write Kiwi "a two-thumbs-up letter" if Kiwi continued to cover for him, and to call his wife on Adultery Fridays and say that Yvans was going to be "in an after-hours conference" with Carl Jenks until the moon rose. Vijay said that he would sign any letter that Margaret put in front of him. That left Carl himself. Kiwi was more deferential to Carl Jenks than he'd ever been to the Chief. He tried to scrub children's vomit from the webbing of the Tongue in a way that suggested deep reservoirs of genius. When a three-year-old Lost Soul came howling around the corner and knocked over a garbage can of Dante's Tamales—which looked like masticated rubies and burned your bare skin—Kiwi righted it. He was monastic, scrupulous. He really hoped that Carl Jenks was keeping track of this.

Vijay Montañez, Kiwi realized, was actually an angel disguised in smelly A-necks and skunk-striped Adidas breakaway pants. Vijay was a wonderful aberration in the World of Darkness's social universe—he seemed to feel a sincere fraternal affection for Kiwi, and he defended Kiwi's dorkiness to the other workers as if Kiwi Bigtree were a country under his protectorate. Vijay was an only child, he lived with his mother and his grandmother and what Kiwi judged to be eighty Chihuahuas, if you based your estimate on the terrible noises they produced through a door, in a closet-size apartment on Regal Avenue—and he'd mentioned right away to Kiwi that he'd always wanted a brother. His father had remarried a white woman, *Susannah.* Technically he did have a brother, Vijay said, *Ste-phen,* breaking the name hard as karate on the syllable. Vijay had never met him; Vijay's father had relocated that family to Grand Rapids, Michigan. For reasons that Kiwi didn't fully understand, he felt certain that this infant in Michigan was the reason Vijay was so kind to him, and so unreasonably loyal.

Vijay was not Kiwi Bigtree's only teacher. Kiwi received many complimentary tutorials from his other colleagues those first weeks. When he'd used the word "pulchritude"—a compliment! he insisted—in unwitting reference to another janitor's girlfriend; he later found condoms full of pudding in his work locker and a new phrase to dissect in his Field Notes, GAYASS ASSFUCKER, etched with a cafeteria knife above the locker gills. When he recited "Ode on a Grecian Urn," hoping to impress Nina Suárez, who was wiping cigarette butts out of the whale ashtrays with a rag, Ephraim Lipmann happened to overhear him and told everybody on the Leviathan crew that Margaret Mead was definitely *gay.*

"No, no, I was *seducing* Nina!" If people believed that he was sexually attracted to woolly, goony Ephraim—if people believed that Kiwi desired to see big-eared Ephraim naked, in any context—his life in the World of Darkness would be over. What was wrong with these philistines? "I read it to her because I like *women!* It's a poem about love!"

Then Nina herself got wind of this—that skinny Margaret Mead was hitting on her?—and now all of Nina's friends who worked in the Flippers were boycotting Kiwi, a political strike against his nerdly advances that took the form of girls rolling their exquisitely lashed eyes at Kiwi in the Leviathan. They touched the hair frizzed above their ears as they passed him as if radioing their disgust to some central intelligence.

To bribe Ephraim Lipmann into reversing his river of calumny, Kiwi offered to work overtime for him. Then he started to recite Keats's "Ode" to Ephraim, believing that the beauty of the poem would be self-evident and exonerate him.

"Fuck, Margaret!" Ephraim said. His reedy voice was loud enough to echo throughout the Coils, the purple foyer to the whale's belly. A few young mothers pushing their whale-fluked rental strollers looked over disapprovingly. "I do not want to sleep with you, dude! God, leave me alone!" He gave Kiwi a little push, hard enough to cause Kiwi to fall backward against a mesh trash can.

"Guys, come quick, Margaret Mead wants to butt-rape me in the Flukes . . ."

Every day, Kiwi's colleagues taught him what you could and could not say to another person here on the mainland. This was a little like having snipers tutor you on the limits of the prison yard.

"My colleagues," you were encouraged to call your fellow stoned, moose-eyed teenage workers. "My colleagues," to sixteen-year-old Nina, who wore her jeans so tight around the plush heart of her ass that sometimes Kiwi had to walk behind the cardboard flames to compose himself. This egalitarian recommendation did not apply to the management, Kiwi discovered—Carl Jenks could call his staffers anything he liked. Carl's "colleagues" were mysterious people to whom he communicated via yellow sticky memos and the telephone. Carl Jenks had a habit of referring to all his teenage employees as "new hires" until such time as he had to fire them. Yes, it makes sense, Carl Jenks joked. Oh, it makes perfect sense that Hell is staffed by teenagers! If there is a hell, I know it's a NASA space station manned by monkeys your age.

Kiwi wondered how things had gone for Carl Jenks in high school. His hypothesis was: Siberian bad. On-the-deck-of-the-*Titanic* bad. On par with Kiwi's early weeks in the World.

After his first disastrous lunches in the staff cafeteria, Kiwi began to eat alone. He brought his pimiento-and-cheese sandwiches into the last stall of the men's bathroom, his back against its broken door. The World entrées each had some stupid name, Hellspawn Hoagie or Faustian Bargain Fish Tacos. Kiwi marveled at his lunch—how could a hoagie be soggy and incendiary at the same time? His eyes watered in the bathroom mirror. The whole theme park was like a joke that someone had taken too far! The water fountains didn't even work here—

Vijay had warned him on his first day. They piped in a manufactured salt water.

"Get it, bro? 'Cause it's Hell."

"Yeah, right, I got it." Kiwi's throat burned from getting that particular joke. Why weren't natal dolphins swimming around in the salt water? Why weren't hospitals using the saline solution to save a baby's life or something?

When he was brave, Kiwi ate his lunch on the deep end of the Jaws. He sat on one of the whale's rock-size plaster molars, a place where any of his colleagues could have approached him (they didn't), but more often Kiwi slid between the teeth. He slumped as far down as he could go on the spongy mauve rubber mats. The gums were always filling up with rogue bits of trash that the Lost Souls dropped as they stepped into the Leviathan: cigarette butts and foldout park maps, doughnut holes grouped like tiny Stonehenges, pretzel paper—once, horrifyingly, a squidlike blue condom that got pasted to Kiwi's elbow. (Not used? Kiwi prayed. Used! Yvans!)

Kiwi sat like that, a toothpick speck in the whale's smile, and pretended to read Plato's *Republic* until his lunch hour was up.

Kiwi often had to remind himself that no matter how badly a day could go at work, this present situation was in every way an improvement over his first week on the mainland. He had food now, access to clean toilets; he had money, a dormitory, a few embryonic friendships. At night sometimes he would sit alone in the dorm kitchen and microwave a frozen cheese pizza that he'd purchased at the nearby gas station, with his own income. He'd count down the beeps with a meditative fervor—if anybody had wandered in and seen Kiwi's face in the microwave glass, they would have thought he was having a numinous experience. He ate the gas station pepperoni prayerfully, peeled the mozzarella off in slow ribbons, tore off warm gluey bites of crust that he swallowed like an animal in the dark. He'd drink a vending machine soda and think to himself, *I've done it!* and feel a twinge of uneasiness— because what had he done really? Used the Chief's cash to make a purchase? And what was he doing here? *Helping,* he thought vaguely. He backed away from this thought and let it hang there, a Monet picture, beautifully out of focus. The colors of it were right; the shapes could sharpen and emerge later. He tried not to think too hard about the

Chief, the girls. The ninety-eight Seths becoming anonymous in their Pit because the tourists had lost interest in that particular story. Kiwi had come prepared to disguise his identity, but nobody here ever mentioned the Bigtree Wrestling Dynasty or Swamplandia! Already everybody had forgotten the origins of the joke about him; they thought his real surname was Mead. Anonymity was a very easy goal to achieve in the Leviathan.

On weeknights, he could hear fat Leonard's heavy breath coming from a dormitory off the kitchen. His snores came in fusillades, once causing Kiwi to jump up and ding his head on the microwave door, and yet Kiwi felt grateful for even this noise, and for all the small and tolerable irritations of dorm living. Leonard Harlblower was a park greeter, a loud, obnoxious young man who would probably go through life disliked by everyone he met and never know it. Sometimes Kiwi would look at his reflection in the bathroom mirror they shared and think: *Oh my God, I pray that I am not a Leo.* Large Leonard, via some athletic self-deception, believed himself to be the most popular employee in the World. He read everyone's behavior backward to fit this thesis: Carl Jenks's open contempt for him became a convivial respect, Kiwi's queasy dislike was shy sycophancy, Yvans's insults became "Caribbean banter," and Nina Suárez and her girlfriends' eye-rolling avoidance of him was just "those bitches playing hard to get." "Ladies love Leo" was his auxiliary hypothesis.

Even Chief Bigtree—an "indigenous swamp dweller" who was actually a white guy descended from a coal miner in small-town Ohio, a man who sat on lizards in a feathered headdress—even the Chief seemed like a genius of self-awareness next to this kid Leonard. Leonard Harlblower was always slapping Kiwi too hard on the back and demanding to be called "Leo Nard-on" and cracking up at his own misogynist puns, many of which Kiwi would later hear repeated on TV reruns of the canceled sitcom *It's a Man's Grand World.*

Oh my God, you are not even an original asshole! You are a plagiarist of assholes.

Kiwi thought Leonard had the worst job in the World—he had to dress up in a whale suit in hundred-degree weather and shake the small children's hands with his flippers, which were made of a hard bubbly plastic and about the size of car doors; the whale head alone must have weighed ten pounds. (The irony here was that Leo's real-life head was also huge, the size of a moai; Vijay sniggered that the foam domehead was probably a snug fit.) You half-expected sweat to come pouring out of the whale's eyeholes.

Kiwi had a PO box now, a mainland address, and he sent away for brochures from the northern colleges. He began to receive pamphlets in the mail with fall leaves and brunettes in toothpaste-colored turtle-necks, modest castles behind them. These were the New England colleges where he could get a liberal arts education. He had taken the number 23 bus to the public library a few times and checked out a stack of outdated books about the college application process. He'd left a message for a woman named Jennifer Davies at the LCPS about enrolling for the fall, and written out a short autobiography that he planned to read to her when she called him back on the World of Darkness pay-phone number.

Kiwi's plans to save the park—or at least to forestall bankruptcy, to keep the family afloat until August or even September—these plans were off to a sluggish start. He had an envelope of twenties, but it wasn't his salary—he had stolen this money from the Chief. This theft had been easy to justify: as an investment, or an early draw on his inher-itance, or as his salary for years of unpaid tribal labor. Rationalizations buzzed inside him as he slid the bills out. *Owed me,* these shrill voices in Kiwi droned on and on, bees swaying in columns in the dark room, until he'd pocketed even the change. Pennies. A lintlike currency, value that collected in corners. He swabbed pennies out of the Chief's wallet and trouser pockets. People thought the worst robbers stole the most, whole vaults. But it was the smallest denomination that you stole, he wrote later in the Field Notes, that was the real measure of your greed.

Kiwi shook out the envelope: $22.12 now. His thumbs found and pressed the two pennies; for some reason this action made him think of Ava and Ossie. One, two. He wanted to save for the girls' college tuition. A doctor or a psychiatrist or something for Ossie. He had drawn up a budget to address the Chief's deficits; Ossie would of course get priority. But given that he had a job flossing a whale's teeth with a sudsy rope and the lowest salary allowed by law, things were not look-ing inspiring. Kiwi took out the repayment calendar he had drawn up on Swamplandia! and flipped through the weeks ahead of him, erasing the naive numbers, subtracting his state taxes, making adjustments based on phantom increases that he planned to receive to his tiny salary.

So he hadn't sent any checks home yet, but he had swiped a stack of greeting cards from the World of Darkness gift store. "I'm Having a Whale of a Time!" read one: a bug-eyed black woman in her seventies or eighties was caught on camera sliding into the Leviathan, her blue wig a full inch above her head. "It's Hell Without You!" read another, this one of a very confused-looking girl in a cherry-pink party dress descending into a hole.

Dear Ava—

Dear Ossie—

He went on accumulating beginnings.

CHAPTER SEVEN

The Dredge Appears

Now that the Chief was gone on his business trip and we'd temporarily closed Swamplandia!, we girls were the queens of the island. The Seths followed the sun around the Pit, the moon continued to whir. I could sleep into the deep yolk of any afternoon, wear my dirty pajamas to the Pit, stow away on the Library Boat and read murder mysteries until four in the morning. I could watch the World of Darkness commercials with the volume cranked. All this possibility made me dizzy with a strange kind of grief. I wasn't sleeping right. On the nights that Ossie didn't come home, I dragged a blanket down to the sofa and left our whole house lit up like a ship.

One Saturday, four or five days after the Chief's depature, in the late red light of June, a black shape appeared on the westernmost edge of our park. At first it was just a mote that I glimpsed between the bay-head hammocks, floating in the blue eye of the island like a speck in jelly. I blinked and rubbed my eyes and the blot stayed put. Then Ossie said that she could see the blot, too.

Ossie and I were a mile from the house, walking the limits of the touristed park. After the Last Ditch the trail became impenetrable palmetto scrub. All day we had been hunting for melaleuca saplings.

Water once flowed out of Lake Okeechobee without interruption, or interference from men. Aspiring farmers wanted to challenge her blue hegemony. All that rich peat beneath the lakes was going to waste!

Melaleuca quinquenervia was an exotic invasive, an Australian tree imported to suck the Florida swamp dry. If you were a swamp kid, you were weaned on the story of the Four Pilots of the Apocalypse, these men who had flown over the swamp in tiny Cessnas and sprinkled melaleuca seeds out of restaurant salt and pepper shakers. Exotic invasives, the "strangler species" threatened our family long before the World of Darkness. The Army Corps of Engineers had planted thousands of melaleuca trees in the 1940s as part of their Drainage Project, back when the government thought it was possible to turn our tree islands into a pleated yellowland of crops. I was raised to be suspicious of the Army Corps of Engineers, with good reason. The dikes and levees that the Army Corps had recommended for flood control had turned the last virgin mahogany stands into dust bowls; in other places, wildfire burned the peat beds down to witchy fingers of lime.

Now the melaleucas had formed an "impermeable monoculture." That meant a forest with just one kind of tree in it. Most of the gladesmen had long ago abandoned the dream of farming their islands. You could sum up the response of the Army Corps of Engineers and the swamp developers in one word, said our dad: "Oops!" Forest fires raged and burned the swamp down to peat. Frosts came and a man could break his knife trying to slice through a glade tomato. By 1950, the dream of drainage was largely dead. The Army Corps of Engineers changed its objective from draining the "wasteland" of the swamp islands to saving them. Unfortunately for my family, the melaleucas were still root-committed to the old plan, the drainage scheme. They swallowed fifty acres a day. Back in May, Kiwi had discovered a punky infestation behind the Gator Pit: saplings the width of mop handles. The Bigtree men swung axes into them, bled them, flooding the world with the smell of camphor. We kept cutting them down, and the earth kept raising them. It was a haywire fertility, like a body making cancer.

Why, the swamp is writing her own suicide note! A visiting botanist looked down and said this to me once on an airboat ride, running a thumb around the pinky-gold rim of his glasses as if he were extraordinarily pleased with this phrase. We'd taken a team of five Corps engineers, hydrologists, and botanists out to a hammock behind West Lake where the new forest had come in so thick that "a chubby wood rat couldn't get through it." The afternoon was full of these "Stanley, look!" kinds of comments from the scientists. Like our dereliction was a zoo for them.

"Fifty trees to an acre, my *God*" was how Stanley the stunned hydrologist summed up the problem; he'd taken a photograph for a journal article.

"Do you folks believe in God?" my dad had asked. "Because that's who I'm praying to now. I'm through waiting on you people." The Chief said that the Army Corps had a funny amnesia about the fact that our crises—the wildfires, the melaleuca stands, the fatal flooding in the gravity canals—had each originated as a Corps blueprint.

"Die, melaleuca!" I'd been hollering all afternoon, swinging my paintbrush. Ossie was cutting the saplings down, and I was painting herbicide onto the stumps. We were tree warriors, I told Ossie. We had come to the Last Ditch for a massacre.

"This is a pretty boring massacre," said my sister. "When is lunch?" I was stirring the bucket of vitreous poisons when I looked up and saw the shape: something black, liquefying and resolving behind the reddish grain of the pines.

It took us five minutes to get through the scrub. Spanish moss and pineapple-like bromeliads waved in tall curtains from the bay trees. The shape kept changing dimension on us between the trunks; I thought it might be a house of some kind. But how could a whole house wash up here?

"HELLO!" we both called into the Last Ditch.

"It's a boat after all, Ava . . . ," my sister shouted, running ahead. But not a boat like we'd ever seen. It was a twenty-five- or twenty-six-foot vessel with a cuddy cabin and a maze of ropes that was in a process of solving itself, the pulleys lying on the stern where some knot had collapsed; a thin crane with rusting struts was attached to its bow. Its dipper bucket was thirty feet above us, like a dinosaur's little yellow skull. Tall palms stretched around the latticed crane as if in competition. My sister punched straight through the willow heads and pulled me after her.

"Hello?" we asked, more quietly now.

"Ava!" said Ossie. "It's a *dredge.*"

"Oh." For some reason the word made my heart speed. Now that she'd found the name for it I saw immediately that Ossie was right—

this boat had a bucket and cables and a crane arm, presumably for bringing up the crumbling muck and digging a road or canal. We had black-and-white pictures of them hanging in our museum: The Dredge and Fill Campaign, 1886–1942.

Ossie was already moving toward it. The canal had swollen to seven or eight feet and twisted and hissed now like an unbungalowed snake; the recent rains would have driven it even higher. I guessed that the dredge would have continued on, too, but it had gotten hung up in the crooked pincers of the mangroves. Something about the angle of its entry made me think of a key that had been jammed hard into the wrong lock. Several buzzards sat on the dipper bucket. Once I noticed the birds I started to see them everywhere: one was slim-winged on one of the crane's ladders. One was eating a squirrel on the hull. There was something canny and bald about their attention, their tiny wet eyes. I felt like these buzzards had been waiting here for us, for a long time.

Ossie didn't seem to notice them; she was intent on reaching the boat. She took the first-moon-man leap over the canal and I followed. The deck was a dull, uneven black. Slick. We got the cuddy cabin door to open, which took a lot of one-two-three!ing and team wrenching. When the door came loose, colors flooded over us. I screamed, too, and covered my face with my arms, and if Ossie hadn't caught me I might have fallen into the wedge of canal between the shoreline and the boat. In that second I knew that I'd been wrong this whole time: that my sister was psychic, that the whole world was haunted, and now a ghost was tuning itself like a luminous string above me. Then the ghost broke into particulates of wings.

"Calm down, dummy, it's just a bunch of moths."

Moths jumbled tunelessly above our heads, kaleidoscoping in this way that looked like visible music to me—something that would be immediately audible to an alligator or a raccoon but that we human Bigtrees couldn't hear. Could my sister hear them? I wondered. She was picking a wedgie on the deck.

"Hear what, Ava?" She freed a tiny, beating moth from my bangs. Moths kept coming at us in unbelievable numbers. "My God," she whispered, "there must be thousands of them in here!"

"More than that."

"You heard somebody in the boat, Ava?"

"No, that's why I was asking. I don't hear anything."

The cloud of moths drew their darker blues across the pale egg of the sky. Now I felt stupid. Nothing about these cake-icing blues suggested ghosts or monsters.

"Well, only one way to know for sure. Ready, Ava?"

"You bet I'm ready." Wings painted our faces. "For what?"

Ossie yanked me into the cabin, sunlight flashing everywhere as we pulled at the door; a second later the moths were outside a dark porthole, and we were inside the machine.

Inside the cabin of the dredge barge we found:

Flaking metal everywhere in these fantastic reds and greens;

The staring socket of a pole sticking straight out of the floor;

A box of lemon candies called Miss Callie's Pixie Dust, which looked like the flavors of spinsterdom, yellow and soda brown;

A man's work shirt, size medium, long sleeves and white-and-canary checks;

A mosquito veil;

A dingy WPA jacket;

A cypress workbench, rotted through, its surface slimed with various life-forms;

A rag beneath this that looked as powdery and dry as the last century, something the last century had used to wipe its lips; it smelled wheaty and sicksweet, like beer, and it stuck to the floor;

A skeeter bar bleached the lunar blue of salt;

A four- or five-gallon bucket with the initials "L.T." scratched in these somehow polite letters onto the side;

Tools I didn't recognize inlaid on hooks along the walls, fishermen's swords, I thought: something like a spear with an antlered tip;

A mucky key—I wiped it golden again on my shirt hem and bit its teeth straight;

A map.

We smoothed the scrolled things: illegible mechanical diagrams, the map and the veil. The wavy mosquito netting was made of an amazingly old and weird material that couldn't be straightened; I tied it over my face like a surgeon and it kept crimping at my nose. I sneezed into its tiny squares. *Haunted,* a frantic voice in me said, *haunted,* but my hands disagreed with this hysterical lady: everything I touched here confirmed itself as solidly cloth or wood or rope.

"Be careful with that stuff, Ossie! The Chief might want it, for the museum . . ."

Ossie was climbing into the galley. I saw cabinets furry with damp greenery, an accordion pump, a sink with a pox of rust around a black faucet. The sink was still full of tiny copper forks and spoons and a squat thermos that for some reason made my heart constrict. I wished we'd thought to bring flashlights. We'd only been inside the dredge cabin for a few minutes but I half-expected to see a moon outside, stars the color of blood, a totally changed world. I peered through a porthole: there was the sun, beaming down at us like a dim-witted aunt. There were the same oblivious trees.

I ducked my head back inside the dredge; Ossie was taking swimmer's breaths with her eyes closed. She was sitting on the floor between puddles of water and clotted oil, the Ouija board on her lap. She tugged her skirt over her dirty knees and blinked up at me like some waylaid picnicker.

"What are you doing? What—you think there are ghosts here?" I tried to use Kiwi's roller-coaster intonations on her (I'd seen his sarcasm work like an ax to break her milder possessions). "Tell *the ghost* it smells like farts in here. Ask *the ghost* if I can have one of his lemon candies."

One eye snapped open. "Gross, Ava. Let me concentrate, okay? Please don't eat the candies from the thirties. Remember how sick you got from the candy corns, and that stuff wasn't even six months old!"

Ossie smoothed the work shirt that we'd found and put it in her duffel. She was always muling around this duffel now, which must have weighed a ton—it contained *The Spiritist's Telegraph,* apple snacks, and her bath-towel turban and various occult supplies.

"Why do you get to have that? What if I wanted the map?"

"You can have the hammer. And maybe the rag."

"Oh, gee, *thanks . . .*" I stared into the crowd of shadows toward the barge's stern. The buzzards had all vanished from the railings. The hull was rocking slightly.

"We should go pretty soon, Ossie. We should probably go *now.*"

But we stayed, opening the years-glued cabinets.

I kept returning to the map, which we'd weighted with a rock on the wormy workbench. The map had the greenish tint of great age and drew a world I didn't recognize: MODEL LAND COMPANY/DREDGING OBJECTIVE read the insignia on the bottom, each word boxed together in gray and red lines like a locomotive car. The initials "L.T." in the left-hand corner again, that same well-mannered handwriting. L.T. had added a date this time: December 12, 1936. Above this inscription, a filigree of golden hairs with tiny numbers (A-7, A-8 . . .) cut through the grid. Water was blue, that was easy to figure out. Also you could see the black powder kegs of the pinelands, and teak shadings that seemed to correspond to the saw-grass prairies. Other lines were drawn in golden pen, each one numbered and lettered—were these supposed to be rivers? A system of canals?

"Ossie! Do you know how to read this thing?"

I pinned the map against the starboard dredge window with my thumb so that sunlight filtered through its onionskin of colors. We crowded in and touched the parchment in the same nervous way, pinching our elbows back in wonderment, because *lookit,* Osceola said: the bottom half of the map was totally empty, just pleated space.

"I wonder why these guys never made it to the Gulf?" Ossie traced the green spindle of our panhandle, letting one long fingernail trail all the way down to the colored line between our swamp and nowhere. "Ava, see that? The map just stopped."

"Ossie! That sounds like a question from a scary movie. Now watch, here comes the part in the movie where a monster bursts out and eats us!"

"You're right. He's been hiding here all this time!" She made claws with her hands and rose onto her toes, pretending to menace me. "Blah!"

We giggled for too long; then we turned to stare at a padlocked hatch door in the center of the cabin. It was stained the thin green of bread mold and wouldn't open. I thought about the silhouette of a man that I had seen or imagined. I could guess what the Chief would say: Girls, that dredge crew just ran out of money. The Gulf route got cut short because this Model Land Company couldn't finance it. Nothing supernatural about *that* fate.

When no monsters materialized, we went back to looking at the map.

Ossie pointed to faint shadings that we thought might be Mahogany Hammock, West Lake, the Wet Lungs, but we couldn't be sure because the map didn't have a key. The names that did appear—Syrup Kettle, Snake Bight, Poor Ashley's Island, Dead Pecker Slough—were different from the ones people used now. Some of the hammocks and camps didn't exist anymore, if they ever had. We marveled that the mapmaker wrote in a lovely cursive, just like our mom. This amazed us, that a muck rat had looped his *p*'s and *q*'s during the Great Depression (as if cursive were somehow our mom's invention). This map was like unfinished homework. Whoever drew it up had missed dozens of tree islands that we had personally explored.

"Eew, Ava, look!" Ossie kicked backward and nearly knocked me over. In the corner a mullet screwed its eye at the low roof, still scaled in gel and gloom.

"You scared me, Ossie! What's wrong with you? It's just a dead fish. You act like some Loomis girl . . ."

A foamy urine-yellow liquid came sloshing out of the galley hole, our movements having caused the great barge to rock on its keel, and we screamed with laughter and disgust as we scrambled up onto the workbench. Perhaps we'd jostled or reanimated something? Because just then the death stink, which I'd barely noticed until now, became overpowering. I hid my nose and mouth under my T-shirt collar and breathed in my mother's perfume. For a moment I pretended to feel a wonderful guilt, like *Mom will hate that we are out here. When she finds out she will punish us for sure.* Our mother had that maternal sixth sense for when her kids were up to stupid or dangerous things. For a second I could really *see* our mother sitting in her wicker chair, humming one of her tuneless songs—in addition to being the world's worst chef our mom was cheerfully tone-deaf. I knew this vision wasn't anything like Ossie's possessions—it was just a stupid, lucid daydream—but with my face inside my orange T-shirt I breathed Mom's smell in the weave of my clothes and I just pretended. Mom was angry, not worried yet. She was drafting punishments. Her brown foot in a lake of sun on our porch, tapping at air, waiting on us . . .

I shivered and heard my breathing getting shallow. The dredge felt like a plummeting submarine to me, even though the portholes were level with the shining leaves.

"Give me that key, Ava."

"What? No! Why?" This was the one item I wanted to keep. I tossed the bag of ossified lemon drops at her instead.

"Hey, I dare you to eat one of Miss Callie's Grossest Candies. I'll give you a dollar."

"Where's the key, Ava?"

"You don't even know what it's the key to," I whined. "One more minute . . ."

Ossie returned to the galley with her Ouija board in tow and let me fool with the key for a little longer. When I next looked up, a dark blue had wrapped around the portholes. Outside I saw clouds rising like bread; one of these turned out to be the moon. A storm was coming, then—on a clear night on Swamplandia! we could see millions of stars. "We should go, we should go," I kept saying, trying the key in various metallic fissures, bouncing on my sneaker rubber to make the barge jump. I touched the puckered rag, my share of the treasure. I was going to leave that candy. I'd read enough myths and fairy tales to know how eating some deadman's candies would end. Most likely they were poisonous or carried some bad enchantment.

"Ossie, hurry up. It's late and I'm starving. If we wait any longer we're going to be like those Donners . . ."

Then I regretted bringing this up. Ossie, to the best of my knowledge, had not yet dated a Donner.

"*You* go. They're not finished with me yet."

Ossie was hunched over her Ouija board, which she'd spread onto the grouty galley counter, where dead mosquitoes turned on little black puddles.

I returned uneasily to our damp treasure: I squeezed a candy and discovered that it was uncrushable; I mopped my sweat up with the elderly rag; I ran the bitter green teeth of the key up and down my underarm. The odd key didn't fit into any slot or box on the boat. When nothing happened I ran the key along my collarbone. I tried again. I could hear my sister humming one of her pig-Latin-sounding spells in the galley. The key bit into the flesh of my neck, two dots of blood appearing. *Turn, turn, turn. Come on.* Do *something.* I glanced over at Ossie and placed it on my tongue; it tasted like a soda tab. I put the key under my right armpit like Mom's thermometer and I waited.

Nothing flew open in my heart or brain. I didn't start speaking in tongues or brim to fullness with some spirit. No hinge swung. So my body was not a keyhole after all.

Then my whole face felt hot and tight as a mask and I realized that I'd been hoping for real sorcery. *The Spiritist's Pathetic Black Telegraph!* It was an embarrassing hope; I hadn't conjured anything but a ragged red scratch up to my armpit, where I'd pushed up my shirtsleeve and tractored over my skin with the key. Disappointment had introduced us, me and the hope—it took the key's failure to teach me what I was doing with the key.

Once Mom and Ossie and I spent an afternoon alone together in her hospital room. We were watching the small TV above her bed politely, as if the TV were a foreign dignitary giving an unintelligible lecture, and waiting for any news from Dr. Gautman. As if on cue, that lame movie from the sixties started playing, *Ladies in Waiting*. A quintet of actresses haunt the punch bowl—they are supposed to be spinster sisters or spinster best friends, or maybe just ugly and needy acquaintances— anyhow, these pink chameleons, voiceless in their party chignons, they stand around the back of a ballroom having flashbacks for most of the movie, regretting older events in their minds, ladling cups of glowing punch from a big bowl, and only after the dying violin note of the final song do they at last step away from the wall. "Oh, but we *did* want to dance!" the actresses cry at the end of the scene, their faces changing almost totally. All these angry multiplying women.

Hopes were like these ladies, Mom told us. Hopes were wallflowers. Hopes hugged the perimeter of a dance floor in your brain, tugging at their party lace, all perfume and hems and doomed expectation. They fanned their dance cards, these guests that pressed against the walls of your heart. Our mom had become agitated as the movie credits rolled: There had never been a chance for them! What *stupid* women. That day we watched TV with her until the hospital began to empty, until the lights went white as a screech and the room grew so quiet . . .

Mom said that she was meeting all her pink ladies in the hospital. She had been hoping for the craziest things! For another baby. For your father to . . . well. For you girls . . . (and in her silence you could hear at least a thousand verbs). She'd touched her IV bag and sighed to us that a wallflower in bloom was very very angry, very scary.

"Okay," Ossie called from the galley hole, packing up the Ouija. "I'm ready to go."

"Who were you talking to?"

My sister reached a hand up to fix my hair, her palm stained a deep maroon from touching the old gaffs. They did not really look like gaffs though. Not in that half-light. They hung flat against the aft wall like long red and black piano keys, or farm tools for the harvest of an unimaginable crop.

"Nobody. Did you hear that?"

"Hear what?"

"Nothing. Ava, I think we'd better go now."

"Hey, are you lonely here, Ossie?"

We were back in our room, dozing in that span of light-headed, hungry time that comes before dinner. "Dinner" didn't really happen anymore—we were defrosters of burgers and Pick Up Club meals—but for some reason we still rolled down the stairwell every night at seven o'clock. In the old days, good smells filled the kitchen (misleading smells, since our mom's cooking strategy was to throw a couple of raw things into a greased pan and wait to see what happened, like watching strangers on a date). Two voices, the Indian braid of our parents' voices, called up to us.

"No." Ossie frowned without looking up at me. "I'm busy, chickee. If you're lonely, go watch TV."

"I don't mean *here,* like in this room. I mean here-here. Where we live. Are you lonely on the *island?* Do you wish we could, I dunno, live on the mainland? Go to high school, like Mom did?"

Ossie rolled over and stared at me thoughtfully. She stood and walked to the windowsill, hugged the raw pillow to her chest—I'd been pretending not to know where all of Risa's daisy pillowcases had gone, making noises of annoyance along with her for weeks, encouraging my sister to blame the phantom of Millard Fillmore, when in fact I had used all the pillowcases in the house to make a carrier for my pet alligator, who was now eleven inches—almost a full foot! I was going to tell my sister about her when she hit a foot for sure. My sewing was bogus and the carrier looked like a Franken-quilt of weird linens. To be honest, I think the red Seth was a little embarrassed to ride around in it.

"The mainland. You're asking me if I'm a Kiwi? If I want to leave home for Loomis County?"

"Yeah. I don't want to go there. You neither, right? I mean, I bet Kiwi likes it. I think it could be okay to go visit him. Remember when we stayed on the mainland during the hurricane? At the Bowl-a-Bed hotel? That wasn't so bad."

Pins clattering in the lobby even after the storm began—that's what I remembered—gutter balls and the occasional strike still audible over the rising wind. Cold sodas and nuclear-orange crackers you could get for a quarter from a vending machine. We'd all piled into a single room. The Chief and Grandpa Sawtooth had climbed onto the balcony during the eye of the storm to smoke half a pack of cigarettes, and eleven-year-old Kiwi had followed to inform them about lung disease. At eight o'clock the power went out. Mom had read the *TV Guide* to us by candlelight.

"Yeah, that time was okay," said Ossie. "I liked the shower cap, remember that?"

"The shower cap! Mom said we looked like actresses in it!"

(To be clear, we were talking about plastic hats. Disposable bath hats, *used,* with black curls of stranger hair in them. My sister and I dug into those jeweled soaps and shrink-wrapped bath hats as if we'd found a sultan's treasures next to the minty hotel crapper.)

"That *was* fun. And all the mainlanders got so grumpy when they didn't have hot water, and the Chief said that a Bigtree could shower in a Seth's spit, remember? How hard he made Mom laugh?"

"But it would be different if we lived there. That time was like a vacation."

We both grinned—the idea of the Bigtrees on a vacation, of the Chief as some dummy tourist! A Loomis *dad.*

Ossie's smile flickered. "I don't think we'd do very well there, Ava. I don't see how we could really ever catch up. What grade would they even put us in, at a Loomis school? I mean, are they going to offer a class for Spiritists? Gym class for you? Gym credits for alligator wrestlers?" She flopped onto the bed and pushed two stained pillows at our ceiling like pom-poms: "Ava—I know! We can try out for the cheerleading squad!"

I laughed, startled—Ossie sounded as bitter as any adult. And Ossie was *never* the wise guy in our family. The jags of intelligence inside my sister shocked everybody, tourists and Bigtrees alike—she'd say something smart out of nowhere and prove to us that she wasn't only a dreamer. Every time Ossie was funny or mean it surprised me; it was like your skiff hitting an intricate reef, all those delicate white fans that wouldn't yield, or like your foot scraping a rock in the middle of a deep empty lake. Even her fantasies had such rocks in them.

"I'll be the prom queen." She grinned a terrible grin at me. "You can be the class president. We'll make *posters*."

"Okay, I get it. Good. I think it's a dumb idea, too. I was just wondering."

Hours had passed since we'd returned from the Last Ditch, and already the dredge had taken on a pleasant, hallucinatory quality in my memory. Ossie did a studious belly flop onto her mattress, frowning down at the Model Land Company map through her white bangs. The map was four feet by three feet and thin as a butterfly wing; its blank half made the Floridian peninsula look like an amputated arm. It covered the whole floor between our beds, and the "L.T." kept catching the light. A tiny lizard scurried over the Gulf of Mexico and disappeared behind the chest of drawers.

On Tuesday night I heard the bed groan at one a.m., the thud of Ossie's shoes as she snuck out. Stars slid away like rain, she was gone so long. It was five in the morning when I heard the door hinge squeak.

"Ava?" she whispered. Outside gray light was tenting the pines. "You're not awake, are you?"

What a dumb question. I cracked an eye at her. My sister looked beautiful, I noted with a grudging pride. She'd copied a style from a magazine. Soft hair floated onto her cheeks.

"Are you okay?" I asked her.

Her smile faltered. "It was wonderful. But he had to leave me; I think it was my fault? I couldn't hold him. I started thinking my own thoughts again." She looked at me with a face I didn't understand, and I hated her new ghost, whoever he was. Was this guy just going to live inside her forever? Could she possibly want that?

"Good! I'm glad that guy is gone. Do you feel better now? Is it like climbing out of the Gator Pit? It sounds like waking up."

But she shook her head sharply and I felt pained now, too, like I was the one hurting her. Ossie's hurt was an airborne virus, it could travel at you fast as a sneeze.

"I'm sorry, Ossie. Don't be like that."

"You don't understand, Ava." She pushed at her hair. "That's okay. Maybe in a few years you will. It's not like waking up. I was awake before. We were together, and now he's gone."

I got up on my elbows in the bed.

"Kiwi says your boyfriend's not real. Or he's real, but he's some Loomis kid you're meeting up with in the woods."

We stared at each other across the channel between our two beds.

"I won't tell anybody, I swear. Is he older than you, this guy?" I paused, running down the list of boys with heartbeats who we knew. "Is it Gus Waddell? It's not Cubby, is it?"

"Oh, well *shoot, Ava!*" she laughed, flopping back on her mattress. "Yes, he's much older than me. He's not some Loomis kid, either. Cubby Wallach, *oof.*" She scrunched her face in a way to further underscore: Not. Cubby. "Cubby's just some kid. My boyfriend is a dredge-man from Clarinda, Iowa."

Her fist contracted into an abacus. She counted knuckles for a while.

"I guess if he'd lived he'd be Grandpa's age. But he still looks like he did the day he died."

"Oh." I frowned up at her. "That's lucky, I guess."

She leaned in and patted my head. "Good night, Ava," she whispered.

"Good *morning,* you mean." This was the fat cherry on the whole crappy sundae because it was obviously morning—the skies were pinking up behind the kapok.

"Not for me. I'm exhausted, Ava. *The Spiritist Telegraph* says some Spiritists sleep for a week after a possession, but I'm going to set the alarm for lunchtime."

"Mmnh." I mummied myself in the bedspread. Osceola could sleep forever, for all I cared. Fine by me. I would save the park by myself. I had important training to do with my red Seth.

"Okay. Getting into bed now." But she sat on the edge of my bed instead. "Listen, I'm sorry I left without telling you. There's a secret I have to keep for someone. Don't worry, okay?"

I did my best to inhale like a sleeping person.

"Hey, chickee, I do wish I could tell you," she mumbled sadly somewhere above my head, the mattress sagging with her weight, "what's happening to me . . ."

Two thirty a.m., about ten days after the Chief's depature: I walked downstairs to investigate an animal rumbling in the kitchen and found my sister gorging on a lump of cauliflower—there was nothing left to eat, she said, and she was *ravenous*. Swamp rats could not have cleaned out our pantry more thoroughly. I saw an apple core, broken spaghetti, six cola cans. Her lipstick had left a glossy print on the plastic we kept our bread in. She'd sucked the stick of butter into a little fang.

"What the heck are you doing?"

"What does it look like I'm doing, Ava?" She shook a box at me. "I'm *starving*."

"But why are you dressed like that? Did you run out of clean clothes to wear?"

"This is my boyfriend's shirt. He asked me to wear it."

I recognized the canary checks, the stains on the collar that had probably set in the spring of 1936. She'd pushed the green cuffs up above her elbows and left the long shirttails flowing over her knees, which looked small and white as clams beneath this big guy's shirt. My eyes settled on the mole just above her wristbone. Ossie had complained about this dumb mole her whole life and it was a relief to rest my eyes on it; I had the disorienting suspicion that this black mole must be where my real sister was hiding. My real sister had gotten sucked inward and in her place was this weird stranger.

"You're probably going to get smallpox from that shirt," I frowned. "Malaria. You'll probably die now, too."

Ossie rolled her eyes. A weak film of light rinsed the stairwell and I could see our shadows bending upward on the far wall like candle flames. At a certain point the tall women of our shadows intersected, became the blank upstairs.

When we were younger, two or three years earlier, we used to play a stupid game called Mountaineering on this stairwell, Osceola on the bottom step and me belaying her with the bedsheets on top. We crumpled Kiwi's looseleaf to make the avalanche; if as a super bonus a pissed-off Kiwi emerged from his study cave, he got cast as our Yeti. It was very life-or-death.

"Remember Mountaineering?"

"Oh, *Ava.*"

"That was a fun game."

Ossie looked stricken.

"Remember End of the World, how mad Mom got when we ruined her towels? Remember that time we got Mom to play, too?" I paused. "The Chief says you're lovesick. He says it's just a phase."

"What? It's nothing like that. This isn't some dumb crush. It isn't . . . I really can't . . ."

Ossie was anguished, or just insulted, I couldn't tell. I was watching her hands move up and down, as if they might be reaching for something the words could not touch.

"And afterward, when I'm coming out of it? When he leaves me . . . ?" she tried to explain.

"Uh-huh." I pictured this withdrawal as something invisible, painful, autonomic, a reflexive ejection, like a Seth disgorging feathers.

"Oh, it's much worse than that stuff you hear on the radio. Your heart breaks, too, but that's just kid's stuff, Ava. Heartbreak is just for starters, for mortals . . ."

Ossie pushed the white apples of her fists into her stomach, as if she were trying to find a new way to feed herself. After a possession came a condition called Spellbreak (*The Spiritist's Telegraph,* page 206). This was when your ghost left you, the end of your séance experience. Ossie said the loss of contact with her ghost was absolute.

"Every time I get afraid he won't come back, Ava. He's my same age, can you believe that? He's a teenager. He's like us."

"Oh boy. I bet we have so much in common." I knew what our brother would say: *Way to pick a winner, Osceola.*

Don't come back, ghost, I thought in a shout. *Leave her alone. Whoever you are, stay lost.*

Ossie thumped the cabinets for more dry food, and I thought of the Chief drumming up a Seth. A jar of gherkin pickles got passed down to me, followed by a brown tin of these prehistoric Little Cheddars, a discontinued brand of cracker. Ossie's hands puffed huge and white behind the aqua light of the jar. I used my alligator-wrestling muscles to open it.

"He needs me to *live*," she said mournfully, crunching into a pickle. "He needs me to hold on to his memories, and to move around the world . . . Death kidnapped him, Ava." She stared at me with dry, serious eyes; for one second she looked exactly like Mom if you netted her offstage and unawares. "He was so young."

I touched her arm through the soft cage of the dead boy's plaids. I had just brushed my teeth but I ate these disgusting foods to keep her company. (That was my grand sacrifice—I ate miniature pickles with my sister. In retrospect, it seems that I might have done a little more for her.)

"Are we playing a game, Ossie?"

"It's no game with him. He's *sincere*. Serious about me. You know what I mean?"

"I know," I said, sick with questions. "Were we playing a game before, though?"

Ossie ignored me. "We are a couple now. We live together here—" She touched her heart through the thin cotton. I noticed two initials embroidered on the shirt pocket in raspberry thread: L.T.

"You and the ghost."

"Me and Louis."

And then she gasped and clapped a hand over her mouth. "Shoot! I wasn't supposed to tell you his real name."

"Louis," I said slowly. Got it. That was easy: the L of the L.T. I didn't like this. Something was changing here, speeding up like a heartbeat.

"Okay. And when can I meet him?"

"My ghost is on the move, Ava," she said—as if her ghost were some prowling scoundrel or a moon on the wane. She smiled at me, her eyes raw and wet. "I think I'd like for you to meet him."

I loved my sister, so it was with some discomfort that I realized I didn't want her to be happy. Not like this, anyways, because of some ghost.

She let slip that her new boyfriend Louis's earthly title had been "the Dredgeman," but she wouldn't tell me any more about him. Who was this guy? When she dated the morgue-fresh dead of Loomis County, she taped their newspaper obituaries above her bed. These were recent tragedies: local sons our age like Camden Walsh, the handsome brunette prom king from Jupiter High, who had drowned in a canal, or Julio Sáenz, a football star and galumphing freckle-spattered sophomore in Fort Pierce who got struck by lightning on the forty-yard line. But I couldn't find Louis's papers in our bedroom or folded inside *The Spiritist's Telegraph*. He wasn't in her binders or pinned up on her headboard. His name didn't seem to exist anywhere outside of my sister.

At noon I did my sleuthing on the Library Boat. Again I couldn't find any trace of him, his origins—no books, no pictures. Possibly she had found something hidden inside the dredge itself, an engineering manual or another Model Land contract? A diary? Old letters from the cook's wife?

"The Dredgeman???" I wrote on a café napkin. Probably Sherlock Holmes carried a pad with him. Fans creaked and spun to life in the quiet café. The generators hummed. Moths were sparkling around our ceiling in patterns that seemed almost meaningful, stitching a violet-brown lace between the blades, and I mopped my face with the blank side of the napkin and waited for more clues to accumulate.

For a week the Model Land dredge barge didn't budge an inch. It remained pinched between the clothespin trees along the canal's eastern bank. It was a delicate and temporary-looking captivity, and I bet the next major storm would wash it further downriver. The boat was always covered in twenty-odd buzzards, and mysteriously denuded of the swamp birds you usually saw out here: anhingas and cormorants and a beautiful variety of heron. The buzzards continued to pour over Swamplandia! in clothy waves; on the radio, the university scientists speculated that the unusual migration had something to do with the late frosts in the Midwest. Disturbances in the raptors' diurnal cues.

That may have been the case, but once these birds got to Swamplandia! it was hard not to take their presence personally. Bundles of feathers quivered all along the Pit walls and the tramway railings, sprouting bright doll's eyes and talons as you drew closer. The flock of them watched over our doings like disinterested angels; at that point the buzzards probably knew more than I did about my sister's nighttime activities. They saw more of her than I did.

"We are in love, Ava," she told me one night while we were brushing our teeth. "We're practically married." Her face in the mirror seemed so sad. "When he left me tonight, Ava? It was terrible. It hurts worse than when a Seth bites you! It's like the opposite of that feeling—like an unlatching. You know what I mean?"

I shook my head. I did not know. Nods weren't going to come cheap anymore. If she wanted a nod, she'd have to do better than her easy, lazy invocation of "love."

"Is it like being hungry?"

"Not really . . . maybe a little. It's hard to explain. You know how light-headed you get when you don't eat?"

"Sure. You feel bad." I licked a pea of toothpaste off my finger. "Starved. About ready to eat Spaghetti Surprise." Spaghetti Surprise was a simple equation for indigestion, invented by Mom: noodles tossed like a blond wig over all your leftovers. Noodles as a culinary disguise for gross, inedible root vegetables: surprise! In a trash can this dish was raccoon kryptonite; even Grandpa couldn't finish it.

"Hey, remember when Kiwi goes, 'Forget the cheese, Mom, you should grate antacids over these noodles,' how hard she laughed . . . ?"

"I don't want to talk about Mom tonight, Ava, okay?"

"Okay."

"We were talking about my boyfriend."

Ossie made her voice shiny, doing her best impression of the mainland girls' gossip:

". . . and people think a ghost is just air but Louis is *heavy,* Ava. There's so much to carry—he gave me his whole life . . .

". . . his death, too." She touched his shirt pocket and shivered a little. She felt cold, she said. Her heart, her vocal cords, they'd gone cold.

"I won't feel warm again until my boyfriend comes back."

I stared at her with the toothbrush in my mouth. Was she crazy? She was crazy—I hardly needed to ask the question. It was 80 degrees in our room. I tugged at my hair with both hands and watched her performing hygiene in the mirror. My sister didn't *look* possessed—we were both wearing the same ankle socks and the striped pajamas that we wore to bed every night. Ossie had a green freckle of toothpaste on her upper lip, her hair was pulled into a high ponytail for sleep purposes, her cheeks were sunburned, she looked pretty and dumb with her same big-eyed, ostrichy features, and all these outside things were so as-ever and ordinary that I wanted to scream at her: *You are faking, you are lying! There is no such thing as your dredgeman.*

"You know who *I* miss? I miss our brother. I miss Mom. I don't miss some invisible *boyfriend.* That's . . ." But the words I tried to stick to the knot I felt all drifted away.

I told myself that I didn't believe in ghosts at all, or at least not with the ardor of my sister, but at night the huge, paperwhite moths flew up to hit or kiss their wings against our bedroom window screens and even the tiniest rasp made me want to cry out.

CHAPTER EIGHT

Kiwi's Debt Increases

The employees of the World of Darkness got paid on a biweekly basis. On his third Friday in Loomis County, Kiwi queued up outside a small office catty-corner to the Jaws, waiting to ask a question about his paycheck. He whistled the new hit single "Haters Will Hemorrhage Blood!" (Incredibly, this turned out to be a love song. It had a violin in it. Very popular that year, Vijay informed him, at area proms.) Kiwi undid a triple knot on his shoelace that had been bugging him for weeks, which felt as satisfying as solving a crime. A bunch of kids were shrieking as they slid down the Tongue.

"We love the World!" an entire family screamed in unison—this was the catchphrase from the World of Darkness commercials. People liked to scream it down the slide from the top of the Tongue, as if to confirm via sonar that they were at the location they'd seen advertised on their TV screen. Kiwi craned around to watch their descent. The mom and tiny daughter were wearing matching skirted yellow bathing suits and foam Whalehead hats. Mere seconds after they vanished inside the Leviathan ride, another family appeared at the top of the slide, their wide buttocks pancaked and drawn upward by the cushioned ruby pads.

Watching people board the ride and get released down the chute was like watching an eerie factory assembly line. Real whales, Kiwi had to believe, were less orderly but more expedient about their consumption of plankton. There were no lines winding around outside their great teeth, no hand stamps and tickets; the real whales just opened wide and destroyed.

At the apex of the Tongue, the ride operators came running out like bandits to pluck the eyeglasses and rings and wristwatches from the startled riders; you couldn't wear these things into the deep inner pools of the Leviathan. You couldn't have heart arrhythmias, spinal injuries, psychoses. You couldn't have a baby growing inside you, either—not if you wanted to plunge headlong into the Jacuzzi steams of the Leviathan! No pregnancies! No stowaway futures! A chubby new hire in a tight WORLD OF DARKNESS SECURITY shirt was escorting a pregnant woman in a pink-and-blue-striped bathing suit down a side stairway just now. "Twins" he mouthed to Kiwi when their eyes met across the long hallway, rolling his eyes, as if he had just caught a nervy shoplifter.

"My mother had a pregnancy that turned into a cancer!" Kiwi shouted back to him, confident that over the roar of the Tongue's salivary jets he would not be understood. Then he pushed a fist to his mouth, stunned. Really, what the hell was wrong with him? (She wanted a baby and she got cancer instead! Isn't that *funny* . . .) The new hire grinned, shook his head. He waved good-bye before disappearing down the stairs with his ward.

The full length of the Leviathan experience, a.k.a. "Digestion," took twenty-three minutes. Lost Souls dropped seventy-six feet from an elevated chute into the first of a series of domed funnels, pools, and bowls meant to replicate the twists and turns of a labyrinthine whale's stomach. Kiwi had never been on the Leviathan ride himself, in part because it would have required changing into a bathing suit, in semipublic. And Kiwi, according to his first paycheck, couldn't afford a bathing suit, or any suit. Or food.

This office had a marmalade-tinted window that opened onto a dark, box-strewn artery of the World. Kiwi wondered how the payroll guy could stand to exist here. You could go a full day inside this part of the Leviathan without seeing the sun. Kiwi made sure to take breaks with Vijay on the roof. Some days he'd go running into the parking lot at noon, nostalgic for clouds and shadows. Finally the door swung open.

"Good morning! How can I help you, ma'am?" the payroll manager asked. He had the crew cut and the saturnine blue eyes of an ex-marine.

He introduced himself as Scott, and Kiwi thought he looked crisp and official compared to the grunts on the World's payroll.

Kiwi hadn't cut his hair in a while; it hung in glossy waves over his ears.

"My name is Kiwi Bigtree," he said politely, and when that didn't help he tugged at the puffy brimstone design on his collar and added, with a note of quiet apology, "I'm, uh, I'm a guy?"

"I'm sorry?" Scott the payroll manager said. He was linking paper clips into a chain that ran across his desk. Scott was alternating colors: blue clip, red clip, green clip, white clip, repeat. They hung over the side of his desk and trailed into his wastepaper bin, swaying hypnotically. *How much does Scott get paid per hour?* Kiwi wondered.

"Well, you see . . ." Kiwi realized that he was unconsciously craning his neck to display his sizable, indubitably male Adam's apple. Evolutionary psychology: he'd read about this. A vestigial, animal impulse to impress his superior. In fact the payroll manager was just a kid himself, a twenty-something in a glittery red World jacket, his black-and-magenta dress socks peeking beneath his ordinary slacks. He had a framed degree from Volmer State, economics BA, 3.2.

(Later, on the rooftop, Kiwi would try to gauge the weirdness of his encounter with the payroll manager by relaying it to Vijay: "I wish you had seen that jacket they make him wear . . . bro. He went to college! I saw his degree. Do you think he is embarrassed to be wearing that?"

"You think you know everything about everyone? Please. You don't know shit about shit, Margaret. Maybe the payroll manager *loves* to dress up like in that jacket. Maybe that's the reason he even went to college—maybe he, like, can't wait to put it on in the morning. Maybe he sets a fucking *alarm,* bro . . .")

"There's been some mistake here." Kiwi smoothed the check on Scott's desk; according to the computer-generated invoice that accompanied it, Kiwi had worked three sixty-hour weeks inside the Leviathan and yet he somehow owed the Carpathian Corporation, the World's parent company, $182.57.

"Well." He wheeled his pencil around the well of one freckled ear. "Well! That's what I'm here for, Mr. Bigtree. Let's do the tally together."

Lunches, those Jumbo Magma sodas that only left you thirstier and the eye-watering Hellspawn Hoagies? They weren't free and neither was his dormitory rent.

Water, AC, electricity, et cetera, mumbled the payroll guy without looking up at Kiwi's face. Instead he stared sternly down at his computer keyboard, as if he were trying to draft a letter with no hands.

Seventy dollars had been deducted for his flame-emblazoned World of Darkness uniform, Scott informed him.

"Wait, they made me pay for this shirt?" Kiwi stared down at his chest, which glowed like a barbecue coal. "Is that hopefully against some law?"

This uniform was starchy, ill-fitting. It had a huge puffy flame exploding out of it. "Like a blister," Kiwi told Scott. Kiwi was no expert, but it seemed like the World of Darkness employees should be the ones receiving extra money to wear these suits. Yvans liked to jog around the ladies in his outfit and blow into an invisible whistle. "Margaret!" he'd shout. "Look! I am the referee for a girls' soccer game in hell!"

Forty dollars had been deducted as well, a "processing" fee for his ID badge and locker assignment.

The lock on his locker cost him $5.02.

Kiwi was paying city and state taxes now.

He was also, unwittingly and against his wishes, saving for retirement.

"Oh," Kiwi said, and "Thank you." Terrific. He smoothed the cotton flames on his seventy-dollar shirt with the flats of his hands and left the office. *I'm turning out to be a pretty shitty Redeemer here,* he thought. He hadn't yet made a penny to send to Swamplandia!

CHAPTER NINE

The Dredgeman's Revelation

When the Chief called us on the kitchen telephone to see how we were doing, I said, "Fine, Dad." And when he asked me about the Seths, I said the same. Everything was fine, everyone was gone. The park was still "temporarily closed" with green tarps drawn over all the airboats and picnic tables. The park was all ours. Without a show to perform, the whole island had become our backstage. The Seths grinned up at us, our only audience. One afternoon Osceola and I fed cookies and whipped cream to the Seths to see what would happen. Nothing happened. I wrote M-O-M? on the Ouija wood, wishing for dark vegetables, punishments.

A few times I walked out to the original gator hole. The baby Seth rode in my coveralls with her fingerling jaws taped up, a little coal in my pocket. My face in the water looked ugly, I thought, bulbous and freckled like some red-spotted frog. Even the gator hole was derelict that summer—algae covered its surface. No mama gator and no hatchlings. Unmenaced, all the fish inside the hole had grown huge and lippy. The bass turned in a thick circle, a clock of gloating life. *You guys think you're safe? The buzzards are going to come and eat you next, you stupid fish.* This time when I ate the saw-grass buds I got a bad stomachache.

Osceola was barely talking to me. I'd trot after her toward the Last Ditch until she turned and shouted at me to leave her alone. One time she sprayed insect repellent at me.

"Ava, *please.* Quit spying on me! He won't come if you're here."

"I can't visit the ditch? It's a free country. Hey, slow down!"

But I'd stop at the end of the boardwalk, frozen in place. "Just tell me, Ossie—who are you going to see?"

One night I finally made her crazy enough to turn and face me. It was twilight, and we were halfway down the shadowy path behind the Gator Pit, my flashlight beam chasing hers along the sticks and rocks.

"I'm going to see Louis Thanksgiving, Ava. His ghost. My boyfriend. That's who. One of the crew of dredgemen who never made it to the Gulf."

"Yeah, right." The lamps glowed. "Your *boyfriend.*" Saw grass bent westward on either side of the boardwalk. Neither of us moved.

"So what happened, exactly?" I finally asked. "Will you tell it to me?"

"What? Tell you what?"

"How it . . . how the Dredgeman became a ghost?"

"Okay," she said after a long pause. "But it's a secret. And it's not a happy story, Ava. Obviously. You sure you're ready? Sit," she said, and the lights seemed to tremble with her voice.

I thought she sounded a little relieved, and I wonder now if the Dredgeman's Revelation wasn't also a kind of burden, a weight that my sister needed my help to carry. His death story seemed very heavy to me, in whatever unit death stories get measured.

The dredgeman had a name, Louis Thanksgiving Auschenbliss; but on the dredge barge he preferred to think of himself as a profession. For the past six months, he'd spent each day and half the night pushing deep into the alien interior of the Florida swamp, elbow-to-elbow with twelve other crewmen, the "muck rat" employees of the Model Land Company. They were the human engine of a floating dredge, a forty-foot barge accompanied by two auxiliary boats—the cook shack and, for sleeping, the houseboat. The Model Land Company was digging a canal through the central mangle of the swamp and the dredge clanged toward the Gulf amid blasts of smoke and whining cables, tearing up roots and bedrock and excavating hundreds of thousands of gallons of bubbling soil. In sunlight and in moonlight, everybody on the barge had to work under billowing capes of mosquito netting—and the weave of that finely stitched protection was what the word "dredge-man" felt like to Louis. Like soft armor, a flexible screen. As a dredge-man, Louis was the same as anyone on deck. And on the floating machine, in this strange and humid swamp, every yellow morning was like a new skin that you could slip into.

At seventeen, Louis was the youngest member of the crew. It was the height of the Depression, and sometimes the men turned to the past for distraction—talking about the girlfriends they'd left mooning after them in red diner booths in Decatur, or their high school teachers, somebody's family store in Rascal Mountain, Georgia, or their army stints, the dogs and the children that they'd left on terra firma, the debts they'd gleefully abandoned. Inside the suck of these other guys' nostalgia, Louis became almost unbearably nervous.

"What about you, Lou?" somebody eventually asked. "How did you get washed down here?"

"Oh, not much to tell . . ." he mumbled. Very little of his childhood before the dredge felt real anymore. In fact, the vast and empty flood-plain that spread for miles in every direction around the dredge's gun-wales seemed to mock the notion that a childhood had ever happened. Two skies floated past them—one above and one below on the water, whole clouds perfectly preserved. "One thing about me, though," Louis said, coughing, trying like the other guys to make his past into good theater. "One sort of interesting thing, I guess, is that I was born dead."

"Well, goddamnit, Louis, you don't need to brag about it." Gideon Thomas, the engine man, laughed. "Born dead—shit, son, everybody is!"

Of all the men on the dredge, Gid was probably Louis's best friend, although it wasn't exactly a symmetrical relationship, since Gid teased Louis without mercy and "borrowed" things from the kid that he couldn't really return, like food.

"I'm not bragging," Louis said, and he wasn't bullshitting the crew, either. He was just repeating a fact that he'd heard from his adopted father—"born dead" was an epithet that he had used to needle Louis whenever he moved too quickly for the old man's fists. And although the old man had boiled the boy's birthday story down to two cruel words, they both happened to be true—Louis Thanksgiving had very nearly been a nobody.

At birth, his skull had looked like a little violin, cinched and silent. The doctor who had uncorked the baby from his dead mother in the chilly belly of the New York Foundling Hospital had begun shaking it to a despondent meter, thinking, *Ah, what a truly rude awakening!* Because this tiny baby—holding its breath, refusing to wiggle—was failing at the planet's etiquette. He did not blink. He was resolute and blue in the doc's blood-soaked arms.

"A stillborn," the doc told a nurse. "And the woman's dead, uterine rupture, terrible . . ." So this kid had missed it totally, then, his windy little interval between birth and death. His life. And the unwed mother, lying naked on a table in the Foundling Hospital, was now no one's mother or daughter.

The doctor lit a Turkish cigarette and let out a little cry, a sadness that registered in decibels somewhere between a gambler's sigh and the poor woman's grief-mad wailing at the end of her labor—and then another cry joined the doctor's. The stillborn's blue face opened like a flower and he started crying even harder, unequivocally alive now, unabashedly breathing, making good progress toward becoming Louis. The baby's face kept reddening by the second, and the doctor plucked the cigarette from his lips like a tar carnation. He would have liked to keep on smoking, and drinking, too, but babies—you could not just stand there and toast their voyage back to nothingness! Although. If the room had been emptied of witnesses, no nurses, no mother, just this baby's squalling eyes, and your own . . . ? Could you maybe then . . . ? *No,* the better doctor inside the doctor insisted. *We can't do that.* So the doc put on his self-prescribed green eyeglasses and massaged air into the baby's chest with the flats of his hands; and when blood and air started to work in tandem and the midnight pigments in Louis's bunched-sock face brightened to a yellowish pink, the doc stared down at the baby and said, "Well, pal, I think you made the right choice." The mother's cracked heels were by this time cooling to putty on the table.

Exhausted, the doctor left the birth certificate blank. L-O-U-I-S read the alphabeads that two nuns strung on a little black bracelet for the baby, because the doctor remembered or imagined he remembered that the dead mother had at one point whispered this American name to him. Louis's mother was an immigrant from a country that Louis could not have pronounced or found on a map—and if Louis ever did hear its name when he was growing up, well, it could have been Oz or the moon to him, an imaginary place.

One of the Children's Aid nuns at the New York Foundling Society came in to retrieve the newborn orphan. Louis lost his true past in a few squeaks of her nun shoes on the linoleum. Carrying him away, leaving that widening blank of a woman behind him, this wimpled stranger wound the clock of Louis's life. The nun (who sometimes dreamed she was a man in advertising, writing copy for Hollywood movies) tucked a paper with a short description of his delivery into his blanket, thinking that this might help him to be adopted by a Christian family at the train station: MISLABELED STILLBORN MIRACLE BABY ALIVE PRAISE GOD FOR LOUIS, THANKSGIVING!

Somewhere down the line the nun's purple comma got smudged and then Louis had a surname.

When he was three days old, Louis Thanksgiving was added to a group of eleven orphans, accompanied by one nun, one priest, and one mustachioed western agent who really did not care for children at all. He became one of those unfortunates who grew up in the Midwest, part of the human sediment deposited by the orphan train that ran from New York to Clarinda, Iowa; and while plenty of boys and girls found their way to loving adoptive families, such was not the case for Louis. The New York Foundling Society had placed a melodramatic advertisement in the newspapers of each of the towns along the railroad route, and dozens of farm families had gathered under a striped awning at the Clarinda station to size up the scabby knees from New York City. Louis was picked up at the station by Mr. Frederick K. Auschenbliss, a German dairy farmer who treated him worse than the livestock—at least the dairy cows got to stand still and swat flies; Louis was up to milk the cows at 2:30 a.m., spreading manure on the flat fields at sunup. Mr. Frederick K. Auschenbliss was not an affectionate father. Picture instead a slave driver who grew into the hard hiss of that name—a hog-necked man with a high Sunday collar, his eyes a colorless sizzle like grease in a pan, half his face erased by the dark barn. Louis was zero when he arrived at the Auschenblisses' farm, sixteen when he escaped it—and even Death, judging by the gaps in Osceola's story, had not yet afforded Louis T. enough time and distance to permit him to tell the story of those lost years.

Louis T., now grown into a bruised and illiterate young man, the brother to no one in that house of twelve, escaped the farm as soon as flight seemed possible. He rode the rails southward on a voyage that had the fitful logic of a sleep interrupted: suns set and suns rose. Forests dispersed into beaches and regrouped again in mountain passes. Lightning sent down its white spider legs outside the dining-car windows and crawled up the pine trunks, trailing fires. He hopped trains that crisscrossed the Midwest, touching golden millet fields and the black corners of the Atlantic before he finally pushed beyond the Florida Panhandle.

Florida, in those days, was a very odd place: a peninsula where the sky itself rode overland like a blue locomotive, clouds chuffing across marshes; where orange trees and orderly rows of vegetables gave way to deep woods and then, further south, broke into an endless acreage of ten-foot grass. This, finally, was the vision that reached Louis T. through the train window: a prairie that looked as vast as the African savanna. A strange weed or wild corn shifted restlessly in the afternoon winds—*saw grass,* said a fellow passenger beneath the slouch of his hat. That was the name for the long stalks that swallowed the WPA men up to the waists of their coveralls. Teams of lumbermen and government surveyors were working up and down the train rides, an eerie counterpoint to the dozens of herons and deer that Louis saw standing in the marshes. Then the dizzying height of the trees in the pinewoods, the thin millions of them extending as far as the eye could see. They were called slash pines for the cat-face scars left by the gum tappers—already thousands of acres had been tapped for turpentine. The slash pines reminded Louis of a stark daguerreotype he had once seen as a child of Lee's emaciated Confederate forces.

These woods were deep but they were neither peaceful nor quiet—they were full of men. Axes swung and fell, a blue glinting on the edges of the woods, and Louis followed the blade handles to the stout arms and the square, heat-flattened faces of the Civilian Conservation Corps lumbermen. It was the Depression, and thirteen million job seekers were surging southward, westward, eastward and massing like locust clouds in the cities. But few of these money hunters had made it to the deep glade. From Louis's window seat in the train, he saw just a smattering of humans. When the train had some mechanical problem outside the Crooked Lake National Forest, they cut the engine and the metal moaned to a full stop in the middle of a wrinkled wood. Out here you could hear the beginning of the wind, the hiss of the air plants and the crimson bromeliads. Oak toads chorused incessantly. If he could hear his own death in all that lively hubbub, he ignored it. *Home, home, home,* sang the rails, and the train lurched back to life.

Louis disembarked in Titusville and signed a six-month contract with the Civilian Conservation Corps. He wrote his name out LOUIS THANKSGIVING, dropped the Auschenbliss, and then looked up and down the dusty street as if he'd just gotten away with a crime. Why did anybody fool with guns, he wondered, when he had just dispatched Mr. Auschenbliss and the cat-eyed Mrs. Auschenbliss with one bloodless swipe?

"There's Indians, but they got their own camp," the recruiter told him in a patient voice, as if this were a concern he frequently allayed. "There's coloreds here, though, we haven't segregated your camp yet . . ." He glanced up from Louis's paperwork to see if this would be a problem. Louis stared incredulously back at him. He wanted to tell the man that he had spent the last sixteen years living with animals and a pack of brothers whose great entertainment on the Iowa weekends was to devise practical jokes with bulls and farm machinery that had nearly killed Louis in the fields. Louis had no problems with any man alive, black, white, or Indian, so long as his surname was not Auschenbliss.

On his first stint he got deployed with fifteen other men, who were introduced to him by their professions ("This here is the cook, the cap, the civil engineer, the lieutenant, the scout . . ."). He was now part of a government team surveying the woods around Ocala. Thirty dollars a month for income and try as you might, you couldn't spend more than five dollars of that unless you were a serious and self-hating gambler— what could you buy on the swamp besides cigarettes, penny stamps, camp equipment? Louis bought a mess kit for fifteen cents. He slept in a tent with five other men, their legs tangled together, the odor of sweat and cigarettes percolating inside the tent's bubble. Outside their tent, rising out of the scraped stone like the earth's own exhalation, came the odor of peat, a great seawall of it, nothing so subtle or evanescent as a fragrance—no, this was stuff with a true *stink.* In open sunlight the peat became an olfactory roar that recalled to Louis Thanksgiving the feculence that hung over Clarinda. *Cow pies,* Louis T. thought, wrinkling his nose, *farm perfume;* but out here the air was salted, the feculence quadrupled. He complained about it good-naturedly, happy to have something to say to the other men at night. *Our legs are tangled,* he realized that first night and every night thereafter, saying nothing and moving not one inch once he found his bedroll, the tent humid with the other men's careful closeness. Every man had to maintain his fixed position; you had to train your body until even in sleep it remained a tethered boat that wouldn't rock. There was news that a surveyor for the train company had been beaten to death south of Tallahassee after climbing into another man's bedroll stark naked—*a fairy, a funny one,* the men hissed.

Nights came and the moon was so bright that it penetrated the tent cloth. Louis was often awake until the filmy predawn, listening to the hum of the mosquitoes as if even this were something holy. He was in love with everybody, with the heat and the stink and the foul teakettle dredge that had cut a channel so far from his childhood. He was in love with the crushed oyster beds and the uprooted trees. He was smart enough, too, to keep these feelings to himself. Osceola described the way that Louis liked to hoard a hairy kiwi all day and then waited until the other laborers were snoring to open it. He'd pushed a thumb through the furry skin and released the kiwi's subliminal perfume through the tent. The first time Louis had done this, he'd watched as the men smiled in their sleep; after that he did it nightly, smiling himself as he imagined pleasant dreams wafting over them. His good mood spilled over into the mornings, and a few of the more taciturn crewmen grumbled that this farm kid must have a screw loose—who woke up whistling in 102-degree heat? What sort of special asshole kept right on beaming at you when his cheeks were flecked with dead mosquitoes and his own pink blood?

"Look who's grinning like an imbecile in the dead heat of noon," the lieutenant said, shaking his head. "You are the most good-natured boy I have ever met, Louis—honestly, it's a little worrisome. You just better not snap and kill us in our sleep! I could tell you stories. Strange things happen to personalities this far out, you know."

Every so often, the captain passed around a flask of purple apple moonshine, joking that he hoped it didn't blind the men. Louis thought the captain's hooch tasted like a mixture of Christmas cider and gasoline—it didn't make his personality any stranger or corrupt his vision, but his smile shrank, and often he had to excuse himself very politely to run and puke over the stern. Louis still had a kid's broad face, a farm face, but with a sharp nascent handsomeness lurking around his cheekbones—he had what you'll hear described as a "lantern jawline," with its presidential thrust, its hint of bedroom avarice. It would have been irresistible to a woman, had there been any such creature in the general environs. The last one Louis T. had seen was the cook's wife, who had a tall and mannish figure with a dishlike face and mean little eyes, a dirty cloud of yellow hair. *That must be the cook's older brother,* Louis T. had thought as he watched them embrace at Fort Watson. *Why is the cook's older brother wearing a dress?*

"She's stately, you bastards," the cook had said, correcting for gossip.

So there was no woman around to tell Louis T. that he had become, quite suddenly, a handsome man. This had not been a foregone conclusion: in childhood, in Clarinda, he had been a bland, doughy creature. The only things that had foreshadowed this turn were Louis's hazel eyes and the promising size of him. Louis T. wouldn't know that he was in possession of this beauty until after his death, when he first appeared to my sister inside a pool of water and she told him so.

The dredge clanked downstream with the dipper handle swinging. For the first time in his short life, Louis had real friends, all sorts walking alongside him into the long glade—calm men, family men, bachelors, ex-preachers, hellions, white men, black men, the childen of Indians and freed slaves; Adams, who had kicked a coral snake away from Louis's naked big toe and saved his life with a casual grunt; ex-army boys who followed the deer into damp hammocks; drunks who took potshots at the queer golden cats that stalked the perimeter of their camp, and missed; gamblers who took all of Louis's money with a pair of jacks and then gave (some of) it back to him at the day's end; all of them, every man was Louis's friend. When there was light in the sky they waded forward. They surveyed the old section lines of the national forest during the workweek, and during the weekends they "rambled," as LaVerl, the buck sergeant said: shooting, fishing, sometimes even gator hunting along the nests that filled the unused railway bed. The cook told Louis to collect two dozen leathery eggs from these alligator nests, and then he made the whole crew a dinner of fishy-tasting omelettes.

When the light expired, they slept. White-tailed deer sprinted like loosed hallucinations between the tree islands. Sometimes Louis fell asleep watching them from the deck and it worried him that he couldn't pinpoint when the dream began: deer rent the mist with their tiny hooves, a spotted contagion of dreams galloping inside Louis. There were bad fires that blurred the world; in the summer months you could see smoke rising almost daily, wherever lightning struck the pure peat beds.

Louis heard from the other surveyors that men all over the country were "hunting a week for one day's work." Sometimes when he thought about this he felt so lucky that it almost made him sick to his stomach. Happiness could be felt as a pressure, too, Louis realized, more hard-edged and solid than longing, even. In Clarinda he had yearned for better in a formless way, desire like a gray milk churn; in fact he'd been so poor in Iowa that he couldn't settle on one concrete noun to wish for—a real father? A girl in town? A thousand acres? A single friend? In contrast, this new happiness had angles. Happiness like his was real; it had a jewel-cut shadow, and he could lose it. Well, Louis Thanksgiving determined that he was not going to lose it, and he was never going back. The Depression was the best thing that had ever happened to him. He had a crisp stack of dollars, a uniform with his initials stitched in raspberry thread on the pocket, pig and grits in his belly.

Elated, wanting never to leave, he signed another contract, this time to dredge a canal clear across the swamp to the Gulf Coast for the Model Land Company. They were going to drain the swamp and develop and sell it, and they needed a team of skilled muck rats to do it.

But nobody had explained to Louis just how deep into the swamp they would have to go now, and how *quickly* their bosses at the Model Land headquarters in St. Augustine, Florida, would expect the crew to drain the floodplains with a single bucket arm—a Herculean task for any machine, especially for the ancient and fumey Model Land dredge, which made the government vessel look like some futuristic spaceship by comparison.

The dredge was there to dynamite the marl, spud down into the blasted muck, and spud up with a bucket of oozing crust. And this task in a swamp where you could sink a support platform through *twenty-four feet* of peat before hitting stabilizing rock.

And the crew had changed, too—none of the CCC boys had signed on with him. LaVerl was going back to his family's horse farm in Savannah, and the lone Indian on the crew, Euphon Tigertail, who had survived subhuman conditions while working on the Panama Canal, decided that he couldn't work in the swamp any longer. He'd been undone by minuscule foes, the chizzywinks, and the deer flies. "You sure *you* want to be a dredgeman for this outfit, Lou?" Euphon had whispered, both of them staring at the hulk of the dredge. Its digger arm was as tall as a house and sunk deep into a quagmire. A pair of enormous cast-steel feet gave the contraption a drunken, donkey-legged appearance. The stack slumped toward the saw-grass prairie, which looked like a drowned and shimmering field of wheat. For a second Louis thought of the distant Auschenbliss pastures and shuddered.

"You'd be better off gum tapping in the turpentine woods. It's all soup doodly in those prairies, it ain't like the pine rocklands. There's nothing piney about it. No elevation, Lou. No lakes or trees or breaks. It's just saw grass till you want to scream. You won't have a dry day again for months. You'll go in there and never come out."

How could you make a mistake when you had one option? Louis felt that his hellish past exempted him from all regrets. But he was humbled by his friends' defection—and a little shocked, hearing their complaints about the last months. Ultimately, Louis felt an almost romantic embarrassment, listening to the grizzled guys talk—it turned out that the same nights and routes that he recalled as heavenly had been, to the other CCC men, "godawful months, a nightmare" and "the valley of the shadow—only full of mosquitoes!" When the dredge anchor hit at Chokoloskee their whole CCC fraternity came loose like a knot, and he and Euphon and LaVerl all parted at the dock like strangers.

His first job on the dredge was described by the splinter-toothed captain as "involved": he had to dive overboard with a knife clenched in his teeth and cut the slimy ropes of cattails away from the dredge's wheel and shaft. "Removing detritus" was what the captain called this labor, which tasted like brine and sour blood. Dee-tree-tus. A name from a book, Louis T. figured as he removed the knife from his mouth and spit copper. He had split his lower lip. Five times his first day he'd had to jump overboard into that stinking gator marinade and hack at the weedy ropes.

"What do I do if there's a gator?" Louis asked the first night at supper.

"You put that knife between the blamed scaly-back's eyes, he'll lay offa you. Or get the base of his neck, sever his spinal cord." Ferguson, one of the cranemen, had gone gator hunting with some white glade crackers once and now claimed to be the crocodile expert.

"Don'tcha go for the eyes themselves, though. The crocs can retract those."

He held up two gnarled fingers and jerked them back into his fist.

"Thanks for the advice," said Louis. He imagined screaming underwater and the tiny needles of salt against his gums and eyeballs. Louis, curiously modest, refused to strip before diving. He jumped in with his pants and cotton underwear on and kicked beneath the dross of slimy marine plants. His legs floated like two planks behind him, every muscle tensed, ready to jerk away from an alligator's teeth.

Louis T. wasn't a particularly quick learner, but he was strong and docile and within one month he was doing all sorts of jobs on the dredge: trimming greenish fat off the pork in the cookhouse, helping the sweating firemen to keep up steam. The men looked like beekeepers in their cotton gloves and mosquito veils, their lungs filling with black mangrove smoke from the smudge fires they burned constantly to keep the insects away.

"Line up, boys! Take your medicine," the cap said, pressing indigo flecks of charcoal and sulfur into Louis's cupped hands. Every time you asked what they were for you got a different answer: ear infections, hay fever, styes, skin lesions. Gideon Tom said the pills were placebos, although Louis noticed that he still queued up to receive them like a good Catholic boy in line for communion.

"Ahhh," Gideon said, extending his chaw-stained tongue.

"Stick out your palm, you jackass, I'm not your damn mother!" the cap howled. If the pills were making a difference, it was hard to imagine how bad you could go without them. Men held their fallen orangey scabs up to the sun and cataloged them like entomologists. Week 1: Men couldn't sleep for the bug bites; scratching at them, and fending off new ones, was an eight-hour endeavor. The insects had been a chronic irritation on the CCC barge, but out here on the marshy open prairie they felt pestilential, their sawing sound filling the air like a cruel ventriloquy of the men's own thirst. Their dense bodies put a fur on the steel hull of the Model Land dredge. More mosquitoes rose out of the cattails at dusk like tiny vampires. Theodore Glyde, the dredge's dour engineer, grumbled that he was working back-to-back shifts on the dredge, quitting the deck at sundown to work a second job as a bug killer. Week 2: Everybody's legs acquired the cracked sheen of cockroach wings. Louis, who had hosted much more colorful bruises back in Auschenbliss country, poured a little vial of alcohol over his shins and returned to work. Back on the CCC barge, they had never been more than twelve miles from a port with a doctor, but now they had entered an unmapped part of the swamp where wounds had the opportunity to fester. Week 3: Sores began to ooze. Of all the dredgemen, only Louis T. was indefatigably happy. He volunteered to haul water off-shift and shared his larded fried eggs with whomever.

"Louis, are you on a diet or what?" Gideon Tom grumbled; he was leaning against the starboard railing next to Louis, gobbling down a plate of Louis's eggs with a guilt-racked expression. "You should eat, kid. It's not good to share the way you do out here. What the heck are you always staring at?"

"The landscape."

"The landscape!" Gid snorted. His broad nose wrinkled as it often did when someone said something he didn't like, as if he were trying to sniff out what was wrong with their reply. "There's something . . . something *womanly* about watching that, Lou."

Louis grinned over at Gideon Tom, shrugged; even the other men's ribbing made him happy. Daybreak, sunset: he liked to watch the red sun pour through the tiny doors of his mosquito screen until his blue eyes filled. Behind the screen he had the face of a man in church.

"Hey, Gid?" he asked his friend when they were baling wastewater later, the sun a pinhead of color behind the green trees. "Gid . . . are you anxious to get back?"

Warily his friend turned to him. "Get back where?"

And what Louis really meant was *Anywhere*. Back to land. Back to themselves, back to their names without jobs, back to any motionless, dirty place—or back to either of the twin poles that the swamp road they'd been digging was meant to connect. He had heard of hydrophobes, and he wondered if there was another word like that, for him. Or for what he was becoming. Terraphobia? It was a fear of the rooted, urban world, of cars and towns and years on calendars. He wouldn't be the dredgeman there, that was for sure. Sometimes, at night, Louis thought in a dreamy way about becoming the dredge's saboteur—plucking parts like flowers from the engine room. It was only a thought, and a crazy one; but the closer they got to the Gulf the sicker he felt. His sweats got worse when he pictured the dawn horizon solidifying—a sudden break in the mangroves that revealed the swallowing saltwater ocean, the big success for which the bosses of the Model Land Company had hired the dredge and her crew.

"Jesus, Louis, you're just like what's-his-name? Greek guy. Narcissus! Just making puppy eyes down at your face in that bucket."

"Sorry. I was getting a little . . . homesick, I guess. So you're excited for the end? For the Gulf side of things?"

"Fool, of course I am!" Gideon laughed, pouring the black water over the railing onto the head of a small and outraged alligator. "Am I excited for a paycheck and a woman and a bed? Am I excited to climb out of this soggy hell and get a pair of pants that's not infested with forty kinds of insects, and get a pair of shoes where I can't count my toes? Goddamn, Lou, I'll be singing 'Ave Marias'! I'll be diving for land!"

Louis spent the morning of his death beating himself at hand after hand of solitaire with Gideon Tom's faded deck. He was off-duty, and free to ruminate. He did not have any headaches that day or dark presentiments. At noon he felt a little hungry, ate some ibis jerky, considered rowing over to the houseboat to bathe. He lit sticks of dynamite and lobbed them into the marl, watched as the white-tailed deer shot off through the elevated hammocks. For every ten hours of work, the canal grew eighty feet longer; they were still months away from the Gulf and the end of their contract.

Louis T. was sitting on the starboard side of the dredge barge with his bare feet swinging, his calves hot against the metal rail, watching a pair of otters mock-dueling in the cattails. When next they appeared they were lovers, their bodies turning in a silly ballet, black volutes beneath the lily pads and the purple swamphens. He was maybe twenty-five feet from the engine room when a roar like a tidal wave rolled forward and nearly knocked him loose from the deck. He turned and watched flames engulf the roof of the engine room in one spectacular red spasm; within seconds a thick smoke swallowed the entire port side of the deck and shrouded acres of the sunlit saw-grass prairie to the southeast.

What Louis saw next came filtered redly through one slitted eye:

A stencil of a man—Ira, Louis thought sleepily, or maybe Jackson—went flailing off the fantail. Louis heard him hit his head on the way down; another man jumped in after him. To save him, Louis thought, proud to have finally made the connection. Foggily, it occurred to him that he should perhaps do a thing, too. This fog seemed to have penetrated his brain from the outer world, because the whole deck of the dredge was lost in a roar of escaping steam. *The boiler head has burst,* Louis thought, and felt his pulse jump. That's what shook the deck. He pushed himself up and started to make his way toward the smoking engine room, where the other men were already hauling water.

Louis held a hand to his face and found it came away sticky. Blood was trickling out of one of his eyes and the other didn't like to open. Suddenly he felt tired, a terribly heavy tiredness. *I could fall asleep right here,* he thought. His own square face surprised him in the water below the barge; he had at some point pitched forward on the railing. His reflection blinked up at him, as if the boy below was trying to remember how they knew each other. The otters, he noticed, had vanished.

"Gideon needs a hospital!" Hector screamed. "He's killed, he's killed!"

Apparently Hector had forgotten the usual chronology of death and medicine as it worked on the mainland, Louis thought grimly—if Gid was killed then it was late now for the hospital. It was almost impossible to push through the wall of steam, and when he finally located the door to the engine room Louis found the scalded body of Gideon Tom. Gid was lying on the floor with his right hand wrapped around his throat. Dead, Louis thought—the steam from the exploded boiler and the still-burning fire must have seared his eyes and lungs. But then as Louis watched the hand began to *move,* massaging Gid's black skin. His eye opened like a blue crack of sky and his other hand pushed flat against the metal wall—and then, impossibly, he was standing up, staring abstractedly at Louis, half his face a sputtering blank. His mouth was moving but no words came. His jaw made convulsive chewing motions, and above this his right eye regarded the deck incuriously, full of a blue ancient calm. *The Mariner,* Louis thought—this line bubbled up to him from some long-forgotten event, a poetry recitation that the youngest Auschenbliss had given at a church assembly many winters ago. *The bright-eyed Mariner . . .*

Somehow Gid had gotten upright and was now lurching toward them, trying to retch up smoke. *This is a bad miracle,* Louis thought as he watched Gid trying to move. *Go to him!*—but Louis was frozen, staring. Gideon took a step toward Louis and then said, with a grievous eloquence, "I believe my lungs are all burnt up, Louie. I do believe . . . ," before crumpling.

"A hos-pee-tal! A—"

"Goddamn you, Heck, shut up," Louis said with the first true viciousness of his life. "Hos-pee-tal" sounded like an imbecile's taunt. What place could they take Gid to? There were no places here. That was the point of the crew's continued presence, that's what they'd all been hired by the Modern Land Company to accomplish: to turn this morass into a real place. The swamp was a waste and men had built the machines to fix it.

Something was happening down below. The whole deck had begun to vibrate. Elsewhere the other cranemen were racing around, hauling water to put out the small fires that had spread now to the houseboat. Flames licked at the bleached planks of the cook shack. The smell of burning metal stung Louis's lungs, throat. Lights rocketed up in the deep swamp like a July fireworks show, and then every bulb burned out at once—the governor belt on the steam engine must have broken, Louis thought, letting the engine run wild and burning out all the lights. This would be an interesting problem come nighttime, assuming everybody calmed down sufficiently to make repairs. The cattails hushed around the dredge, shushing each other and brushing close to the ship like alien observers. That's what Louis remembered, the purple sky and the grasses winding upward—the world felt as though it were a bubble curving in on itself.

"Pop, pop," Louis mumbled. Trees stood wide-armed in the river. He felt as though his thoughts were drifting loose from him and popping on the skeletal branches. Something or someone came crashing down onto the work deck on the stern of the dredge and Louis didn't turn to look. The blood on his hands had become the blood in his brown hair, he noticed, the blood on his neck, on his dungaree jacket. Hector came to tell him that the backing drum was reeling in its cable; Hector's scream had dropped into his shoes and now he was staring at Louis with a goggle-eyed, just-awakened look. He pointed at the engine room, where two coal lumps—two feet, Louis realized, Gideon's boots—were sticking out. His legs were limp, and the soles of his shoes flopped outward from the heel in a heart shape. From the waist down he looked like a man relaxing on deck.

"Take his shoes off," Louis said. "Please, goddamnit, just somebody take them off . . . ," but the other men stared at him and moved to give the flailing Louis space, as if afraid to get contaminated by his raving. Several of the crew had gathered now. Nobody knew what had caused the accident—corrosion, the captain speculated. He'd seen a two-inch rent in the boiler head. "It was Gid, it was Gid's fault!" Hector said, then made the sign of the cross as if in apology to Gideon. "May he rest in peace," he mumbled, staring down at Gid's shoe soles.

As the men stood huddled on the starboard side of the barge, a now-familiar shape began to populate the sky: buzzards appeared and dotted the watery horizon in twos and threes, dozens more behind these. They moved so swiftly they looked like pure holes advancing through the air, a snowfall of inky holes. Talons began to hail down on Gid. The first batch dove and took Gid's hat, tore at the buttoned collar of his shirt. Hector shot wildly at them and a bullet grazed the captain. "Put the gun away," the cap screamed. "You're liable to kill somebody . . ."

Everyone was watching the buzzards. These buzzards were nothing like the red-headed turkey vultures they'd been seeing since Long Glade; these were huge birds, black and wattled, and with their wings folded they made Louis think of the funeral umbrellas dripping rain along the stone walls of the St. Agnes Church in Clarinda. Several of them formed a heaving circle around Gid; within moments one had flown off with his cigarettes and another had torn his shirtsleeve loose from the elbow. Two buzzards worked industriously to tug the black shoe off his foot. Louis couldn't move or think: his mind was helium light. The taste of screws and pennies pumped into his mouth until Louis felt sick with it. Around him the cranemen were hollering *Fire!* at a pitch that canopied the dredge.

What rolled through Louis's mind were like the shells of thoughts, a series of *O!*'s, round and empty, like the discarded rinds of screams. A fine tooth of purplish glass marked the spot on the deck where Gid's eyeglasses had been and Louis got down on his knees to retrieve it; when he felt a prickling on his neck, he looked up.

In a scene that seemed as plausible and horrifying as Louis's worst dreams, the birds descended on Gideon Tom and hooked the prongs of their talons into his skin; perhaps a dozen of them lifted him into the sky. Gid's body shrank into the cloudless expanse. The sky that day was a bright sapphire, better weather than they'd had in weeks; for a long time, the men could still see the shrinking pinpoint of Gid's black head. It was the only part of Gid that was not held by talons, and it lolled below his shoulders as if Gid were trying to work out a bad crick in his neck.

A strangled quiet came over the men after that. It felt like hours before anybody moved.

"You boys ever seen birds do anything like that?" Hector asked, close to sunset. His voice was a child's squeak, and Louis thought there was real bravery in the act of speech. Louis's own throat was a desert and he couldn't have gotten a word out for one million dollars. No, Louis thought, you saw a thing like that and you went deep inward, you didn't want to make a single ripple in the air.

"Never," the launchman said behind him. "Never seen a bird behave that way." His tone was mild and genial, as though he were discussing unseasonably cold weather, or food with a peculiar taste. Hector, in his panic, didn't seem to hear the answer. Some of the men were still staring at the spot in the sky where Gid had disappeared into a bone-white ridge of cloud; some, including Louis, had fixed their attention on the spots of blood on the deck. The moon was rising. Louis, able at last to overcome his vast, black speechlessness, noticed something interesting that he pointed out to the other men—the buzzards were returning.

People began screaming, babbling obscurely; someone went splashing overboard. Louis heard the wet, frantic beats of arms on water. The birds had completely swallowed the dredge now. They were perched all along the trusses and gunwales and the cabin roof so that the whole structure looked upholstered in black velvet; it didn't seem possible to Louis that there could be so many birds in all the world. Louis saw a buzzard that looked as large as a man lift and stretch its wings; some part of Gid went winking from its beak and fell into the water. Finally Louis felt a scream tear loose from his throat.

"Oh, shut up. They're just birds," Theodore Glyde, the tall, sallow engineer, kept repeating crossly next to him, gesticulating at no one. "They're just filthy buzzards, they shouldn't hurt us at all, anyhow, men, we're *alive* . . ." He went on and on like this as the buzzards grew in size and definition—how could more be coming? Louis wondered. Hundreds more were coming. He stood there and waited with a pale, uplifted face. He might have looked courageous from the outside. Theodore Glyde was still throwing his arms around as if he could argue his death back into the hole of the moon.

"Here they come, fellas," Louis T. said quietly, and beside him Theodore snorted with disgust and crossed his long arms in their slate-blue sleeves as if he were impatient to prove a point.

Oh God, Louis thought. He didn't feel any more horror—just pure sadness, because he was seventeen that summer and he didn't want to go. His real life had begun less than a year ago. *I'm next.*

And, Osceola told me in a whisper, he was. We sat there for a full minute listening to a wild gator clawing through the brush that lined the boardwalk. Afterward, she swore me to secrecy.

"You cannot tell *anybody,* Ava Bigtree."

"Gee, okay. I'll try . . ."

I pointed backward at the dark windows of our house and for some reason we both broke up, laughing and laughing. I made binoculars with my hands and pretended to scan the boardwalk for tourists.

"Got that, everybody?" I said. "It's a secret!"

But then I saw, through the open fists of my binoculars, that Ossie's pale eyes above her laughing mouth were filling with tears. It was strange to watch a face having that kind of secret disagreement with itself. For some reason I flashed to a dry, sunny day last year outside the hospital, to the Chief's deadcalm eyes over his screaming red mouth.

We walked up the steps to the Bigtree Swamp Café and ate two pistachio cones while a storm rolled in. The longer I thought about the Dredgeman's story, the more convinced I became that Louis was or had been real. How else could Ossie know about his death in such detail? My sister could memorize obituaries but tonight's performance had been different. She hadn't stuttered at all, she'd used words I thought she couldn't possibly know. And then there was her face as she told it— she had reacted to her own recitation of the Dredgeman's Revelation like a first-time listener. My sister's eyes had turned melty and black as the cook shack fire spread. We'd both gasped when Gid died, and when the white sky had swallowed him cold. When the dredge wrecked, we'd been truly *afraid*.

Now Ossie crunched into her cone. "You want more ice cream, Ava?"

A tumor-headed buzzard cocked its head and looked at us from behind the café glass, not quizzically like a sparrow or a gull, but with a buzzard's bored wisdom, and I imagined then that this bird, too, must also know the story, and that all the quiet trees and clouds had always known the story. I ate the second stale cone my sister handed me, licked green drops from the back of my palm. We polished off a tub of sprinkles. They covered our hands like magnetic shavings, and we were still giggling about our "gloves" when the power went out.

"Ava? That's you, right? Don't move. It's okay. I'll get candles."

"Why not ask your boyfriend to do it?" I whispered, waiting to see if the café light would flicker on again. Louis Thanksgiving could be just outside the café windows. He could be inside this room with us, I shivered, riding out the storm. *Ossie,* I almost screamed, until it occurred to me that the ghost could also be inside of her.

Later, back in our bedroom, my sister unscrolled another, smaller map. She said she'd found it in the cuddy cabin on one of her dates.

"Look, Ava," she whispered. "Louis says this is where the door to the underworld opens . . ."

"Na-uh." I squinted at the map. "That's the Eye of the Needle."

I recognized the coordinates she was pointing to—we labeled this place on our own souvenir Swamplandia! maps and place mats. The Eye of the Needle was an Indian landmark. Grandpa Sawtooth had been fishing out there. Good red snapper hole.

"Of course it's a real place, silly. But it's also one of the thruways to the underworld. A gateway to the world of the ghosts."

"The underworld? You mean, like, hell?" Just the word made my mouth go dry; I didn't even like living this close to Loomis County. "Does the Chief know?"

The Eye of the Needle was a full day's journey by airboat from our island—at least that, given how difficult it was to navigate the narrow mangrove tunnels between Swamplandia! and the Gulf-side shell mounds. Tourists certainly couldn't get there, and we kids had never been. Grandpa Sawtooth took a photograph of the Eye of the Needle passageway during his rambles in the forties: a gray channel cut between two twenty-acre islands made entirely of shells. These islands looked like twin boulders to me, or like one island that lived next to its echo. Two intricate skulls rising out of the river. They are hundreds or maybe even thousands of years old—the Calusa Indians contructed the mounds out of clay and every kind of local shell: oysters and conchs and whelks. The Calusa Indians were well established in our swamp when Ponce de León arrived in 1513, and they probably hugged the shoreline of Florida for hundreds of years before the European contact; by the late 1700s their tribe had disappeared, undone by Spanish warfare and enslavement, and by microbes: smallpox and measles. The Calusa shell mounds, these seashell archipelagos, had outlasted their architects by at least five hundred years. You can find them scattered throughout the Ten Thousand Islands; visitors will drag their kayaks up a shell mound's glittery shores and picnic there. On the Gulf side a 150-acre shell mound supports a modern township. But the Eye of the Needle was a special landmark, known only to locals, and very remote.

"The Chief doesn't know a thing about this passage to the underworld," said Ossie. "Nobody living does, except for me, and I only know because Louis told me on the Ouija board."

"So how come Louis knows?"

"Uh, because he's a ghost? It's a doorway to the *underworld,* Ava. The whole dredge crew is there. It's where Louis goes when he's not with me—he crosses over."

Ossie pronounced the word "underworld" with great authority, as if we were talking about Cincinnati or Peru.

I got excited then. "Have you been there, Os? To the, ah, the underworld?"

"Not yet."

"So you don't know what it's like . . . down there?"

"Not really. Louis can't describe it to me. Louis says it's the kind of place you have to see to believe."

"Okay." I was thinking that we might find our mother in this place, and I was also thinking that my sister was officially nuts. "You'd think Grandpa Sawtooth would have mentioned something about all this, though."

Ossie smoothed a wrinkle in the old map and met my gaze with clear, violet eyes.

"*Grandpa?* He's a great wrestler but he's no Spiritist. I'm sure he thought the Eye was just a pile of rocks. He didn't have a clue what he was looking at."

Weekend 3: The Chief is still gone.
   Seths: Ninety-eight.
   Sisters: Two.
   Brothers: Zero.
   Tourists: Zero.
   Ghosts: One.
   Park Hours: ?
   Mom: ???

Gus Waddell came by late Saturday to see how we were doing.

"Most awesome, Uncle Gus," I said from the kitchen table, not looking up. The mail crashed onto the dark sea of wood around me—I was coloring. Even I knew that I was years too old for this baby activity. Next I'd be playing dolls like some mainland girl. Using my gator noose as a jump rope. *Well, somebody stop me,* I frowned, snapping a blue crayon.

"Whatcha drawing there, Ava Bigtree? That sure is—huh."

I had filled in a dozen sheets with single colors, our Bigtree tribal colors: Indian red and heron blue. The whole time I was coloring, I lived a second life in my head. I'd glance up at the kitchen clock every minute or so and think: *Now is when our matinee should begin. Now is when the Chief flips on the blue lights. Gold, clap! Orange, clap! Red lights. Now here comes the song—ba-da-dum! Now Hilola Bigtree is climbing the ladder, waving at all the tiny cheering people; now she is running down the diving board; and here, ladies and gentlemen, she hits the water!* . . .

Behind me, Uncle Gus coughed.

"I see you, ah, you like the color blue there."

"Yup."

Uncle Gus smelled like eggs and diesel and I wished that he would please go away. We had our food, our mail, we were *all set.* Uncle Gus seemed to want to pat my back, but perhaps couldn't figure out how or where to touch a kid for sympathy purposes; his large hand hovered near my right ear, then dropped back to his side.

"You sure you're all right? You know, I told your old man this already, but you girls are welcome to spend the night at our place, anytime. Mrs. Waddell would love to have you over."

"Thanks. Maybe next week. We're going good, Gus. I fed the Seths a few hours ago. Ossie is good, Judy Garland is good. It's good here. Quiet."

That morning I'd found a half-dead gator in our Pit. She looked like the drowned gators that wash up after storms, their blond tongues glittering with hundreds of decaying minnows. She was alive but I couldn't tell what was wrong with her—disease was so infrequent among our alligators that scientists from the University of Florida came out once a year to take samples of their blood. I'd let her rest her leathery head against my shoulder while I touched the saffron plates of her neck. The Chief says it's a terrible sign when a monster gives you this kind of access.

On Tuesday, it seemed that good news had come at last! Gus brought me another letter. This one came in an envelope with Loomis University's orange-and-green seal on it.

Dear Ms. Bigtree:

Thank you for your inquiry. I have done some research on your behalf; unfortunately no such Commission or Committee or alligator-wrestling competition has ever existed. You

might visit the Miccosukee Indian Reservation to watch a
live alligator show.

.

Regards,
Amalia Curtis
Secretary to the President
University of Loomis

I tore up this letter within seconds of finishing it, put the bits of it
into a plastic bag, and shook the bad news out over the Gator Pit. Later
I caught some sunfish for the red Seth—she was eleven and three-
quarter inches now, and very healthy-seeming, not sluggish or inap-
peteant or anything, a few more centimeters and maybe it would be safe
to share her with Ossie and the Chief. Not tourists, though, I frowned;
I really did not want strangers to see her yet, even though I knew that
was the ultimate point of our training. I practiced with her for two
hours. I had her to where she would walk this perfect debutante circle
around my Swamplandia! ball cap. She would bite my finger with a
precocious viciousness. We were going to get famous and save the park.
My dream kicked painfully inside of me, and I was surprised to find
how easy it was to go on working toward it as if I'd never heard from
Mrs. Amalia Curtis.

I didn't try to write the commission again, but I did begin a letter to
my brother.

Dear Kiwi,

I tapped the pencil against my lips. How to explain Louis Thanksgiving? Already I had amassed a stack of Bigtree postcards that I
planned to send to him in bulk just as soon as he wrote with his new
address. Weeks and weeks of postcards, our mother's face on most of
them. I liked the satisfying clack the stack made against the edge of our
dresser, like I'd collected Time itself for my brother. Kiwi could just
read these, come back to the swamp, and pick up where he left off.

Dear Kiwi,

How are you? Good, I hope. Are you in a college yet? I
wanted to tell you something: last night I met Ossie's boy-

friend. His name is Louis, and he is a dredgeman. I don't know, Kiwi. I think I maybe believe in this one? You know what, as far as ghosts go he is really not so bad. He sure got a raw deal in his first lifetime. Ossie is saying that he's "the One," which means that we could have a ghost for a brother-in-law, haha. Poor Ossie. I guess I'll have to tell you the rest in person . . . hint hint. We miss you.

Your sister,
Ava Bigtree

Now that the Chief was gone I left the TV news on all the time. I knew about the gas hike in Loomis County and the famine in Uganda, the mayor's "fiscal indiscretions." Kiwi's bulb burned like a lighthouse at the top of our stairs. In the new emptiness I'd made a series of discoveries. For example, if you stared out our bedroom window you could see a forest of dark, inverted trees in the pond beyond the kapok. Pop ash, the kapok, mahoganies, all draped with the irregular lace of Spanish moss—the pond was about fifty feet wide, but it repeated every leaf and branch in a deep layer of endless colors. This second forest had a watery, independent life. Where did the real woods begin? you'd start to wonder after a while.

Two cinnamon lizards blinked at me from behind Ossie's unmated work boot. Earlier I'd searched the park for her and then given up to read my *Bandits of the West* comics. Cowboys were still the closest things to alligator wrestlers I had found in kids' literature—they lassoed the killing horns of steers and smoked like Dad, drank like Grandpa, wore Mom's secret smile. That night I gave myself fifteen pumps of Mom's perfume. Then I let the whole bottle drop onto the floor. Glass flew everywhere. Our bedroom became a terrible canopy of artificial roses. The glass shards I left alone until the thought of my sister cutting her feet on one grew unbearable and I swept them into the dustbin. *Ossie is going to really lay into me,* I thought. But dawn broke and my sister's bed was still made. She strolled up to the house at noon, smiling cheerfully, with huge bags under her eyes.

"Where were you?" I asked dully. I felt exhausted just looking at her. After hours of pumping up for a big speech my anger turned tail on me, slinking away.

"A secret. But don't worry, Ava," she smiled. "Louis takes care of me out there."

Wednesday was the same, and Thursday—she stayed out all night. When she came home she slept through most of the day. On Friday, I did the usual: fed our gharials, visited the red Seth and brought her fresh water, checked on the incubators, gave Judy Garland her raw tarpon and berries, went back to the house to make myself a jam and jam sandwich. When I got to the kitchen I saw a white paper rolled small as a cigarette—someone had pushed a note through a rip in our screen door:

PAYMENT FOR SERVICES RENDERED REQUESTED—

Yrs, The Bird Man

"You don't think some tourist left it?"

"A tourist from what planet? Ossie, the ferry hasn't even been here today."

We were in the cypress dome, gathering petals and roots for one of her spells. The interior trees in a cypress dome are one hundred feet tall, with roots, or "knees," that stick out of the water and breathe for them; with their veins of vines they look like petrified rain. Really, it feels like you're walking through the weather of the dinosaurs. The gray-blue fossil of a storm, now dropping small leaves. I watched my sister stand *The Spiritist's Telegraph* against a live oak, her mouth full of flowers.

"Anyways, that doesn't make sense, Os. Why would a tourist want payment from us?"

"Well, Gus will probably know what to do." My sister yawned. Her eyes watered behind a flume of swamp violets and orchids.

"Hey, P.S., you look super really ugly," I said. Ossie was wearing all of our mom's makeup at once. "Your eyelashes look like spider legs."

"You don't own her, Ava. Anyway, you're too young to wear mascara." She blinked her clotted eyelids and shook the note. " 'The Bird Man,' " she laughed. "How silly. Maybe Uncle Gus is playing a trick on us." She handed it to me. "Write one back." She shrugged. "Put the Chief's mainland phone number on it, let him deal with this."

Once you exited the cypress dome, you followed a little dip in the elevation of the island and wound up in a swampy meadow on the banks of a brown canal that was often more mud than water, a place we called the Last Ditch. It was about two miles from the touristed park, at the extreme end of our wanderings; you couldn't penetrate the mangrove scrawl on the opposite side of that canal without a machete. Osceola was wandering around the Last Ditch, picking a bouquet for herself. She kept reaching up to them on her tiptoes, huffing like those ladies in neon unitards we sometimes watched doing *Stretch for the Stars!* on Grandpa Sawtooth's rabbit-eared TV. She'd amassed an armful of cowhorn orchids, an epiphyte species that grew on the sunlit side of these trunks.

We'd been collecting the orchids all afternoon and we were both panting and crosshatched with scratches when Ossie spotted a cowhorn orchid wrapped serpentlike around the uppermost branch of a live oak.

"That one," Ossie said, pointing at the lone blossom on a spindle of raveling bark almost twenty feet above our heads. "That's the one the ghost wants."

"Of course it is," I muttered, wedging my sneaker into the crotch of the tree and hoisting myself onto one of the strongest-looking branches near the trunk's base.

"Hey," I hollered. "Tell the ghost to pick another one. That branch won't hold me."

"I didn't ask you to do it," she called up to me. "He did." And here she jerked her thumb at the black wreck of the Model Land Company dredge.

"Ossie, I *can't,*" I yelled, already halfway up the bald cypress. A fist of wood broke off under my hand, and for a second I saw long stripes of ants run like wet paint; I swung my leg horizontally as high as I could manage, huffing air. A prong of little ants went running over my left hand. The world swooned below me.

Now I made the time-honored, biblical and mythical and TV mountain-climbing movie mistake of looking *down:* my sister was small as a rag doll. Birds whirled like paper scraps around the bottom of the trunk. I saw where a long metal blade from some quartered machine was sunk into the earth like an ax head buried in some giant's green scalp. The dredge rocked gently on the canal.

I tipped my chin skyward: the yellow orchid was two feet above my outstretched hand. The wind lifted the tiniest hairs on the back of my neck and I was reaching blindly, clumsily for the yellow orchid, hugging the trunk with one arm and swinging wildly with the other, scraping the same tough nub of bark and getting fistfuls of air. On the third grab I *got* it. Something shuffled the air below my feet and a cormorant streaked cobalt mere inches from my face, upsetting my balance; I righted myself, panting.

"I almost fell," I screamed down at Ossie, wanting to get credit for this. It had started to rain lightly. Below me, I could hear it landing on the roof of the dredge barge with a tinny *drub-drubdrub*. I began my one-handed descent down the tree. Lightning cracked the sky and then I did fall, crashing down the tree. My T-shirt rolled up as branches snapped, Ossie squealing at me at top volume. For a crazy second I worried that my belly was going to peel away, torn off by the rough bark. Then it was over; I was a jumble of limbs in the marl. Somehow I managed to hang on to the thin stem all the way to the bottom.

"Here!" I screamed, thrusting the crushed orchid at Ossie. "Your ghost is a jerk. Do you want *me* to die and haunt you? Because I swear I will."

If I were a ghost I would ride that pointer around her Ouija like a little white Cadillac, giving her so much grief! I would—

Something flashed inside the dredge cabin—half a man's face. His nose and neck and lips were plume-thin. Then he disappeared into the glare on the porthole.

"Did you see that?" I asked softly.

"Yeah, wow. That fall looked like it hurt. You okay?" She gave me a squeeze and dropped my hand. "Thank you for doing that. But look, the spell said we needed tree-growing orchids. See? Nothing terrestrial." She tapped at a line from a torn page of *The Spiritist's Telegraph*.

I looked back at the dredge porthole and saw nothing and no one behind the dirty glass.

"Ava, will you hold these for me?" she asked, handing me a bunch of loose spells with titles that seemed to have come straight from the headlines of a woman's magazine (sleep enchantments, 479; a spell for happiness in marriage, 124; magic herbs to enhance beauty, 77). Ossie lifted and winged the hem of her dress so that her yellow orchids slid into the middle. Fat raindrops were sliding down both our noses now.

"Okay, Ava. I have to go."

"It's time for your date?"

Ossie nodded. In the compromised light of the Last Ditch my sister's skin took on a watery, greenish cast, like the palest rings around a watermelon.

"Don't wait here, okay?" she said.

"Okay," I said, as I leaned against a swamp oak to wait for her.

"Ava . . ."

"You go. I don't mind. I've got nothing better to do. I'll save your place here," I said, and drew a little X with my sneaker toe where she had just been standing.

"Ava, listen. You have the Chief's number? You remember where he left the money for us?"

I nodded. I thought we were talking about this Bird Man's debt and I was annoyed that Ossie was going to leave me to deal with that.

"I—"

Then she swooped in and hugged me. Coming from Ossie, a hug like this was very unusual, but I think it's hard to ever hear your own happiness as an alarm bell. All that I suspected in that moment was that we loved each other, and that things between us might soon return to what they'd been before. I threw my arms around her neck. *Stay in your body, Ossie.* She kissed my cheek and then released me with a little push.

"Go already, please? Ava, he's waiting on me . . ."

She set off across the muck as briskly as a mainland woman who is late for her ferry. Her footprints filled with groundwater and as I watched a dozen tiny lakes opened between us. Rain blew in from the east while out west the sun burned through a V in the trees, bright and gluey-gold as marmalade.

Halfway across the ditch, Osceola reached a hand up to her braid, tightening her purple ribbon; then, just when I imagined she was possessed again and had forgotten all about me, she turned back and waved at me. Her face didn't look so happy any longer—she looked old to me, older in age than our grandmother's picture, and scared. A mood could age you a hundred years in a finger snap, I now saw.

I was still standing there when my sister Osceola pulled herself across the brown canal and into the dredge barge, and shut the door.

* * *

Quiet rode outward like wildfire after that, engulfing the ditch and me inside it. I held on to the flashlight with both hands. I listened for my sister's movements inside the dredge; instead, I heard the creaklings of quick, hunted life inside the ditch and the groans of the taller trees in the center of the dome. When you wrestled Seths it was clear when something was going wrong—even indoor people knew what to do when they saw blood, heard screams. But if Louis was at all, he was invisible, and I wouldn't know from where I was standing if Ossie needed my help.

I swung the flashlight like a little sword, made a combat hiss. *Kshhh! Kshh-kshh!* No moon tonight.

"Ossie?" I called once, after fifteen minutes. The dredge hunched motionless on the canal. My throat felt raw and I wondered if I was maybe getting sick. Yes, I decided, I definitely was. I concocted an elaborate fantasy about how I'd break it to Ossie that I'd gotten pneumonia while standing in the rain, waiting for her to reappear. The leaves opened a low green heaven above me. Next I made up a language with my flashlight, a sort of luminous pidgin tongue, a battery-powered Morse code for my mom or whichever of the ghosts was watching me. The day was peppery with rain and darkening. I held the flashlight under my chin, the plastic ridges against my throat feeling somehow deeply comforting, a fuzzy portal opening onto my sneakers. There were eyes in the grass down there, lizards and bugs. I tried to wiggle my goofus slicker on—one of Mom's picks, a Goodwill special with off-brand cartoon rats dancing on it—and when I looked up again I saw something high in the trees: two shoes. Two burgundy boot toes, brightly polished with rain, the long thin laces wagging down below the cypress leaves. These boots, when tracked backward with my flashlight beam, sprouted two thin legs. Above these I found a feathered torso, and added to this a puffy white face on which—compared to the boots and the patchwork outfit—looked almost ordinary. The man was blinking violently down at me, caught in the light, his pale lips twisted in a grimace. I could calculate a Seth's age from its battle scars or the girth of its tail, but I was bad with adults generally and this man's age was impossible for me to guess. He was younger than my grandfather and older than my brother. His eyes were something terrifying.

"Jesus, kid, get that out of my face."

"I'm sorry, sir." I lowered the light a few inches and tried not to gape at him. "You're lucky I didn't scream. I didn't know you were up there."

"Did I frighten you?" He smiled. "Well, shoot, kid, you scared me, too. I was just getting to the last of your buzzards."

"Huh?"

Droplets of rain seemed to tremble singly along a thin wire between us. I tracked up the tree with my flashlight but I didn't see any birds.

"I cleared out those buzzards for you. Strange, the numbers of them out here." He lowered himself delicately from the tree, pushing up from the branches as easily as a mainlander lifting out of an armchair. "Chief Bigtree pays me every year. It's a service I'm providing for you islanders."

I know what you are! I thought, triumphant. I should have guessed it right away. The heavy, tussocked coat, the black wooden whistle for birdcalls, the bright eyes in a shingled face. He was a gypsy Bird Man. There are several such men who travel around Florida's parks and back-waters, following the seasonal migrations of various species of birds. These men are like avian pied pipers, or aerial fumigators. They call your problem birds out of the trees and send them spiraling over the sloughs; then they wait for them to alight on another person's property and repeat this service. It's rumored that even the Florida Wildlife Commission employs them when the more traditional methods of animal control are attempted, fail.

"Did the Chief call you to get rid of them?"

"No. What's your name?"

"Ava."

"Ava." He shook my hand. "Can you keep a secret?" He reached his gloved hand out and pressed two fingers against my lips. "Listen to this."

The first three sounds he made were familiar to me. A green-backed heron, a feral peacock, a bevy of coots. Then he made another, much deeper noise, as close to an alligator bellow as I have heard a human make but not quite that, exactly. It flew up octaves into an other-worldly keen. A braided sound, a rainbow sound. I stepped closer, and closer still, in spite of myself. I tried to imagine what species of bird could make a sound like that. A single note, held in an amber suspension of time, like a charcoal drawing of Icarus falling. It was sad and fierce all at once, alive with a lonely purity. It went on and on, until my own lungs were burning.

"What bird are you calling?" I asked finally, when I couldn't stand it any longer.

The Bird Man stopped whistling. He grinned, so that I could see all his pebbly teeth.

"You."

The Bird Man told me that he'd be leaving our island in the morning, now that the buzzards were cleared. "I saw that you folks could use some help," he said, his feathered shoulders heaving up and down in a shrug. That was how he operated these days, he explained. He wasn't one for drawing up contracts.

"You're welcome to stay the night at our house," I heard myself tell him. "At the moment we have plenty of room."

I was an alligator wrestler, accustomed to bold movements. On the walk back I took this Bird Man's hand in my own without looking up at his face and was shocked and pleased when he didn't release me. *Now we are friends,* I thought hopefully as we slid sideways over the muck-soils. My roof was a stern-looking triangle above the trees. I'd left every upstairs light on; behind the palm trees our house looked like a fat man taking little yellow breaths in the dark. The Bird Man let me squeeze the empty thumbtip of his leather glove. He'd heard about our shows, he said. The Bigtree Wrestler Spectacular, Swimming with the Seths. I had to explain to him about Mom's death, which was always hard to do. It felt like killing her again.

"I'm very sorry about your mother. What is your performance like without her?"

"Oh, we haven't been wrestling much lately," I said. "Our show is really famous, though. It's gotten written up in a bunch of newspapers and we were on the seven o'clock news once, the Bigtree Wrestler Spectacular . . ."

The Bird Man soared vertically above me, taller than the Chief, six three or six four, and thin as a scarecrow, and walking next to him I felt like a yapping dog, each of my stories about my family and the Seths like a tug at the stranger's trouser cuff. He didn't ask many questions, but he slowed down so that I could keep up with him and he smiled as I babbled about the Seth of Seths, my grandparents, my favorite alligator-wrestling victories. He was such an interested listener that I wondered if it was possible that this Bird Man had been lonely, too.

We were a quarter mile from the house when the Bird Man asked to see my show. To see me, specifically, wrestle an alligator.

"Oh! Sure! You mean . . . now?"

With my ears buzzing, I led the Bird Man (a tourist!) toward the Gator Pit. When we reached the stadium, I showed the Bird Man to an orange seat in one of the middle rows. Out of habit I began to set up as usual but my heart was thumping. I didn't know how to work the follow spot or start the music; I was too short to reach the rack of gator nooses. I turned the popcorn machine on. I pulled on a wrinkled brown bathing suit I found backstage, its leg holes very loose on me, the material shivery and dank, and then I climbed the ladder to the diving board. I did not tell the Bird Man that while I had watched Hilola Bigtree's Swimming with the Seths act hundreds of times, and even practiced swimming in the Pit with her, tonight was going to be my first dive. I stared at my bare feet on the stenciled stars and took a jittery breath.

I peered down into the water—I couldn't see any of the alligators. I'd figured out how to work the control panel for the auxiliary lamps that glowed along the edges of the Gator Pit and lit the stairs up the stadium rows, but backstage the follow spot sat lidded and dark.

I took a final breath and I was flying. Water flooded my nostrils. When I opened my eyes, I could see the Seths' dim shapes from below, their great bellies that look like prehistoric pinecones and their dinosaur feet. I could see the glint of a Seth's claws, curled motionless at the mountains of its sides—an alligator's tail does all the work of swimming. Little starbursts of teeth, pebbles over lips. A three- or four-hundred-pound Seth sailed over my head, and I watched a thin jet of bubbles rising from my own nostrils. Far above me peach ovals opened on the water—a column of milky illumination from the stadium lamps. They seemed to gasp back their light as I swam for them, like good dreams on waking.

I swam as smoothly as I could for the edge of the Pit. My palms scooped through little nets of algae and something thicker. (*Don't look, don't look,* cautioned my mother's voice inside me—often during shows

I could hear her in my mind's ear, directing me. She'd scream at you good if you goofed a move; she got protective at odd moments. Our mom was her most conventionally maternal when she was watching one of us fight the gators.) A Seth floated above me as serenely as a souring iceberg, its huge legs contracting. Bubbles fell like crystals of salt from its thrashing tail. I surfaced as far as I could get from the Seths and scrambled up the ladder rungs. "Ta-da!" I said lamely. Without the Chief to hit the switch, the end of the show was harder to pinpoint. I caught my breath, my hands on my knees; then I walked around the Gator Pit fence to find the Bird Man in the stadium. He was standing up in the middle row, giving me a kind ovation.

"Beautiful, kid." The Bird Man clapped his gloves together as I shook the water from my hair and grinned.

I had a feeling like I was still moving, still flying up and up toward the next surface. The stars greeted me like a second challenge. After months of the bad feeling—months of the sensation that I was evaporating, of practicing for wrestling shows we were never going to perform again—I could taste the old Bigtree victory. Suddenly I remembered: I am an *alligator wrestler.* This Bird Man's eyes were like new lamps for the old performance. He kept smiling and smiling at me, and when his gaze rolled over my skinny legs, the pins of my knees became twin suns.

The Bird Man waited for me to finish drying off with one of the grungy towels we kept slung over the pine railing.

"That was really something, kid. You say you learned that from your mother?"

"Yup." I smiled happily and squeezed my toes against the pool ledge, feeling suddenly shy. I got dizzy looking into the pure whites of his eyes. The alligators slid through the murk beyond the railing: lamplight opened there in soft petals between the black water and the alligators' sand mounds. I switched the lights off; I knelt and checked the temperature of the Pit water with one finger. Then I led my new friend to our house.

This Bird Man was not what I'd expected a Bird Man to be; for starters, he was very kind. He did not conform to any of the common stereotypes of his profession: redneck exterminators, mangrove gypsies, backwoods ornithologists, black magicians, feathered druids, scam artists. This Bird Man volunteered very little about himself, his age or where he came from, but he told me that he'd been working hard all spring on account of the unusual migration. I wanted to ask, but did not: *You do kill them, right? Or is that a rumor? And if you don't kill the buzzards, where do you take them?*

"Want to see something else?" I asked him as we walked down the wood-chip trail and turned at the shed. "It's a real miracle."

My flashlight found her first, its beam falling through the crepe of the palmetto straw. At her new length of twelve inches, the red Seth was almost too big for the tank now. She twisted her head and let out a dry hiss in the light.

"Beautiful," the Bird Man said. He said it exactly right, with the whistling wonder that I had dreamed the red Seth would elicit from a tourist. I thumbed her jaws open and flipped her over to display her checkering of belly scales, which tapered to the single row of scales down her tail (which was still fully half the length of her) as proud of her as if she were my own design.

"See? This is her palatal valve, the same fire-type color, pretty impressive, right? And these are her dorsal scutes . . ."

"Well," he smiled, "I've never seen anything like her."

He thanked me; he still hadn't mentioned the money we Bigtrees owed to him for his avian removal services. This made me feel grateful and a little nervous. We couldn't pay him, obviously. I was embarrassed, imagining handing him my dad's voice on the phone. The Chief would offer him coupons instead of cash.

When we got to the house it was very quiet—Ossie hadn't come home yet. I didn't think she would tonight.

"I haven't slept indoors in such a while," the Bird Man told me absently from the bottom step. He touched our wall the way a child might touch the flesh of a strange animal, flattening his hand against the polished grain of the wood and frowning at it for a moment. The indoors was exotic to folks from the remote swamp, I guessed.

"Thanks again, kid." He smiled at me. "Beds and linens. It's like a little vacation."

His coat made a shuffling sound against the wall of the stairwell.

"See you in the morning! The sixth step sags a little," I called idiotically. "The towels are sort of dirty?"

I watched him disappear behind my brother's bedroom door, trailing wispy blue-black feathers behind him. They floated on a slender flume of light from Kiwi's bedroom, dreamy nicks suspended in the dimness, so small they seemed like molecules of night or visible scent. Should I offer him water, a toothbrush? Did he want a cookie or a sandwich before bed, like I did? For a swamp kid, a visit from a Bird Man was like a dark Christmas. I wished Mom or the Chief were there to help me work out the etiquette of the visit.

Within minutes I could hear our guest snoring behind the wall. I sank beneath a dirty cloud of sheets and lay open-eyed on the pillow. I tried to match my breaths with his snores. I had a feeling like I was dreaming although I was wide awake, staring at the beige cracks overhead and floating happily on my mattress. Maybe this was how a possession started? The Bird Man was no ghost, though, and I was grateful for his company. I had childish fantasies about this man: I wanted to hold his hand in the woods again. I wanted to put my ear on his chest, something I used to do with Mom. To listen to the thud-thud-thud of another heartbeat. For the first time in what felt like months, I slept all the way through a long furrow to dawn.

When I woke up from a dissolving dream of great happiness, Osceola was not in her bed. Light filtered through our window and when I read the clock I felt a little sick. I pulled on yesterday's socks, my muck boots, and tied my grimy shoelaces. I tromped past the wax-fruit shine of the smaller reptiles' plastic cage lids, still waking up. Searching for her from the crow's nest of the kapok tree house, I felt chilled and annoyed. This time she wasn't in the Gator Pit. I followed our old footsteps from yesterday's trip to the ditch, which now felt like it had been a thousand years ago. Then our footsteps ran out, and fear unspooled through me as slowly as a yawn. The ditch that I returned to was empty. I remember it as being calm and wet, and very peaceful, flat as a pasture in the blue light.

As I approached the live oak in the center of the Last Ditch my heart began to pound—a glowing square was taped to peeling bark: a blank sheet of paper. No, I saw, hurrying forward, not blank, just white. There was a beautiful handwriting on it that I recognized:

Dear Ava,

I am eloping with Louis. That means we are going to the underworld to get married. Do not stay here by yourself. Get

Gus to take you to the Chief. Ava I love you very much. Tell the Chief I love him too, and Grandpa and Kiwi. I will see you maybe.

—Ossie

All I could think was: *Her spelling is perfect.* I pictured Ossie in Kiwi's empty room, looking up each word in his dictionary. Slowly I got up and walked to the bank of the canal, which that morning was swollen with rainwater and stained from the cypress roots. We'd checked our rivers against Louis Thanksgiving's map, and it seemed possible that this canal in our backyard could be the very same artery that the Model Land Company dredge had dug out during the Great Depression. I peered around the river bend, saw only thin trees and moths.

Oh-no. Please-no. Mom . . .

Moths flapped in mute hysterics all along the canal. I counted hundreds, flying downriver like a second water.

The ditch is empty, I realized.

The dredge is gone.

CHAPTER TEN

Kiwi Climbs the Ladder

From the roof of the World, the pigeons looked like falling stars. It was a shame you couldn't relax and enjoy the Olympic splendor of this, Kiwi thought, on account of how the pigeons kept shitting on everything. Their timing was uncanny, malevolent—the pigeons had gotten him twice this week, down his open work-shirt collar and splat across the back, and the King Suds Laundromat off I-95 was yet another mainland luxury that Kiwi couldn't afford. Kiwi didn't even have the bus fare to get to the King Suds Laundromat. He did not have sufficient quarters to pay tribute to King Suds, the mustachioed monarch who ran it. Instead, he took his uniform shirts and his losery boxer shorts into the dormitory showers and washed them with Leo's dark green dandruff shampoo, which burned like acid on your skin. Somehow it had gotten onto his balls and into the webbing between his fingers and the shit just *hunkered* there like cold fire. He had developed a rash or a pox, something purplish and specklesome on his bony thighs that he was determined to ignore until it went away, or killed him.

"Ahh, Leo," Kiwi moaned into the mildewed nave of the showers, "why is this shampoo so *thick?*"

Was Leo trying to regrow hair or something? In the break room his colleagues plugged their noses and made a big show of asking, "What smells like formaldehyde, yo?"

During their break hour, Vijay sighed and tugged at Kiwi's slimy shirt hem. "I told you, I will lend you quarters to do your fucking laundry, you retard."

"Laundry is my last priority right now, V."

"Shit, I'd rethink that! Have you smelled you? I will, like, sneak your laundry into my house, bro. My mom *loves* doing laundry, it's like this Immigrant Mother disorder? She uses Lluvia de las Montañas detergent—it's so badass. You'll smell like Costa Rica!"

The last thing Kiwi wanted was some other kid's mother doting on him. Just the word "mom" still made his stomach flip.

"Ha-ha. Yeah. I am none to be fucked with."

"Vijay. I need another job."

"Yeah, I hear you." He sighed happily and rolled his pant legs up. "Who don't?"

The boys were sitting on the sooty edge of the roof overlooking the eastern side of the main lot, watching someone in a BMW double-park. An awesomely jawed man in chinos got out of the car, took a furtive look around, then sprinted on his loafer toes for the park entrance. Banker/lawyer, Kiwi thought, ticking down his taxonomic chart. Silk tie, comb-over, tassels. Something about his gait made the double-parker seem almost jolly; it was like watching an elf leave a Christmas surprise.

"Sing it with me now, Margie: what a d-d-*douche.*" Vijay was smiling his breaktime smile. You could tell time by that smile—5:45 must be just around the corner.

"D-d-d . . ."

Far below them, the Loomis traffic roared. A pigeon waddled along a pipe, lifting its mauve wings like an acrobat. Kiwi felt a stab of the unpredictable homesickness.

"How much do they make over there?" he asked quietly. He was pointing at the row of businesses that abutted the Leviathan hangar, which looked small as a ring of petrified rocks. As if someone had planted them around the World of Darkness, Kiwi thought, thinking for some reason of *The Spiritist Telegraph.* Those diagrams in the appendix of sacerdotal magic.

"Where? What are you talking about? The gas station? Don't you read like every newspaper that was ever invented? Don't you know the facts? People who work at gas stations get *shot.* They get *capped,* Marge."

"No, no. The restaurant." Kiwi pointed through the scrim of pigeons to a neon *B*.

"The Burger Burger? I would not really call that place a restaurant, bro. You can buy a cheeseburger there for a fucking *quarter*. You think the Burger Burger is going to pay you big money? Leo calls it the E. coli factory!"

"Leo eats there all the time."

"They pay a dollar less than here and you smell like dead cow forever and all the girls are skanks, which is fine with me, but I swear to God they all got herpes."

"Oh. I see."

Kiwi wasn't 100 percent on what that meant. What was the use of talking about anything? He needed to make a thousand dollars this month and he didn't see how that was possible.

"Check their lips, bro."

"Okay. I will. Poor girls." Kiwi was sure he'd read about this ailment somewhere but he couldn't quite recall the etiology—he would have to do some research later. *Regardless of my findings, I am going to wolf like twelve of those burgers.* Kiwi stared at the neon *B* and felt his mouth flood. Hellspawn Hoagies were eight dollars and he had thirty-two cents on his employee card.

Vijay was looking at him strangely.

"You cannot work there. Not to sound arrogant, bro? But without me around, they will *destroy* you."

"What are you talking about?" Who could he mean, "they"? The skanks?

Vijay blew hair out of his left eye and looked at Kiwi darkly. "*Everybody*. The people who hear you talk."

"Oh."

Kiwi pushed greasy hair out of his own eyes—he couldn't afford a haircut at the moment, either. On Swamplandia! Ossie had taken this duty over from his mother, surprising the other Bigtrees with the steadiness of her hands. Their compliments had irritated her—"Well, I'm not a chimpanzee, you guys. I can use scissors. I can cut in a straight line." Now Kiwi had hanks of red hair that crimped in the heat like sea serpents.

Yvans had offered to shave Kiwi's skull bald for him ("For free, Margaret!"), but that seemed to Kiwi like a move of premature despair. Possibly he would bleed to death from lacerations on his head, or more likely he would be exposed to the cruel hail of female mockery. Also Yvans had more than once confessed to suffering weird ailments like "the shakes," which didn't seem, as the girls of the World would say, so super compatible with a razor.

"Do you know any way I could, uh, supplement my income?" Kiwi asked. *I'm going to save the park,* he beamed out across the parking lot toward his sisters, in a direction that he believed led to their water—he could see one small bird rowing its wings into the sun over the interstate, centered up there like the face on a coin.

Vijay was staring at him. "Are you asking me to rob a bank with you? Maybe you want me to pimp you out as an erotic dancer by the airport?"

"Exotic."

"Erotic. Whatever, bro. Same thing."

Was it? Vijay lifted his shirt and rippled his abdomen like a belly dancer. Kiwi watched Vijay's belly button pinch inward and roll sinuously back into existence, which was mesmerizing.

"Quit acting gay, Vijay," said Kiwi. "I'm serious here. I'm in trouble."

"How much do you think I could make, Marge? With moves like this?"

"Zero dollars and zero cents." (*Bro!* Kiwi remembered, too late now.) "Hey, I really don't think you should be touching your abdomen to this roof like that? Because you will notice there is glass everywhere and you're putting yourself at risk for tetanus . . . ?"

A seaplane made a noisy loop above them, fangs painted on its black nose in a simulacrum of an alligator's grin. *Don't scream,* he heard in Ava's small growl. For a moment they were in the shadow of its wings, the roar of engines sucking their speech upward.

"What is that?" he managed.

"New ride. You didn't hear about it?"

Kiwi's heart was in his throat—the seaplane was landing on the moat that surrounded the World, coming in so close that Kiwi thought its propeller would crash through the Leviathan windows. He dropped his head in anticipation of a phantom shower of glass, but when he looked again, the seaplane was skimming the surface of the moat. A heavy spray exploded around the seaplane's fixed wings. Something about the way it landed, floats first, gave Kiwi the impression of teeth entering the water, the jet floats biting into the red-dyed water like two bright fangs. *Probably just the effect the World of D. is going for here,* Kiwi thought. Part of the grand theme.

The seaplane blew red jets of foam across the water for another hundred yards or so, stopped with the whiskers of its propellers trembling near the Leviathan.

"Oh my God," said Kiwi.

"Right? Say. You know who makes bank, Marge? Those pilots."

The World of Darkness had its own flight school, Vijay said. The managers were recruiting from inside the World, instead of doing outside hiring, because then they could pay the pilots less—$45,000 a year, said Vijay. Kiwi would have to sell his greenhorn sperm and platelets for a decade to make anywhere near that.

"It's not even that hard, *supposedly.* It's like driving a bus of the sky."

As far as driving was concerned, Kiwi had once driven the tram into the side of Grandpa Sawtooth's house. Sky-wise, he'd fallen out of Ava's kapok tree house at age ten and broken both arms.

"Huh. Forty-five thousand dollars. And how does one enroll in the, uh, the flight school?"

Kiwi should have guessed that some new ride was under way. For weeks he'd heard the ear-splitting construction on the northern lot. From the roof he'd seen Caterpillars pushing the moat into an artificial harbor, the crews installing a slate dock on floating supports that looked like huge gray boxing gloves. The attraction was called the Four Pilots of the Apocalypse: a play on the Bible's book of Revelations, of course, but also an allusion to a real event. In the 1940s, the Four Pilots of the Apocalypse were heralded as Loomis County heroes. They were young men, out-of-work supply pilots contracted by a private millionaire who had purchased great tracts of swamp from Henry Disston, the potbellied Florida land baron, whose baronial hairstyle was as black and wavy as charred bacon. The Four Pilots carried the granules of their particular plague in restaurant salt and pepper shakers. They dumped thousands of Australian melaleuca seeds from the windows of low-flying Cessnas, shaking them all over the salt marshes and the saw-grass prairies and the tree islands. Would-be farmers dreamed of nights lit by fragrant globes of citrus, yellow fields of corn, and Angus cattle black as jackboots, the worthless saw grass vanquished, the alligators dead, the water drained.

Then in 1981, at the crest of a fitful wave of public interest in the swamp, the famous late-night talk-show host J. P. Twomey had done a series called *The Four Pilots of the Apocalypse* about the unwitting villains who had planted the seeds of the swamp's destruction. It still got screened on channel 2, Loomis's "cultural" station. J. P. Twomey had interviewed the surviving pilot, Mickey Hotchkiss, now a white-haired man with a voice as small as Michael Jackson's wearing what appeared to be women's palazzo pants. Mickey Hotchkiss was no longer entirely with it, was the implication of his wardrobe choices. He seemed shy but also happy to be on TV. After denouncing him for nixing a unique ecosystem—"putting the whammy on the wetlands," as Twomey put it—J.P. forced Mickey to look at photographs of the melaleuca's conquest. A haunting slide show commenced: acres and acres of new forests composed of a single multiplying tree, the melaleuca; fires burning on the drained land in northern Florida, where blue-green sheets of water used to flow from Lake Okeechobee all the way to the Gulf of Mexico; a final grim view of the swamp from above, silver corridors of melaleucas flattening whole islands into one color like a trick involving mirrors. Mickey's smile faltered but remained in place. Once or twice the old pilot had clucked politely, as if he were being shown photographs of grandchildren whose names he had forgotten.

"I did this?" he'd asked in a sly, guilty voice, like a child trying to figure out why he was about to get punished. "When?"

Kiwi had watched the Four Pilots program with his dad twice. The Chief had railed against the advance of the melaleuca woods the entire time, even during commercials, but he wasn't angry at this pilot. They'd agreed (Kiwi and his father could sometimes meet at the intersection of their two angers, like neighbors drawing up to the barbed stars of a fence) that the old guy looked like the original scapegoat, Grecian almost, with his wispy beard and baffled ovine eyes.

Vijay explained that the new ride was a tour of ecological devastation. You could take aerial pictures, with a fancy rental camera, of "the Floridian Styx." You could murmur over the gray blight and eat a sack lunch. You could ache for lost species of flowers and trees for twenty minutes and touch your forehead to the cockpit window's glass to find "Swamp Acheron" and "New Lethe," and then fly back.

"That's my home," Kiwi mumbled. "That's where I grew up."

"Yeah, right?" Vijay sighed and rolled over on his side. "That ride sounds pretty fucking lame to me, but Carl says the Carpathian Corporation is 'capitalizing on a local fear' or some dumb shit. Same stuff they make us watch the videos about. They're only running the Four Pilots tours in Loomis, though. Like a test run." Vijay was lying half in shadow with the sun on his chin and his eyes shut. His chest rose and fell like an old cat's. Even stoned and half-asleep, Vijay could somehow roll sideways and, like a bird-shit clairvoyant, avoid getting bombed by the pigeons.

"If it goes good they're going to do one in Fairbanks. Bush pilots are going to fly Lost Souls to the melting ice caps, so they can, like, cry like babies and get competitive about how sad they are and shit. Get photos of those snow bears. Be like, 'Hey, bear! Sorry we fucked up your summer, bro!'"

"You mean polar bears," Kiwi corrected automatically. "Or possibly the Kodiak bear. *Ursus arctos middendorffi.* Hey, how come you know about this ride already?"

"You didn't get the memos? Look around your locker," Vijay told him. (Kiwi had been avoiding his locker, where ASSFUCKER still glowed lithium white against the metal.)

"Oh, okay. Right-o."

Vijay cracked one reddened eye at him.

"Right-o? Are you Sherlock Holmes? Have I taught you nothing?"

"I meant, right on. I mean, thank you." He kept his eyes on the sun. "Really." A cloud moved and light poured over them. It suddenly occurred to Kiwi that he and Vijay both looked bronzed and goofy, sitting up here in their Thinking Man poses. Like statue rejects that some sculptor had in a paroxysm of shame hidden on the roof.

"No problem, Margie. I hope you get it." Vijay waggled his bare toes at Kiwi in farewell, one arm flung across his face. Break had ended fifteen minutes ago. He giggled into the crook of one elbow: "Take it to the skies, Margaret!"

Kiwi stood. He spent a final minute staring at the black seaplanes with their torpid propellers, now drowsing like huge dragonflies on the bloodshot moat. Time to go find Carl before he could second-guess himself. His body prickled with dull anticipation, cell memory—it would be freezing on the stairwell. Often Kiwi felt like he was eavesdropping on the conversations of his own body, committee meetings of muscles and ligaments that didn't seem to include him. Whenever he'd gone onstage to wrestle the alligators, he'd always felt like the last to know about his own terror. It was a disorienting lag. Even the behatted, popcorn-munching tourists in the stadium got the scoop on him. His parents, his grandfather, his sisters, the alligators, his own deep tissues—everybody had him figured for a coward, but Kiwi wouldn't catch on until he heard his own scream.

Kiwi stood for a moment longer outside the cherry-red door that led back into the World of Darkness, enjoying the feeling of the warm outside air against his back. The outermost rail of the overpass glowed in a thin gold parabola at this hour, like some interplanetary racetrack. *Somewhere our Seths are clawing onto their rocks,* he thought, staring out across lanes of Loomis traffic.

"Hey, don't puss out, Marge!" Vijay called. "Threaten him! Tell Carl that if he doesn't let you fly the plane, you'll quit and leave for the Burger Burger."

Kiwi found Carl Jenks spinning on his office chair. He frowned at the tiny cactus plant on his desk as Kiwi spoke.

"And I have excellent hand-eye coordination, sir," he coughed, "and a good foundation in aeronautics, physics . . ."

Carl pressed his lips to near invisibility. Possibly Carl Jenks had at one time wanted to be a kind man, a decent and charitable man; and then puberty had come along and slapped this almost translucent blond mustache across his face. The mustache was Carl's most distinctive feature—the hairs grew in achromatic and already bristling.

Kiwi heard himself speaking faster and faster; he resisted the urge to lean in and do spontaneous calculus for Carl on his clipboard.

"Are you crazy?" Carl said when he'd finished. "Two weeks ago you broke the vacuum. Nina Suárez complains that you're sexually harassing her. Ephraim Lipmann says that you're sexually harassing *him.* Every time I turn around you're tripping over something, or coming down from the roof stoned out of your gourd. Shut up, Bigtree, I don't want to hear it."

Carl Jenks, who had started this disquisition in his usual wry tone, was suddenly breaking on his vowels. His voice shook. He seemed to have accidentally stirred himself to real fury, as if Kiwi's request were the last in a long string of impossible ideas, inappropriate and painful ideas, that Carl Jenks been asked to entertain in his lifetime.

Carl said, "Scout, our payroll manager—"

"Scott."

"*Scotty* tells me that you do not understand *numbers.* That you cannot do *basic arithmetic.* And we're going to train you to fly a plane?"

"Yes?" said Kiwi.

"Tell you what, Bigtree. We'll train you on the chair and see how that goes."

"The electric chair?" Kiwi was picturing spikes, white forks of summer lightning running through a tin cap.

"The lifeguard chair. Down in the Lake of Fire."

Carl Jenks sighed and reversed the direction of his chair-spins. He had an office chair, Kiwi noted, with cushy armrests to prevent strain and fatigue.

"Dale Bonilla is our lifeguard now, but I'm moving him. Tell me, Kiwi, can you lifeguard effectively if you are reading pornography? Can you safeguard the lives of preadolescent children if you are busy shooting half-human, half-tiger monsters in an imaginary jungle on your portable *video* console?"

Kiwi had played that game in the dormitory: Were-Cats Attack IV. The bad guys had tiger paws for running and human thumbs for guns. Kiwi made it to level 7 with Leonard one Tuesday morning in the dormitory, where they'd been defeated at last in an interspecies massacre outside the gray digitized ruins, ambushed by a roaring horde of bipedal tigers with machine guns and big clawed feet bursting out of their khaki pants. Silence on this topic seemed prudent.

"That sounds irresponsible, Carl. It's against the World of Darkness policy to use personal electronics on the job."

Carl rolled his pale eyes. "Quit being such a shoe-licker, Bigtree. What I'm saying is, does Dale Bonilla even know how to swim? Do you think Pam in HR asks the tough questions when she does new hires? I don't think so, Kiwi, personally, because here *you* stand."

"Okay." Kiwi ran a hand through his hair. Violence was contemplated, then rejected by Kiwi as counterproductive to his larger financial stratagems. He thought, *The Chief would have you by the neck, Carl Jenks.*

"So I'm not going to be a pilot?"

"Nobody starts at the top, do they? You have to work your way up." Carl was grinning now, a messy grin that spilled all over his face, his blue eyes sparkling with improved humor, as if this were a joke they could share: Kiwi climbing the ladder.

"You'll need to get CPR certified." Carl actually giggled, then relaxed into silence again, as if good humor were an athletic stretch he couldn't hold. "And you can request your Rescue Stick and your little bathing suit from HR. The ladies are in for a treat, eh?"

At the mention of a bathing suit, Kiwi cinched Cubby's jeans in his left hand.

"Is this a promotion, Mr. Jenks?"

"Sure." Carl smiled magnanimously, swept a hand over his moon-white skull. "Why not think of it that way?"

CHAPTER ELEVEN

Ava Goes to the Underworld

"Therefore, for your sake, I think it wise
you follow me: I will be your guide . . ."
— Dante Alighieri, *The Inferno*

O n the morning that my sister eloped with Louis Thanksgiving, the Bird Man gave me his own version of Virgil's advice—a swamp aphorism, he said, a maxim commonly uttered by the moonshiners, the glade crackers, the plume and alligator hunters, by the famous bird warden Guy Bradley and the Seminole and the Miccosukee tribes alike, and he was surprised I'd never heard it:

"Nobody can get to hell without assistance, kid."

When I burst into the kitchen I saw the Bird Man grinding coffee beans with Mom's little tin mill, an artifact I had forgotten about.

"Found this in your museum," he said without turning. "Haven't seen one of these in ages. Your tribe has some really interesting stuff out there. Hope you don't mind that I borrowed it—"

Ossie's note was crushed against my chest and I couldn't get my voice to work. What I remember feeling was a kind of stage fright, as if the curtains were about to lift onto a new and never-rehearsed show.

"Well, I guess I sure made myself at home," he said, a red smile in his voice. "I'm making us eggs—" He turned to face me, shaking grease angrily from the spatula grill. "Jesus, kid. What happened?"

My sister never came home.

A ghost has kidnapped my sister.

"Read this, please," I managed.

The Bird Man scowled down at the wedding notice like the Chief reviewing a bill.

"Is this somebody you know, kid?"

"Osceola, she's my sister. She's missing?" I moaned the information into a question. "She wants to marry this guy, Louis . . . but he's not, ah . . ." I pushed a fist into one eye, tried to slow my breathing.

"Your sister is getting married? Today?"

"She ran away with her boyfriend. What should I do? Who do I call now?"

I glanced at the clock: twenty-two minutes had passed since I'd found Osceola's note.

"Deep breaths, kid. Sit down. Nobody's dying here. Now, let me just get my head around this . . ."

The Bird Man had opened all the windows in our kitchen. Rose curlicues shivered on Mom's brown curtains, a fabric garden, and suddenly I missed my mom again with a pain that was ferocious. She was everywhere and nowhere in the kitchen. Pale brown eggshells rocked like little cradles on her cutting board. Salt, pepper, a jar of ancient Tabasco lined her countertop—the Bird Man had even found her real china, mainland stuff from her Loomis mother, these plates that were the hard white of malt balls. It was strange to see her cup and saucer in this stranger's hand. The Bird Man had disappeared into his odd clothes again, the long coat in the death heat of summer, his ankle-laced boots. The coat had a layered ruff of black feathers and tumbled all the way down to his boot laces, like a trench coat. The feathers put a furlike gleam on his shoulders, which hunched together each time he sipped from my mom's cup. *That coat must be so heavy!* I thought. *How can he stand it?* But he moved through our kitchen as if he weren't wearing anything at all, as nimbly as any animal.

The Bird Man brought the coffee over; he motioned for me to sit, like we were going to have breakfast together. Black feathers sprayed around the orange handle of Mom's mug. The kitchen was already hot and I could *smell* that coat today, the oily feathers trapping an unplaceable aroma. He poured us both cups of coffee and milk and his voice was very calm, as if we were discussing a misplaced key.

"You say the whole machine is gone?"

"The dredge barge."

"And somebody is with her? Her, ah, her fiancé?"

I stared at him for a moment. "I don't think anybody is with her right now, actually. I mean . . . I think she's the only body on board. She makes stuff up. We don't think she really has a boyfriend."

"Okay. And does your sister know anything about engineering? Would she know how to pilot a dredge like that by herself?"

"I told you, I don't know." My face felt hot and huge. "I don't think so. But the dredge must be running again, right?"

"How do you figure? Your sister—"

"Because it's *gone*, Bird Man."

"I see. Your sister. How old is she?"

"Sixteen. She's not an alligator wrestler like the rest of us, though— she's not real strong or anything. Could she have gotten the dredge down the canal on her own, is that possible?"

The Bird Man frowned, which turned his long nose into a blade. "It's possible. The dredge was in the water already, correct? So if she carried an old outboard to the ditch, got a rope around it, and hooked it onto the back . . ." He shrugged. "It's possible. But would she know to do that, do you think?"

I felt my teeth part around a "no," then paused. We underestimated Osceola. Just when you thought she was a lost cause she'd surprise you with a funny proficiency. And we girls were always underfoot when the Chief did repair work on motorboats, airboats, the Pit plumbing . . .

"She might know how," I amended. "She's been carting all kinds of stuff out there."

You track the buzzards. Do you know, I almost asked him, *have you heard and do you believe in a story called the Dredgeman's Revelation?*

I'd assumed the bags Ossie had toted out to the ditch were full of flowers and candles, her séance stuff. But the Chief kept all kinds of old equipment in the museum. We had electrical relics piled up to the roof: spark plugs and the gouged eyes of Chevy headlights; a box of gold grommets that the Chief and Mom used to collect like metal seashells after hurricanes. Glass chutes, fire wheels, daisy-shaped gears. Antique tubing. Red and orange wires kelped in boxes. All these parts might mean something to a ghost mechanic like Louis.

"Plus she had help."

"Help?"

"The ghost is helping her. Her boyfriend. His name is Louis Thanksgiving"—I felt my cheeks heat up, hearing how this sounded—"and he used to operate that dredge. He's seventeen, or at least he was on the day that he died."

"He's a dead kid. Your sister's helper."

"My sister can talk to them."

"To ghosts . . ."

I stared down at my coffee. "My dad says that she's going through something. A phase . . ."

"Okay. And you don't think she had someone *real* to help her, kid? Someone besides this . . . Louis?"

"No," I said, startled by the force of my voice. "No, it's Louis who's behind all this."

Somehow it was easier for me to imagine a secret wind unbending the pins of an engine than any tanned and red-blooded helper, some local boy or fisherman fixing up the dredge and piloting her away. Who besides us had even set foot in the dredge? Who alive would know how to run it?

So I did believe, finally, in the ghost of Louis Thanksgiving. I believed, in a waterfall rush, in the world of the ghosts. An underworld—I pictured blue mist, rocks so huge the dredge barge rolled between them like a marble.

"I know where the ghost is taking her, too!" I blurted out. "The Calusa shell mounds. The Eye of the Needle. That's how she says you can get to the underworld—you go between those shell islands."

The Bird Man got a funny smile on his face. "Right. The underworld."

"Stop that," I said angrily, surprising myself again. "What I'm telling you is real."

But the Bird Man didn't say—as I'd expected him to—"That's ridiculous. Your sister is lying to you, or else she's crazy." He didn't tell me what I'd been secretly hoping to hear: "I believe in ghosts." Instead he ground a pale fleck of butter into a piece of burned toast and smiled sadly at me. Belief didn't even come up.

"Oh, I know it is, Ava. I know it's real. It's just that your sister is pretty young to make that trip."

Then the Bird Man sipped cold coffee and told me that there was a real underworld.

"This whole swamp is haunted, kid."

I felt my mouth go slack as a fish. "Haunted? Really?"

"Sure. Your sister is right. I'm sure you folks have sensed it your-selves, wrestling the alligators, living way out. And there are thousands of openings in the limestone and the eastern mangrove tunnels. What the old gator hunters and plumers called the Black Woods."

I nodded reflexively. We called these tunnels the Mangle or the Walking Woods. Far south of our island the mangroves grew in impen-etrable tangles. Their prop roots lifted balletically out of the mud, as if each tree were about to take a step forward into the water.

"Way out there, that's where you'll find those shell islands. Most people go from one side to the other and they never get to the under-world. If you're a first-timer—if you're alive—and if you want to make the return trip, well, kid, you need a guide."

I looked down and saw that I was holding on to our kitchen table with my strongest wrestling grip. I nearly gagged at the sight of milk clouding the coffee cup. The whole world was funneling through a crack and reconstituting itself: this ghost was real, my sister had van-ished with him, there *was* an underworld, just like Ossie's book had claimed—and this stranger knew how to get there. Was it possible for girls like us to get there? Living people? I remembered the map that my sister and I had pasted to the dredge porthole: a wide empty south-west. The sun splashed through a blank grid. But maybe a Bird Man had a special gift for reading blanks? If he could understand the birds' silence, maybe he could find a country in that emptiness.

The Bird Man had turned to face our door. Was he going to leave soon? I couldn't let him do that. I couldn't tell the telephone what I'd done—losing Ossie to an invisible kidnapper, losing her when I was supposed to be the boss of Swamplandia! I felt a grogginess and a terri-ble, terrible lightness, as if I might let go of the table's edge and blow away. The clock and the telephone stared at each other from their oppo-site walls, like parents who refused to advise me. To teach me a lesson. To make me decide this for myself.

"We should call someone?" I pointed at the phone, in case a Bird Man was not familiar with house technology. "I have Chief Bigtree's number here. Or Gus Waddell, he could search from the ferry. Park Services . . ."

I frowned down at my fingers. I didn't want to call them.

"Yes, you can call the mainlanders. Your decision . . ." His forehead creased beneath his hood. He reached into the feathers and produced a brown cigarette, lit it. "What I'm afraid of, kid . . . Well, look, they are not going to believe you. Not Park Services, not anybody who you contact on the mainland. And their technologies aren't going to find her, either." He ashed into his coffee with the serene sadness of a man accustomed to the worst news. "Not if she is heading to the underworld with this ghost."

"Louis."

"With this Louis."

What would the Chief say, if he could hear me now? What would my brother do? Kiwi would be on the phone to the ranger Whip Jeters and Park Services, using Latin words to describe the crisis. (But Kiwi hadn't heard this Bird Man calling to me in the woods, I thought, and just the memory of that sound caused many bright fibers I had not known existed inside me to tighten.)

"So she won't be found, you mean?"

"Oh, they might find her. Of course they might find her."

The Bird Man's voice got too gentle. He sounded genuinely sorry for me, like our tourists used to when I explained about my mom. "I can't tell the future. But if they do find her, well . . . I might worry about that, too. I might prefer to find her *myself* if I were you."

The Bird Man explained to me that mainland authorities remove children from their families—that this was not uncommon. If the family or the child was deemed "unstable." (He hissed this word like a buzzard, like the wind in feathers.) "Eloping" would be a red flag for the government agents, he said, and "eloping with a ghost" sounded much, much worse. The Bird Man gave me a look of odd complicity above his feathered collar.

"Ask Chief Bigtree. Your father can tell you: the mainland authorities are no friends of ours. Swamp people are this country's last outlaws, kid. We have to stick together."

I grinned back at him, happy in spite of everything to be bundled into the word "we."

"Okay," I told the Bird Man. "When the mainlanders ask me why my sister ran, I'll lie. I won't mention Louis. I won't breathe a word about the underworld."

I wasn't going to lose Ossie a second time. Not to a government agency. On the Library Boat, Kiwi once showed me a mustard-yellow tome, *Child Psychiatric Medicine,* Vol. A-4. What struck me was a black-and-white photograph of a teenage girl in an asylum, bare-kneed in a claw-footed tub with her hair in a kind of translucent cap, like a shower cap but tight to her scalp. She had unblemished skin and these wafer-light eyes. You could see her blond hair through the cap, wrapped around metal curlers like waves of leashed, disciplined thoughts. The *scary* part was that you couldn't tell, from this girl's scrubbed and ordinary face, that anything was the matter with her. "That place is an asylum, Ava," Kiwi had told me, explaining the word's several contrary-seeming definitions. And now this Bird Man told me such prisons for girls still existed: *There is a place on the mainland where they hide girls like your sister.*

"Well," he said, following my gaze to the phone. "The thing about that plan, you see . . ."

His voice took on that cushiony layer that adults use to pad the worst news, a kind of sonic insulation, as if they are afraid their words might otherwise electrocute a child. "The problem, Ava, is that if your sister has already crossed over to the underworld, they won't find her." He coughed amiably, continued. "Park Services will be useless to your sister. None of their dogs and helicopters can track a ghost."

"Why can't we help them find her? Can't we show them how to get there?"

"Who? The rangers? The dogs, maybe." He laughed. "You think we can direct the Coast Guard's ships to the underworld? No, kid. That's impossible."

"But you said you did know how to find it once . . . ?" My cheeks felt feverish. "You could draw those guys a map . . ."

"But I can't—kid, the paths are always changing. Even if I *could* help them, it wouldn't make any difference. Nobody at Search and Rescue is going to listen to a Bird Man's directions to the underworld—they'd probably drag me to the loony bin. They'd take you with me, kid."

"That wouldn't happen. I'm an alligator wrestler," I explained. "I would fight them."

"And then who's left to find your sister? Do you think that Search and Rescue is going to believe either of us about your sister and her . . . companion?" Golden crumbs were suspended on his feathers. Incredibly, he was buttering another slice of toast—Gus Waddell had brought us a fresh loaf of white bread with our groceries that Saturday. "Would even your father believe us?"

"Oh, my dad?" My eyes fell. "No. Probably not." The Chief would not understand the Dredgeman's Revelation. Our dad would look for Ossie elsewhere, drowned or on the broken rocks of Gallinule Key. I did not think his heart could take a search like that.

"If Ossie and Louis make it between the Eye, can we get her back again?"

"Who knows, kid? This is a problem. I deal with the migrations of birds, not people."

"You could go after her. We could go."

The Bird Man steepled his long fingers. His whole face puckered up inside his hood, as if he were weighing something—*me,* I realized. Calculating if I'd be strong enough to make the trip. I tightened my grip on the table and flexed my wrestling muscles.

"It's a difficult journey. We'd have to take my skiff. No engines. You have to use the old Calusa waterways—way too narrow out there for an airboat. We'll be extraordinarily lucky if we can pole it this time of year."

"I'll help out. A lot. You saw me last night—"

"Alligators aren't the fauna we'll be dealing with down there." He shook his head. "No, look, you're years too young for this. You'd be the youngest passenger I've ever taken . . ."

"I can wrestle the biggest Seth in the Pit. My grandfather says I can wrestle better than an adult man. I'm strong and I don't get scared. We'll pay you," I added quickly. "How much do you want? I can pay you. When the Chief gets back . . ."

Taped beneath the telephone was our father's mainland telephone number. The Chief always stayed in the same room at the Bowl-a-Bed hotel in east Loomis. (I can still hear the song of the numbers that we dialed for his hotel room, although it's been years since I could recite the numerals themselves: _ _ _-_ _ _ _.) I held the earpiece against my damp face, and I listened to the tone for too long without dialing, until my heartbeat disappeared into the telephone's terrible hum. *Dial. Dial.*

I dropped it onto the hook. Why call him, why risk all that fear and disappointment, when this whole situation might be resolved before noon? Why should anybody ever have to know that Osceola ran away? If I made the right choice now. If I acted *fast,* with the reflexive courage of a Bigtree wrestling a Seth . . .

The Bird Man, meanwhile, had shifted verbs on me. He had detoured from the realm of theory and begun talking *plans.* "So we're going to be discreet about this, we don't need to attract any undue attention on the water. We'll want to leave as soon as possible, before the tide goes out . . ."

I watched my hand scratch out a note to my father, in case he got home before we did. The note was very formal. "Sincerely, Ava," I wrote, because the Bird Man was watching me and "I love you" or even just "Love" struck me as a childish sign-off.

Then I took the telephone off the hook. That way if the Chief called us before we got back he wouldn't worry, he'd think we'd just been careless. So: we were going. The rose gardens on my mother's curtains continued rippling. The lizards clung to the window screens, motionless. We left her china plates in a pretty stack.

We packed in a hurry: cans of pork and tuna, red beans, powdered coffee and milk, dry curls of macaroni, a skillet, the Chief's fishing knife, a package of ground hamburger, envelopes of the powdered orange drink Ossie liked. I grabbed knives and old gallon jugs. But the Bird Man said we should bring more food, more water. Nonperishables. It seemed to me like we were overpacking; how long did a trip to the underworld take?

Two hours after I'd discovered Ossie's note tacked to the tree, we started down the trail toward the island's muddy shoreline.

"I never tie off at your dock—that's a public spot, and you've got that fat ferryboat captain puttering around, minding other people's business . . ."

"Gus." I felt a little pang. "He's nice."

The Bird Man's feathers heaved up and down—he was only shrugging again.

"I try to protect folks from their own curiosity about me. My profession. Not too many Bird Men working the islands these days. This way, kid. I'm over on the lee side."

In addition to food and water I had decided to bring the red Seth in her wooden carrying crate. It wasn't a practical or a kind decision, and I whispered a little apology through the breathing holes; if it was any consolation, I told her, by this time next year she would be too big and fangsome for me to carry. Her stint as my pet would be over. We would have to become rivals, I explained a little sadly, a world-famous duet of muscles and scales, we would pioneer new holds and we would invent our own championship if we had to . . .

The Bird Man glanced down at me. "Who are you talking to, kid?"

"Nobody. I'm, ah . . . I'm praying."

"Just keep that thing taped up. If you're dead set on bringing it, which is a pretty stupid move—but I noticed that you didn't ask my opinion."

My hand tightened on the carrier's handle. We were deep into the underbrush now. He paused to make some grunting adjustment to the red cooler's weight, sliding cans and jugs around, when a fish crow cried out, a long squawk. The Bird Man stood up.

"Hear that? That's our augur. Hell's doorbell. It's time to go."

"That's it, really? That's hell's doorbell? A fish crow?"

This cawing was a sound I heard and ignored a dozen times each day. I would have expected something more impressive, like *Phantom of the Opera* music or the boom of a chasm opening. But this crow sounded like any old crow sounds, foreboding and hoarse, like a psychic who is indifferent to your fate. We entered a stand of madeira trees. As we walked beyond the strains of the crow's last, dry cry, the Bird Man ticked off instructions on his thumb:

"One, keep your arms and legs inside the boat.

"Two, keep your questions to a minimum.

"Three: Some of the Ten Thousand Islands on the way to the underworld are inhabited." The Bird Man's voice seemed to issue from the pool of shadows beneath his hat. "The people who live along the Riptides of the Dead . . . these are not people you should trust, kid. A few of them aren't even, to get real technical, people. Don't get too loose and free with the details about your sister, either. Anybody asks, I'm your cousin. We're on a fishing trip."

"Okay. No problem, cousin." I tried to grin. "Are you a Bigtree then, or am I a . . . you? One of your kind?" But the Bird Man didn't like this game. I smelled salt and a skunkier odor, and knew that water must be hidden behind the yellow pines.

SWAMPLANDIA! AND BEYOND read a wooden sign at the edge of the grounds.

OVER 1,000,000 ACRES OF WILDERNESS!

"We can find her, I know we can," I mumbled. "How far can she have gotten?"

The Bird Man didn't respond. He lifted a low cocoplum branch for me: the glare of water dazzled in. Through the bushes I saw a treeless spit of sand.

"See that, kid? A hidden harbor." I saw a horseshoe of earth around shallow broth. A glade skiff made a long snaky beak along the sand.

"You wait there." He flipped the skiff and began wading out with it, the gravied water covering his boots. Grasses got crushed and sprang back around the hull. "You know how to paddle?"

"You bet." I'd been kayaking through the Ten Thousand Islands before. I used to go rare-flower hunting in the spring with Mom and, on summer nights, gator hunting with carbide lanterns and .22 rifles with my grandfather. This would be a different kind of voyage, I thought, and felt a little yellow slurry of excitement. Sister hunting. Ghost seeking. Squeezing through the Eye of the Needle to another world.

The skiff was a fourteen-footer. I saw that he'd built it following the old Seminole blueprint, with penny nails and a cypress transom, a poling platform in the back; he waved me forward and offered me a glove. I hesitated—a second later his gloves hooked my armpits and swung me onto the bow seat. Up close, I noticed that the Bird Man had the finest purse of wrinkles around his mouth, so that he seemed older or younger depending on where the sun hit. His chin was pocked and small as a red potato.

"So you don't think my sister is crazy?" I asked happily. Now that I could feel the current tugging at our boat a knot was loosening in my stomach.

"I don't know your sister."

"But you do think that ghosts are real? You think it could be true, that she's been talking to them all this time?"

Feelings tumbled through me.

One was: *Ossie does have powers.*

And another: *What if I follow her to the underworld and find my mother?*

The Bird Man, tightening the screws in the poling platform with a doll-size tool, didn't respond. I started babbling about Ossie and Louis then, as his silence deepened. I wanted him to agree with me that she wasn't "sick," like Kiwi claimed. Even at her wildest, I told him, even while possessed, my sister had certain ideas about herself that you couldn't change, fixed in place like the burning constellations—who could love her, who couldn't or would never, what she could ask for on the Ouija, what she was likely to get.

"I'm too ugly for him," Ossie had told me one October day with the dispassion of a much older woman, checking her reflection in the back of a café spoon. I had only been joking, telling her that she should conjure Benjamin Franklin. "Didn't Benjamin Franklin invent a car that runs on lightning or something? He's too good for me, Ava. He won't come if I call."

Even in her trances, even while possessed, my sister was very shrewd about her prospects. A fantasy would collapse like a wave against the rocks of her intelligence. Madness, as I understood it from books, meant a person who was open to the high white whine of *everything.*

"Okay, kid. She doesn't sound crazy to me. Enough, huh?"

The Bird Man kept shooting looks at the coast.

"Listen, did you hear something? Did you see anybody following us?"

I shook my head. It wasn't a Gus day.

"Good."

"Also—I swear this is the last thing, okay?—it's not like my sister believes she could summon just *anyone.*" I paused. "She can't contact our mother, either."

Ossie said a spirit's voice was as fine as a needle, tattooing her insides with luminous words. I'd seen a picture of this in *The Spiritist's Telegraph.* A young Spiritist levitated a full foot above her bedsprings. A ghost was curled like a blue snail inside her chest, and it was so tiny! It burned through the lace of her old-fashioned dress like a second heart. A musical staff wound in a thorny crown around the Spiritist's forehead, so that notes ran down her cheeks in a loose mask of song. Her eyelids were blacked out—and I saw this again and again in nightmares about my sister. Her eyelids had the high polish of acorns. But her *ears:* that was the truly scary part. Great fantails of indigo and violet lights spiraled into her earlobes in an ethereal funnel—what the book called the Inverted Borealis. The caption read: "A ghost sings its way deeply inside the Spiritist."

Now the Bird Man seemed really interested. "The Inverted Borealis. That sounds like a big event for one girl's body to host. Must get awfully bright in there. Does your sister wear sunglasses? Is there a 'Sunblock for Spiritists'?" He chuckled once and stopped. "Aw, hell, kid, don't look that way. Just a bad joke."

"That's okay. It's not so funny when it happens to her."

"Does she like talking to them, these ghosts?"

"I don't know." I shrugged. "She sure likes talking to her . . . to this guy Louis." I was horrified—I had almost said "her husband." *How exactly does a person marry a ghost?* I wanted to ask, because a very very bad thought had just occurred to me.

"And what do these voices tell your sister, I wonder?"

"The voice. There's only ever one voice at a time, I guess, and she and it . . . converse. The ghost tells her romantic stuff. Stuff like you hear in the movies: that it loves her, that it needs her. That she, you know . . ." I frowned and hoped that he believed me. "That she smells like flowers."

This bluff embarrassed me because I had no idea what two teenagers in love might talk about. My parents had their own language for that stuff that involved the alligators, and us. TV movies and radio songs were the only models I had for love transmissions, a boyfriend-girlfriend conversation.

"That's mostly it, I think."

The Bird Man nodded distractedly. He was knee-deep in the water with his pants trailing threads, his coat slung like a pelt over one shoulder. He pushed his trousers up and shook out a lighter from what I thought of as the left wing of his coat (it was hard for me to think of it as a *sleeve*) and held it up to a cigarette. I watched his lighter jump. Aside from the cranberry brightness of the flame against his slick feathers, everything else checked out. I examined his ungloved fingers, his chewed nails surrounded by little flags of skin—what had I been expecting, claws? Talons? His legs were very ordinary. His shins were slightly hairier than my brother's. Hyacinths slid around them and stuck to the boards of the transom.

"Oh, wow, you smoke my dad's brand of cigarettes."

"Sure do. I took the carton from your house. A little advance on my fee."

Then I started noticing other acquisitions. The Chief's fishing knife was under the stern seat and the Chief's beer was in the cooler. I saw a knot of antique Heddon lures from Grandpa Sawtooth's tackle. The Bird Man had raided our fridge and our museum. This gave me a dizzy feeling, as if we were only going on an ordinary camping trip together, a family trip. I caught myself listening for squelching footsteps, my mother and the Chief and Ossie and Kiwi lagging behind us on the trail.

"Took a few more things from your museum, kid. Useful stuff. You can bring it back after we find her."

"Sure. Okay." We were poling faster and faster now. Through the peeled branches I saw a dense, soft shuffle of wings. "Bird Man? I thought you got rid of them. Are they coming, too?"

"Of course they are coming," the Bird Man said. "If I am the navigator, the buzzards are our stars. They're our map, kid. Nobody can get to the underworld without assistance, myself included."

Buzzards filled the trees along the riverbanks. They panted their wings at us, scattering water droplets like slavering dogs on high perches.

I peered up at the sky where a few birds were getting knocked around by the wind. I tried my best to see a map there. Maybe a map to the underworld worked like an optical illusion—you had to train your eyes to see it. I thought of Kiwi's gray M. C. Escher print of a stairway that I could never bring into focus.

"Oh, yeah, there it is. I think I see it now." I paused. "You can read that map? We can get there, for sure?" Doubt felt like a lash caught in my eye, a little hair I had to blink out if I wanted to find Osceola. "You promise it's a real place, Bird Man?"

"What a question. Do I promise that hell is a real place?" He chuckled at me, as if to reassure me, but his eyes were bright and cold as snow banked in the valley under his hat. "Hell's real, all right. We can be there tomorrow, or Wednesday at the latest. So long as you want to go."

He'd stopped poling, and I realized that he was waiting for me to say something. *Hurry up! Our map is getting ahead of us.* A fat mosquito blimped through the air between us; I watched it crawl inside the open throat of my water canteen and slip down the plastic walls like a coward's tear.

"I . . ."

The skiff was pointed at the bend in the channel, where dry grass exhaled yellow butterflies. If we could get around that bend, I'd feel better.

"I don't want to go there," I said slowly. "But I'm not scared. And maybe we can find my sister before she and Louis get married."

The Bird Man extended a glove; at first I didn't understand what he wanted. I grinned and shook his hand. Then he resumed his ferry work. We poled around the scummy crystals of the oyster beds and made a beeline for the mirrorlike slough. I watched a line of water creep up his pole as the channel deepened, like the mercury in an old-fashioned thermometer, and then we broke into wild sun.

"Put your hat on, sonny," he said, and grinned back at me so then I knew that he had been making a joke. "Put on your sun cream."

I laughed, startled, because the Bird Man sounded so much like an anxious mainland dad. We were bringing actual sundries to this underworld: sun lotion and aloe, itching powder, blond jugs of mosquito repellent, iced-tea mix from the café, a Ziploc bag of bandages and unserious medicines to treat a traveler's minor aches and pains. To this cache the Bird Man contributed a half-full brown jar of pink bismuth antacid tablets. If indigestion was one of the dangers that we were preparing for on this trip to hell, I thought, then I was going to do just fine.

"I didn't plan to make this trip again, you know," he said softly at one point, and not really to me.

"Thank you. We are going to pay you, I swear, Ossie and me . . ." I studied the sky, trying to see what he saw. So the map to the underworld was not a secret, static document like the paper map we'd recovered from the dredge but alive and legible above us, beating its wings. I leaned into my knees and tried to lift off my tailbone a little, get settled on the skinny bow seat. The Bird Man began to perform a strange call—it took a minute before I realized it was our own English language:

"*And and and and . . .*"

The Bird Man told me that he was singing a transition song. He dipped his pole into the shallows and parted clumps of golden periphyton.

"*And and and . . . ,*" he called, poling steadily faster. Again I fought the desire to cover my ears. *Please stop,* I thought, but after a few more measures the droned melody snuck inside me, it was infectious, and I almost wanted to sing along. After a while the song wasn't a language anymore but a note like a skipped stone—a melodic conjunction. The bull gators were sopranos compared to the Bird Man's deep pitch. I knew then that this person had a real magic. My pet Seth's crate wobbled between my sneakers, her eyes two pins between the slats. We made a keyhole turn around the coast. The Bird Man's pole kept clanging over rocks, his song like a cog in his throat, and I watched my home pull away from us.

CHAPTER TWELVE

Kiwi Goes to Night School

Vijay was wearing his red bandanna and doing twenty over the speed limit, and for once Kiwi didn't say a word. Kiwi made no mention of the study he'd read on vehicular manslaughter or the difficult medical ethics of life support; he didn't comment on the alarming flap-flap-flaping of Vijay's unbuckled seat belt against the door lock; he didn't ask if Vijay was a registered organ donor, or call attention to the many drivers flipping his best friend the bird: no, tonight Kiwi Bigtree was ready to endorse reckless speeds. Kiwi's name was second on a green-and-white computer printout from the LCPS: Álvarez, Ruben, and then Bigtree, Kiwi. It was 7:01, and he was late for his first night of school.

"Buckle up, bro," he'd mumbled at a light, but Vijay had stared sightlessly forward. Kiwi sighed. Out of kindness—perhaps as part of some private philanthropic project—Vijay was now pretending not to hear the dorkiest things that Kiwi said.

They flew onto a bridge that spanned downtown Loomis. Huge, luminous pharmacies pushed at the darkness like giant cruise ships at anchor. Kiwi spotted a billboard that the Chief used to lease, SWAMP-LANDIA! in green-and-sapphire circus letters above his mother's beautiful face. Now it advertised the Bigfoot Podiatry Treatment Center of America. There was a grinning Bigfoot in a karate suit on it, kicking a hirsute monkey foot at traffic.

"Can you maybe crack a window, bro?" Kiwi asked in a small voice. "I feel sort of carsick?"

The neighborhoods went from bad-historic to bad-dilapidated, then recovered their lawns and flowering trees again in mere minutes of highway travel. The Loomis Children's Hospital appeared on the other side of the bridge, a putty-colored complex ringed by the world's saddest playgrounds, with medieval-looking bucket swings on rusted chains and the pastel skeletons of bouncy-horsies. Next door was a church. A group of stone angels gathered like hunchbacked hitchhikers in the garden. A boarded-up movie palace called Casa del Encanto had become a lion's den of hundreds of stray cats—Kiwi could see dark and pale fur coursing around the ticket booth. The strip malls and the XXX . . . And More video stores gave way to stucco coffee-colored office buildings, drab apartment complexes, a few hallucinatory glimpses of the sea.

"So what's the deal with this XXX . . . And More chain?" Kiwi muttered. "What's their business angle? That you can rent pornography *and Bambi* there?"

"*Bambi!* Ha-ha. That's about a baby deer. Shit. You're sick, Marge. You got weird tastes."

But Vijay was only half-listening. He kept craning over, checking out the two girls in the car next to them. Kiwi liked them instinctively. The larger girl had a face as round and white as a clock and she kept touching a spot near her heart and exploding into a laughter that shook her every frizzy curl. The driver had an acned face and musty-colored bangs and laughed without teeth. Kiwi wondered if they were sisters. Something about their ease with one another and all the happy, feckless ugliness in that car made him think of sisters. They were singing along to the radio, acting much younger than their ages. It was clear that these girls didn't care who was watching them through the clear panes. Kiwi wondered if they would step out of the car and shrivel into individuals, grow self-conscious again.

What are Ava and Ossie doing today? An easy thought to erase. Sometimes Kiwi wondered if he was also a genius at Zen Buddhism, he had become such an expert at annulling certain attachments.

The rap song playing now was one that Vijay had been trying to teach Kiwi for weeks. It was called "Gas Hose" and the title seemed to be a metaphor for oral sex. One of the verses Kiwi simply refused to sing: it rhymed "big old tits" with "my catcher's mitts," and then, most bafflingly to Kiwi, "cricket bits"—Kiwi *believed* that was the lyric, he could be wrong, because behind it was a chorus of moans and what sounded like a thousand air horns. "Cricket bits" [n]: could this be yet another mainland synonym for female genitalia? The party slang of entymologists? Either way, the rhyme really unnerved him.

On Swamplandia!, the crickets sang to announce the day's transition to evening, the flash of pink to black time that meant: deep summer. Vernal currents, an air as lushly populated as seawater, deer flies and damselflies, a whole cosmos of mosquitoes: all this iridescent life rose out of the solution holes at dusk. Seths bellowing in gravelly eruptions, launching that strange sound at the sky until you braced yourself for an astral landslide. Crickets meant that the moon was up, that a tide was rising, that his mother or the Chief would soon be calling for them across the mudflats . . .

"Oh fuck," Vijay muttered. "Traffic."

The Volvo was trapped inside a tunnel, sedans and a crocus-blue delivery van and one snouty limousine beeping all around them. Kiwi felt his lungs fanning open and shut, the first white tinge of panic. He shut his eyes and pictured the ocean. Vijay was twisting the knob of the radio, and Kiwi heard the "cricket bits" song fly past on three different stations. He heard the jingle for the World of Darkness: "Jo-nah sur-vived the Le-vi-a-than . . ." Finally the cars began to move. When he opened his eyes, Kiwi saw a slab of blue night up ahead—and then the stars began to fly. The Volvo jumped forward. A rain-soaked banner sagging from the roof of a two-story building read LOOMIS COUNTY COMMUNITY COLLEGE.

"Have a good first day at school, son," Vijay giggled.

"Okay!" Kiwi waved Vijay off the premises. "Thank you! I can take it from here."

Night school was held in a chilly top-floor room of the community college, now dark and humming, the moon floating like a buoy just outside the window. Kiwi opened door after door onto empty classrooms. "Hello . . . ? Uh, is this . . . school?"

Kiwi had purchased all these rainbow multiclip folders, which he carried fanned against his chest, like a float in search of a parade. The floors squeaked under his sneakers. The same moon greeted him in all the empty rooms. Kiwi wondered if he'd messed up the time and date.

"Are you looking for Miss Arenas's class?" snapped a janitor. "You're on the wrong floor."

"Cool. Thank you." Kiwi could feel the janitor's hatred rising out of the darkness like heat from a vent; this was another new mainland experience for Kiwi: to feel immediately hated, to be anonymous and hated. "Wow, those are some quality gloves, sir. I work at the World of Darkness and the management is really parsimonious about our supplies . . ."

The janitor, a whiskery man with blue exhausted eyes, gaped up at him.

From the stairwell, Kiwi heard the always-intimidating squeal of mainland girls' laughter—a wolf pack howling for blood on an open glacier would have been less terrifying, the bellow of a thousand Seths would be a lullaby—and he followed their voices to a crack of light below the stairwell. When he touched the knob the door swung back.

"No, I don't want to hear excuses. You're late. I was about to lock up."

Had he missed the class? The teacher was a tall, unsmiling woman in high-waisted pants with a nickel-bright Afro. Her body had a switch-blade beauty that Kiwi was not encouraged to continue appreciating by her face.

"You just going to stand there? Shut your mouth, find a desk. One warning. You can't get here on time, don't bother coming."

She wrote her name on the board and underlined it with a defiant lit-tle flourish: VOILA ARENAS. "I will be your instructor," Voila Arenas said, chalking urgently, as if human life were an equation they were going to solve together in the next hour and twenty-two minutes. Facts screamed at meteoric speeds across the board.

"We're all adults here, so you can call me Voila."

Somebody in the back left corner made a crack about a magician's hat and a vagina and the room roared.

"Excuse me? My parents were first-generation immigrants." Voila locked black eyes with Kiwi as if she suspected him of being the joker. "It's a beautiful word."

"My name is Kiwi," Kiwi offered.

Everybody had to introduce themselves and say something about why they had chosen to enroll in Voila Arenas's GED class. When it was Kiwi's turn, he told the truth: "I am a Bigtree alligator wrestler. I'm here because my dad put us under a mountain of debt, and I need to make money, and to do that I need to get my high school equivalency." He paused. "I aspire to get a scholarship to a four-year university."

"I ass-pire to fuck a bitch with great ass cheeks!" The kid behind him giggled.

"White boy's here to tutor us," said another white boy, a corncob-haired Midwestern-looking kid. "Community service! White boy try-ing to . . ." Kiwi heard sniggers and a few affirmative grunts. The insult drifted into something unintelligible. It took a beat to realize that he was the joke here, the punch line—he didn't think it came naturally, to see yourself as an object. It was like conjugating your own name in a foreign tongue. So: in Loomis County he was a "white boy," apparently. This was news. *Well, it's not like I can disagree*—Kiwi stared at his skin in the pencil's aluminum rim. He wished he could explain the island to these city kids, though. Could tell them about Chief Bigtree's "Indian" lineage; how as a kid they'd put makeup and beads on him, festooned him with spoonbill feathers and reptilian claws; how at fourteen he'd declared: "I'm a Not-Bigtree. A Not-Indian. A Not-Seminole. A Not-Miccosukee." This category "white" gave him a whistling fear, a feeling not unlike agoraphobia. "White" made Kiwi Bigtree picture a vast Arctic plain, a word in which one single person could never survive. *Whitey, white boy*—Kiwi didn't like getting snowballed into a color. But maybe everybody felt that way about their adjectives, Kiwi thought. He remembered the feeling of coming down the Loomis ferry dock with his battered Swamplandia! duffel into a wilderness of faces.

Kiwi wondered if Miss Voila Arenas always began the class with this question. Several female students in the class had gotten pregnant and had to drop out of regular school; one slight young man had escaped a horrific home life, alluded to by the student in monotone; several admitted to having fallen into Loomis solution holes of drug use or unintelligent, repetitive crimes and crawled back out again; or they were ESL, new arrivals from Ecuador and Pakistan and Cuba. There were many older folks, too, older women especially. The oldest student, a woman with sparkling, hooded eyes, was wearing a bomber jacket worn to peach fuzz at the elbows and had brought a stack of old text-books with her from her high school in Havana. She'd covered them in plastic. Kiwi disliked her immediately. How stupid could you get, carting all your Communist books to Loomis County? It wouldn't occur to him until their fifth class together that his classmate's stack was perhaps not so dissimilar from his own Field Notes and the soggy 1962 encyclopedias shelved in his bedroom at Swamplandia!

That first night Voila passed around a sheet. Diagnostic Test. Kiwi's neck ached. He could hear the clock tick and the distancing breaths of the other thinkers, the way their cognition seemed to be happening down long, echoey corridors, somewhere impossibly remote. Words he hadn't understood in the questions appeared again, in new orders, in the choice of answers. It was like an evil game of musical chairs. Names crowded into his brain, a drunken stadium of names, refusing to get quiet and organized.

Part I: True/False/Uncertain

"The fact that total revenue rose when half the crop was destroyed indicates that demand for coffee is *inelastic . . .*"

"Substituting in the information about price and utility, we get . . ."

"Cross-multiplying for *x,* we get . . ."

"Five minutes," said Voila, turning the page of a bodybuilding magazine called *Bulk Up.* A woman with an Arctic-white smile and scary bauxite skin grinned out at him from the cover. Skinny Voila was underlining something, her face pensive.

When Kiwi got stuck, which happened every third question, he would stare up at this grinning bodybuilder. He felt as puny, as desperate as he ever had during the Bigtree shows. In his sweaty fingers his pencil kept slipping; he'd already broken one. Kiwi had taken many tests on Swamplandia!, his pencil moving at a steady clip in the ever-green light of his own kitchen; he couldn't understand why his intelligence wouldn't make a fist now, and pound reliably, like his heart.

He couldn't remember the quadratic equation, or which one the rhombus was, or whether the perimeter of Griswald Wallace's fence would be fifty-four meters or seventy-two, given the area of his out-house and the volume of his well. Where the Christ did Griswald Wallace live, anyhow? Why did Griswald Wallace need a fence around his outhouse? Kiwi couldn't make sense of the reading comprehension portion, either: some excerpt from a poem about a sick dog and blueberries. "What is the <u>theme</u> of the passage about Rochester the dog?" "What do the blueberries <u>symbolize</u> for the dog named Rochester?" Kiwi's eyes were swimming. He began to bubble in indiscriminate letters.

They had to sit at their desks while Voila graded the diagnostic tests. She put his scored test paper facedown on his desk: 38/100. She handed Kiwi a *Remedial Algebra* and *English II,* the same textbooks that the Cuban woman in the bomber jacket got. They eyed each other over the beet-orange covers of their books with the perfect contempt of equals.

Vijay showed up twenty minutes late, which gave Kiwi time to read and reread all his mistakes. At 11:33, Vijay came screeching into the parking lot with several greasy bags of fries and two girls in the backseat. Vijay had (hypocritically, Kiwi thought) seduced them away from their registers in the Burger Burger and now they were all going to see a movie. That new one, the box-office leader, starring a very popular obese gay Polynesian comic actor who, in this latest cinematic vehicle for his self-loathing, starred as a prince attending a royal ball in drag.

"That's our plan? We're going to pay six bucks to see *Cinder-Ralphy?*"

"You're not coming, Margie. These girls, see . . ."

"Good." Kiwi chewed his lip and watched the Volvo make its way onto the highway. "Thank God. That film looks terrible."

The two girls spent the whole ride whispering and doing horsey eye rolls and hand mannerisms in their mysterious female language. So far as Kiwi could tell, they managed to agree that Rollie, a mutual friend of theirs, was in fact a fat bitch and *not* their friend, and also that Enormous Gladys needed to get some *self-esteem,* stupid! But Kiwi assumed a second, secret conversation must be happening below this. Otherwise how to explain all the gesticulating? Wrists and elbows went flying through the air in some jujitsu of lady-empathy. Kiwi thought that he should take down Field Notes but he was still smarting from night school and his testing hand was actually cramping.

The girls never bothered to exchange names with him. But at a red light one of them poked Kiwi through the seat-back hole and asked: "Right that my friend is pretty? Right, nerd?"

Four intricately painted and lined eyes glared at him in the rearview mirror.

"You're both pretty!" he gasped. "Equally pretty!"

The clock on the dash flashed 11:42. Vijay was bulleting down the freeway, talking to the girls in his Seductor Voice, a creamy baritone that made him sound like he was on muscle relaxants. Eleven forty-three. Eleven forty-four. *I want to go home,* a voice in Kiwi whispered, raggedy as a child. The Leviathan loomed in front of the Volvo; it seemed a miracle that Kiwi's tiny staff key ring would let him into a place that size. As Vijay pulled into the World's parking lot, Kiwi's eyes found the bright blue door for late-night entry; the door led to the elevator that led down to his bedroom. All he wanted now was to study: he imagined sliding the contents of each of these night school textbooks into his brain as easily as a pillow goes into its case. He clutched the exam to his chest.

"What are you holding there, bro?" Vijay asked. "You think somebody's going to steal *your paper*?"

"Test. It's a test I took."

"Well, son," Vijay clucked, reaching across the gearshift with a goony smile, "what's the verdict? Are we a *genius*?"

"Fuck you." Kiwi hopped out of the car and started loping away, hands deep in pockets; he was halfway to the World when he had to pivot and jog back and open the door again to snatch his folders and textbooks, his face the lopped red of a watermelon. The girls twittering behind him like birds.

CHAPTER THIRTEEN

Welcome to Stiltsville

A re we there yet, Bird Man?"

"Kid, you are making me crazy. New rule: you are not allowed to ask me that question."

The Bird Man sank his pole into the river with a furious curl to his lips and I flinched, instinctively drumming my knuckles on the red Seth's carrier. I'd been doing that all morning, a request for luck.

"Okay. Sorry. I was just trying to make a joke." I tried grinning at him. "But what should I be looking for, Bird Man?"

"Hell's a special place, kid. You'll know it when you get there. Everybody does."

We were poling through the glitter of high noon, and even the Bird Man's voice sounded sweaty. Still he insisted on wearing his coat, on straddling the poling platform with his elbows bent, the black hood of his coat looming like a gloomy sun over the gunwales.

"I'm going to pay you when we get back, you know . . . ," I mumbled, to make myself feel better. I felt guilty imagining how tired my friend must be—the Bird Man had been standing ramrod straight on the poling platform for three hours now. He didn't take breaks. I sat in the bow seat and paddled hard around the strainers. No sign of my sister on the river—no sign of any vessel, really, besides a bleached dinghy hung up in a swamp oak, a beard of vines and flowers tumbling out of it. But for some reason I wasn't worrying anymore; in fact a small, indecipherable part of me hoped that we wouldn't find Ossie right away. On

Swamplandia! I wrestled alligators for hundreds and maybe thousands of tourists, men and women from fourteen countries and every U.S. state (except, weirdly, Oklahoma—the Okies had other vacation plans, I guess). But the Bird Man was the first adult besides Grandpa Sawtooth or Chief Bigtree or my mother who'd spent more than an hour with me.

At one o'clock, we poled into a place where the water level suddenly rose again, a channel glutted with rain, and the Bird Man had to climb down and sat behind me in the stern seat. We moved our gear forward to bring the bow down. The skiff was well built and didn't tip. We both rowed for a while, passing islands of lightwood—the old pine stumps west of my house—and sundews. It was deep enough here to dip our oars through the golden brown algal mats without scraping bottom.

At three o'clock there was still no sign of Ossie.

At four o'clock we broke clear of the mangroves and now the horizons seemed to speed away from our boat, receding in both directions. A fuzzy black cloud line striped the bayheads. At five thirty the red Seth was agitating in her wooden crate, and I felt guilty for bringing her, and also glad she was there. As we poled deeper, I used my rain slicker to seine minnows and wiggly, translucent cricket frogs the size of my thumbnail for her.

Around six o'clock we got doused by a nasty chop on the narrow bay. A strong wind was blowing in out of the northeast and sending four-inch swells over the skiff's low gunwales. The Bird Man showed me how to roll the boat with each wave, keeping our hull as parallel as possible to the waves. We couldn't tack straight and the Bird Man took the brunt of the swells; within minutes his coat was soaked through, its outer feathers slimily adhered to his arms. He grimaced when the waves hit but he didn't complain.

"Drink some water, kid. We'll have to stop soon," the Bird Man said from the poling platform.

"Thank you so much for doing this, Bird Man."

"Sit down."

"Thank you for taking me to find her. Thank you. Are you tired?"

"No."

"If you're tired I can pole, I'm much stronger than I look." I waited two minutes and then I was spitting words at him again. Fits of grateful or fearful language kept rising in my throat, embarrassing but unstoppable—they felt almost like knots of phlegm that I had to cough up.

"Really, thank you so much. You're sure you're not tired? If you hadn't showed up, I don't even like to think about . . ."

"Sit down, kid. Calm down. If your sister's smart she's not on the water now. She and her friend are making camp somewhere."

"But did she come this way, you think?"

I leaned into the hull: I saw nothing. Rain fizzing in the near distance. A vague red sun behind the trees.

Seven o'clock: we were on a drift slough now, small oak trees and cocoplums rising along the water's edge. Butterflies flecked the air in pale triangles, so pretty that I concluded we must still be a long ways off from the underworld. The sun was lowering itself behind the tree line at an angle, as carefully as a round man descending a ladder. Two bullnose turtles craned their black caramel necks at us from a rock.

Instead of camping on a hammock, the Bird Man said we were going to spend the night in a "sky house" at Stiltsville. "Stiltsville is our Swamp Roanoke," the Chief liked to say, giving the place a black-ice twinkle for the tourists. ("Stephen, did you hear that! *Everybody disappeared.* Oh, it gives me the chills to think about it! What a morbid riddle!") The truth is a lot less interesting: Stiltsville emptied out when Park Services took over this part of the swamp. Residents of Stiltsville abandoned their platform houses and moved to townships on the sloping rock of the continent. The sky people had mailboxes now, elms and gardens; their houses no longer resembled arks. The last family moved out of Stiltsville in the dry season of 1952; in the intervening decades it devolved into a wooden rookery. The name "Stiltsville" had always made me picture a cloudland of these acrobatic palaces, but the reality was pretty modest: just a collection of ten or twelve houses mounted on fourteen-foot support pilings.

"Do you think anybody lives here anymore?" I asked the Bird Man. "Do you think there are any ghosts here?"

"We'll find out."

Each house had a shadow beneath it, a sort of liquid basement. Small waves rose midway up the platform supports and collapsed into a thin foam. The temperature dropped tens of degrees whenever we poled beneath a house. Above us, the rotted planks and greenish white crossboards looked like they'd been nailed shut by some lunatic carpenter— I saw the glint of what seemed at a distance to be hundreds and hundreds of nailheads. *Barnacles*. Not nails but shells, dark red horns spiraling out of every surface. Some of the houses had disintegrating dinghies tethered in their "garages." Some had holes in the floor that aligned with holes in the ceiling, and you could see the sun pinwheeling cheerfully above the ruined kitchens and bedrooms.

"Know any good knock-knock jokes, kid?" the Bird Man asked, and for some reason this made me laugh hysterically. "This whole place looks like a joke that got knocked over, doesn't it?" He touched a support where tiny brown-and-red crabs clung like bottle caps to the wood.

Be alive, Ossie, I beamed over the monotony of water. *Be safe.*

We poled under a porch where a bobcat was shouldering through a cracked blue door frame. For a second it paused to look at us. Ancient blue and red flowerpots sat all over the deck, heavy enough to have survived who knows what. I saw spiders, the long absence of flowers. The bobcat slunk around the maze of ceramics, broke free, leapt through a gray space in the porch slats, and easily cleared the six-foot channel between two of the houses, its white belly fur flying above our skiff. The creature landed soundlessly in front of a second doorway, bulled its flat head through the screen, disappeared into another house. All told this took maybe twelve seconds tops.

The Bird Man sucked air between his teeth.

"We'll make sure to find an empty house tonight, kid. No ghosts or cats."

Above us a hundred birds screamed. I watched a snow cloud, a pale blue cloud, a black and crimson-edged cloud, a green cloud, a nickel cloud explode into the sky.

"Are you making them do that?" I asked the Bird Man. "That's you, isn't it?"

The Bird Man didn't answer me and I hadn't heard him chirrup or whistle, as he'd done back on Swamplandia!, but the birds danced in a weird clockwork above us and I guessed that he had something to do with it. The sun was a low, red ball behind gray clouds. I felt scared, watching the cormorants and the ibis obey his secret commands, but this was a wonderful kind of fear. It was nothing like the metal-in-your-mouth terror I got thinking about Ossie and Louis. It was an exhilaration, the way you feel when you are wrestling a Seth and it nearly knocks you loose. Kiwi, my smug brother—I wanted to tell him that I was watching real magic.

We paddled zags through Stiltsville until the Bird Man found a house he said was good for us to sleep in. He tied off on one of the southern pilings. Wooden steps rose eleven or twelve feet to the front door.

"Okay, pal. Up, up, and such."

"You first. Please." I was still thinking about the bobcat.

Inside the house was bare wood. Smells bloomed in the dark, a mix of salt and bird droppings and deep rot, but the structure itself was in surprisingly good condition. No Seths, no hawks, no raccoons, no trespassing felines. The main room was about three hundred square feet, and the roof was low enough to scrape back the Bird Man's hat. There was almost no furniture, but what remained was arranged in the patterns you'd expect: a dining table, twin beds bunked in an alcove that opened like a walnut mouth behind what had been the kitchen, a small black desk that looked so weak that I didn't even like to rest my eyes on it. Black and white specklings covered the walls, these grim starbursts of mold on the pale wood that made me miss with a random stab my acned brother. A huge hole in the middle of the ceiling opened onto a clear night sky: it looked as if some great predator had peeled the thatched roof back, sniffed once, and lost interest.

Immediately the Bird Man began setting small smudge fires in pots along the holes in the wall to smoke the mosquitoes out. I climbed down to the river again to change out my Seth's water dish. Outside I watched clouds sail over the neighboring houses, which stood on tall and lemon-gray legs like a flock of herons in the shallows. From the bottom of the ladder I watched the sun fall behind the many wooden legs of Stiltsville; you could almost hear the splash. Soon afterward the river became a looking glass for stars. Now it was our first night on the water. I climbed the ladder to a plank where I could see the Bird Man hunched over our Coleman in a yellow round of light, his shadow flung far back against the wall. I paused there for a while, watching him.

For dinner, the Bird Man cooked up some fatty hamburger meat on his one-burner camper stove and sliced two small, golden onions into the oil. "Eat up, kid," he said, "because this stuff will spoil rotten by tomorrow night." (*Tomorrow night?*) We ate in silence at a gimpy three-legged table. It was the only piece of furniture left in the kitchen. The original chairs were long gone but the Bird Man had scavenged two from the adjacent house and they were unexpectedly beautiful, a matched set with swirly black rails painted with pink roses. We both sat down gingerly at opposite ends of the table; when the chairs held our weight our eyes met, surprised. *Maybe he will dance with me later,* I thought out of nowhere, and felt a quick flulike joy. Back home I never got to dance during our mock proms that we girls held after hours in the café; Ossie always made me be the disc jockey. Being the DJ meant feeding a black poker chip on a string to the jukebox. Ossie and her invisible partner twirled in front of the windows, her purple skirt going full as a balloon as she spun around the empty tables. Once a ghost had tried to dip her near the fryer and she'd fallen and given herself a shiner.

"Hey, Bird Man?" I asked him abruptly. "Do you have another name that I could call you? Like, I don't know, Alan or Paul or something? Stanley? A regular name?"

The Bird Man glanced up as if this were a shockingly rude question. "I had a name when I was your age. Not anymore. I guess I don't see enough people in my line of work that I feel a name is necessary, kid. Who would I need to distinguish myself from?"

"I don't know. Other men?"

"Not too many other men out here in the first place, and my customers aren't much interested in getting to know me. Generally speaking, I mean." He gave me a small smile. He was garnishing a third hamburger with slick onions and green slices of tomato. "So I don't mind being the Bird Man to them."

I nodded, but I felt hurt—here he had a name like an ace in his pocket and he didn't want to show it to me. Didn't he know that a Bigtree alligator wrestler was trustworthy?

But I guess the Bird Man was right to keep the secret of his name from me, because later that night I broke my promise to Ossie. I told him the story of the Dredgeman's Revelation. It happened by accident—I was only planning on asking him if he knew or had known a man named Louis Thanksgiving, and then I watched as one sentence after another exited my mouth like those knotted magician's scarves. Louis's death story came out unstoppably; I didn't even feel so guilty about breaking Ossie's trust. As I babbled onward the Bird Man removed his gloves and settled his warm, bald hands on my knees, as if this were the polite thing to do. The whole time I spoke his slate eyes were liquid and dog-kind above the camp lantern. He didn't tease me like my brother would have done but instead regarded me with an attentiveness that felt wonderful, like relaxing into a net over a wide ocean. When I got to the part about the buzzards he whistled softly and began to nod, and it occurred to me with a cold wonderment that he might have seen this species of bird himself; in the underworld he might have sailed beneath the very flock that got Louis.

"What an ending," the Bird Man said when I finished. "A vanishing point. And what do you think the Dredgeman's Revelation means, kid?"

I paused. *Is he testing me?* I wondered, and wished that I could crane around and peek at what the Bird Man knew, as if he might have an answer card hidden behind his back.

"Oh, I think it means that . . ."

I thought about Louis Thanksgiving's hands, Louis's freckled knuckles curled around the dredge railing at the end of his story. I could see the black dredge in greenish storm light, and how brave he'd been then, staring down that darkness. I thought of how he'd left his surname "Auschenbliss" floating miles behind him like molt feathers or snakeskin.

"My mom had a name that she tore off, too," I heard myself saying. "Like Louis. She had a mainland name—her maiden name, it's called. She used to be Hilola Owens. So she wasn't always a Bigtree. And then she only got to be a Bigtree for eighteen years, you know, and now she's nothing."

Why had Louis died so young, before he could even become anybody? On Swamplandia! my sister and I found the dredge crane's bucket frozen at a noon tilt, filling with sunlight and moonlight. That light, I felt like it belonged to Louis Thanksgiving. The world owed it to him, it was his child's inheritance. He should get to drink that pink light through every pore and every follicle, every cell, the way our basking Seths ate the sun through their wet skin! *Death is a theft, a crime, a cry in the sky, that's what the story means to me, Bird Man.* But as soon as I opened my mouth I sounded like a dumb kid again.

"I guess I don't know what it means." I tugged on my shoelaces like tiny reins, embarrassed. My sense of it had dissolved back into the old hurt in my chest. "I wish that Louis had never died. I wish that Louis and Hector and Gideon Tom and all the rest of them could have finished digging their road to the Gulf of Mexico. Then Louis Thanksgiving could have gotten married, and had a wife and a son—not to my sister, you know? But maybe married to some nice lady from his, ah, his own time. And he'd grow up to know for sure that he was handsome and good. And he would be an old man now."

I paused. I hadn't known that I wanted all that for the ghost.

"So you wish that the dredgeman Louis was still flesh and blood?" the Bird Man asked. It was a serious question. He took me seriously, and I did feel taken up by his musing tone and carried, lifted onto the ledge of adults.

"Right. That's not really a revelation though, is it?"

That night we unrolled our bright blue tarps onto the floor of the central room, which gave the wrecked wood a planetary look. I wanted to play the End of the World, a cheery game Ossie and I had invented in our bedroom, back when the worst threat we faced was Mom's Spaghetti Surprise. We rolled blankets down the stairs and pretended that we were reupholstering the dead world. The towels were the grass and the seas. Ossie always wanted to be the Creator and fluff the prairies, and then I'd burst in as the Destroyer and kick at stuff and roll everything up again. Mom hated this game because all her towels ended up on the floor. Before the ghosts showed up, we played all kinds of silly games like that, doing a theater of personalities for each other. Ossie liked to be the sweet and kind one: saints, princesses, Vanna White. Not me! Even in games I liked to play myself: Ava Bigtree, World Champion Alligator Wrestler. I was as strong as ten men, ferocious. Ossie always let me be the hero.

The Bird Man grumbled that he wasn't in a great mood for pretending. He shuffled inside the foil of his bedroll. On the sill behind him, the wind kept trying to pluck the orange petals of our fires. Mosquitoes waved angrily just beyond them. Through the saw-cut boards I could see the empty neighborhood of Stiltsville. Pilings bolted down the water, where the moon boiled.

"What the hell are you doing over there, kid?"

"Nothing. Can't sleep. Just praying."

"New rule, kid: don't fall out."

"Dear God," I prayed awkwardly, unrolling the tongue of my bedroll, "let me not veer away from this darkness amen."

Our mother grew up in a churchgoing family on the mainland, and Grandma Risa was an Italian Catholic who collected these truly spooky Virgin Marys carved out of raw abalone on her trips to Key West, but we kids were never raised to religion. "God" was a word I used as a spell-breaker. Sometimes it worked, and sometimes it didn't. "God," I'd whisper, feeling sometimes an emptiness and sometimes a spreading warmth. If a word is just a container for feeling, or a little matchstick that you strike against yourself—a tiny, fiery summons—then probably I could have said anything, called any name, who knows? I didn't have a normal kid's ideas of the Lord as an elderly mainland guy on a throne. The God I prayed to I thought of as the mother, the memory of love. She was my own mother sometimes, baggy-eyed and smiling in the Chief's heavy canvas work clothes in the morning, one of the Chief's cigarettes hanging from her mouth. The Our Father and the Hail Mary I'd picked up somehow by osmosis but it was her name I invoked out there, her memory I summoned like a wind I could lean into, and I liked this prayer much better:

Mom, please help me to find Ossie. Please help me to make the net.

The next thing I knew light was pouring through all the holes in Stiltsville: dawn light screaming through the doorways that hung on their hinges, the broken windows that birds could fly through, the plank lace, the cheesed metals. Red sunbeams burned through the tin panels above my head. *Where am I?* I sat up. In the daylight I saw that parts of the room were sprouting a fuzz the spring green of scallions. An empty bedroll on the floor was halfway into its stuff sack. *Ossie?*—and her name was like a trapdoor latch that brought the whole predicament tumbling down on me.

Across the room, the Bird Man's antique boots were coming toward me, the toes addressing the air like sniffing noses, and slowly I gathered up the long length of him: trousered legs, brace of feathers, face, hat. Today the Bird Man wore a strange expression. He crouched inches from my bedroll, staring right into my face—he reminded me of a tourist touching his nose to the ferry porthole, his eyes coming slightly unglued and his breath on me. It gave me a little chill. Something about his gray eyes seemed urgent and vacant at once. We had known each other for hours and miles now, but I thought that he looked even stranger, even more like a stranger, as if the currents that governed such things were blowing him backward. Stubble peppered his cheeks and I missed my father.

"I just talked to a fisherman out of Chokoloskee. Says that yesterday he saw a strange ship at dusk. About two miles west of us." His voice was as excited as I'd ever heard it. "Sunrise at six a.m., kid. We're going now. We've got fifteen-knot winds against the tide."

CHAPTER FOURTEEN

The Drowning Chain

Kiwi Bigtree was in an *excellent* mood. He had just dropped a fat check in the mail, made out to Samuel Bigtree in the amount of one hundred and forty-seven dollars and twelve cents, a check he'd sealed in an envelope addressed to Swamplandia!, c/o Chief Bigtree.

YOU ARE WELCOME, DAD, he'd written on the flap.

His essay about the Glenfinnan Viaduct for Voila Arenas's class had received a purple check-plus mark, not just a check for credit. To research the paper, he'd taken the bus to the Loomis Public Library—the two-story brick building near the courthouse downtown, with large, placid librarians moving through the stacks like human galleons and glass-green plants in pots. This place was nothing like the Library Boat, with its smashed hull and its stink of hydrogen sulfide. He'd spent four hours in the Non-Circulating Room next to a homeless man in a bloodstained Christmas sweater who had introduced himself as Rudolph. Rudolph kept screaming "Wheel . . . of . . . Fortune!" and dissolving into a guttural laugh while Kiwi frowned and traced mechanical diagrams of each of the Glenfinnan Viaduct's twenty-one arches. Rudolph spit his gum on one. The title of Kiwi Bigtree's paper was "That Scottish Wonder." His report had a glossary. He'd made two appendices. Rudolph had admired them.

"This assignment was one page," Voila had written lightly under her check-plus.

Victory 2: Kiwi passed his CPR exam. Monday was his first day of work as an indoor lifeguard. Which meant he had only to survive a last weekend as the Leviathan's janitor. One Friday, one Saturday, one Sunday—more or less what the original Jonah of biblical fame had done.

Weekends, inside a whale: Kiwi worked the nine-hour Friday shift inside the Leviathan and for that period he forgot all about Swamplandia! He dragged his wheelie bucket through the Flukes and he forgot his mother, his sisters, the Chief's impossibly stupid Carnival Darwinism, his anger, his mission, his genius burning inside him all day like a grounded rocket. After a few hours of cleaning the tunnels and slippery chutes in the Leviathan, Kiwi found he couldn't worry about his family anymore—it was as if his mind itself got soapy-fingered. His mind lost its grip on the future.

By five o'clock, Kiwi's thoughts had been sucked into the vacuum's hum.

By nine o'clock, it was all he could do to manage a "Good night, Mr. Jenks" before punching out. There was a sort of grimly lit, fluorescent party happening in the break room. The party was catered by the girls who worked in the Dorsal Flukes, who had stolen a bunch of pizzas and soggy boluses of garlic loaf after their shift ended. About fifty kids were crammed around the sofa, shedding their uniforms. It was a frenzied scene, their weekend-night molting—Kiwi caught sight of several belly buttons and boxer waistbands and the wide hot pink strap of one girl's sports bra as everybody peeled down to their regular clothes. Kiwi shoved four breadsticks into his pants and grabbed a two-liter bottle of diet cherry soda and fled. At 9:17, he shuffled off the elevator deck to his dormitory cot and fell open like a palm.

Monday finally came, and Kiwi celebrated by washing his face. The Lake of Fire was in a concrete grotto dug out of the same limestone shelf that ran beneath the entire city of Loomis; this shelf itself was artificial bedrock, dynamited out of the blue bay by dredge crews in the early century. The Lake of Fire had a separate admission fee for visitors. Kiwi had to use a swipe card and a special elevator bank to get there.

"Going *down*?" the recorded voice inside the elevator car kept asking on a demonic loop. "Going *down*?"

At the Lake of Fire, Dale Bonilla was waiting to orient him.

Little kiddies in their swimming trunks and their rental goggles engaged in gleeful masochism around him, shrieking, pounding one another's sopping backs and buttocks, and giving indiscriminate wedgies. The mothers were all bone-dry; they slumped against one wall. The mothers' faces were so slack with exhaustion that they looked almost rapturous—Kiwi thought so, anyhow, watching waves of electric light ripple over them. The Lost Souls' expressions mirrored his own weekend stupefaction inside the Leviathan.

Dale Bonilla walked Kiwi down the left side of the Lake of Fire, his hands clasped behind his back and resting in the little coulee just above his swimming trunks.

"This is a cake job, Margaret, you're going to love it. Look, here's your Rescue Stick. Push the button here and give it a shake, see, like an umbrella, and it springs into a net."

Kiwi sprang back as what appeared to be a commercial fishing net burst open from the Rescue Net. How many people was this thing designed to save, a wedding party?

"That's for when you got to fish a kid out of the Lake."

The Lake was a hundred-foot-long pool, twelve feet deep at its far end. Dye turned the water the color of dead rose petals, which Kiwi found beautiful in its own disturbing way. But this tenebrous dye made it next to impossible to see the swimmers' bodies.

"I can't see anything, Dale."

"Right? Visibility *blows*. Here, though, I got the manual for you—"

Dale gave Kiwi what appeared to be an enormous cardboard coaster. It folded out into a kind of daisy-chain checklist of the forces working counter to a lifeguard.

THE DROWNING CHAIN

Lack of Education
Lack of Protection
Lack of Safety Advice
Lack of Supervision
Inability to Cope

Kiwi opened and closed the coaster-thing like an accordionist. *Excellent,* he thought, surveying the list. *Check, check, check. It would appear that I am drowning right now, Dale.*

"Allow me to demonstrate," said Dale, pointing at a pair of feet kicking up spume the color of melted bricks. "See the feet? Watch the feet. The feet are, like, the flags of the body."

Really, it didn't seem possible that Dale was using this Rescue Net correctly. He dragged the kid's kicking body toward the shallow end, and the kid, a skinny white boy with a crew cut and froggy eyelids, began to scream: "Let me go! Idiot! I was just diving!"

"Sorry, bro!" Dale released the kid from the Rescue Stick, smiling dreamily down at—so far as Kiwi could tell—nothing. He stirred the Lake of Fire like a giant punch bowl. "I used to work at the Red Lobster in Fullerton," he said, "so I'm good at getting the squirmers."

"Hey," Kiwi said. "That's great. I think I can take it from here."

"Awesome." Dale stooped to retrieve some of the trampled rental towels. He had the extreme pallor and off-kilter good nature of a TV serial killer. Possibly Dale wasn't evil at all, Kiwi thought, just extraordinarily sleepy. His voice when he spoke was cryptic, academic: "Look, man. Just don't let one drown."

Thus ended Kiwi's Life-Saving Orientation.

Every twelve minutes a high-speed fan blew pressurized air into the caissons, transforming the Lake of Fire into a turbulent wave pool. The water shivered up into red pyramids while the swimmers screamed with surprise. This happened twenty-eight times during Kiwi's shift. When the waves receded, Kiwi watched the ruby dye congeal in the deep end. He thought about the wings of roseate spoonbills, their brilliant plumage. He thought about the July skies over the saw grass. In this way his mind emptied very naturally into thoughts about home, his sisters and his mom, Grandpa, his delusional father. Kiwi had to paddle a long ways back before he could focus on the Lake.

During his lunch break Kiwi wandered the tunnels until he found the payroll office. Nobody had cashed the checks he'd signed over to his father yet. Had they even gotten to the island? Was his asshole dad trying to make a point? From the pay phone, Kiwi spoke to "Holly," a loan officer at the Sunshine Community Bank.

"I'm a relative. No, I'm not Hilola. I'm her son. I'd like to pay down Samuel Bigtree's debt, ma'am. Can we maybe work out some kind of deal? I'm interested in buying my family some time."

Kiwi meant this very literally. At his current wage of $6.50 an hour he probably couldn't afford to purchase Swamplandia! a month or even a week, he explained to Holly. But to forestall their homelessness he was willing to negotiate the price of minutes, hours—how much would a minute cost?

The woman on the other end of the line laughed sadly.

"Honey, are you a signer on this account? No? Then you need to put your father on the phone."

"Okay, Holly? That's not possible. Could you just tell me the dollar amount that we owe you?"

But she couldn't, not legally. She informed Kiwi Bigtree that *he* did not owe her employer anything.

"Are you guys going to foreclose on us?"

But she couldn't tell him that, either. What she could do—she put the phone down to get her supervisor's consent—what she would be very *happy* to do was apply any moneys Kiwi sent her toward Swamplandia!'s "substantial debt load."

So after work, Kiwi mailed a money order directly to the bank. Fourteen dollars and twenty-two cents, the change in his stupid World trousers. What was left of his salary after food and rent. He watched his signature swirl over and under the mint line and licked the little stamp, feeling sick in his gut.

Lifeguarding was exhausting. Kiwi moved from his chair only to take bathroom breaks. Vijay returned to smoking on the roof without him. Kiwi spent most of each shift doing a mental good cop/bad cop narration in the Lake's general direction: *Please, children, I am begging you, nobody drown,* followed by, *You bitches better not drown.* The Lake of Fire was adjacent to Beelzebub's Snack Bar, where Lost Souls ate fourteen-dollar boxes of Dante's Tamales "for the experience." What experience? A Dante's Tamale was a mutant breed of tamale from Cienfuegos, Mexico, that was, without exaggeration, the size of a wind sock. A grown man ate a Dante's Tamale and wept into his wife's hair. Toddlers ate the Dante's Tamales and turned unhealthy shades of purple.

"Smile!" The itinerant photographer wandered through the Lake of Fire and snapped candid pictures of the Lost Souls—the itinerant photographer was a graduate of a prestigious art school in Rhode Island and everyone agreed that his shots were very creative. At the end of the day Lost Souls queued up to buy a $29.95 picture of themselves printed on a mug or a calendar, glossy assurance that they had suffered in Hell.

A new World of Darkness jingle, sung by a deeply ironic gospel choir, was being piped in through the World speaker system: "The Leviathan, the Leviathan, what a bargain! All that pain in a single afternoon!" The chorus was like a virus, playing in a self-replicating loop in everybody's brains. Sometimes whole winding lines of Lost Souls would all at once burst into the song.

Swamplandia! had its own jingle, too, which nobody seemed to know. It wasn't conventionally "catchy," although it sometimes almost rhymed. Risa Bigtree had written the original lyrics, with old Sawtooth on the uke. His mother and the Chief had sung it for the radio ads—the Chief, whose voice rumbled like a washing machine full of shoes, and his mother, who happily admitted that she didn't understand what pitch was. Fortunately, the Bigtree tribe never had the bucks to saturate the mainland airwaves with it. Kiwi and Ava and Ossie were on the recording, too. They shared a middle verse.

> We Bigtree children wrestle gators
> With the skill of our forefathers
> With the steel of our foremothers
> We Bigtree children tame our gators . . .

From the tall lifeguard chair, which rose nine feet above the Lake and overlooked the deep end beneath an ornamental black umbrella, Kiwi blew his whistle—a Korean kid had just beaned his twin sister in the head with a BrimStone, an enormous inflatable beach ball (rental units: $8.75; on the weekends hundreds of BrimStones blew in from the Vesuvius Blast Off, which meant an extra hour of cleanup for Kiwi). When the screaming began, he thought this roughhousing was the reason for it, even though the Korean boy's mouth was a seam.

It was whole seconds before he saw the body.

A blot appeared and spread in the pool's deep end. It stopped and shivered in place. Arms rose out of the blot, flailing and falling a little ways, rowing again. This T shape in the deepest part of the Lake was a girl or a woman, Kiwi realized, floating there with such gracefulness that at first Kiwi thought her posture must be deliberate, part of some show, her arms fluttering and black tendrils lifting and separating from her head. He guessed what must have happened: she'd gotten a foot or leg caught in an open drain. Kiwi rose onto the platform on trembling legs and began to blow into his whistle. The crowd in the Lake was screaming at him.

"Help her!" he shouted back to them. "She's drowning!" It was the crowd's howling, finally, that got Kiwi to leap, and not the girl at all— he wanted only to escape the sound of the strangers' terror.

When Kiwi jumped from the lifeguard platform, he shut his eyes. Everybody was screaming but he could feel his own silence unfurl and flutter in streamers behind him, like two black ribbons tied to the soles of his feet. Then Kiwi hit. The Lake water rushed into his nose and unhinged his jaw, flooded into him, and this felt like swallowing a gallon of melted pennies, swallowing everything the wrong way, a mucoid sting. He made it over to the girl, found her wrist and closed onto it and held on, and he was worried that he was going to break all the small bones inside the girl's fingers as he gripped a hand and then an arm and pulled at it, blanking on all his reading and certain now that he was injuring her, doing her some terrible and irreversible physical harm; but then as he tugged her toward the surface Kiwi could feel the wake of her legs kicking alongside him. For a hallucinatory second, just before surfacing, he came face-to-face with the girl under the lava globes in the water. *She is staring at me!* Their eyes met. Her hair was rising and twirling continuously into a slow fountain above her pale temples and her two eyes were open, black and alert. *She's conscious,* Kiwi had time to think. Awake under the lake. Then they were both kicking for the surface together, their arms linked at the elbow like twins. When they broke the surface the girl immediately went limp again.

"Hey, come on," Kiwi gasped, jerking at her arm, "what are you doing?" She wasn't moving at all now. Her eyes (had he imagined them open?) were smoothly shut. He hooked an arm around her and dragged her in, and throughout the great cavern of the Lake of Fire he could hear the Lost Souls cheering.

"The lifeguard got her, Mommy . . . !"

"The lifeguard *saved* her . . . !"

Shut up, he wanted to growl. The girl was growing in her sleep, becoming so heavy inside the crook of his arms. He kicked his right foot out until his toes curled around the ladder rung.

Kiwi dragged the girl up and out on her back. "Are you okay? Are you okay?" he shouted moronically into her ear before bending close to deliver two rescue breaths. Fernando, his World of Darkness CPR instructor, had told him that he was "too nicey-nicey." He tapped harder. People were watching him; he could feel the familiar onstage lurch of his body beginning to panic.

Okay, genius, this is a human person, this is not some alligator that you have to wrestle. But Kiwi had muscular amnesia. What came next? His fingers clutched at his rib cage as if he were holding his own guts together. *Her,* he had to help *her.* This girl was pretty. She had coal-black curls in a crazy sprawl on the towel and a narrow squint of a face; she was his age or even a little younger. Kiwi fixed his lips over the girl's lips. He pinched her nostrils shut, one hand floundered against the alien slickness of her black swimsuit—she was breathing, Kiwi realized, he'd forgotten to listen for breaths. A fraction of a second before Kiwi exhaled his air into her, the drowned girl's eyes flew open.

Kiwi sat back on his heels. He stared stupidly at his own hand, which was still pasted to the thin black fabric on her stomach. Both of their eyes were running clear ruby tears, their fingernails brilliantly stained, their lashes clumped and dark.

"You're okay? You feel okay, huh?"

She sniffled and nodded, rubbing at her eyes.

"You *were* okay, though," he said suspiciously, but the girl didn't hear him. Her lips opened in a joyful shout:

"You saved me . . ." Even as she spoke she was turning from Kiwi to the crowd, beaming at the two dozen or so swimmers gathered at the Lake's edge. "This lifeguard saved me!"

"What?" Kiwi mumbled. "No, really, I didn't do anything, you just needed to catch your own breath . . ."

"What's your name, son?" someone called, and without thinking Kiwi answered truthfully:

"Kiwi Bigtree."

"Thank you, thank you," the girl kept whispering, her lips opening and closing so delicately against the cleft above his left shoulder that he could feel the buzz of her gratitude on his neck—but what did she think he had done for her? Why were these other people agreeing with her? Rumors began within earshot of him:

"See that young man, son? He was all action. Fell back on his training. He's a hero."

"Did you watch the kid *move* down there? He freed her hair from the pool drain, the whole production took him under a minute, she wasn't even breathing . . ."

A woman in a yellow sarong at the far end of the Lake with five duckling children thronged around her started clapping: "Bravo, young man!" And then the whole crowd around the Lake of Fire broke into a standing ovation. Applause like he remembered from the Bigtree Wrestler Spectacular echoed around the vaulted ceiling—directed, incredibly, at him.

(With his eyes shut, with his face turned toward the din, he could see his mother standing in sunlight so bright it looked like slick ice on the wooden stage, waving at all her tourists indiscriminately, a sea of red ball caps and cellophane visors. H-I-L-O-L-A B-I-G-T-R-E-E! He could see himself at thirteen, selling bags of popcorn to her great admirers. When he watched his mother wrestling Seths onstage he'd felt proud and ashamed of her in shifting ratios—his mother's tourists he just hated. Hate like that was an easy, monochrome feeling. *Look anywhere but at my mother,* he'd think at thirteen, and also: *Stand up for her ovation, you assholes.*)

Someone was taking a photograph of him, and others followed suit. Someone patted a thick towel around Kiwi's shoulders. Kiwi heard the ricochet of the word "Kiwi" throughout the grotto and he felt a smile spreading messily on his face. He stood, dragging the girl up with him. After so many days and nights of being anonymous, a Margaret, his real name had a narcotic effect. He put one hand around this girl, and his free hand lifted in a wave.

CHAPTER FIFTEEN

Help Arrives, Then Departs

S tiltsville was miles behind us and there was as yet no sign of my sister. We were traveling southwest with the current, alligators sprawled on either bank. My oar head was white and scummy with grass. A skipjack landed in our bow and I cleaned it and fed it to the red Seth. Behind me, the Bird Man's pole kept clanging against limestone bedrock. Was the Bird Man angry with me? His hood hid the clue of his face.

Touch me again, Bird Man, I thought urgently. *Tell a joke, say anything*—because I was having the convection feeling. As if my skin were rippling, dissolving. Kiwi describes this phenomenon, "convection" [n], in his Field Notes: the rapid cooling of a body in the absence of all tourists. Even Kiwi, King of Stage Fright, admitted to feeling it on Sunday nights. Convection caused your thoughts to develop an alarming blue tinge and required touch or speech with another human as its antidote (Seths didn't work, not even my red Seth, I'd tried). Sweating could feel dangerous if you were alone in the swamp, as if droplet by droplet your body might get whisked into the sun.

When I baled water I leaned sideways and grazed the edges of the Bird Man's black coat. My fingers came back wet, with tiny black feathers stuck to them, which reassured me that neither one of us was a figment. At noon the basking lizards slid into the water to cool off. The river began to pick up speed.

At twelve thirty we ate lunch inside a Park Services chickee hut to avoid the mosquitoes. When you rowed into a cloud of skeeters it was loud as a tractor but there was nothing there, just these tiny molecules of sound. Some ranger had borrowed the Seminole design and erected a modern chickee here to use as a campsite, since there was nowhere high enough on the surrounding tree islands to pitch a tent. The inside smelled clean and dry, like a hollowed-out stump. We weren't the first people to use this shelter, either—overnighters' trash filled the corners. Their beers and soda bottles looked shiny as treasure. On the back platform I found a dead anhinga furred in mosquitoes, and a single, mysterious crutch. The poor bird had a broken left wing. The crutch belonged to a human invalid, presumably. Someone on our same mission, maybe, limping toward a wife or daughter in the underworld.

"Uh-oh," the Bird Man said, shaking the crutch at me. "A bad thing to forget, huh? Wonder what the story was there."

"Can you talk to that one?" I asked the Bird Man, indicating the dead anhinga, and he looked at me with an adult's generic formula of pity and irritation; I was disappointed in him. Given where we were headed, I thought my question was a good one. We made our tuna sandwiches and scooted under the palm window.

"There are lots of Seminole ghosts out here, did you know that, Bird Man? My sister told me."

"Of course," he nodded, as if I'd just told him there were lots of sheepshead minnows. "We might see them later."

"My sister is named for a Seminole chieftain. The whites killed him with malaria. He died in Fort Moultrie, South Carolina. Do you think he's in this part of the underworld?"

"Who knows, kid? Maybe we'll meet him."

After the Indian Removal Act was passed in 1830, the Seminole people were hunted like animals. They built the palm-thatched chickees for use as temporary shelters, hiding places. President Jackson sent a letter to the Seminoles that we reproduced in our museum, the last line of which reads:

"But should you listen to the bad birds that are always flying about you, and refuse to remove, I have directed the commanding officer to remove you by force."

Few mainlanders know that the Seminole Wars lasted longer than any other U.S. conflict, longer than the Vietnam War and the American

Revolution. By the time Colonel Loomis declared the end of the Third Seminole War in 1858, thousands of Seminoles had been slaughtered or "removed" to the western territories. My sister was named for the Seminoles' famous warrior and freedom fighter, War Chief Osceola, who, legend has it, said, at a time when General Jesup was upon them, and all seemed lost:

"If the Great Spirit will show me how, I will make the white man red with blood; and then blacken him in the sun and rain . . . and the buzzard live upon his flesh."

Ossie said the spirits of Seminole babies killed by Major Francis L. Dade's men still haunted the swamp, as did the ghosts of hundreds of army regulars who were murdered out here. So our home was actually a very crowded place.

These Seminoles, the "real" Indians that the Chief envied in a filial and loving way, were in fact the descendants of many displaced tribes from the Creek Confederacy. This swamp was not their ancestral home either, not by any stretch—they had been pushed further and further into the swamp by President Jackson's Tennessee boys and a company of scarecrows from Atlanta, a militia that was starved and half-crazed. We Bigtrees were an "indigenous species" of swamp dweller, according to the Chief and our catalogs, but it turned out that every human in the Ten Thousand Islands was a recent arrival. The Calusa, the shell builders—they were Paleo-Indians, the closest thing our swamp had to an indigenous people. But the Calusa vanished from all maps hundreds of years ago, and it was not until the late 1800s that our swamp was recolonized by freed slaves and by fugitive Indians and, decades later, by the shocked, drenched white pioneers shaking out wet deeds, true sitting ducks, the patsies of the land barons who had sold these gullible snowbirds farms that were six feet underwater. And then by "eccentrics" like the Bird Man and my parents.

Florida itself was a newcomer to these parts, you could argue. Kiwi did—he said that Florida was the "suture" between Africa and North America three hundred million years ago, when all the continents were fused. According to the geologic clock, our state was an infant. Our soils contained the fossils of endemic African species—my brother said these feathery stencils of the past in our bedrock sort of gave the lie to the Chief's ideas about the purity of our isolation.

"So, is your sister like the war chief Osceola?"

"Oh, no! She wears barrettes and stuff. She's a real girl-girl. She's not like us." I paused. "Hey, Bird Man?" I watched a bead of sweat travel down his neck and disappear below his collar of feathers. "Why do you always wear that coat?"

"This old thing?" The Bird Man smiled and ruffled a sleeve as if he'd never really considered it, fanned his grimy leather glove at me with a funny coquetry. I didn't laugh—I didn't know if I was supposed to— and his face soured.

"Oh, habit, I guess. I've been wearing it for so long that I feel naked without it."

"Okay, wait, I have another one. Where did you get your, ah . . . that?" I pointed at his black whistle. We were two days into our journey and the Bird Man had yet to use it.

"My birdcall?" He picked it up and held it between his lips, took a long suck of air; for a moment I felt my own belly muscles contract. Then he spit it out and laughed.

"It's just a whistle, kid. I made it."

"When?"

"I was even younger than you when I started up with the birdcalls. Ten, eleven."

I tried to picture the Bird Man as a child—just some runty kid whistling into the leaves. Already odd enough at eleven to give women misgivings.

"When did the song change so that you heard it as words?"

"I don't hear birdsong as words."

I had pictured the birds' strident calls trembling through the air and dying, and then all of a sudden those same cries taking on a coloring— red, black, blue—until what had previously been an empty hissing splintered into a hundred separate dramas: males squabbling over carrion, a lover's quarrel, a chick and its four siblings protesting their hunger.

"That's beautiful," the Bird Man said. "I wish it had been that way." He sounded tired. All the dark storyteller's charisma in his voice had vanished, and now his eyes had the absent sheen of my dolls' eyes. "Really, kid, I couldn't tell you. It's still birdsong. One day I heard patterns, that's all. I'd row out to Black Gum Rookery and I could hear a logic under all that shrieking. Peaks and valleys. Once I could use their calls to get them out of trees, I started to tour the swamp."

"So you don't—"

"No."

"But do you—"

"No more questions for a while, Ava."

We ate the rest of lunch in silence: tinned ham and little pinkie-length fishes packed in oil, most of which I fed to the red Seth. Our food was running low now. We had, what? Cooler 1 contained six hard-boiled eggs. Crackers, we still had two greasy brown tubes of those. At the bottom of the dry-foods box I found a jar of blackberry jam that had been left for Mom by the Pick Up Club, the little green ribbon still tied to it. Some lady had used scissors to curlicue the ends.

(Q: Why did those good Christian women volunteer to ornament a loss? With their terrible pity, a glittery pity, as if Death were a holiday like Christmas? We kids got a load of gifts and sweets from the neighbor women, all wrapped up in paper and bows. My brother told me that he was only "intermittently certain" that their intentions were good . . .)

"I'll pass," I said, but the Bird Man wanted some jam. With his coat on, and hunched over the tin jar lid like that, the Bird Man looked like a huge crow intelligently attacking a piece of metal.

"You should try some," he said, extending a black spoonful. "It's sweet. Tasty."

Stands of pond-apple trees were adorned with long nets of golden moss and shadowed a kind of briary sapling I didn't recognize. Air plants hung like hairy stars. We poled through forests. Twinkling lakes. Estuaries, where freshwater and salt water mixed and you could sometimes spot small dolphins. A rotten-egg smell rose off the pools of water that collected beneath the mangroves' stilted roots. If Osceola was out here, even with the ghost helping her, I thought she must be so tired by now—she would be thirsty, and very hungry, blood-sucked by all the chizzywinks and mosquitoes, she'd be aching, she'd be wondering why she ever left our island in the first place . . .

"Can we take another break, Bird Man?"

"Not a chance," he said with his grave cheer. "No more breaks, my friend. Not if you want to come to a rescue."

All day the horizon was inches from our noses. We'd been poling the leafy catacombs of the mangrove tunnels for hours. Any changes—palings of the sun that dropped the temperature a degree or two, or a brilliant lizard hugging the bark—felt like progress. More than once I'd think a tunnel was truly impenetrable. We'd pole into a green cone of water lapping at the trees' wickery roots: the end of our journey! I'd think. And then we'd slide through a stew of crimson propagules, duck through a wishbonelike mangrove root, pop out. At one point an osprey's nest crashed onto the poor red Seth's carrier, knocked loose by our boat; that time we had to pole out stern first.

The Bird Man could always find us a way through. Often it took several tries: a tunnel would appear to be plumb shut and he would lift a branch, pull the skiff into sudden darkness, and slingshot us forward into the undergrowth. Blossoms dropped in a delicate static around us. The mosquitoes hid in wait for us, even in these shadows.

"You don't see her, right?" I kept asking. "You don't see anything yet?"

Eventually I stopped asking when we were going to get there. I stopped studying the buzzards, or worrying about whatever future was snaking upstream to meet us. At first it alarmed me to watch the buzzards drop into the thick palms; our map to the underworld kept rewriting itself, and how could anybody read a map like that? Half the black atlas would vanish into a hardwood hammock.

"Bird Man?" I asked at one point. "There goes our map again . . ."

But the Bird Man snapped in a tired voice that I should leave the navigation up to him. (*The buzzards are our stars . . .*) I took his advice; I didn't let my mind wander anymore. Too dangerous. Instead I sent my thoughts flying backward. Certain memories I could reenter like safe rooms, and I had this one in particular I liked to turn the knob on: once when my sister was fourteen she had led the afternoon tour of the Bigtree Family Museum. The Chief was away on a business trip, and Mom was taking some Lithuanian schoolkids with weird haircuts backstage to see the alligators' incubators. I was in a mood. I told Ossie that I was sick, and convinced her to do the tour. You used to be able to get Ossie to do anything for you—Ossie was the kindest member of our tribe. Privately I thought my big sister was weak and pitied her a little, for her softness and her status as a nonwrestler. She used to be so very quiet, back before her possessions started up. During these tours she read from a script that the Chief typed up for her. She stuttered *t*'s and said her *s*'s adenoidally. Her hands would shake. I still made her cover for me. I was passing by the museum window, eating a lemon ice and feeling like an expert deceiver, when I heard her voice float out:

"Ava Bigtree is only eleven years old. But she is already one of the best-t-t alligator wrestlers in the history of Swamplandia! She is Hilola Bigtree's daughter and my sister. Remember her name, because one day she will be the best alligator wrestler in the world."

Maybe Ossie was already home? I pictured Ossie sitting Indian style on the burgundy sofa in her polka-dotted pajamas. Watching TV, the mainland stations. News programs. Cartoons. Ossie eating popcorn while Tom and Jerry beaned each other with mallets. And then the TV went black, and the house was empty again. My giggle turned into something raw and terrible—accidentally, I'd just met this part of myself that no longer believed my sister was alive. *Your sister,* an old voice told me, as frank as noonlight, *is lost forever. You're too late. There's not a shadow left for you to chase. You'll go home and you won't have a sister.*

"Stay put, Osceola!" I'd put in the note pinned to our refrigerator. "If you beat me back home, sit tight. Don't come looking for *me* now . . ."

"Look out, kid—"

I watched a water moccasin wrinkle slowly across the river. We passed her; we were gaining speed. Gray and rustling branchways arced above the skiff like dried-out rainbows. The magnolia leaves turned green or black with the always-changing light.

"Al-most," the Bird Man whistled. He sank his pole into the water near an enormous frizz of roots. A hundred-year cypress lay on its side in the middle of the water. Roots shot outward from the hollow at the base like desiccated sun rays. Bright leaves like butterflies impaled there. *Closer and closer,* I thought, *we are getting closer and closer to the land of the dead.* The Bird Man pointed at the buzzards, then turned our bow until our boat was nearly facing upstream. We poled hard against the grain of the river.

The current grew stronger. It wove our skiff in an S-shaped path. In certain places now, the river was so narrow that trees on opposite banks could touch.

*   *   *

Some hours later I realized that we hadn't seen a melaleuca in miles. No more threat of "monoculture," as the scientists called it. The trees out here were a dark variety.

"You sure this is the river to hell? This place would be heaven to my father, all the hammocks out here." I pointed at a stand of bearded trees whose flowers gave off a syrupy perfume as we paddled beneath them. "I don't even know the names of some of these twisty ones . . ."

"Hey, kid, look where we're going . . ."

We had to go onto our backs, flat as water moccasins, to pull our skiff through the next tunnel. My head was on the Bird Man's lean stomach as we entered a net of branches. I could feel him breathing in a careful way under my damp scalp; each exhalation sank me a little. A black maze of branches moved over the sun. Leaves, round as pucks, waggled their tongues at us.

"What happened here?" The Bird Man touched the flaky spot on my knee where I'd scraped hard against the chickee ladder. "Poor kid. You okay?"

"Huh? Oh. Yeah. I don't even remember how I got that one."

He kneed forward in the skiff with his black feathers moving in wavelets, slid something from an interior pocket. The next thing I knew the Bird Man was uncapping a jar of green fluid. He drizzled a cool ointment over me and crisscrossed a bandage on my cut.

"There. Home remedy. 'Home' being a fluid terminology, in my special case." He smiled. "There you go. Nomad medicine. Works better than anything in a first-aid kit, that's for sure."

Love.

"I love you," I blurted out. The Bird Man laughed; for once I had succeeded in startling him.

"Are you feeling okay, kid? Do you need some water?"

I shook my head. "Sorry . . ." My eyes were burning. "I, uh, I thought . . ."

We ducked the subject of love by swapping water from the canteen. But now I had an embarrassed feeling and I wanted to explain myself to him; I didn't want him thinking I was some idiot kid. So between sips of water I started telling him about my mother's show. That show was my model for love, the onstage and the backstage parts. In this goony kid way, I think I must have been hoping that my story might get the Bird Man to love me the way my mother was loved by the Chief.

"You know, my father trained himself to be my mother's sun, electrically speaking."

That was exactly how my dad described the job of love. The Chief rigged the lights for Mom's act years and years ago, on their fourth date—he dreamed up the lights and the choreography for her show before she'd ever so much as touched an alligator. This was a popular story on our island (Bigtree Museum, Exhibit 12). After she became a wrestler and started doing evening performances, he operated the follow spot. I'd always try to find a way to be backstage for this part. Love, as practiced on our island, was tough work: the blind eye of the follow spot took all your strength to direct and turn. Every night the Chief ratcheted its yellow-white iris around my mother's muscular back on the diving board. The follow spot we used was decades old, heavy, with poor maneuverability, and the Chief struggled to hold the beam steady. I remember his hands better than his face (I was a short kid): the square nails discolored against the metal, his big knuckles popping from the pressure of his grip like ten white valentines.

My mother did her breaststroke inside the spot's golden circle of light, growing smaller and smaller as she headed for the deep end. "Now watch *this*," my father would say, smiling at me as he changed the color filter and adjusted the iris diaphragm. By the end of her performance his shirt was soaked with sweat.

Now I mopped my own brow and stared at the Bird Man with my knees stowed under my chin, waiting to see if the story had worked.

"Sounds like a nice show," he coughed.

"I saw posters of your mother all over the islands, you know," the Bird Man offered almost an hour later, breaking a long silence. He said this like we'd been in steady conversation, like he was answering my question. "She was a beautiful woman. You look just like her, Ava."

I burned in the bow seat. I thought this was the kindest lie anybody had ever told me.

*   *   *

On the skiff I made up a little credo for myself:

I believe the Bird Man knows a passage to the underworld.

I believe that I am brave enough to do this.

I have faith that we are going to rescue Ossie.

Every doubt got pushed away. Kiwi's voice *(There are no such things as ghosts)* I ignored. Faith was a power that arose from inside you, I thought, and doubt was exogenous, a speck in your eye. A black mote from the sad world of adults.

When I shut my eyes I could see the underworld: a blue wave in front of us. The painting from Ossie's book sprawled behind my eyelids—*Winter on the River Styx*—and if I really concentrated I could get this painting to *snow.* Dark flakes falling into our near future. It was hard work to keep believing that we were going to get there, but I persisted. Faith cupped and kept the future like leaves on the hidden water that (I believed) we were rowing toward. Where Ossie was waiting for me, and maybe my mom.

We kids cultivated a faith in all the Bigtree legends—I'd heard them so often from my parents that they seemed to me like memories I'd made myself. At the time, I also had faith that my pet Seth and I would be champions—how could it be otherwise? In fact I sort of thought this future must exist somewhere, the year of our triumph floating in utero in outer space, as small as the pinheads of stars.

Sometimes when I caught the sun sinking and felt a rinse of panic, I risked a look back at the Bird Man. *Imagine the thousands of birds this man can summon!* I told myself. Armies of birds, whole rookeries. Colors on their underwings that I thought were the prettiest part of our universe and here this man could paint the skies with them. Most incredibly, he had called me.

"Ava." The Bird Man's voice sounded preoccupied; he was trying to backferry us around some rocks. "Tell you what, kid, I'm going to sit and paddle for a while. You're tired, why don't you rest here? Lean back, huh? Put your head on my lap if you want. I'll wake you if I see signs of your sister."

I shook my head. This kindness was so sudden and extravagant that it made me, for some reason, want to cry. In a very different context, I had responded the same way when Mrs. Gianetti on Gallinule Key had offered me fancy chocolates once and I'd declined to eat even one, intimidated by the blue satin ribbon around the box. The Bird Man's gaze rippled over me, calm as clouds.

"Suit yourself."

We were traveling so slowly through the mangrove keys. The bark on the trunks here wove together brilliant magentas and silvers, which reminded me for some reason of the old tourist women's dye jobs, that funny mix of rubies and milk, age and vanity.

"Those tourists are sure going to love *you*," I told the red Seth in her crate. It was three, I noted, the time of our Swamplandia! matinee. "When we get home . . ."

The red Seth squirmed unhappily in my palm, like a little dinosaur dreaming of amber.

Where was the dredge right now? I wondered. Where was the fisherman who claimed to have seen it?

Waves of feeling seemed to heave and smooth in me to the tempo of the actual waves. Big-mouthed fishes sucked whirlpools between the prop roots.

"Ossie?" I called into miles of trees. "Ossie, it's me . . ."

At some point, our waterway disappeared, dried up, and we had to carry the boat overland. In *The Spiritist's Telegraph*, Lethe was described as a deep, reliable channel. Well, that was not the situation we encountered in the Ten Thousand Islands. The sun was a white hole. I was walking with the wet prow of a boat on my head through waist-high marsh grass and the hundreds, the thousands, very possibly the *millions* of mosquitoes.

"Hey, can you use your whistle to call these bugs off?"

We were seeing a part of the swamp that I was unfamiliar with. The distant saw grass waved like wheat that silvered at its tips. I was grumpy, then scared: what wind could it *possibly* be moving in? Sweat covered my forearms; the clouds hung motionless.

It was a terrible portage—the Bird Man stood beneath the skiff's rough yoke and my job was just to steer us, and it turned out I couldn't even do that well, mud everywhere and flies in my eyes and my nostrils. I imagined we made a strange insect, our four feet moving beneath the boat's flipped hull.

Very suddenly we drew up to the ruins of a bridge. Wooden trestles spanned a canal that was fifteen feet wide—it looked like part of a skeletal roller coaster. The Bird Man told me that wild-cotton crews employed by the U.S. Department of Agriculture built this bridge in the 1920s. They were hired to eradicate the red cotton borer, a wild species of cotton that threatened the commercial plantations in northern Florida; they'd been working on a network of roads and bridges through the swamp to get their trucks and equipment out here before the infamous Labor Day hurricane of 1935 struck. Hundreds of World War I veterans died when the train sent to rescue them departed too late and every car—all but the locomotive—got swept into the sea. Broward, Bolles, the private contractors, they all ran out of money. Money appeared to be the one species that couldn't take root in the swamp—and this blight was a killer of dreams, the Chief said, more potent than the red cotton borer.

I nodded hard to indicate that I knew my history well. (Please! Ladies and gentlemen of the mainland, I cleaned the history, I dusted dead mosquitoes off the history on summer mornings.)

"Sure, I know all about that. My grandfather survived the Labor Day hurricane. He took photographs of all the bodies."

Black laborers had drowned by the thousands in the vegetable fields, and, because they were black, the laborers' deaths never got recorded in the official tallies. Few tourists lingered over the framed pictures of their bloated bodies in Taylor Slough, 1935, that floated on our museum wall, preferring instead the photos Mom had taken of obese baby Kiwi in his water wings.

Most mainlanders hear "homeschooled" and they get the wrong impression. There were many deficits in our swamp education, but Grandpa Sawtooth, to his credit, taught us the names of whole townships that had been forgotten underwater. Black pioneers, Creek Indians, moonshiners, women, "disappeared" boy soldiers who deserted their army camps. From Grandpa we learned how to peer beneath the sea-glare of the "official, historical" Florida records we found in books. "Prejudice," as defined by Sawtooth Bigtree, was a kind of prehistoric arithmetic—a "damn fool math"—in which some people counted and others did not. It meant white names on white headstones in the big cemetery on Cypress Point, and black and brown bodies buried in swamp water.

At ten, I couldn't articulate much but I got the message: to be a true historian, you had to mourn amply and well. Grandpa ate rat snakes and alligator meat even after grocery stores made frozen dinners available; he bit that one guy, Mr. Arkansas; but I don't think these facts disqualify him from being a true historian, a true egalitarian. Tragedies, too, struck blindly and you had to count everyone. Grandpa taught us more than any LCPS Teach Your Child . . . ! book about Florida hurricanes, Florida wars. From his stories we learned as children how to fire our astonishment at death into a bright outrage.

After the carnage in the marshlands, the federal government took over the Swamp Reclamation project: its new stated mission was "flood control." Nobody was trying to drain the swamp anymore, although the Army Corps' new system of hydrological controls seemed just as shortsighted and failure-prone as their original plans. We had an exhibit in the Family Museum called The Era of Swamp Reclamation, which seemed to give strangers the impression that this era was over—as if the Army Corps weren't still turning those faucets on and off, sponging phosphorous for Big Sugar, opening the canal locks for the farmers in October and telling the water where to go.

"It's a wonder this bridge is still standing, isn't it, Ava?"

The Bird Man looked like he had just crawled out of a lake, he was sweating so badly. We leaned the skiff on the ant-covered bridge supports while he toweled water from his brow.

"I guess." I was proud of myself for feeling no surprise—I'd been instructed by the Chief to think of mercy as "the wind's oversight" and miraculous survivals as "a lucky malfunction; a fluke in the weather system." Streamers of pale marine grass had swallowed the trestles.

"Did the cotton pickers know they were in hell?" I huffed. It was close to five o'clock now, and sweat trickled down my hairline; I could feel a splinter worming inside my palm. The sky above us was a pure and cloudless blue.

"Oh," the Bird Man said. "I imagine so."

Forty minutes later we were back on the water, poling around the glacial spires of a long oyster bed. At first I didn't hear anything; the Bird Man flinched before I did. He whipped around with his burnished eyes dimming. "Go flat," he hissed, and then he was pushing me down.

After a moment I heard the buzz of an approaching outboard. A beige-and-black Park Services boat pulled around the grass-fringed slough, water spudding off the boat's rigging, and then abruptly the engine cut out. When I saw who it was, I nearly shouted at the happy shock of a familiar face: Whip Jeters, a park ranger who often patrolled the waters around Swamplandia!, was standing in the stern with his hand on the sputtering Evinrude. Whip Jeters was a tall, once-fat man who wore his uniform khakis in a size that swallowed his new frame. He had a painful sunburn, and when he removed his sunglasses I saw a raccoon pallor ringing both eyes. Then I felt hands on my shoulders and my eyes were level with the tackle box, my cheekbone pushed against the wood.

The Bird Man, still seated in the stern, turned and waved. "Howdy, friend!" His voice was unrecognizable. "How's the fishing over yonder?"

"Kid." Without looking my way, he murmured in a cold monotone, "If you tell this man where we are going he will take you away from me. He could arrest me—he has the grounds to do that. We are almost to the Eye of the Needle, but this man will not believe you if you tell him the truth about what we are doing. We need to be *smart* about this . . ."

Whip began to motor over; above me, the Bird Man put on a big grin that made his face unrecognizable to me. It rejiggered his features so that they were at their most ordinary; even his eyes seemed pale and normal. Who had I been traveling with this great while? How could you change so completely when another person showed up, like a chameleon shifting trees? I was impressed. I didn't want to be the one who screwed this up.

"Who's hiding down there? You running aliens, sir? Illegals?"

"This is my young cousin." He touched my back with the butt of his oar. "We are on a fishing trip."

"I'd like to see your permit for that. Your cousin, huh? Well what's wrong with her? She sick or something?"

"She's taking a nap," the Bird Man said in an avuncular voice I barely recognized, patting my knotty hair.

"I'm taking a nap," I confirmed, sitting up.

"Why, you're one of the Chief's! One of the Bigtree kids!"

I am, I am! I nodded so hard my teeth hit. Hearing my tribe's name spoken out here felt like being wrapped in a warm blanket. Mr. Jeters had known me since birth, he had been a childhood friend of the

Chief's, and I think he would have been shocked to know how grateful I felt at that moment. Just his friendly gaze was clothing me.

"I hear from Gus that your brother's living on the mainland now? You believe that?" He shook his head with mock amazement, and I loved him for making Kiwi's defection sound dumb and temporary. "I bet the Chief said jack-crap to that. And how's he liking it, your brother?"

"I don't know, Warden Jeters. He doesn't call us."

"Well, that'll change. What is he now, seventeen? He's probably too proud to call, wants to wait until he's got something good to report. Listen, hon," Whip said, his voice still casual but his eyes cutting over at the Bird Man, "it's a funny question, I know, but I got to ask: is this guy your for-real cousin?"

I followed Whip's gaze to the Bird Man and of course I understood why he had asked. Black feathers shirred along the ruff of his coat and he licked a long finger to tamp them. Behind him the slough had turned the same mix of iron and wine purple as the sky and the wind was blowing the plants apart. "Storm's coming," the Bird Man said politely, picking at his teeth.

I nodded. "He is, Whip. The Chief thought it would be good for me to get off the island. We've had a tough summer over there."

"Whose side are you on?"

"My mother's," I said.

"Her father's," said the Bird Man. We all looked at one another. "The Chief's," I corrected myself. "Sorry, I got confused, I've been thinking about Mom a lot today . . ."

The warden said nothing but let his eyes roll over the length of our skiff.

"No offense to you, sir, but you're an odd sight on the water . . ."

Whip Jeters was some intermediary age between the Chief and Grandpa Sawtooth, and he had been a friend of our family's for so long that there was a picture of him on our museum wall under the heading Honorary Bigtrees. *It's really him, it's Whip Jeters,* I kept thinking. I smiled at the zippered life jacket he was wearing—we'd been forced to pole our way for half a mile because the water was only three feet deep. I was so grateful to see his big ears and red bulbous nose that I worried I might start crying. Whip, misinterpreting my look, rubbed at the floury stripe around his eyes. "Yes, well, I guess I had a little accident involving a nap and the sun. But it doesn't hurt nearly so bad as it looks, although that's not saying much, is it? Ha-ha . . ."

Whip patted the seam of his mouth with his checkered collar. He politely squelched a burp.

"Pardon me." He gave me a wink and a slightly goofy grin, and I realized with a pang that he was embarrassed. "Say, why don't you come over here for a minute, Ava, stretch your legs on my boat?" The Bird Man gave me a curt nod and so I stood, placing my hands on Whip's broad shoulders and letting him swing me on board. We were floating beneath black clouds shaped like anvils and I hoped the rain would hold.

"Have you folks eaten?" Whip offered me a red canister of a mainland brand of crackers. He bit into a cheddar round. He chewed into the terrible quiet between our boats.

"You know, these things are delicious? The wife made me switch over from the potato chips, for my cholesterol, but now I actually *prefer* them. You want to try one, Ava? Sir? Cracker?" He was staring at the Bird Man's greatcoat.

Whip, I'd noticed, was sidling around the Bird Man with a strange formality, and when he addressed my "cousin" his voice shot an octave higher than his usual genial baritone. After a few minutes I put together that this stiffness was not the product of Mr. Jeters's natural awkwardness. He was jumpy around me, too, and when his pant leg snagged on his engine he let out a little yelp. He was very polite—I guess he saw no cause to deviate from marine etiquette—but I could tell that something about this encounter had him miserably flustered. He listened to me talk with his knuckles pressed into his red cheek, and when he removed them I saw they'd left a pale indent.

The Bird Man was watching us talk from the skiff, mining his grimace with a toothpick with his legs flat in front of him. At one point he raised an eyebrow in my direction and clicked his teeth against the tiny splinter of wood—*He wants you to be quiet,* I understood. The buzzards hung in such eerie patterns in the thermals that I felt as if they had paused, too, waiting to see what would happen next. I heard myself telling Whip about Carnival Darwinism and Grandpa Sawtooth's new home and the Chief's departure.

"Say," said Whip. When he spoke his tone was very studiously nonchalant despite the fact that he'd just interrupted me midsentence.

"Just curious, where do you and your cousin keep all your fishing poles and whatnot?"

"At our fishing *camp*," the Bird Man snapped from the stern of our skiff. He had drifted maybe twenty feet from us. "Been in the family for years. You know Mammoth Key?"

"Sure." Whip scratched dead skin from one wrinkled knuckle.

"Want some cortisone? Some aloe vera?" I heard myself offer in a stranger's hospitality voice.

"Nah, honey, thank you. So your cousin here has got a camp over on Mammoth! I haven't been out there in five years. Good bass fishing over there."

We all watched as single droplets of rain hit the water. Duckweed dragged like a wedding train behind our transom. I had seen a small alligator following us earlier, I told Whip, just half a snout and the olive bumps of her eyes visible, but she had disappeared.

"They're a lot more skittish out here than your folks' gators, that's for sure." Whip coughed. The Bird Man was plucking white bits of down from his coat sleeves and flicking them onto the water—*He was bullying Whip!* I realized. He had picked up on his fear and now he was tailoring the show for him. "My cousin has been telling me stories about her mother. I never knew her, regrettably—wrong side of the family," the Bird Man said.

Whip shot me a look. "Your mama was a great woman, honey. It's a terrible, terrible shame what happened . . ."

What happened, Whip? Even the few facts I did have about her last weeks tended to float away from me like shining leaves on water the more I tried to get a picture together.

"We're doing okay. We want to get the show up and running again next month, with that cannon. The Juggernaut. Did the Chief show you our cannon?"

"Not yet. Looking forward to seeing it." Whip gave me what I guess you'd call a rueful smile, which I understood as a kid to be a smile without joy. A smile with a pretty bad joy:knowledge ratio.

The Bird Man was rustling behind me. His black coat went huge on a sudden gust of wind, and the feathered sleeves swelled big as balloons around his stringy, freckled arms in a way that might have seemed silly on anybody else, almost clownish. Whip's face was very still.

"What in the hell is wrong with your cousin, honey?" Whip mumbled, almost to himself. "He thinks it's Halloween or something? That's some coat he's got." He munched another tiny cracker. I said nothing but crowded so closely to Whip's elbow that the boat rocked. The Bird Man and I locked eyes across the channel. We both knew that it would take one sentence now to end our trip to the underworld. I felt suddenly powerful—I could say the Bird Man was my kidnapper, or worse, and I would be believed. Whip Jeters would take me home on his patrol boat. But none of that would help my sister.

"Hey, Whip?" I said, lowering my voice. "You haven't seen anybody else out here, have you? Or a funny-looking boat?"

"Nope, I haven't seen a soul. Funny how?"

"Just funny-looking. Almost like one of those old dredges from the 1930s . . ."

"A dredge! You're more likely to see a Chinese junk in these flats than a dredge launch. Those old jalopies would have to be fifty, sixty years old now . . . Where'd you get it in your head you saw a thing like that out here?" Now he sounded worried. "Because a suspicious-looking vessel this far from Loomis don't portend one good thing. It's drugs or poachers would be my guess, human smugglers coming up from Cuba . . ."

"The Chief says I have a wild imagination, Mr. Jeters," I babbled. "Poor eyesight. I wouldn't worry, it was probably nothing." I leaned in and touched his elbow. "But if you see a dredge scow, Mr. Jeters, will you stop it? Will you . . . will you grab whoever you find on it?"

"I will, I will do that. Believe me, if there's a dredge out here that's still seaworthy I will have some questions for its operators." He made a noise in his throat, laughter or disbelief. "I'll put out a call on our station. You have a good fishing trip with your cousin, Miss Bigtree," he said with a wink. He winked again, like a friendly tic he couldn't control. He didn't look at the Bird Man again, and I got the sense that Whip didn't want to see anything that would hinder his exit. He had decided to believe me, I guess, but I think it must have been the sort of believing that requires a special paradox, a vigilant blindness. Whip Jeters wouldn't look at my face, and he quit sneaking glances at my "cousin" in the glade skiff. Behind him, the Bird Man lifted his chin at me. Now his eyes were shining in the familiar way but I don't think Whip could see this.

The rain was coming on fast. Whip switched on the flashlight at his belt loop and flashed the beam of light rapidly, twice, onto the stern. He paused, and then lit it once more. The yellow circle of light covered my sneakers and shut again for good. I don't know if this was just Whip fumbling with the flashlight or if he was trying to get a message to me. There was no time to ask him; the Bird Man had already rowed over to receive me.

(I was a fairy-minded kid, a comic book kid, and I had a bad habit of looking for augurs and protectors where there were none. So who knows what sense Whip made of the pair of us? It's just as likely that his blinking flashlight was a malfunction, an unlucky one, and not a signal I missed.)

Whip Jeters swung me back over to the Bird Man's skiff, and my fingers sank into the oily feathers on his shoulders. The Bird Man got me settled in the bow seat with my paddle.

"Good-bye," said Mr. Jeters, no longer disguising his desire to get away.

"Good-bye," we sang out together, the Bird Man's voice a gravelly accompaniment to my high whine. Rain had started blowing in from the east, and I wondered if we'd paddle through the afternoon showers or hunch in one of the little coves around the mangroves and wait them out.

I didn't tell the Bird Man what Whip had said to me as we parted ways. Before he'd returned me to the Bird Man, Whip Jeters had done a curious thing. He'd leaned in and let his dry lips brush my cheek. It felt stiff and formal, less like a kiss than some strange benediction. He'd put a warm palm on my shoulder and gotten close enough to whisper:

"Be safe, Ava."

CHAPTER SIXTEEN

Kiwi Bigtree, World Hero

The reporters talked him into hair and makeup. Some TV crew assistant had deflated his water-logged trunks by pounding on Kiwi's actual ass, cheerfully conversant as he did this—as if Kiwi were somehow not attached to it, the ass. Great tinfoil sheets and lunar caps of light went up around the lifeguard station. The World of Darkness had closed an hour before and without the crowds the Lake of Fire felt newly eerie, water jetting from its sides in bruise-colored clouds. Kiwi flinched; a short, ebullient male stylist from the *Loomis Register* was combing the snarls from his hair. His mother used to powder his cheeks by the Gator Pit, using some sort of drugstore magic to transform her acned son into a wrestler of Seths. *This is fraudulent, Mom! This is a dubious project.* He'd pumped up his anger with big language like a bicycle tire.

"We think this might run on the front page, love."

The front page of a mainland newspaper! He hadn't allowed himself to be photographed for the Swamplandia! brochures for years; in the most recent one he was fourteen, wearing his sister Osceola's red ribbon around his forehead and furious about it, a feather sticking up behind his head like a middle finger.

The stylist licked his thumb and tamped down Kiwi's owlish eyebrows. "Gawd! Stubborn! We don't want you looking like a *warlock* in the photograph, do we?"

"Well, I guess you're going to need more gel, then." Kiwi rubbed at his forehead.

The newspaper photographer made him pose in his trunks, which hung flabbily down his chicken legs, still loaded with water. He stood shivering on the cement edge of the Lake of Fire. Emily Barton curled herself against Kiwi's shoulder and arranged her hair so that it curled in a pretty raven lock around Kiwi's right nipple. Kiwi didn't want to touch it, the raven lock. It seemed to have its own important agenda down there. Kiwi badly wanted a T-shirt. The stylist, meanwhile, was circling Emily's head with the hairspray like a maniacal bug exterminator.

"Emily, babe, don't move? We want that hair to stay put."

Emily kept tugging one black strap and wiggling closer to Kiwi, until he could feel the dampness of her black swimsuit pressed against his side—she, too, was still wet from the rescue.

"Thank you for saving me," she told him breathily. "For saving my *life.*"

"Sure. I mean, no problemo." Kiwi felt a little sick.

"Emily, babe, when you stare at him? Can you look a little more, *you* know—" The photographer made a noise like a popped balloon and Emily shuffled her hair back, nodded like she understood this directive perfectly. "Like: *wow.* I am so happy to be alive. Like, give this man a medallion."

Kiwi straightened at the word "man." Instinctively, he clenched his pectorals.

I didn't save her, Kiwi was going to answer honestly if the question came up. They were cheek to cheek, and he could feel all the smiling muscles tensing in her face.

"Bag-tree," a female reporter asked him, "how do you spell that?"

"It's Bigtree. As in Hilola Jane Bigtree," he said. And it felt wonderful to say it, like swinging an ax into the glass case of his Loomis identity. "I belong to the Bigtree tribe of Swamplandia!"

"I'm sorry?"

"B-I-G-T-R-E-E. We do an alligator-wrestling show? Have you seen that billboard on I-95? Big guy in a headdress?"

Her smile went vast and glassy.

"Channel seven came out a few years back to film a segment about us? We advertised in all the local papers. We call the alligators Seths," he added, as if this fact might spin some tumblers for her.

The pen hovered an inch above her pad.

"Okay, give me that, I'll write it for you," Kiwi said. "Can you at least put her name in there? It's H-I-L-O-L-A."

Kiwi started talking faster. He heard his voice taking on the Chief's ringleader intonations. *This is how I can help them.* If he could pull it off. He pictured an article that would drive the mainlanders seaward like lemmings, pushing them deep into the swamp, toward his father and his sisters and the patient Seths, toward Hilola Bigtree's glass tomb in the museum, a hundred new tourists clutching dollars, a hundred new mourners come to pay his mother the tribute that counted.

"... and that's why I'm working this job at the World of Darkness in the first place ..." Kiwi heard himself urgently quoting his father. "... we're just sizing up the competition, building capital for our Carnival Darwinism expansion. I'll level with you, ma'am, Swamplandia! is the superior park. Best value, biggest thrills. Catch the late show, Saturdays. Alligators! Starry nights! It's like Van Gogh meets Rambo. We're got ninety-eight true-life *monsters*."

Kiwi frowned—had he just seen the nib of her pen trace a little star in the pad's margin? "Did you catch all that? Could you perhaps list our showtimes in there?"

To his left, Emily was sipping a bottle of orange soda inside a crescent moon of reporters. She wasn't so much giving an interview as she was performing respiration for them. "I saw a tunnel," she was saying—"of light!" she added, to clarify that she wasn't talking causeways. The TV crew formed a little carousel of approval around her, nodding and *ahh*ing. She sucked air as if air were a milk shake, demonstrating the joy of life.

"One last question, Mr. Bigtree: is this the first life you've saved?" The reporter's glasses made her eyes look far away, like tiny moons.

"Yes? I mean, I guess so."

She smiled with creamy indulgence. "That's quite a milestone."

Kiwi felt himself redden. The photographers were zipping their cameras into silver bags when he stopped them.

"Wait, ma'am? My quote was not entirely accurate. I just wanted to add, apropos of your last question ..."

The reported looked over with a white, harried face. "You just said—did I get this right?—'a porpoise of your last question'? Is that supposed to be a Leviathan joke? Afraid I missed that."

"*Apropos,*" Kiwi repeated, touching a finger to his new mustache. "Would you like me to spell that for you?" In fact, Kiwi had once again mistakenly said "a porpoise." He had been bungling his SAT building-block words for months now—he pronounced "fatuous" so that it fit the meter of "SpaghettiOs." He'd been using the word "meningitis" in compliments.

"Well, I'm a wrestler, ma'am." Kiwi kept his eyes on his big hands but his voice grew in conviction. "I used to tape up alligators . . ."

Several people had turned to stare at him now. Kiwi corkscrewed his fists into Bigtree Wrestling Grip 7 for the Circumnavigator trick. Was that it? All his fingers looked smashed and broken on the tiles.

"So, ah, viz-a-viz your, your inquiry?" he coughed. Behind him the Lake of Fire gurgled benignly, a cleaning solvent fizzing on its surface. "Can you change my answer? I guess I've saved my own life before."

Saturday night in the World of Darkness! Kiwi Bigtree had been alone for his whole small life and he was ready to *party.* He had mainland friends and a reason to drink with them. A hero's welcome awaited him at Lotsa Shots, on the Paradise Level of the Sunrise mall next to the Have a Shakee Shack and Gamenesia. Kiwi borrowed one of Leo's polo shirts and his El León cologne. When he and Leo stood next to each other now, they smelled like a fire hazard. Their polo shirts might as well have been rags soaked in kerosene.

"You sure you're okay to drive, Vijay?"

"What, do *you* want to drive, asshole? No? You want to walk? All right then."

The skunk lines of the road whipsawed in front of the windshield. Everybody had piled into the shitbox Volvo, two of the girls from the Dorsal Flukes and Leo in the backseat and Kiwi representing for Team Safety and Legality by wearing his seat belt in the front. Had there been a crash-test helmet, he would have worn it. Someone thunked a flask against Kiwi's head.

"Ow! What was that for?"

"Make a note of this, Bigtree," Leo giggled. "We earth people call it a *flask*. It's for transporting awesome feelings. Getting-laid juice."

"Fuck you," Kiwi said, but he was exhausted. "I know what a flask is for."

Red orb after red orb floated dreamily over their car roof. Vijay's huge sneaker stayed flat on the accelerator. Stoplights swayed yellow and green over the Loomis intersections, like air plants, the mainlanders' epiphytes. I-95 extended from Florida to *Maine,* and that faraway syllable made Kiwi fantasize about college, snowfall . . . Kiwi found his reflection in the side mirror: his eyes squeezed black and small above the ruddy poles of his sideburns. This face appearing in tomorrow's newspapers, everybody!

"Running *lights*!" Vijay crowed, a yellow globe pinging to red in the side mirror. "You know why, 'cause we can't crash, bro, we got the fucking hero with us! *Kiwi Bigtree!*"

Everyone in the World of Darkness was calling him Kiwi Bigtree now. How had this happened? It was anthill intelligence. Even Nina Suárez and her moussed coterie of World girls were kissing his cheek in greeting; they tiptoed up and called him "Kee-wee" at close range, like they were talking into a phone. Margaret Mead, RIP. Kiwi seemed unable to collect and absorb it, this happiness he knew he should now possess.

KIWI BIGTREE: SON OF THE SWAMP. He hoped the newspaper printed the name of their park. It would be a Trojan attack inside an article about the World of Darkness.

The bouncer at Lotsa Shots was a white man with ratty wheat-colored hair, his arms a lewd sleeve of nude blue fairies.

"You boys having a good time tonight?"

"So far, bro," Vijay said, just as Kiwi slurred, "Heretofore."

"How old are you boys?"

Vijay nudged Kiwi forward. "My friend saved a girl's life today."

My *friend,* Kiwi grinned. He was trying to remember his phony birthday—according to this card he was twenty-seven. These IDs were the handiwork of Vijay's cousin's boyfriend, a dimply Cuban-American kid who had introduced himself to Kiwi as Street Magic.

"It's true, you don't believe me? He did CPR on her! Check it out, that bitch is right over there. She could be *dead* if it wasn't for him."

Oh no! Kiwi thought, because Emily Barton *was* here, at the bar. She was sitting on a stool, talking to the bartender, rowing her arms like a hockey player. She looked a little goofy. At the same time she was oppressively beautiful, with waist-length ebony hair.

"Congratulations, hero," the bouncer said sourly, flipping their IDs. He waved them through a frail parasol of cigarette smoke. "I hope she blows you."

"Asshole!"

"Not worth it, bro," Kiwi said gravely, thinking it came out sounding pretty good. Being Vijay's friend felt a little like being his personal accountant—girls, aggressors, who should Vijay invest his time in?

Everybody wanted to buy the heroic lifeguard a drink. A menu board listed 301 different kinds of shots—NO REPEATS!! someone had boasted in marker on the wall. For the first hour of his party, Kiwi, afflicted with a booze-specific lexical insecurity, kept asking everybody in his loudest voice, "Hey, am I really drunk? Like, drunk-drunk?"

Leo clapped Kiwi's back and cheerfully offered a diagnosis: Kiwi was *wasted.*

Carl Jenks had come out, too. He stood behind the pool table, next to the wooden cues like he was trying to blend in with them, and his face looked so swollen with distress that Kiwi wondered if Carl was holding his breath. *Why is he here?* Their boss's face was like a stubborn sun that refused to set, burning uncomfortably late into the night. He took off his wire-rim glasses and glanced around blindly. Nobody was talking to Carl Jenks; Kiwi watched him nervously set one of his orc books, number 7,012 in that series, on the edge of the pool table. He was staring into a sunset-pink cocktail.

Kiwi stared at Carl Jenks. For a second he had the disorienting feeling that he was looking into a mirror—that somehow Carl Jenks's miserable expression reflected something truer about Kiwi than the strip of glass behind the bar. *I should go talk to him . . .*

But Kiwi couldn't talk to Carl Jenks because he had a girl on his lap. Yes: Emily Barton, a beautiful girl, had volitionally climbed onto Kiwi's lap and was now, with a dreamy casualness, as if she were reaching up to touch her own face, stroking Kiwi's cheek. Just above his nouveau goatee-thing. Nothing like this had ever happened to Kiwi before.

Emily Barton was speaking very eloquently on the topic of herself. She was the only child of the only child of the CEO of the Carpathian Corporation, who had been visiting the Loomis World of Darkness chain on the day of her near-drowning. She was also, on her mother's side, an heiress. She had a red-gold locket with her own childhood picture in it and her black hair smelled like peeled oranges.

Whenever one of Kiwi's colleagues came over, she began talking in a singsong little-girl voice about her brush with *"l'morte." Quit calling it that.* She kept touching Kiwi's face with a small, repeated pressure, the kind of coy gesture that pretends to be void of intent; after a while Kiwi began to feel like a door that she was pushing at. Onto what? He had a feeling that whatever room he opened onto could only disappoint her. *You are a liar,* he thought, stroking her back. *We are lying together.* To date he hadn't saved anybody—not this brunette mainlander, not his mother, not a single human or reptilian member of the Bigtree tribe.

"You *know?*" she'd ask after nearly every sentence. But Kiwi never did. He managed to touch her ponytail once, very lightly, with enough frail resolve to seem both timorous and creepy. The deep citrus smell of her hair was deranging him.

Emily was an only child but that had not made her *spoiled.* She skied with a famous Ukranian, Trainer Bart, in a mountain town in Colorado. Her father was a "cheese enthusiast." He toured wineries and he collected big rocks of art with fabulous price tags for their "hideaway" in Putney, Vermont—her family was rich enough to have these alien hobbies.

Emily giggled at something bland and declarative he said, kissed the tip of his nose—sort of fell there, actually. Her head crashed into Kiwi's shoulder. He could smell and taste that she was very drunk.

How strange, Kiwi thought, that you could want so badly to insert a part of your anatomy inside someone who you hated. Kiwi had never once seen a pornographic film. Henry Miller's books had aroused but confused him. At some midnightish time he put a hand on Emily's forehead—smack on it, like a TV athlete palming a basketball or a shaman attempting an exorcism—and tried to kiss her. Did he miss? His lips grazed a left eyebrow. The attempt was not repeated.

Much later Emily announced that she would give Kiwi a ride home.

"No, thanks, it's way too far." She was going the wrong way on the highway. Then he remembered where he lived now. "Home" was one of those magnetic words, it would stick to wherever you slept. "Home, you know what's so funny about it . . . ," Kiwi slurred. His epiphany about the origins of species dissolved into unnameable feeling ("You are drunk as a skunk, bro," he heard Leo tell him). "Wasted" [adj]. The road in front of them billowed and fell like black parachute cloth.

Emily moved a hand from the wheel to her own thigh, and Kiwi watched this descent with a great disturbance that he did not yet know to call arousal. She tugged his hand down to join hers. Fortunately the hand, compared to the rest of Kiwi, seemed courageous and self-possessed. It caressed her knee, rucked the fabric of her tights. The hand slid up the length of her leg with the confidence of a psychic, as if it knew exactly what was coming next. *I surely hope one of us does,* Kiwi thought, watching the hand disappear. He touched the band of her underwear and then stopped; now the hand just sort of hung out there, under the skirt, not really doing anything. Like a bookmark. Apparently it was just going to hold his place until Kiwi developed a spontaneous literacy of the female body. Did Emily wish for the hand to be there? Was she just sort of tolerating it on her thigh for now, like a benign starfish that had become mysteriously attached to her? He ran a finger around the thin band. At the intersection on Segovia Road, Kiwi leaned over and with his free hand touched a barrette or possibly an earring? He had to duck a chandelier of jewelry to find her lips. Then they *were* kissing, a long, sloppy kiss, an incredulous kiss—Kiwi's first.

Behind Emily's head, Kiwi could see the tall buildings of downtown Loomis. Large ficus trees became a blotter for electric light. He gulped a moan and shoved her hand beneath the roomy waistband of Cubby's jeans. *Don't ruin this, brain, please.* He hoped this amazing thing that her hands and her warm mouth had committed them to could proceed without another word.

Forty minutes later Kiwi got dropped at the World of Darkness, no longer a virgin. His predominant emotion: confusion. A headache swaddled his thoughts like cloth. *Don't come back, brain, ever again.* The few dreams he had were bad and broth-thin: Ava turned up in some of them, and Osceola. The Seths were an undersea quilt of lantern eyes and teeth. He woke up half a dozen times to a feeling of pins and needles— as if the entire length of his skinny body were a numb foot tingling awake, resigning itself to the pain of sensation.

By 4:30 a.m. Kiwi wasn't drunk anymore, or a hero—that whiskey shimmer had been reabsorbed by his skin. *I hate you,* he thought, and this thought floated serenely outside of him, because who could it attach to? He couldn't even pretend to hate the Chief at this hour. He missed his family too badly. *I hate who?* Carl Jenks? What about Dr. Gautman? Emily Barton? Every tourist? The Chief's loan officer? Failure! He couldn't hate any of them, he couldn't find one person to use as a tether; the rage was like a balloon that drifted heavenward and broke free of its string. Kiwi, who considered himself a grammarian of human emotion, knew that anger required a direct object. (I am angry at ___. I hate ___.) "To hate" was a transitive verb. Anger needed an anchor, a plug, a wall. (I am angry because of ___.) Otherwise you had a beam of red feeling searching vainly through the universe. You had a heart that shot red light into space.

Kiwi shivered in his sheets. These, too, were rentals. "Prison linens," Leo called them, although Kiwi sort of liked their stripes, which were wood-duck gray and a mustardy gold and indisputably ugly and which made Kiwi feel strangely at home. They looked like something his mom might have thoughtlessly plucked from the Goodwill bin. His mom in the Goodwill was like a girl in a field of dismal flowers.

I hate you, Dad, he tried again—but that old trick wasn't working. Lately his dad had started to shrink in his mind, too thin to blame the big crimes on (loss of home, loss of life).

Kiwi Bigtree contracted into his smallest self. He smothered his face with the pillow. At one point he opened his closet door and stared at the green poster of his mother, closed it. Minutes dripped red light down one edge of the bedside clock. He stared at the closet door and he called this state "sleep."

When Kiwi woke up at 7:09, he was a hero again. Everybody pounced in the break room. Barb from ticketing joked that she wanted Kiwi's autograph. Half a dozen employees who had seen his article blocked his path to the time clock. Yvans shook the front page of the *Loomis Register* at him. KIWI BIGTREE, "HELL'S ANGEL" the headline read, and below this, WORLD OF DARKNESS HERO.

One line four up from the bottom read: "And Kiwi Bigtree is no stranger to the water—he grew up on an 'alligator farm' in the swamp!"

A farm?

Two-thirds of the article was about Emily's "tunnel of light." Specialists were quoted next to their boxy photographs: a famous surgeon who claimed this tunnel was the happy fiction of a body deprived of oxygen, and a priest who called the light God.

Their debate on the cosmos was allotted one paragraph. Kiwi skipped it irritably, wondering: *But where is my* family*?*

Kiwi's real name appeared in every paragraph, but with each successive mention the words "Kiwi Bigtree" seemed to grow more remote from his own understanding of himself until the newsprint looked like runes, glyphs, an obsolete equation for sound. Kiwi read the letters K-I-W-I B-I-G-T-R-E-E as if he were staring at two squads of ants.

The final line was a quote from a World of Darkness director, Mr. Frank Saleti, whom he'd never met before: "We couldn't be prouder of his performance. Kiwi Bigtree is one of our finest employees."

"And that girl you saved was on *television,* Kiwi, did you see it?" Yvans spun him toward the mounted television set as if Kiwi might appear there again this moment like a face in a mirror. "Channel five, how you call that show with the crazy lady? The large-butted one with hair like a squirrel's tail? She seems like she is bipolar or something? Very hyper-acting?"

Kiwi knew the program. "Emily Barton was on *Jenny Just Spills It?*" This show was Loomis prime time and very popular with a certain histrionic-lady demographic. The eponymous host Jenny drank pots of coffee on air and often wept with her guests. Rescues were a regular feature. Kiwi had once watched Jenny interview a fire-truck dalmatian.

"What did Emily tell her? Did she use my real name?"

"That she had like a kind of a vision underwater." Yvans grinned with all his teeth. "She says she saw an angel. *You,* Kiwi."

Kiwi's shoulders flew up around his ears.

Deemer and Floricio, two of Ephraim Lippmann's thuggish buddies who had shunned Margaret Mead for weeks, now knocked into Kiwi Bigtree—in the friendly way—or punched him, in the friendly way, in the halls. "Saw you on TV, motherfucker! You're big-time!" Kiwi smiled warily back at them.

Nina Suárez stopped him in the Flukes to gush, "Did you watch the news? It's like we're *all* famous now!" She'd seen her bike in the parking lot when the news crew camera panned out.

"You must feel wonderful!" strangers kept insisting. "You must feel . . ."

But from eleven to two fifteen Kiwi felt like puking, and when that feeling at last subsided he felt nothing.

When Kiwi was three or four months old, the Chief had photographed him in a wicker laundry basket on a sandy kink of land in the Pit. Kiwi wasn't sure what the inspiration for this shot was: baby Moses meets Robert Louis Stevenson? Inside the photograph Kiwi had company: rat snakes and scarlet kings, thin ropes of them, and hatchling Seths with their yellow eyes bugged and wild around his clothespinned diaper. "My son didn't cry at all," the Chief told strangers at every opportunity. Everybody agreed that this was an auspicious image for a Bigtree wrestler. Baby Kiwi was wrinkled up with laughter, his pudgy fists swinging for the lens.

His parents had turned this image into a ten-by-fourteen-inch poster and sold hundreds of them to the tourists over the years.

"See, son?" The Chief liked to say, tapping the baby Kiwi in the poster. "What happened? You were brave as spit *then*."

Gus Waddell will have brought him the newspaper by now. He pictured the Chief lowering his coffee. His son, a World of Darkness employee! But a "hero," now. Did those two facts cancel one another out? Possibly the Chief would take the bus to the World of Darkness to look for him, he had to be prepared for that. Maybe the Chief was rolling toward him right now with a slow, inexorable rage, like a bowling ball . . .

Kiwi caught himself smiling at the thought. He smiled so hard that his eyes narrowed into crescents and began to water. And it was this grin that broke the news to the rest of him—Kiwi realized then that he would really love to see his father.

Attendance at the Leviathan spiked by 20 percent during the week following the "Hell's Angel" story. People wanted to meet him, to pump his hands and thank him for some reason, as if he had saved them personally. They posed for snapshots in front of "the Lake where it happened."

"Are *you* religious?" Lost Souls asked him. "Do *you* believe in angels?"

"No," Kiwi replied seriously. It was his kid sisters who believed in ghosts, angels, life after death, conjuring spells. "I am not. I do not. Who knows what Emily Barton thinks she saw down there, but I can tell you with one hundred percent certainty that I am not a literal angel, no."

He gave several dozen autographs as Kiwi Bigtree, Hell's Angel. As he signed he'd feel the bones inside his back clench against these credulous people, unaccountably furious.

"Ticket sales are up twenty-two percent this week," Mr. Jenks reported grudgingly on Friday, reading off an enormous legal pad that said MEMOS. Many of Mr. Jenks's managerial accessories were labeled in a font sized for the legally blind.

"So enjoy your fifteen minutes, Bigtree . . . ," Carl grunted through the roll of tape in his mouth. Back home a roll of duct tape in your mouth meant you had an alligator's jaws in your fists, but Carl Jenks was just taping up cardboard.

"Can I help you, Carl?"

"No. I know how I want my things."

Carl was moving, or "being removed," by his own boss, the Carl of Carls, to the other side of the World. Lamentably, he said, he would still be Kiwi's supervisor. Orcs and pencils disappeared into the box.

"I hope you know how lucky you are," Carl Jenks muttered. "The training alone is a huge company investment. They've hired a private CFI who brags that he taught his semideaf nine-year-old niece how to fly. Promises even you can pass the check ride. If you ask me you're a bad investment—who is going to remember this Lake of Fire story a week from now?—but Tom Barrett saw your picture in the paper this morning and he's just giddy about it. Thinks we're going to get all this free publicity, and new clients from the 'crystals-are-my-medicine' crowd. New Agers."

"Right. All that miraculous bullshit." Kiwi felt the stab that accompanied all thoughts of Osceola. He could see her face smiling under the goofy puple turban.

"Barrett doesn't get many ideas, so when he has one he likes he throws a lot of money behind it."

"Yes. Got it. Ideas need money to become a reality."

Kiwi rocked way back on his red-and-black sneakers ($22) with his hands in his pockets, as if he were vying to become a Human Slingshot. He had no idea what Carl was talking about.

"What I'm telling you, Bigtree, is that HR is casting against type. The Loomis directors want you as one of the Four Pilots. They think it'll be *cute*—" Carl's smile went taut. "That girl Emily Barton is going on all the news outlets and calling you her 'angel.' So that's how they want to bill you."

The office was almost empty now, the walls bare except for glue and pegs. A World of Darkness calendar was the last thing left to pack, and Kiwi felt a rueful stab as he thought of the Bigtrees' own calendar. Kiwi's face was always the mascot for July, and for one month each year he grinned out at himself from the gift shop's walls with a ferocious self-hatred, desperate for August to come.

"To be honest, I doubt they'll let you fly in the end. What are you, twelve? I'm shocked it's even legal for you to get a pilot's license, frankly. Probably they'll use you as a stewardess. Give you a little beverage tray and a catcher's mitt to nab the Lost Souls' vomit, you'll excel at that. I'm just telling you for your own sake: Don't get your hopes up. Don't let your hopes get higher than your girlish hips."

Kiwi reddened; it was true that he'd become a little pear-shaped. Burger Burger portions. All the pizza.

"Excuse me, Bigtree."

Carl patted Kiwi's wingless back and picked up a large box.

That afternoon, Kiwi conducted an intake interview with the Take to the Skies flight school on Carl Jenks's new office phone, with Carl Jenks's forehead visible behind the computer. Kiwi felt an incredible power over this man. To be envied was a new experience. Just the sound of Kiwi dialing made Carl's forehead wrinkle and smooth. His boss's skin was the pasty, poreless color of cake batter. Sad evidence, the Chief would have said, of a lifetime spent indoors. *And when the Chief sees me skyed inside a cockpit? What will he have to say about that?*

"You're that Hell's Angel kid?" a voice was saying. "The one that saved Teddy Barton's girl?"

"I'm Kiwi Bigtree."

"Well, you sure screwed up these forms that you faxed us pretty good, Kiwi Bigtree. They're just about illegible. You're how old, son?"

"Eighteen. Almost."

"Almost. So that would make you seventeen, correct?"

"Right."

"Excellent. You can fly solo at fourteen, but older is better. How tall?"

"Six five," Kiwi lied, shifting his weight onto his toes in Carl's office.

"What on earth are you doing, prima ballerina?" Carl muttered from behind the computer.

"How's your vision? You got your medical certificate yet?"

"No, sir."

"You need to get that. High school diploma?"

"I'm attending the Rocklands High nontraditional student program, sir. Night school."

"Degree expected?"

"Oh!" said Kiwi, misunderstanding the question. "Yes, definitely. I want to get several. The MA, and the PhD as well."

"What *year* will you receive your high school degree?"

Kiwi was silent. Somehow he could more easily imagine his graduation from Harvard University in five years than any of the intervening steps. The prospect of actually passing Miss Arenas's final exam next month and transferring his single credit to Rocklands High School was so overwhelming to him that it temporarily short-circuited his brain.

"It's sunny out today, Mr. Bigtree, why not be optimistic? I'm going to put down 'September.' Okay, you're all set in the computer. First class is Tuesday. Three thirty. You can do the lesson modules at the public library. I'll put your Reach for the Skies! packet in the mail."

Life was a phonograph in an empty room. The World was a silent record, turning. *Whatever song we are making in this place, we are going to die without hearing.* Such was Kiwi's stoned thinking on a rainy Tuesday at 1:30 p.m., with five hours and fourteen minutes of his shift left to go. He was back to pushing the vacuum again, filling in for Leonard.

"Cover for me," Leo had commanded Kiwi that morning. "My thumb feels wrong."

"Your thumb?"

"Both of them," Leonard said slyly. As a dedicated malingerer Leo set a new standard; even his lies were lazy. "Both thumbs hurt now. I think I slept on them or something. You have to cover for me."

Which was fine by Kiwi, because now he'd have ten hours of overtime this week. After taxes, this boosted his salary by $43.12.

Yesterday—two Mondays after his "miraculous resuscitation" of Emily Barton—he'd gotten on the number 14 city bus after his shift with no real destination in mind, happy to pay a buck seventy to get out of the World. He'd wound up riding it all the way to the ferry docks. It was raining when Kiwi climbed down from the bus. A black cat was stalking a fat, doofy pelican across the cement landing; Gus's ferryboat and a few misused U-RENT kayaks were moored there. The ferry had received a fresh coat of paint, a spectacularly ugly gourd orange. Nobody was around. FERRY SERVICE SUSPENDED UNTIL FURTHER NOTICE said a sign on the gangplank. Kiwi sat through the intensifying rain for an hour and fifty minutes, the time it took for the bus to repeat its loop, and for that entire period he stared in the direction of the island. Slowly it sank in that he couldn't get home that afternoon, even if he'd wanted to. Kiwi could feel this thought descending from his brain to his lungs, where it winnowed like a noose. *You're stuck here, kid,* Kiwi imagined the Chief saying in his microphone voice, a booming, put-on friendliness. *We need you and you're nowhere.*

Lost Souls percolated around him in the Leviathan, sightlessly munching at diabolical corn chips or tugging up their bathing straps. A few of the tiny kids were wearing Whalehead hats, foam skullcaps in orca whites and blacks that looked vaguely French, monastic, cost $17.99, and disintegrated—Lost Souls were always complaining—in the wash. Kiwi Bigtree seemed to have hit minute fourteen of his fifteen minutes of fame. It had been over a week since Emily Barton did her last TV interview about "the angel" whom she had seen underwater and later pegged as the human lifeguard Kiwi Bigtree. Since Monday he'd signed only three autographs. Lost Souls still stopped him in the halls, but most of them needed to validate their parking ticket, or urinate.

Heaven, Kiwi thought, would be the reading room of a great library. But it would be private. Cozy. You wouldn't have to worry about some squeaky-shoed librarian turning the lights off on you or gauging your literacy by reading the names on your book spines, and there wouldn't be a single other patron. The whole place would hum with a library's peace, filtering softly over you like white bars of light . . .

Kiwi grunted; someone had written BOOTY FUCK THE MOTHER-FUCKERS on the wall beside the escalator to the Jaws. Where was his paintbrush?

Heaven would be a comfy armchair, Kiwi decided, rubbing at expletives with his elbow. Beige and golden upholstery, beige and golden wallpaper (what he was actually picturing here, he realized, was the pattern of his mother's brown rosettes on their curtains). You'd get a great, private phonograph, and all of eternity to listen to your life's melody. You could isolate your one life out of the cacophonous galaxy—the a cappella version—or you could play it back with its accompaniment, embedded in the brass and strings of mothers, fathers, sisters, windfalls and failures, percussive cities of strangers. You could play it forward or backward, back and back, and listen to the future of your past. You could lift the needle at whim, defeating Time.

Roaring erupted from the high, angled vents that lined the Leviathan—it began all at once, as sudden as a flood of rainfall. The white intrusion that makes you aware of what the silence had been before. Kiwi paused with his hands in the bucket.

Mom? Kiwi shuddered, feeling immediately stupid.

"Whadduppp, Bigtree!" Sergio from concessions appeared in one of the labyrinthine hallways, wheeling a trash can behind him. His name tag was coming loose on its pin and the great red moose fans of his devil horns hung around his scrawny neck.

"I thought I was the last fool in the World. Weird to be inside the Leviathan so late, right? That air conditioner sounds like a fucking hurricane, bro! I'm *freezing.*"

On Monday, Kiwi got special permission to leave work early and get his medical certificate for the FAA licensing requirement. He'd thought about making the appointment with the Bigtrees' family physician, Dr. Budz, a liver-spotted Ukrainian man who was sort of mentally spotty as well—who did not, for example, require that his patients have insurance or even legally viable surnames; who'd instructed the Bigtree tribe to call him Al in an accent thickened by his weird humor, and whose office was above a women's gymnasium. You could hear the basketballs drumming as he stethoscoped your heartbeat. No one had seen Dr. Budz since the previous fall, when Hilola's medical needs introduced them to a new class of death specialist.

Instead, Kiwi made the appointment through the World-contracted flight school with an AMA-accredited physician. The office was in the fanciest part of Loomis, where the buildings were identical pastels and weepy-eyed with windows; even their decorative plants had this sort of futuristic sheen that said, "I'm germless."

Kiwi had to answer pages and pages of questions about himself. Nope to measles, never to mumps, scabies, diabetes. He'd had two weeklong bouts of weird dreaming and terrible chills when he was six that his mom referred to as "grasshopper fever," but who knew how that illness translated into mainland etiology? Old crackers in the swamp used bear piss to cure chicken pox. One section of the form was called "Family History." *Well, for starters, my sixteen-year-old sister is crazy, she has aural and visual hallucinations . . . my youngest sister is an equestrian of Mesozoic lizards . . . my father wears a headdress . . . my grandfather bites men now . . .*

The doctor's office smelled like lemon disinfectant and even the big-shouldered leather furniture made him very nervous.

"Oh, Mr. Bigtree!" the receptionist called after him. "You forgot one. No, don't get up, hon. I'll fill it in for you. I just need your home address."

"The World of Darkness" fell lightly from his lips, Kiwi noticed.

The private CFI the World of Darkness had hired to train him was an ex-army guy in his early sixties, Dennis Pelkis, or Denny, as he kept encouraging Kiwi to call him. "Relax, relax," Denny would say, and then he'd proceed to regale Kiwi with some story about a former student who fell out of the sky. In every case these tragedies had occurred because the student pilot failed to obey the teachings of Dennis. He kept referring to "Denny's ground rules" and "Denny's philosophy on that issue," with open arms and a tour operator's smile, as if he were giving Kiwi a cultural orientation to the country of Denny. Dennis Pelkis had silvery chest hair and a satyr's physique. He smiled at Kiwi in a sightless, professional way, a smile that faltered only slightly when Kiwi asked him, apropos of nothing, if he and Mrs. Pelkis had ever been to a place called Swamplandia! to see Hilola Bigtree wrestle alligators.

"I'm sorry?"

"Sorry," Kiwi mumbled, which was the usual volley. "Thought you looked familiar . . ." Really, Kiwi had hoped that *his* face would look familiar to this Denny. On those rare occasions when Kiwi found a mainlander who knew about Swamplandia!, even secondhand, he went after their memories like a magpie tugging at bright string. He'd strike up conversations with the Lost Souls in the Leviathan and engineer an opportunity to ask them, *Say, have you ever visited Swamplandia!?* A few days ago he'd met a couple from Sarasota, Florida, who began nodding immediately when he mentioned the Bigtrees.

"Oh, right, those alligator people," the wife had laughed. "I remember that place. Swampy Land. That woman alligator wrestler, Don, what was her name, we used to pass her billboard on the way to your sister's . . . ?"

Hilola!

Whenever tourists remembered her name, men with beards included, Kiwi wanted to passionately kiss them. Her name in a stranger's mouth was a resurrection: however briefly, she was alive with him again. Even that little shove could roll back the tomb. On those rare and wonderful occasions when he found an entire mainland family who had seen his mother's show, Kiwi could watch the strangers' eyes brighten with recognition and picture a tiny Hilola Bigtree climbing a tiny ladder in each of their brains, walking out to the edge of the green diving board.

Dennis Pelkis coughed once and resumed a rolling discourse about the World of Darkness floatplanes versus "terra firma" aircraft. He punctuated his major points by jabbing a lit cigarette at the sun.

"Soon it will be time to fly," he concluded. This was also the title of the 630-page flight instruction manual that he handed over to Kiwi. Kiwi had a polynomials test this week in Miss Arenas's class and he was picking up shifts for Yvans; lately Kiwi felt like an understudy in his own life on the mainland, stumbling over his lines and missing important cues and waiting with less and less patience for the real actor to show up.

"I can't wait," Kiwi said sincerely. He was thinking about money.

From Denny's explanation of the pilot licensing requirements, it sounded like he and this cheerful and alarming man were going to spend forty hours together in the plane and twenty more in ground school—four months.

"Longer than a Vegas marriage," he grinned, and Kiwi let out an accidental whimper. The kind of grief that shows up at a Halloween party with its costume in tatters, swears "I'm a chuckle!" What if Swamplandia! went into foreclosure before he got his license, his pay raise?

"Ha-ha! Four months does sound like a long time. And there's no way to, ah, expedite the process?"

"Ex-speed-ite." Denny frowned. "You sure that's how it's pronounced? We can't speed anything, Bigtree. Same FAA rules apply for heroes."

Kiwi frowned down at his fingernails. "Your hands are damn pretty," Sawtooth used to say accusingly. Like most alligator wrestlers, Sawtooth Bigtree had lost substantial chunks of several fingers. Part of his thumb was somewhere in the Gator Pit, remaindered by one of the Seths. Even Ossie boasted scars from an accident that took place when she was four years old and a juvenile alligator had snapped at her hand while she was pulling up weeds along a riverbank. Kiwi was the only Bigtree with zero injuries—no stitches, no scars. He'd once cut his pointer finger opening a can of cherry soda after a wrestling match. He tried to imagine his ladylike hands throttling up inside a floatplane.

"Do you happen to know, sir, what my ranking is going to be? Second? Third?"

"Huh? That ain't how the check ride gets scored."

Kiwi nodded. "I recognize that I probably won't rank as the First Pilot of the Apocalypse, given that I am an airplane greenhorn. But do I necessarily have to be the last one?"

Denny exhaled two cool gusts of smoke through his nostrils and stared at him.

"You're a funny young man, Kiwi."

On Thursday, Kiwi found himself ducking the crack in the break room door, where he got a brief glimpse of a bunch of flame-clad staffers

watching TV, and then he was pinball-whizzing out of the World:
upstairs, downstairs, through staff-only hallways. There was an empire
of supplies down here: pyramids of toilet paper (single ply; this was
Hell), boxes of BrimStones that spilled over the cardboard like collapsed speech bubbles, devil horn hatbands and devilish ribbons for the
ladies. Finally he exploded through the same small service hole that
spat out garbage. Yvans was standing right there by the Dumpster,
waving at him.

"Where you going, Kiwi?"

So much for the secret mission.

"Nowhere," he said, hurrying past Yvans. Really, he had no time
today to listen to Yvans complain about the complaints of his wife.
Kiwi's secret destination was the gas station. You couldn't really skulk
there, you had to walk across the highway. Kiwi walked through four
lanes of stalled traffic. A knotted sock of quarters bulged in his pocket.
The pay phone was at the end of the candy aisle. It was the nearest
semiprivate phone that Kiwi knew about. He hunched between the
black- and yellow-jacketed candy bars and the gigantic freezer. For
twenty minutes Kiwi kept plunking the same quarter in the phone and
dialing Swamplandia!

"Answer," he commanded the receiver. "Pick up."

The phone was busy. Busy! Busy! Busy! Busy! it told his ear in black
starbursts.

Weird, Kiwi thought, which became:

Bad.

Wrong.

Really fucking worrisome, as a mainland kid would say.

The busy signal whammed into his head in a series of right hooks.
He rolled his quarter out, dialed again. "Ava. Ossie. Chief," he said
between teeth. After a while he switched the speed and order: "Chief-
Ossie-Ava. Ossie-Ava-Chief. Pick. Up."

The owner dropped his newspaper and stood. He was an older Afro-
Cuban man with powdery hair and eyes like acetone. He didn't like
Kiwi—he'd sell Black and Mild cigarettes to Leo and Vijay but never to
Kiwi. The cigarettes cost one dollar and came in two flavors: wine and
apple. The last time Kiwi had tried to buy a pack with his fake Kiwi
Beamtray ID, the owner had shouted at him to get out of the store. A

curtain of pink and green lottery tickets hung level with his forehead, which gave him an exotic, Scheherazade look.

"Hey! In the back!" He unlatched the little gate to the register. *"¿Qué haces?"*

"Hey, sir!" said Kiwi. "Good afternoon?" *Maybe he thinks I'm making sex calls,* Kiwi thought, his ear smashed and rubbery against the receiver. *Masturbating into the CLOSET OF ICE!*

He dropped another quarter into the slot, watched his fingers hopscotch across the dial pad onto his home numbers. *Last try. Okay, no, this is the last try*—he began threatening the receiver, trying to bluff the universe into giving him an answer.

"Hang up the phone, *maricón!*"

"I'm not doing anything wrong here. I'm a hero, sir. Hell's Angel. Don't you watch TV?"

Kiwi hung up the phone. He tried to mad-dog the owner and then gave up, felt his face tremble and collapse. On the way out he knocked over a display of gummies.

"Sorry," he said, rubbing his cheeks with his fists, a teenage mantis. "God, sir, I'm really sorry."

The owner held the door for him. He patted Kiwi's left shoulder.

All that day and into the next his head felt clouded. Where was everybody? Were they visiting Grandpa or something? Had the Chief instructed the girls not to answer the telephone—were they avoiding the creditors? Probably he was overreacting? Kiwi pictured all ninety-eight Seths in the pit lifting their great warblers' chins at the sun while just inside the screen door the telephone rang and rang and rang.

Kiwi Bigtree, Hell's Angel, got a leather jacket from the World of Darkness management with his new epithet emblazoned on it. He got a free Friday. He stood in his jacket and waved sightlessly into the lanes of traffic until a green Toyota that was batwinged with dents on its left side honked at him, screeched to a halt well before the intersection.

"Hello again, Mr. Pelkis."

"Oh My Christ Son the Light Is Green Get in the Car!"

Kiwi was relieved when Dennis Pelkis told him that they were just going to eyeball the plane. He drove Kiwi to the papaya-colored seaplane hangar off Route 302 where the flight school conducted their lessons. He taught Kiwi how the water rudder and the floats worked and walked him through a preflight checklist. It took Kiwi two tries and a rump-assist from Denny to scrabble over the gap between the dock and the plane and get inside the cockpit.

Later Dennis drove Kiwi to his house in the Coconut Creek development, in a suburb of Loomis, so that Denny could have black coffee and a roast beef sandwich that was hemorrhaging horseradish, treat a corn on his big right toe, watch the ball game; and also so that Kiwi could take a test on the pitot-static instrument family. Kiwi felt sort of forgotten about. Kiwi pictured his existence in the mind of Dennis Pelkis: a tiny Kiwi politely letting Dennis's other concerns cut in front of him in line at the register until he was the last priority, the afterthought.

The test was easy. Kiwi had retained most of the colorful facts from the textbook:

A white arc indicates the arc in which it is safe to use flaps.

The green arc is the normal operating range of the aircraft.

The yellow arc is the caution range for the airplane.

"More apple juice, Kee-wee?" asked Denny's dotty wife, whose hostessing strategy was to remove each item from her refrigerator—a carton of juice, a pie slice with lime green filling, a single egg—and offer it to Kiwi. She did this with the serene efficiency of a crazy person; was this a custom of the suburbs?

"No thank you, ma'am."

"Too bad they don't make *kiwi* juice, right?"

"Ha-ha, right. Thanks, Mrs. Pelkis."

I am going to be a pilot, you bitch! Kiwi thought. His rage felt wonderful, like cake icing in his mouth. Pure lipids dissolving onto his taste buds. Kiwi didn't care for middle-aged women. He found them all to be ugly, flighty, soft. Their wrinkles enraged him. Their dyed or graying hair. All the obvious, dimpled evidence that they had enjoyed years and years of life.

Coming into the kitchen, Denny rolled his eyes at Kiwi and barked at his wife: "Kid has to take a test, Nancy."

Now that Kiwi had at last made it to a suburb it was easy to want the swamp. What was this fresh hell? The World of Darkness seemed like a cozy and benign place compared to the sprawl of these stucco boxes, these single-family houses. Kiwi saw no coconuts and no creeks. The Pelkises had a poinciana tree dragging magenta combs over the grass and a bunch of rusting croquet wickets in the yard. Inside, they had a Wurlitzer piano and a mantel covered in what appeared to be hundreds of tiny porcelain cats. The Pelkises' decor was such a clean and pleasant variation on the Bigtrees' cabinets of gin and lizards that Kiwi found himself holding tightly to the edge of the Pelkises' Lysoled table, as if these shiny surfaces were trying to buck him. Instead of a Juggernaut Human Cannon, they had a green Toyota. Instead of a Gator Pit, their backyard had a shrunken plastic house that contained an animate cotton ball that turned out to be a dog.

"That's the wife's Pomeranian," Denny said, following Kiwi's gaze. "Vol de Nuit. She gave him a French name. Do I look like I speak French, son? The wife does a lot of things that just mystify me. Totally worthless animal."

My dad would feed your dog to the Seth of Seths.

"How we doing?" Denny asked forty minutes later. He was on his fourth plain doughnut and listening to baseball on the radio. He looked over the page in front of Kiwi.

"Well! You must have memorized that whole dang chapter." He planted the doughnut into milk. "But you know, son, this test, strictly speaking, doesn't count for anything? These are for practice. It's the FAA written exam you gotta pass. And then you gotta actually fly the damn plane."

Kiwi nodded. "Right." He covered his test with his palm and slid it toward his edge of the table.

"See you next Friday. We'll see what happens when we get you airborne."

The Jaws were terrifying at night. Something gaseous seemed to shimmer around them, a trick of the weak lighting and the ventilation. The molars shone like huge basalt blocks and everything looked suddenly, impressively real to Kiwi, the giant cave of the maw arching forty feet above him, the web of puce and ruby mesh shot through with dangling yellowish gray threads on the roof. A luxury of being the only rider in the Leviathan was that you could drift for hours. You could let the current conduct you. Also it was a good study break, Kiwi thought.

At two o'clock, after finishing the last of his homework, Kiwi stripped to his boxer shorts and climbed the frozen escalator up the Tongue. He crossed his arms in the SAFEST POSTURE depicted on the sign and he flew down the slide into the first of a seemingly infinite number of brachiating chambers—caves of water, some neck-deep and others shallow as dishes. The Leviathan felt bigger than he had ever imagined, impossibly big. The white points of his knees looked like distant buoys in the darkness. Kiwi's mouth slammed shut and his teeth hit together as he flew around a bend in the Esophagus, and then he was submerged in deep water, his feet cycling and touching nothing.

Usually at this juncture one of the more athletic park employees would drag you up and bully you out of the pool and into another tortuous line—the Leviathan staff moved four hundred people through the ride each hour. Some kid's feet would be punching into your back.

Kiwi shut his eyes and breathed very slowly. At night he felt less like a kid than a sick calculator. He ran the same problems and numbers in his head. *What am I doing here?* Kiwi wondered. *Why don't I go home?* The longer he stayed in this place, the less he understood about his own motivations. *But the World of Darkness gets me!* Kiwi thought. *The World has me gotten.* The World of Darkness seemed to understand its workers the way that floating sticks got understood by a river, and studied to splinters, and undone by it.

Kiwi floated from room to room with his palms up. He got sucked beneath a grid of radiance, little stars that glowed blue and lime green above him—as if the roof of the Leviathan had suddenly opened onto the real sky! And with his own eyes filling with salt and his total spatial disorientation, the slow flow of the water, the turgor of a nonsensical hope in his body that grew and grew beneath the stars and left him airless, bewildered, so very unexpectedly happy—over the roar of his own happiness it took Kiwi a long time to understand that the blue and green galaxies spooning above him, blinking down in some holy binary, were actually banks of emergency lights.

CHAPTER SEVENTEEN

Ava's Eclipse

There were thousands of stars above us—that much I knew from the neon hour blinking on my watchface. We couldn't see any stars from our skiff because they were trapped behind the storm. Fifteen minutes after Whip left us, rain began to pound the slough.

"I'm sorry. I got nervous."

"Jesus, kid."

"I shouldn't have told about the dredge."

"You almost blew it for us. You almost cost us our best chance at saving your sister."

"I know," I said miserably.

A mosquito crawled out from the feathers at his collar. It drifted up and landed on my nose, its little wings sawing the air. *My sister is alone out here,* I remembered, watching it bob between my eyes.

"That was a close call." When the Bird Man was angry, he sounded like anyone to me, like a blue-haired tourist demanding a refund. "We could have both gotten into some serious trouble. Imagine the hassle that man could have kicked up for me . . ."

I nodded, blinking mightily. The mosquito flew off. I was thinking that I had made a bad mistake, maybe. We were miles from any telephones, from the airboats with their UHF radios, from the city ferry. Back home, I could have placed a simple call to Search and Rescue and the whole rescue operation would have been out of my hands. I could have called my dad . . .

"You want to turn back?" The Bird Man peered out at me from the rain-sleeked hood of his coat. His mood was on the downswing now. Light caught on his whistle and in the soft, wet curls of hair around his ears, but his eyes were dull as gunmetal. "Say the word, kid."

I took a breath. "I think I want to turn back, yes."

"Kid, I've been poling for two days. We're knocking at the door."

"I'll still pay you when we get home!" This came out as a cry, startling us both. I hadn't expected my voice to sound that way. The Bird Man gave me a sidelong look of bad disappointment. For a while there was no noise from the stern beyond the air in the oarlocks, the hull's regular lift and slap. The glade skiff nosed forward.

"I just . . . I'm really worried here?" I kept my gaze fixed on the blue quicks of my fingernails. "I think we made a mistake."

"You need to be brave now, Ava," the Bird Man told me seriously. I scooted forward a little and snuck my knee under his gloved hand. I liked the weight of the heavy metal buckle on my bare skin. When I leaned into him I was safe, I was pinned in space.

"Have you ever heard of Bianca Defiore and Michael Taylor?" the Bird Man asked quietly.

I shook my head.

"They went on their first date on Michael's airboat, launched from Viper Bight at sunset for a little scenic tour. And then Mikey got lost."

"Out here?"

"In a similar nowhere. He hit a tree that cut their gas line. He stranded them on the saw-grass prairie with food and water for one night. Bianca had a diabetic attack while they were waiting for Search and Rescue and she died, Ava. With all of their technology it was fourteen days before they found Mr. Michael Taylor, half-looney with his dead acquaintance in his arms."

I shivered. "So, they goofed up one time. The swamp's a big place . . ."

I got an image of Whip Jeters putzing around on his boat with his anemic flashlight.

"And don't forget, these are people who have gotten into bad scrapes, yes, but they are *here*. They are in our world. They *can* be found by Search and Rescue," he said slowly, checking my eyes for understanding.

"Right . . . I know." I took the Bird Man's hand. I was close enough to see the red canoes above his eyelids, the hazel lines that shot through his gray irises. You could stand this close to a Bird Man, or any man, I thought with wonderment, and still not guess what was in his mind.

While we were talking I let my fingers slide through his fingers, not really thinking about what I was doing, and he relaxed his own long fingers, squeezed down. The knit of our hands on his lap looked so distant from either of us, like a sculpture we'd made. My small fingers pushed inside the pallid roses of his knuckles. One knuckle had a raised scar on it, nasty as a tattoo; I saw older scars, too, from beaks or maybe talons. I figured this for evidence that the Bird Man was a powerful fighter, like my father and my mother and my grandmother and my grandfather, and hopefully, one day, myself.

"You've got a wrestler's grip there, kid," he said, smiling down at our fist. "Look, Ava—"

He jabbed a thumb up, and I started at the chaotic movement of our map. Three buzzards were crashing around on the wind a little ways behind us.

"You think Search and Rescue can find the back entrance of the underworld? You think Mr. Jeters can read a map like that? You're on the edge of the universe, kid, and you don't even know it."

We rounded a bend and I groaned inwardly. The wind tilled the saw grass for miles and miles in every useless direction. We were going to have to carry the skiff for another long, mucky stretch. "The edge of the universe," I repeated, and picked up the dripping handle of my oars.

Another portage of a quarter mile, and hard rain when we got back on the water. We both had pulled our slickers on—it was strange to see the Bird Man's feathers pasted below the yellow plastic. He kept scratching his head, and he seemed more genuinely agitated now than I'd seen him at any point on this trip. It was a little frightening. He'd scratched his thin hair into a pompadour—it looked as though every wire were coming disconnected in his brain. I thought about making a joke about it (we used to tease Kiwi when he woke up with Amadeus Mozart hair, for example), but the Bird Man's eyes warned me away from doing so. They mirrored the storm.

And then my breath caught, because we had arrived. Two great humps rose in the rain before us. I could see the gigantic swells of them not fifty yards away.

"We made it? That's the Eye?"

The Eye had been described to me as a kind of Calusa Scylla and Charybdis, and I'd seen Grandpa's grainy photograph, but I hadn't been prepared for the overwhelming strangeness of seeing the mounds' weird, pyramidal shapes up close. They rose out of the river like twin volcano peaks. They were perfectly denuded of trees or any green growth, fogged over by the rainstorm and made of what looked like lunar cement, whelk, and conch. The two middens that formed the Eye were a kissing cousins' distance from each other. A tall man could have easily jumped from one mound to its neighbor. Water cut between them in a perfectly straight gray line; the channel couldn't have been much more than four feet at its widest point. It was going to be a squeeze for us; no way could an entire dredge barge pass through the Eye; if Ossie and Louis had come this way, they would have had to abandon the barge somewhere and use the dredge scow, a tiny red canoe hung over the barge's stern like a wooden eyebrow. The scow didn't have a motor; she and Louis would have had to paddle *hard*. Which was exactly what the Bird Man wanted me to do now, apparently—to push our skiff into the portal.

"Come on, kid, put some real muscle into it."

The Bird Man's hair was hanging in his eyes and I didn't understand the expression on his face. *Maybe he's scared, or angry? Because he's been this way before,* I thought, *because he knows . . .* but I couldn't begin to imagine what he might know. We paddled hard against the wind and current and yet we weren't making any progress; it felt as if our skiff were pinned beneath the wind's great thumb.

"You think we can get through that?" I shouted. "Shouldn't we find a place to wait this out?"

We paddled into the chop with spray flying at our faces. An easterly knocked us sideways and we aimed our bow for a blue breath between the rocks that I did not think we could make.

"This is our window, kid."

The humps of broken shells rose around us. We had to pull ourselves through the passage with our hands—if the bow had twisted a few inches to the right or left we would have gotten hung up. The Bird Man put on his helmet and switched on the headlamp, it had gotten that dark. Shells glittered on either side of us like defunct treasure, washed a pearly rose and dish blue that glowed against the sky. The water was as narrow as a hallway, lapping the tall white walls of shells, and the green column of air on the other side of the tunnel stood open like a door. The underworld is coming next, I thought, and the muscles in my stomach tensed the way they did before a show. "Where is my SISTER?" I moaned through my teeth, too tired now for real hysteria but more determined than I'd ever been to find her.

Probably if I had waited even a few seconds longer to glance at the sky, I wouldn't have seen her ribbon: a flag of purple snagged amid the toothy piles of whelk. "Ossie!" I shouted out loud, but the Bird Man didn't hear me over the wind. I imagined the ribbon catching there as she tried to squeeze through, her hair flying out in a white fan around her face. I stood up, keeping my arms on the shell mound so that I didn't overturn the skiff, and I reached onto my toes to grab it; in the process I nearly fell out of the shallow hull, and the Bird Man had to grab my waist and jerk me down again.

"Have you gone crazy? Sit down, sit down!"

I gaped up at him.

"I said *sit*," he screamed over the wind. "This is nowhere to capsize!"

"I just wanted a souvenir," I called, and showed him the opal fragments of shell that I'd dislodged into my palm when I went for the ribbon. The ribbon itself I stuffed quickly into my pocket and didn't explain. I still don't know why I did this; somehow it seemed a smart secret to keep for the moment. I thought this ribbon must be a message from Ossie and I wanted time to puzzle it out on my own—it could be an arrow pointing me toward her, I thought. Or a new kind of map. It didn't occur to me then that there might be a darker explanation for my discovery.

"Ava! Ship your paddle, kid, use your hands . . ."

He seemed angry with me but there was no time for a lecture: we were midway through the Eye. There was no space to row anymore so we were pushing our way forward with our palms on the brittle sides of the middens. Behind me I could hear the Bird Man's pole striking shell. The air gushing into my throat felt hot as exhaust, and it was all I could do to keep my hands moving along the walls.

The rain stopped as suddenly as it began. After five minutes we were totally clear of it. In the clarifying light that spilled between the live oaks I looked for proof that we had arrived in the underworld.

"I keep telling you, kid, this is the *shallow* end." The Bird Man rubbed at the creases on his forehead. Why did adults always do that? I wondered. What if a face really worked like that, like rumpled trousers, and you could smooth out your bad thoughts from the outside in? I had thought he might share my happiness—we had made it through, and now we could find Ossie! Wasn't that right? I crumpled a little; we'd arrived but there was no celebration or encouragement in his pale eyes.

"I got cut really bad," I said, to say something. "On my hands." Wordlessly he tipped a few drops from his bottle of green medicine onto our deepest cuts and we watched the white bubbles open like a million tiny mouths. This time I did not say one word about love.

"The freak show happens inside the circus tent, kid; we're just at the entrance to the fairgrounds. No ghosts, not yet. Does that hurt you?"

I shook my head. He petted my hair and I smiled back at him help-lessly, Ossie momentarily forgotten. With a twinge of shame I mussed up my hair again, hoping he'd lean in once more and smooth it. But the Bird Man did not touch or look at me again; he stretched the knit of his fingers and returned to his poling platform. I placed the red Seth on my lap and let her sun, soothed by her small weight there. Her sides col-lapsed dramatically with each exhalation and her belly felt cool and dry.

Already I had seen a few gars in the water, and tiny green herons. They had all looked conventionally alive to me, although who knew what the rules of this underworld were? I'd expected the weather to be icy, or at least a few degrees colder. I touched my hand to the rocky beach where we were resting and let a golden bug crawl onto my thumb. Dozens of legs combed up my bare arm, and for a second I felt almost joyful.

"Ossie!" I called. "Ossie?"

You be alive, too, I told her. I looked down until my vision blurred and watched the beetle crawling onto my shoulder.

"Do you think we'll run into the rest of the dredge crew out here?" I asked. I had just seen something squatting on all fours behind the cab-bage palms. A crocodile, I thought. You can tell from the teeth.

The Bird Man pulled his hat down. "It's possible, kid. Stranger things have happened."

"Do you think we might run into my mother?"

I picked up a clot of moss with my paddle, dunked it. I hated how little my voice sounded when I asked the question.

The Bird Man gave me a look I couldn't read and then nodded once, quickly. "I told you, it's possible. Anything's possible. Right now we're only in the shallows of the underworld, the threshold . . ."

After that we didn't speak again for a long time. The underworld was unbelievably fecund. I saw snail kites, which I hadn't seen in such numbers since I was nine or ten, and a virgin stand of mahogany. Wood storks' heads appeared like ancient doorknobs along the branches. *We are in the* underworld *now,* I thought, kneeing forward in the skiff and looking around. *We have crossed over; we could at any moment find my sister!* But the pink sun was so hot here, and this landscape was not the landscape promised in the book. This landscape looked like our backyard. I saw lonely pine keys, cormorants, broken rock.

We stopped in a brush-filled cove, drank from the canteens. A Seth blinked incuriously at us, curled on the dark sand amid the palmetto fronds.

You could become a fossil in your lifetime, I'd discovered. I'd seen the eerie correspondence between the living Seths in our Pit and their taxidermied brothers in our museum. The Chief could achieve an ossified quality, too, with his headdress skeletally flattened against the sofa back, drunk and asleep.

"Is that one alive or dead, Bird Man?"

He was busy with the baling bucket and he didn't hear me, or maybe chose to ignore me. I threaded all my fingers through the wooden holes in the crate carrier; the red Seth regarded me from a triangle of shadow. The wedge of our bow pushed into a dark spot on the water, where rain came shaking off the trees. I'd tied Osceola's purple ribbon around my wrist—so tightly, the Bird Man grumbled, that it looked like a tourniquet. I waited for him to ask where the ribbon had come from but he seemed to think it was one of mine, original to our journey.

Somewhere, possibly just a few hundred yards to the east or the west of us on one of these tree islands, Ossie's hair was blowing in this same wind that rippled the water at our bow. The Land of the Dead was windier than I had expected and as flat as a cracker and I had so many bug bites on my shins that the bumps overlapped. Mosquitoes were just as vicious here. I'd have to remember to tell that to my brother, I thought dizzily . . . I stared at the black mush on my ruby bruise where I'd slapped one and felt myself beginning to be sick. Kiwi would be taking assiduous Field Notes on the shallows of the underworld. He'd be skimming specimens off the water, or sketching the wings of undead mosquitoes. But why were the mosquitoes in the Land of the Dead so thirsty and noisy? Why did the fish jump just as high here as they did anywhere?

"Everything is alive here, Bird Man," I whispered, not wanting to offend anyone—it seemed a funny thing to mention if there were ghosts around.

"So far. Watch out that we don't get hung up on that—" The Bird Man pushed his pole against a submerged rock. "You'll find a mix of the living and the dead in the shallows."

"Oh. Right. That makes sense."

There are estuaries near Swamplandia! where salt water and fresh-water mingle, and it's a crazy party down there: manatees and ten-foot saltwater crocodiles and freshwater alligators, bottlenose dolphins and bluegill, soft-shell turtles.

"Hey, do you want to play twenty questions or something?" I called over my shoulder. At this point we were twenty minutes beyond the Eye. "Do you want to, uh, to talk?"

The Bird Man shook his head and held the thick finger of his fal-coner's glove to his lips. He seemed jumpy to me. Once I turned to look at him: we were paddling in a deep lake into fierce open sun, and sweat slid down the closed window of his face.

I am almost there, Osceola, I thought, as the little waves imploded. *Keep breathing.*

Five o'clock and we were still on the river. Now the Caloosahatchee had become the Styx. The water here was clear as a blue lozenge. Large, bril-liantly winged moths trailed our oar handles for a mile. We moved through a labyrinth of canals that felt identical to the route we'd taken yesterday, just as shallow and confusing, just as chokingly hot. Occa-sionally you would see something new: on one tree island, for example, hundreds of cabbage palms felled by a storm covered the ground. Ferns had swallowed the stumps: resurrection ferns and saw palmettos, hundreds upon hundreds of waxy blooms with a brilliant red center. I told the Bird Man they looked like dwarfs in tuxedos and he smiled. Then I thought I saw a shape moving behind a screen of vines—it was two-legged, short but humanoid—and I hollered at the Bird Man to stop our boat.

"No," he said, poling us evenly forward.

"What do you mean, no?" The island was curving away from us.

"I mean no. We're not stopping. Not there."

"But I *saw* somebody back there. What if it's my sister?"

"It's not her. Pick up your paddle, Ava."

I caught my muscles making sly preparations to jump out and swim up current.

"Ossie!" I yelled behind me. "Please, we have to at least check . . ."

The Bird Man's hand flew out and retreated so nimbly that at first I didn't know what had happened; I saw colors, felt my teeth snag on my lower lip; I touched my cheek, confused; *He hit you,* explained the smart voice that narrates pain to your animal parts; on the platform he resumed poling forward. The skiff turned away from the tree island. He hadn't done it to *hurt* me, he said angrily. The last thing he wanted was to *hurt* me, but what the hell was he supposed to do if he couldn't trust me to keep quiet?

"You better start paying attention, if you want to get out of this place alive. That wasn't your sister, believe me. That's not a good island to stop at. We have a very small window to find her and we can't waste time chasing some shadow, kid."

"It wasn't a shadow. What I saw—"

"You can get *stranded* out here, kid. Did you know that? Did your sister's book include a tide table for the underworld?"

The Bird Man turned my chin to face him.

"Look: have you ever heard of someone getting trapped on a sand-bar?" I stared at him. My mouth stung. "Trust me on this one. Remember the rules? Remember what I said about the riptides?"

I nodded. The water was five feet deep here and clear to the bottom and my muscles twitched to jump. *Believe him,* I thought. *He's gotten you this far.* But then who was that girl? As he poled forward I craned around to watch the island recede, wanting very badly to see her shadow—but this time there was nothing. Just a wall of leaves and a cradle of water, shining. The Bird Man was struggling mightily to keep the skiff straight—it had become so narrow in the mangrove tunnel that when we got turned even a few inches sideways we hung up on the brambles. At one point a felled mahogany blocked a channel, a huge tree with shaggy roots, thirty or forty feet tall, and he had to pole us out stern first.

"Ossie!" I screamed one last time at the bend in the river, and the Bird Man shot me a warning look. Two buzzards swung through the silk of the rain. It was six o'clock by my watch, the underworld becoming muggy and preternaturally dark.

Dusk again. The pig frogs were throating their joy in the cattails. Sometimes I forgot for whole minutes what we were doing out here, who we were looking for.

Through her cage slats the red Seth blinked up at my face with florid eyes.

We wove through a long ridge of pinnacle rock. The sun glittered behind what sounded like the roar of the surf, as if the twisted pines hid a long seabed, a tidal hum so convincing that you could almost make out the Gulf foaming behind the trees—mosquitoes, the ocean's tiniest mimics. I swabbed their iridescent green-and-silver corpses out of my ears and crusted nose and continued to peer into the scrub, my heart pounding.

I was baling water in the bow seat, the Bird Man poling behind me, when I heard the crackle of a song I recognized and shot up.

". . . bye, bye, Miss American Pie, drove my Chevy to the levee but the levee was dry . . ."

Somebody on the tree island was listening to a radio! There was no mistaking the moody AM crackle—it was a station I knew, WCAM, Glen Winter's Golden Oldies show. Who had a radio out here? I saw tall shapes moving between the black mangroves: gator hunters. I guessed this from their canvas gear, the steaklike crimson of their faces beneath their hats. I knew a fair amount about that messy business, not from the Chief but from Grandpa Sawtooth, who used to hunt everything without discrimination before Park Services took over. I'd watched him cutting out the brain cap, salting it, stripping the skin before the scales slipped. "Hornbacking" meant taking everything, the whole hide. During the worst years of the Great Depression, hunters sold even the heads and claws to the seaside artisans who turned them into pocketbooks. "People were tacky in those days," Grandpa Sawtooth grunted by way of explanation.

Through the holes in the trees, I saw something flashing. Long and scythe-bright: knives. Handles that connected to fists. Two men were cutting at something splayed on the ground that I couldn't see, a radio bleating fuzzily behind them. I rotated by careful half degrees in the skiff. I didn't want to upset our equilibrium—who knew the rules of this place?—but if there were other living people in this underworld I wanted to know if they'd seen Ossie. And these guys seemed like happy drunks, not ghosts.

"No," the Bird Man said before I could ask. "Better keep your mouth shut. Those men are dead, kid."

Dead? "Are you sure?" Already the river was hurrying us away from them. "They looked just like ordinary people. Like any hunters." My voice broke into agitation like a rash. "They've got a *radio . . . ,*" I whined.

"Do they?" the Bird Man hissed. "Did you see if they had knives, also? Did you see, with your superior vision, what they were skinning behind the trees?"

"Alligators." My voice sounded faint.

The Bird Man sped us downriver. But I could still hear the chorus of the radio song and the men's cheerful voices shouting the lyrics above it, sloppy with drink:

". . . and them good old boys were drinking whiskey and rye, singin', 'This'll be the day that I dieee, this'll be the day . . .' "

"Sit tight. Don't mess this up now, Ava. This is the dangerous stretch. We'll tie off soon. We'll get there before midnight."

I swam my oar head through the river and watched a fist of brown moss dimple and sink. We were already in the underworld, right? So his promise didn't make a whole lot of sense. Where would we be before midnight? But I saw the Bird Man's face and knew better than to ask. For what felt like a long time I could hear the perfect radio version and also the drunk overlay of the hunters' voices, and I could see it, the dry levee, and for some reason the picture made me very afraid for my sister. *Those men are alive, Ava.* I heard the stern, tiny rudder of her voice, my mother's voice. *You know they are.*

"Help!" I hollered, scaring myself worse with my own screaming. "Help, can you hear me? If you're real, come help me! We're over here on the water . . ."

I was fumbling for the cooler and trying to get the red Seth inside my bib pocket; I wasn't going to jump without her. Then the Bird Man was covering my mouth.

"Oh shut up, shut up," he groaned. "Now why would you do that?" His glove tasted like sour fur.

He clamped hard against my mouth to smother my second scream and I thought dizzily that this was how our Seths felt. Like a Seth I was too weak to do anything, to bite down or force my jaws open. When it was clear that the men weren't coming he loosened his grip. His eyes were full of a funny sadness, like a digust—disappointment. I couldn't slow my breaths enough to get air down. Air looped shallowly through my nostrils. My vision darkened. For just a second, black snow shook across the sun, and I thought with a misled excitement about the painting *Winter on the River Styx.*

"If I let go," he said directly into my ear, "can I trust you to keep your mouth shut? Please, I am trying to *help* you here. Jesus H. You cannot go *screaming* around the underworld, kid."

This felt like one of Kiwi's English tests: was the Bird Man scared *of* me or *for* me?

If it was the first one I knew that I should probably bite down or scream again. If it was the second one I needed to stay quiet. *Oh but Kiwi, I can't guess the answer from his voice.*

"Kid, pull another stunt like that one and you will get yourself killed."

I nodded my chin into his hand. For an alligator wrestler this posture is very humiliating. It didn't seem like I should move though, or really even could have.

"You're going to get the both of us killed . . . ," he pretended to repeat, but I knew this was different from what he'd said the first time. The first time, I was alone in the sentence.

I sat in the boat, mouth shut now, and balanced the oar on my knees as he poled us toward a soft little piney key. The mud was a loamy red-violet color. Pines and magnolias waved their flags at an elevation of six or seven feet. We flipped and dragged the boat onto the deep beach, our feet sinking a few inches. I got out the taped-up alligator and I was holding her with her claws scrabbling on my shoulder, all twelve inches of her fighting toward the floor of the skiff. She flipped and clawed and twisted redly, almost slipping out of my grip as she dug heavily into my knees, but I nabbed her. As if my heart had sprouted claws and was trying to escape my body. I pocketed her. Right next to my heart, the poor Seth kept it company while it boomed.

The Bird Man squatted and asked if I was okay.

I was.

Was I going to scream like that again?

I was not.

He sighed heavily and told me to relax and get myself together, that he was going to take a piss. *Re-lax, Ava,* he said, watching me struggle with the writhing alligator. He hung his hat and his coat on a pronged branch—both of us were sweating hard. The whistle dropped from the branch's spindly fingers like a black cocoon, a pendulum of secret music; the wind pushed sound soundlessly around. I thought, *Make my call again, be the Bird Man.* If he repeated the call from our first meeting, I knew I could get back into the boat.

But if I observed my friend and ferryman from a different perch in my brain, I saw that the Bird Man could be an anybody. He could blend quite easily into the crowd of panhandlers and businessmen on the streets of Loomis: a tanned, middle-aged man with a few scars on his knuckles. Just a fleck of foam on that sea, as my dad would say. My dad would want me to get a good description of him. I sat on a rock and watched him remove his coat behind the saw palmetto. Okay: How would he look to a ranger, or a mainland person? Okay: he weighed a skinny number like my brother's, whatever that might be. He had brown hair with gunmetal streaks in it. Scars on his palms and arms. A thin outdoorsman's face. "Off the grid," my dad might have added with his chieftain's squint—because there was in fact something unwashed and wobbly about the Bird Man when you got up close.

"Ava," the Bird Man barked—to let me know he could *see* me, I thought with a little shiver. "Keep an eye out. Stay with the skiff."

The Bird Man was a bone-thin shape behind the willow head. His magic dulled and swirled beyond my ability to recall it, like an island that shrinks to a point behind your boat. All of a sudden the dimensions of my problems changed on me, like rocks coming out of the darkness: Now I was lost. Now I hoped that my sister would find *me*. Mentally I called out to her: *Ossie? Louis? Help me.*

Why, there isn't any ghost of Louis, the frank adult voice informed me. This voice was very primitive. It was some amalgam of the Chief and my mom and a much, much older creature. A dry rasp like a fingernail, a scale. *You are both alone out here, you and Osceola, if your sister is alive out here.*

I stared down at the purple ribbon and felt a sour rise in my throat.

I could hear the Bird Man zipping up behind the leaves maybe fifty yards from where I was sitting. I walked over to the tree where the whistle was swinging. I caught it, held it to my own lips, winced in preparation for the shattering sound. I'm not sure what I was expecting to summon—a gale of birds, an army of birds. I could see one great blue heron watching me from the river with her slate feathers blown smooth. I inhaled hard, I emptied my lungs into the whistle. Not a sound came out of it.

Oh no, I thought in a tiny voice. *Oh-oh.*

When the man returned he stooped and peeled a tiny stray feather off my collarbone. He was smiling at me—his grin was very gentle, wide enough to frighten. His eyes reminded me of two sweating water glasses. I pictured a stalk of cold water running from the burgundy toes of his boots to his scalp. Then his gaze deadened on me—like he could still *see* me but he wasn't really looking anymore, some plug knocked loose—and his new eyes went rummaging around the green corridor behind me, where saw palmettos squeaked along the water.

"Don't sulk," he said, and there was an elastic snap in his voice as his mood turned on me. "You've been a good sport this whole trip, why ruin it?"

His voice surprised me. Inside it I could hear a wounded note, like a dog's keen, almost, but not *only* hurt. Something else in it, too. Our dog Yallo used to howl when it got its big paw caught in our doorjamb, and you could hear his feelings waffle: rage-pain-rage. But I didn't understand what doorjamb the Bird Man could be caught in—we were safe now, weren't we? Those men weren't coming.

"Why would you do that to me?" he mumbled. "Aw, kid, you're going to screw it all up. Do you know what I'm risking here? *For you.* Ava. Do you know what could happen to me, if they find me with you . . . ?" His voice was half a growl now. "Do you have any *idea*?"

I was thinking that those hunters had been real and that we might have missed our chance to save my sister. I was really quaking with anger now, gathering breath—and then I saw his eyes and immediately shut up my face. Something bad here, I thought. Something going awry. The air between us felt like dry powder.

"Come on, kid," he said, and his voice had changed completely; it was charged with something that was almost kindness, that quivered like a finger of syrup. "I sure wish you had not done that. Do you want to find your sister or not? Come on. We're wasting time."

On this shoreline I couldn't hear any voices but ours. No radio song. All the little umbilicals to the world collapsed.

"Let's get you dried."

I was crying now. I stared down at the purple ribbon on my wrist, all that I had to show for two days on the water.

The Bird Man's hat hung from the branch above him, swinging slightly on the breeze; beneath it the coat opened its magnanimous arms. Feathers swirled out of its plumy mat. Black sleeves hung unwizardly almost a head above me, ballooning with wind. Birds moved above it by their own power. Nobody was controlling them.

This coat was just a rag, I realized. My heart froze. A crazy person's disguise.

"You were lying to me," I said dully. "There isn't any such thing as the underworld, is there? This is just the ordinary swamp."

"Aw, kid, don't say that." The man shocked me by pouting, his face bunching into a childish purse. When it smoothed I was scared worse than before. "Don't be ungrateful. Didn't I get you through the Eye? Aren't we having a little adventure? We can even keep looking for your sister if you want, why not?"

He took a step toward me and I watched his hand swing through space and come to rest on my shoulder. He crouched low and his pale lips sprouted teeth and I couldn't remember how to see this face as friendly.

Who are you?

Somebody was grinning at me. I could hear the wind fluttering his empty sleeves.

CHAPTER EIGHTEEN

Kiwi Rolls the Dice

Pa-Hay-Okee Gaming was a forty-minute drive from downtown Loomis. The casino's glowing sign marked the periphery between the city and the undeveloped swampland that stretched forty miles to Chokoloskee Bay. Gus Waddell's ferry departed from a marina just a few minutes down the road, hidden from the two-lane highway by a large commercial strawberry and tomato farm. This was the closest Kiwi had been to his family's island since his trip to the ferry docks. Proximity to the park made Kiwi feel like he was snorkeling, getting air from a winnowing tube. Night fell around the car like a lake. If only he could lift his head, he would see what he was so afraid of. Home, he thought, peering suspiciously through the windshield.

"Would you calm the fuck down?" Vijay asked. "You're breathing like a drunk. You're breathing like a sumo when the elevator's out." Vijay grinned at the rearview mirror, pleased with this last one.

"You're breathing like *me,* bro!" fat Leo wheezed from the backseat.

Pa-Hay-Okee Gaming was the southernmost Seminole casino. Sawtooth and the Chief had come out here once or twice, but Kiwi had been too young and too haughty to join them—too afraid of losing, really, in front of the tough public of his dad and his grandfather. His mom had come here as a kid, she'd told them. When she lived on the mainland as Hilola Owens. No photographs existed from that period in the Bigtree Family Musuem. (It was all BS, the Chief joked—Before Swamplandia!) His mom said that Loomis teens used to haunt Pa-Hay-

Okee Gaming before the Sunrise mall and multiplex opened in the seventies. Hilola and her girlfriends would walk around the perimeter of the casino like it was the deck of a luxury ship. They'd get the bouncer to bring them champagne flutes and narrow cans of Hula-Hula pineapple juice from inside.

"Are you sure we can get in?" A part of him wanted to travel the weeds outside, to do a little pilgrimage. He pictured his mom as a skinny girl his age drinking her Hula-Hula juice with no idea of the havoc that her death was going to cause, the violent way her death would rip through space. What a weird future awaited her in the past! (Or: what a weird future had survived her?) Alligators, his sisters, his father. Ninety pounds of her was going to sink an island.

"They'll serve us beer in there, no problem," Vijay was saying. "You brought your fake, Kiwi Beamtray?"

The Volvo was one of two dozen cars in the casino lot. A busy night.

Pa-Hay-Okee Gaming supplied the only legal gambling available in Loomis County. A few wiseacres called it the Jesus in the Temple Casino, because the main building used to be a Catholic Church. In 1947, the Seminole tribe had bought the ruins of the church, which had been blown to large bits by Hurricane King. Thirty years later the Seminole transformed the former rubble into a gambling hall.

Once inside, Kiwi pulled a lever arm on one of the slots and won three dollars in quarters.

"See that?" said Vijay. "You're on a roll this week, bro."

Two slots over, Kiwi watched a man in a wheelchair win ten dollars in nickels.

"You jealous?" His eyes looked as gold-bitten as old Midas's. "Take a picture, it'll last you longer."

"Quit staring at people, bro," Vijay said irritably. "You're always *staring* at everybody." He frogged out his eyes and pulled his hair up in an imitation of Kiwi.

"Is that what I look like?" Kiwi was heartbroken. "Electrocuted?"

Both his friends nodded. "Yup," Leo said drolly. "You do. Maybe your brain is full of electricity. Maybe that's why you talk so crazy sometimes."

He and Vijay exchanged an almost parental look, arch and dark, like this was a theory they had previously discussed.

"There is a documented correlation between unconventional speech and genius," he said, patting at his hair. But nobody was listening to Kiwi anymore. They went upstairs to the dining room. For $5.99 you could get a surf and turf buffet.

ALL*U*CAN*EAT*STEAK*AND*LOSTER.

"What's a loster?" Kiwi asked, feeling weirdly implicated by the name on the chalkboard, a combination of "lost" and "loser."

"Lobster, bro."

The single lobster left in there looked like some kind of mystic, trailing long curls of whitish seaweed back and forth around the tank.

"That guy looks like the last unicorn or something," said Leo. "Where's the beef?"

Leo helped himself to two steak tenderloins that were globed with fat and several paper cones of ketchup. Vijay got a ladle or cut of pretty much everything but the baked scrod. Kiwi couldn't figure out how to work the crank ice cream dispenser and returned to their table with a bowl of maraschino cherries.

Vijay jabbed a spoon handle at Kiwi's cherries and made some jokes about virginity.

Leo handled the requisite surf and turd jokes.

Ha-ha-ha-ha, was Kiwi.

You couldn't take jokes about your own asshole personally on the mainland, Kiwi had learned. Other dudes would rattle off "your asshole" jokes with blank faces, like cops reading you your Miranda rights—as though reciting from a script, as if legally this simply had to be done. After a minute Kiwi said, "This looks like Leo's dick," and held up a shriveled walnut to approving laughter. Vijay ate a baked potato. They headed back downstairs.

Kiwi froze on the second-to-last step. "Oh wait. You dudes go ahead. I forgot something."

Adrenaline ate its way through Kiwi Bigtree's body. He wanted to run but he couldn't move. On the opposite side of the room, in a sandbar of light, a tall, bald white man wearing a bolo tie got down on his knees. He was getting a show ready; twelve LIVE GIRLS were standing in the wings. The girls looked a little less lively than advertised. They smoked cigarettes and kept listlessly touching each other's hair. For many of them, Kiwi observed, girlhood had ended decades ago. The casino stage was shaped like a banjo, the long runway strung with rows of white and violet lights.

The man was on his knees, hooking a microphone into an old-fashioned set of speakers. A black cord was looped around his left shoe. He stood and then the cord was underneath the sole; *oh no!* thought Kiwi. It was the sort of prelude to an accident that makes bystanders feel like psychics—and when the man tripped he fell *hard*. He had to push off on one knee before he could stand again. When he got to his feet the first thing he did was examine his own big hands. He frowned at his palms as if he were reading a newspaper, then shined his knuckles on his navy trouser knees. Even these odd gestures were familiar to Kiwi, because the man in question was his father. Chief Bigtree, disguised as an employee of the casino.

The Chief sat down at a small table. His wrestler's fists joined into one tremendous, pale stone under the microphone; he stared sightlessly out at the crowd of slot machines. The first thing Kiwi noticed was the complex graininess of the Chief's skin. (Was his dad really sick or something? What on earth was he doing here?) The second thing was that the Chief was wearing his glasses.

Oh *no*. Kiwi stepped backward on the stairwell, wondering if the Chief had already seen him. These glasses were a bad sign. On Swamplandia! the Chief had been contemptuous of various drugstore aids: bifocals, Ace bandages, hemorrhoid creams, luminous jellies for poison oak and bee stings; he was even a little unsettled by flavored toothpaste. Crutches were bad for business, the Chief liked to say. "Why announce your infirmities to the tourists, kids?"

Can he see me? Do I want him to? Kiwi blinked out of the shadows, mere feet from the seething lights of the casino floor. The walls smelled of old seediness, throw-up, and wood pulp. Behind him he heard a wine-red laugh and the tinsely clatter of forks and knives falling off a buffet table.

"Pick a direction, fuckface." Someone shoved past Kiwi on the stairs, a blur of pale skin and tattoos flickering on a bicep.

"Sorry, sir, excuse me . . ." He felt seasick from the billiard greens and neons shooting out at him from every angle of the room. The roulette wheel turned its tiny spikes. Kiwi's back was drenched in sweat that turned freezing in the air-conditioning. The Chief had switched on the microphone:

"Get your ballots out, folks, because this is going to be one *stiff* competition, har har . . ."

The Chief's laughter burst from the speakers like brown water from spigots. Apparently a "beauty pageant" was about to take place; men were using squabby pencils to fill out a voter's card. How depressing! The Chief's gaze crossed Kiwi's square of carpet twice—three times! four times!—before settling on the stage again. Behind his large glasses, Chief Bigtree's eyes were lost in the neon snow of the show.

"Well, don't just stand there, folks," the Chief growled. "Look alive! How are you going to judge a beauty pageant with your eyes shut?"

This was how Dad was raising money for Carnival Darwinism?

The humans who answered his dad's summons were sad quarry, Kiwi thought—pervy-looking old guys or catatonic gamblers, men with nothing else to lose tonight. The faces he saw under the lights were grim with an insuperable boredom, or in a kind of dreamy agony. One man with a tight, bloated face kept shuffling at his crotch in full sight of everyone.

Vijay and Leo did not join the huddle. They were busy chatting up two old women, two gargoyles in flowery pantsuits near the roulette wheel, hoping to find "female patrons" to support their gambling. They had a little routine, which they'd explained to Kiwi in the car. "The pitch." It didn't sound particularly sophisticated. The plan seemed to involve (1) talking to older ladies, (2) listening to older ladies, (3) asking older ladies for one hundred dollars. In denominations of twenty, if possible.

Vijay and Leo were working hard; Leo had a grin stuccoed to his face, and Vijay kept throwing his head back in a spectacularly phony laugh. Neither of them seemed to have noticed the white man behind the microphone. An aging Bigtree Indian with knotty hands and purple bags beneath his eyes whose face looked—if you really looked—exactly like the face of their friend Kiwi.

What were these women—strippers? dancers? Kiwi wasn't sure what to call them but they seemed underwardrobed for air-conditioning. They were all lined up for the pageant. They scintillated in a sort of depressing, fish-market way. A brunette with a jowly, friendly face walked out first. Bouncing Bella. She guffawed for some reason when the Chief called her onto the stage, as if her name were a complicated joke that she had at last understood. A redhead in a padded bra that looked like it was made from an extinct species of hot-pink Texan snake kept sneezing. The Chief held the microphone in his huge grip and ladled his compliments over each of them, as if he were trying to clothe them in words.

Easily it was the saddest pageant that Kiwi had ever seen.

"Okay!" The Chief cleared his throat. "Let's get those ballots in, gentlemen . . ."

Does my dad do this every night? Kiwi wondered. Only Tuesdays? The Chief was the proudest man who Kiwi had ever met. How had he survived a job, any Loomis job, for so long?

The Chief started using phrases Kiwi recognized from Hilola Bigtree's show:

"Did you forget that they made women like this, folks . . . ?"

"Now, believe me, this girl has got more talent in her *pinkie finger . . .*"

A few things were making sense now, in the scarlet hue of this event. It would appear—it would make sense, timewise—that Kiwi's dad had been working two jobs for quite some time. Years, possibly. Which life did the Chief keep a secret from whom? Kiwi wondered. It seemed unlikely that these mainlanders knew his father as Chief Bigtree of Swamplandia! For a second, trying to assimilate this fact, Kiwi felt his whole childhood turn translucent.

So: the Chief's "business trips" had been to this casino, or perhaps to equally shitty places of employ in Loomis County.

Kiwi's mother used to describe the business trips to her children as "Sam's ventures" in respectful, careful tones. Dark and sparkling tones—that was Hilola Bigtree, monologuing about her husband. Whenever one parent talked to him about the other one, Kiwi got the uneasy feeling that he didn't know either person at all.

"Oh, your father is meeting with the investors, honey. 'Investors' are mainlanders who pay us more money than any one tourist. They are big fans of our show."

As Kiwi got older and angrier, his mother would reveal a little more: "Your father is doing hard work for us on the mainland. He gets lonely in that hotel room. He wishes he were here on the island, believe me. I know you miss him, Kiwi," she'd add. "I know you love your father."

By the end, she seemed to say "I know you . . ." out of a deep anxiety for the future that she wouldn't get to oversee, the same way she begged: "I know you're wearing deodorant" or "I know you're practicing with the Seths" or "I know you'll take good care of your sisters, Kiwi."

"Brush your teeth, son!" she'd screamed at him once from her hospital bed, nine days before her death. "You're not brushing, are you . . . ?" and the pleading and suspicion in her voice belied the stupidity of this accusation. She was all doped with morphine.

"Mom, I'm seventeen," he'd said quietly. And then, when he saw what her face did, "Thank you for reminding me, Ma. I'll keep brushing."

All his mom's requests had become huge and tragic at the end of her life, like magnificent tropical flowers at the suicidal peak of their blooming. Kiwi was studying them, the angiosperms of tropical systems, for a future test that Kiwi planned to give and take. Perhaps he would be a horticulturist. As a genius, your career options abounded, and with his background he was set: horticulture, herpetology, oncology, radiology, the mortuary arts, museum sciences, he pretty much had his pick.

After her cancer was diagnosed, all business trips had stopped.

Always Kiwi had viewed his parents as coconspirators, confabulators. But Kiwi had assumed the conspiracy part was Swamplandia!— all that bullshit about the island and the Seths and their "Bigtree tribe." He hadn't guessed that a bigger, sadder secret existed on the shore, a backstage to their family's story way out here in Loomis County. Carnival Darwinism seemed more impossible than ever before, now that Kiwi understood how the Chief had planned to fund it.

Onstage, the Chief was handing the Queen of Beauty a metal crown and a fountain of white carnations. His bum leg stuttered on the carpet.

"Another winner!"

"Another winner!"

"Another winner!"

A golden-toned computerized voice announced this good tiding over and over while somewhere nearby metal rained into a pan.

"Hey, Bigtree!"

Kiwi started. Leo showed up swinging a bottle of beer in each hand.

"There you are, bro . . . Are you watching this? Fucking unbelievable, right?"

He rolled his eyes toward the stage. There was something puppyish about the conflict on Leo's face. He was clearly torn between his first impulse toward wonderment, a panting and ignorant enjoyment, and his obedience to their pack of three. You weren't supposed to enjoy a spectacle like this.

"What I mean is, it's sort of gross. Pathetic. These bitches are *old*. The whole thing's retarded. What if that was, like, your mom?"

Then Leo made a joke about Vijay's mother, an analogy that compared her to the Lucky-U-Can't-Lose Slot Machine. Leo's mother's vagina was alleged by Vijay to be wide as a bus. Punching commenced.

"You guys? You're going to get us kicked out of here," Kiwi mumbled. Across the room his dad had started to cough. The Chief had an instinct for professionalism: when his coughing fit began he switched off the microphone. From the shadows, Kiwi watched his father's silent convulsions.

A thickset man in jeans and a knotted red bandanna was approaching his dad's table; he leaned in and thumped the Chief between his shoulder bones—too hard, Kiwi thought. The man had a skinny ponytail that jumped against the small of his back with each step, as if this guy thought he was a mobile rodeo. *My dad's boss,* Kiwi realized with something like horror. He watched his father's head tilt forward a fraction of an inch, as if in prayer. This was a humility that Kiwi had become familiar with, via Carl.

So that guy is my dad's employer.

"Sammy!" It was an angry summons. The boss had a voice that carried crystalline across a room. The Chief listened with an odd smile. *The Chief is going to destroy you, guy.* Once, when Grandpa Sawtooth made some snide remark about his son, the Chief had bodily lifted the old man and chucked him into the slough. He waited for his father to throw the first punch. What the heck kind of wrestling move was *this*? Kiwi wondered, watching the Chief's palms lift and separate. Some kung fu trick?

With his huge palms held outward, the Chief shaped a prodigious apology on the air.

"You fucked it up, Sammy, you really *fucked it* this time . . . ," the shorter man kept screaming. "You want to see the records? You got petty cash amnesia again? Or do you remember what you did with my two hundred dollars?"

Kiwi didn't hear what the Chief said after his boss exploded. Kiwi did not run, exactly. "Excuse me . . . ," he kept saying, pushing past low tables covered in empty pitchers.

If anyone follows me I'll pretend to throw up, he thought. *With any luck I won't even have to fake it.*

But no one was following him.

A craps table got him good just above his hip bone; it was going to bruise badly. Ecchymosis, his brain helpfully reported. "Owww!" screamed Kiwi, knocking into the disgusted dealer.

In the back lot a few motorcycles and one dust-red Chevrolet were parked beneath the lamps. The night was a bowl of heat. No moon, no stars.

Kiwi was surprised to see the Chief working here, but it was a dull and terrible surprise. With a grim, spiderlike lacemaking Kiwi's brain knit his surprise into a dull and terrible knowledge.

This was not Kiwi's first experience with the spider. That was Kiwi's nickname for the complex neurophysics that processed your shock into horror. Spun love into fear. In January, for example, he'd seen his mother's chart on Dr. Gautman's wall. The spectacled doctor had entered and paused by the window. A pat of sun slid down the doctor's biscuit-white face. He leaned by the tinted green window shades, watching Kiwi with his clipboard ("I imagine you'll have some questions for me, Mr. Bigtree . . ."). But Kiwi Bigtree had turned his head quickly; nope, he didn't have anything to say. All the questions that had gone hooking through his bloodstream abruptly straightened— aha! And: eureka! Now Kiwi understood perfectly what was happening. *Okay,* he blinked. *Okay, sure. All right.* His blood flow was red and serene. His mom was dying. In two months, if all went according to schedule, she would be dead. Like a genius he'd understood this, without any help from the doctors. A prodigy of the buzzing fluorescence. T3 c, A+!

He read the chart through twice. Afterward, all his uncertainty about his mother's cancer—all that optimistic darkness—drained right out of him. He didn't tell Ava and Ossie, and when they learned it for themselves from Dr. Gautman he'd felt an evil satisfaction. He'd watched his sisters' calm faces fall away like scabs and become something else, something more terrible than he could have imagined. Ava's and Ossie's mouths were perfect Os. Meanwhile the doctor had tried to hedge the word "death" for them. He made it sound like the best thing for her; anyhow, there was "nothing left to do."

"Imagine, children," he'd said with a false, gentle grin, as if death itself were the miracle cure they'd all been waiting for. "At last your mother will be at total peace!"

You thought you couldn't stand not to know a thing until you knew it, wasn't that right? Who had said that, the Chief? Some poet from the Library Boat, maybe.

Knowledge at last, Kiwi's mind recited dutifully. *The fish's living eye: glass.*

Sometimes you would prefer a mystery to remain red-gilled and buried inside you, Kiwi decided, alive and alive inside you.

Kiwi gulped air and went back inside the casino. The scene was unchanged: stale cigarettes, the slots expulsing tokens, all these heads bent in a dying garden over the machines. The old women's wigs looked to him like faded flowers, dull oranges and carmines and silvers. Horrifically, impossibly, the pageant had started up again. This was good news? His dad was still employed, at least. He spotted Leo and Vijay at the bar. His friends looked a little lost next to the tyrannosaurus drunks, old men whose tiny, atrophied arms curled whiskey sours against their Hawaiian shirts. The Chief's voice swam everywhere in this nicotine aquarium:

"Let's all welcome lovely *Bella* to the stage!"

For a second, Kiwi swore he locked eyes with the Chief. He lifted one hand in a stiff wave. The Chief, if he recognized him, didn't wave back.

Kiwi stared over the wide expanse of rug and strangers and machines. Why couldn't he cross a square of carpet to get to his father?

Kiwi counted out the money he'd brought—sixty-two bucks in pristine singles and fives. Kiwi would have ironed his salary if it were possible, he was that careful with it. He stuffed the bucks into one of the dealer's envelopes.

"Miss?"

The woman who took the money from him was one of the Live Girls. Bouncing Bella. She stared down at the cone of twenties, and when she stared up at him her face had transformed.

"We have a place around the back where we can go, honey, it's real nice . . ."

"Oh, no, I'm sorry . . . ," Kiwi yelped as if a great weight had just fallen on his toe. "Oh, my God, ma'am. You are misunderstanding me. We are having a misunderstanding."

Well, his dick was stirring regardless. He noted this with dismay, his penis dumb as a beagle jumping for this woman's gartered leg. Kiwi stared down at the red nails she'd hooked through his belt loop. Fantastic. Luckily yards and yards of Cubby's heavy denim concealed his arousal from anybody. Somewhere in the suburbs of Loomis, Kiwi imagined Cubby Wallach making his seventh ham sandwich, grabbing a pie slice, adding to his empire of girth—that friendship seemed impossibly remote to Kiwi now, impossibly childish. Bella dropped her hand and frowned at him.

"This money isn't for . . . that. I'm here to repay a loan. Miss, could you give this to that man over there?"

"Who? Bobby?"

"May-be . . . ," Kiwi said carefully. "Which one do you call Bobby?"

"Bobby's our boss. The floor manager. You a friend of his?"

"No, no, the, ah . . . the other one. The older white man."

"Sammy?" Bella's eyes regarded him milkily. "Why don't you give it to him? You should give it to him yourself, he's having a rough night. I'll take you over there. He's a nice guy, isn't he? We all love Sammy. He makes us feel beautiful."

"He's good at that," Kiwi agreed. "Good with words."

"Say!" Bella said, peering in at him. "Do I know you from someplace? Are you that kid who was on TV a few weeks back, the angel?"

"No, ma'am. I'm no angel, ha-ha." Kiwi held his hands up. "Falsely accused."

Bella began to tug Kiwi across the floor.

"Can't do it . . ." Kiwi left her holding the envelope, already pushing back into the crowd. ". . . really busy, so . . . thank you!"

No signature, no note—Kiwi didn't see how he could write a letter to his father *here,* on the edge of a pool table. It was a communication so private even Kiwi wasn't certain what he was trying to tell his father. With the money he was saying "thank you" and "keep this job." So far as he knew. Maybe he was saying something else entirely and they'd both have to wait to find out what. Kiwi was starting to think that certain gifts were like hieroglyphs that could take years to decipher.

He'll know it's from me, at least, Kiwi thought. Who else would address Sam Bigtree as "the Chief" here? He watched the Chief accept the envelope.

"Let's go," Kiwi said. He found Vijay chatting up a woman with hair like chamomile tea and pink, alcoholic eyes, who was at minimum four decades his senior. Whatever they'd been talking about was causing her eyes to water with pleasure and Vijay was laughing, too, his braying, abort-mission laughter, desperate as a fist punching the ejector button. When he saw Kiwi he rolled his eyes and grabbed him by the wrist.

"Kiwi! Meet my lovely friend Clarisse—"

"We're going. Right now."

The Chief was on his feet, walking through the rows and rows of machines. He held one stout, hairy arm out, like a farmer dowsing for a spring. The chewed, stained fingers on the end of the arm were Kiwi's own. Same length, same fingernails even. Their eyes met again, and this time the Chief held his son's gaze. Or seemed to; it was difficult to tell behind the big glasses. Light filled them like drink.

"I'm sick." He grabbed Vijay by the elbow and swayed a little to demonstrate.

Vijay rousted Leo from the men's room and they were off—it was immediately clear from the colorful dribble on his chin that Leo was legitimately ill. But Kiwi pushed his way between his friends and flung his arms around them, transforming them into de facto bodyguards, his neck contracting into his shoulders like a turtle. *"Go,"* he hissed. The three boys passed an elderly couple on their way out, and Kiwi turned to watch the casino doors shutting on the old man's walker, and Kiwi watched as his Jamaican caretaker stooped on the AstroTurf green rug to yell directly into his ear: "Freddy, you gotta move. *Move!"*

"We'll come back soon," Kiwi heard himself saying as he searched for the Volvo. "Tomorrow, even. We can come back tomorrow."

"Unh." Vijay nodded sleepily, his head wobbling unsteadily on his neck. The road itself seemed to hiccup as he drove. In the backseat Leonard was already snoring.

One Cyclops eye burned in the rearview mirror: the prison watch-tower. Kiwi felt really sick now. Behind the prison, the swamp flew outward in every direction. It occurred to Kiwi that at this moment, he and his father were both within twelve nautical miles of Swamplandia!

Turn around, he considered saying.

Turn the car around, please.

Turn the car around now. *Oh guys, my dad is in trouble back there.*

A light rain patterned itself on the Volvo's hood.

"Tomorrow, okay?"

Kiwi could hear his promises to himself becoming vaguer.

Had his father recognized him? Would his father come looking for him? In the backseat, Leo was snoring heavily; in a trough between snores, with a shocking tenderness, Leo mumbled the name of a girl whom Kiwi had never heard him mention before. Amy? Annie? So everybody in this car had a stowaway.

"Wake up!" he shouted into the backseat. Vijay turned to stare at him.

Kiwi buckled his seat belt, shocked into old habit. In the rearview mirror the casino blew backward into darkness, and the white candle of the security tower got snuffed.

CHAPTER NINETEEN

The Silently Screaming World

A s I've mentioned, the Loomis County Public Schools used to mail us workbooks and videotapes. The year that Kiwi would have entered high school as a freshman we received a brand-new slide projector, a Kodak Ektagraphic III Carousel. It looked a lot like the old slide projector, only free-er. I don't know if some gentleman altruist was donating this equipment to us or if it was a state-sponsored thing—or if the Chief and Mom paid for it; I suppose that's not impossible—but the packages showed up every September via Gus's ferry, addressed to our parents. Once, on a rainy day in Grandpa's shack, Kiwi and Ossie and I watched a 1950s nature slide show called *The Silently Screaming World*. White letters scrolled across a black screen: "When the world screams in its sleep, we rarely hear it. Sheets of lightning fall across the empty prairies. Earthquakes echo at depths that would burst a human eardrum. High on the Altiplano, canyons cave inward like mouths."

The footage was grainy, and the black-and-white palette gave the slides an eerie, immutable feel: a wall of solid flame in the Andes, Alaskan glacial collisions, the great thumbprint of an old comet in the Yucatán. What frightened me more than the images was the silence that accompanied the jumpy stills. Kiwi made us after-hours caramel popcorn and we screened these cataclysms on the hairy tiki walls of the Swamp Café, the three of us crunching loudly.

"Lie down, Ava," this man said, spreading a green tarp for us, and I did.

Lying flat, I could see plants with leaves that flared outward like living Victrolas. Their throats were a pale green that winnowed into organlike tubes and disappeared. Ants crawled out of the throats of these plants. At first there were just two or three of them, dotting the broad leaves.

Then ants came streaming onto the leaves in the black millions. A hard root was poking into the top of my spine. I closed my eyes, and waited, and when I opened them again the man was still on top of me. I couldn't speak. I blinked my eyes and the ants streamed wetly, then spiraled into a black kaleidoscope. Above me the yellow moon kept traveling behind clouds, and the mosquitoes filled the clearing with their static. Leaves lost their transparency for whole minutes. I stiffened and my eyes flew open and when the pressure eased I could hear my breath again. The man cupped a dry hand under my neck and said something that I didn't understand. I stared up at him; my fingers fidgeted, my wrestling hand cramping nervously, filtering dirt on the other side of the tarp. He smiled at me, pushing the hair from my face, and automatically I smiled back.

Even after I realized what was happening, I held very still. *Oh, this,* I thought, and got a counterfeit déjà vu from the stories I had read and overheard. He pulled me forward along the crackling plastic, sliding the birds of his hands under my back. You could get my type of coveralls off by unhooking the two bottom snaps and sliding the straps down, but I was too embarrassed to tell the man this and so I watched as he popped all of them, even the useless little latches. Then I kicked when he needed me to help again.

The Bird Man coughed once and I felt a wetness on my cheeks. His wrist bone was level with my eye. I had never seen his arms naked from wrist to shoulder before; they looked like anybody's arms. His undershirt smelled like deep July. Little belly hairs crushed into the sweat on my belly. Now the Bird Man was breathing funny. He wouldn't look at me at all, not at my face, and this made me feel a little lonely, as if we were rooms away from one another. All I could see was the gray slice of one cheek.

My eyes rolled toward the blank sockets of the plants. Inside they were washed green, so pale, I thought, too pale to really qualify as a color. Blind light, luminous. Tiny blind bulbs at the funnel's end. Pain collected into deep pockets and I was aware of this pain but somehow I could not seem to feel it. It was like a body-deafness. How strange, I thought, frowning into the plants. Once I saw a police car in Loomis with the sound cut and this feeling was like that, just a sweep over the grass: blue-red, red-blue, a mute bleat.

And then I did hear it, then the sound exploded. The man pushed harder and got inside of me. This pain was dazzling. He grunted and he pushed into me again, he pushed again, he pushed on, until I understood that the pain was going to continue happening. I thought: *Oh, my sister doesn't know a thing about this.* Now I knew deep in my gut what my sister didn't. Ossie's ghosts, her love possessions, those had to be something else. This part had never been what she was talking about.

I closed my eyes then and tried to breathe through my nose only. Dimly I was aware of cold air on my belly; a little shiver of disgust drifted up between my legs. My neck kept getting ground against the hard knot of a root and all my embarrassment seemed to concentrate and grow acutest in that one spot: he would know now that I didn't shave my legs, that I didn't even wear a bra yet. *Your legs are still hairy, he'll think you're a kid.*

"I'd like to go back now," I said. "Please."

We walked back from the hammock in silence. We passed the same trees and their same orbiting bulbs, the same white flowers, the same sour, creamy ponds, but everything looked changed to me now. The moon had a bad charge. I followed the Bird Man's feathers through the trees, staring over his left shoulder to the gray sea glint. A small alligator curled like dried spittle in the radish-colored reeds. As I walked I held a punch against my abdomen, wishing that I could throw up. My big toe pressed up in a hole in my left sneaker and I watched this, fascinated. With each step the toe dilated the mesh. It was like watching the movements of an alien organism. My sneaker laces were still undone. When I bent to tie up, red threads of pain went whooshing through me. I pushed my knuckles angrily against my crotch— somehow I wasn't adding up right anymore. My parts weren't summing into myself.

Why didn't it occur to my body to run then? My body's best idea was to stare at the ground. At no point had I tried to fight this person. Less than two hours ago, when we were poling through the dusklight, I had boasted to him that I, Ava Bigtree of the Bigtree Wrestling Dynasty, could defeat a thousand-pound alligator. Instead I trailed his elbow. I talked nervously, like a tourist girl; I remember noticing out loud that the stars on this island were very very white.

I won't tell Ossie, I decided with a sudden viciousness. *I don't have to tell anybody about it.* "It" was this bloat. Already the thing had somehow grown so big and slippery inside me that I didn't see how I could get it to adhere to any story. Anyhow, I didn't think that Os would understand what I had done with the Bird Man. Way deep in my gut I hoped she wouldn't, and deeper than that I hoped or wondered if she maybe could. Her Spiritist possessions—the ones that I had seen in our bedroom, anyhow—they looked clean and solitary. I pictured ghosts coiling in a glittering and spacious place inside Osceola, ghosts rolling through my sister like a fog and then lifting again, no harm done. (While dressing I'd touched the sweat on my legs and found a salmon-colored film that I'd mopped up with one pant leg, my face hot, as quick as I undid or hid messes in the Pit. I'd pocketed the red Seth, who had been dozing under the leaves.) I knew now that I didn't know anything. Those nights with the ghosts belonged to my sister so completely that I couldn't guess at them, I realized, the way that this thing was going to be mine.

No, I don't have to tell a soul about this, I promised myself. When you are a kid, you don't know yet that a secret, like an animal, can evolve. Like an animal, a secret can develop a self-preserving intelligence. Shaglike, mute and thick, a knowledge with a fur: your secret.

"Ava, come here," the man said to me again—shouted, really—in his new voice.

In the history of sound, nobody has ever said a girl's name that way before. Like it was a string you could pluck. "A-va."

When I didn't come over right away he stood and stretched, opened his mouth in a kind of angry yawn. His smile grew larger and stranger until it was almost unbearable, at which point he began walking toward me.

"Ava, honey . . ."

I wanted to go to him then? Not all of me but the same part he'd just hurt. I don't understand this pull, still. I think it must be a really dangerous physics, the gravity of wound to fist. You can see it happen to the other animals. When a hunter or trapper begins kicking at an alligator, its body curls to accommodate the withdrawing foot.

Once, at Argyle Murphy's fish camp, I watched a little Scottie dog get a Gulch bottle broken across its back and then go loping, tongue lolling, toward its owner with the man's beer and its own blood stiffening on its fur—not to attack him, as I'd originally thought, but to lick and lick at the emerald bits lodged in his hand.

"Ava, I need you to help me over here . . ." The Bird Man's voice was full of squishy feeling that sounded to me so much like tenderness, love. Like he really did need me, too. It was a voice you could see, like green glass sparkling in a palm.

At the same time I heard my mother telling me something I should have figured out hours and days ago, something I must have been on the brink of knowing since Stiltsville. I don't mean that my actual mother told me this, like one of Ossie's ghosts, but it was her voice I heard in my head:

The Bird Man is just a man, honey. He is more lost out here than you are. The Bird Man has no idea where he's taking you, and if he does, well that's much worse, and you won't find your sister anywhere near here, Ava, and I would run, honey, personally . . .

What I did next was all instinct, as if my muscles were staging a coup: I felt a movement in my breast pocket, the red Seth clawing against the cotton ticking; I pulled her out and untaped her small jaws and flung her at him in one fluid motion. The Bird Man was surprised into reflex. His naked hands flew out like catcher's mitts; I could see past him to where his falconer's gloves were hanging off the keel. He caught the Seth hard against his chest. There was something almost funny about watching this, hysterically funny, but terrifying, too, a bad hilarity that lights up eel-bright in your belly. A hideous squeal went up through the trees but I don't know what happened next, if the red Seth bit him or clawed at him—I was off. I disappeared between two trees and felt my upper body career forward as I slid on the deep peat beds. I caught myself, monkey-swung my way out of a liquidy nick in the limestone. I sucked air on the jumps and splashed through pools of vegetation.

When I got up a little higher I dodged the willow heads and tried to avoid the obvious holes where female gators had piled and clubbed down brush.

Even running, I kept waiting to feel a hand fall onto my shoulder. The only noise I heard was my own progress through the cypress dome, my breath rocket-shipping up and up through a heavy tube of sky. *He is letting you go, you can stop running,* but I crashed through the dim hammock. Two great white herons stood like marble statuary in a belled opening in the trees and they opened their wings and they blew away from me and oh I was running so fast their flight looked like smoke; I fell and screamed, my hands sinking into a foot of water, and it took me many many seconds to get up.

The elevation crept up. I burst into a meadowland, reentered the woods, felt my toes curl inside the suck of deep, spongy peat. Curtains of Spanish moss caught at my hair like fishermen's nets. The night had developed a suffocating wetness—breathing felt like drowning in a liquid you couldn't climb out of. Collapse seemed like a wonderful option to me—to fall sideways, to curl into a ball and wait in the braiding weeds for help to come . . .

Sometimes you are able to keep moving because you are not really yourself anymore. Your entire brain can shrink to one pinhead of cognition, one star in a night. I was acquainted with it, this bright spot, because once or twice before it had taken over during my fiercest wrestling matches. Encapsuled in this pinhead lived a brute, a swimmer, a thirst, a hunger, a fire-hater, a grass-jumper. The same as anybody's, probably, as any living person's. I'm sure that yours and mine would push up for air with the same force:mass ratio. Would fin up, would open its frog mouth for air, would claw up, would gallop. This new self had all the personality of a muscle. Its haunches charged ahead of my heartbeat, leaving a wake of blood in my ears: KICK. KICK. KICK.

I ran for what felt like miles before allowing myself to slow, first to a trot and then to a wheezing walk. My vision got squiggly, and for a bad moment I thought that I would throw up. A saw-grass prairie had speared up all around me. I've read stories about Midwestern farmers who became lost in their own tall crops and I can imagine what that would be like—the saw grass went on for miles in every direction. I could make out little yeasty-rises of trees, bayhead islands, but no towns and no people.

"This is the stupidest thing you've ever done, Ava Bigtree." My voice did not sound much like my mother's. It spiked against the hum of the saw grass—on the horizon I saw a brown, serrated sea. I did not see an exit, an end to the echoing plants. If I could get back to the Calusa shell mounds, at least I'd know I was going the right way: north and east, homeward. Against the river's grain, the blue grin of the water. "A house," just the idea of a walled place you could enter, felt like a dream to me. I turned a circle in the tall grass, and every horizon looked like a step in the wrong direction.

As I sloshed forward, the song that we'd heard on the hunters' radio yesterday began to play in my head—"Bye, bye, Miss American Pie." The singers' cheerful voices had gone soft as wax between my ears, and I couldn't stop the chorus from looping and looping. Those lyrics put bad pictures in me: a gushing, a cherry-red spill onto the wide reeds, a Chevy's somber drive past the dry levee, and men inside the car, strangers crooning a farewell, their faces as mournful as blue dogs behind the dirty glass of a windshield. I pushed my face into the last dry square of my T-shirt. Ossie was dead, I was almost sure now. I felt pretty solidly that I was going to die out here. I toweled my eyes and kept walking.

Whip Jeters had seen me the previous afternoon, outside of the Eye, I remembered with a sudden fierce relief—but he thought I was on a fishing trip. Would he maybe contact the Chief to check my story out? I did not think so. I did not think he would. Why not keep things simple, go home to his wife and his dinner and his television, believe what I had told him? Was the Bird Man, my "cousin," looking for me? I thought about the two possibilities:

Yes (you will be found by him).

No (you won't be found by him).

Inside me these words took on the dimensions of rooms. To escape them I tried to recite multiplication tables as I walked, then weird-sounding state capitals like Bismark and Honolulu and Carson City, then my family's birth dates, and then the galloping da-dum, ba-dum of the Tennyson and Edgar Allan Poe poems that I had once memorized to impress Kiwi (". . . with a *love* that the *winged* ser*aphs* of *heav*en . . ."), anything to keep me moving. I was walking east, I thought, toward a large hammock, a place where the saw grass shuffled into a gloam of hardwood trees and boggy water. I felt the first tickle of thirst in my throat and this exploded into panic, like a germ flowering into a full-blown illness. (DRINK-DRINK-DRINK-DRINK! screamed my body at me, all sums and poems swallowed up by my thirst.) I put a palmful of rusty water into my mouth and spat it out—I wasn't thinking clearly. I couldn't afford to get sick, throw up, dehydrate myself further.

Then I convinced myself that I was being followed. I hugged a crusty root and hunched in two feet of water. Something came splashing through the cypress dome and I closed my eyes, struck by the crazy idea that the flash of white gel in my eyes would give me away. What did I have to defend myself with? I did a depressing inventory: wet clothing that at this point was truly coming apart at the seams. Ossie's ribbon. I had no food, no water. Okay. Okay. My mind chattered on, chewing through its own defenses. I had gone sprinting into the middle of the night. I had just run away from the only person who knew I was here.

You might be surprised to learn that I didn't know how to use a flare or start a fire. I'd lived in the swamp my whole life and I had no idea about the Essential Next Steps, what a person should do to save herself. Okay. Okay. Okay. Grandma Risa, my mother, Grandpa Sawtooth, the Chief, any one of them would be halfway home by now. Kiwi would have invented a radio with crystals from the river and made a genius escape.

I thought that Kiwi would have done me one better. He would never have come here.

Soon I was thirstier than I'd ever been in my life. It wasn't the actual thirst but the imagined thirst that was killing me, the picture of myself a few days from now crawling through the mangrove woods without a water bottle. Like Bianca and Michael, I thought (or: *like my sister*). And whenever I thought this, for just a second I'd miss the Bird Man so badly, his weird and sanguine whistling on the poling platform, his maps and his sunbursts of kindness and especially his promises that we would soon recover Osceola.

The woods were all sound. It was too black to see anything from where I was squatting but I heard a barred owl singing its whereabouts to a phantom mate until I longed for Grandpa's shotgun, to silence its relentless romancing. Didn't the barred owl know who might be out

here with us? Mostly I heard the mosquitoes. A soupy splashing somewhere far behind me that I thought might be an alligator. A branch
fell, sending up a lot of froggy chirruping like a little sonic dust.

Every year Search and Rescue saved a dozen novice fishermen, kayak-
ers, and canoers from the carnival halls of the mangrove tunnels not
four miles off the Loomis coast. Water made endless mirrors and the
small islands repeated themselves like a bad stutter, confusing the fishermen. These "terrestrial echoes" were the "swamp's echolalia," according to Kiwi, who liked to make geography as pretentious as possible.
"The Ten Thousand Islands" pretty nearly described their number. Park
Services marks the touristed canoe and kayak trails with white skunk
lines on the shoreline pines; in that alphabet of ranger paint, every turn
is spelled out for you. If you deviate from these popular loops, the stern
rangers warn, and try to chart your own course through the labyrinth,
you are entering a kind of Death Lottery. Kiwi called this claim
"administrative hyperbole." The Chief said we kids better stay on the
goddamn trail and travel in a pack or *he* would kill us, guaranteed, no
lottery required.

"You'll have to be very brave, kid," the Bird Man had said when we
rounded the first blue bend, gesturing at all the humming greenery
that ringed our stern. He'd made this same emptiness seem so exciting,
like a field for real magic. I bit my lip and I thought about how good it
had been that first day, back when I was separated from Ossie by twelve
hours, tops. Just one meridian, really, one sunless wedge of time. Who
knew how many hours separated us now?

One excellent luckiness was the moon. It was full and enormous, and
without it, I doubt I could have made it even half a mile through the
swamp that night. Water the color of hard cider slid between the trees
and everywhere I looked I saw schools of tiny red and black fishes. I'd
never seen fish like this before (although they looked very ordinary, it's
not as if they had coals for eyes or anything) and I didn't know any of
their names. Linty flowers covered the floating twigs. The air was
smelling saltier to me; perhaps I was nearing the Gulf.

By this point I had given my sister up. Not for dead—I don't mean
that—but I'd given up on the idea that I was going to find and save her.
I had failed her so completely that my mind would not permit me to
think about it. I kept sticking my finger into the bib pocket where my

red Seth had been, wiggling it around the way you do when you've misplaced your house keys and you keep checking the same four places with compulsive hopefulness. Where was she, my alligator? The Bird Man had killed her, I thought, kicking a rock and unearthing a squeal of ants. Even if she'd gotten away from him the prognostications were grim—alligators with unusual pigmentation can't camouflage themselves in the dust-and-olive palette of the swamp. Their skin is spotlit for predators. That's why you don't see albino Seths in the wild. Once an alligator reaches a size of four feet its only real predator is man, but during the first few years of a hatchling's life it has to worry about predation by pretty much everything: wading birds, buzzards, garfish, raccoons, snakes, the cannibal kings in our Pit.

I myself felt naked without her, as if I'd been wearing an armor composed of one scale and I'd thrown it away.

Ossie, I'd think in spasms, *I'm coming,* but these promises were like mental hiccups. Just thoughts, mindnoises, because I didn't feel strong enough to voice a promise. Sometimes I'd stumble on the rocky glade and not really want to get up, and then I figured out how to use the promises like poles or crampons. Just the name "Ossie" could hook me up.

The moon moved so slowly through the clouds above me, high and white, with a frightening grace, and I wondered how we'd never recognized the terror of the moon before, this big thing that you couldn't alter or ever reach. If I lived I was going to alert my brother and my sister to this interesting feature of the moon. Kiwi used to come running for us beneath the Perseid shower: "You are missing it, everybody!" he'd flail evangelically. "The end has already begun!"

Something caught at my shoelace, and when I looked down I was startled to find the dirty bowl of my face reflected on the water. My eyes rippled up at me. I didn't look anything like an alligator wrestler, I didn't even feel so much like a girl anymore.

Right at daybreak I started drinking the water. I'd stood sweating in the dome all night, until my thoughts shriveled up and I was just one feeling at a time: COLD or SORE or HUNGRY. All the cypress trunks were sopping up the limited sun and blushing against a gray sky. I crawled forward and bent like an animal over my own dumbstruck face, washing and cupping my hands in the shallows between the roots. The stick-and-needle-flickered brown water floated around the trees, and I drank and drank. This particular cypress dome was huge: I'd covered at least a mile of it and still it pulsed outward, the goliath trees ceding to six-foot dwarf cypress stumps at the perimeter. Skylight poured through the trees and reappeared in the cup of my hands as I crouched in the water. I drank in hot, foul gulps. One day without water should have been easy to tolerate; the torture part was thinking about the future of my thirst. It would grow and grow and do what with me? Thirst was bad, but the idea of night falling on me out here a second time was worse.

I have to get to higher ground, I decided.

"Think!" I commanded my brain. But my brain was a roaring liquid between my eardrums—"thinking" felt like trying to get a river to flex. This I guessed was panic. Pounding everywhere, timpani to bridge a waterfall. A headache throbbed from my temples to my earlobes. I'd never felt this way during a wrestling show; I'd never realized how much the tourists were helping me, just by holding down those chairs. Fear onstage was a thrilling feeling—often it was the prelude to a Bigtree victory. Fear out here was a new species. The sky above me got torn to small crystals by the cypress leaves and as the sun rose it went blue and deeper; some creature shouted *kee-ow, kee-ow* in the middle distance. I did and did not want to be found by the Bird Man. You couldn't fool yourself into thinking a discovery like that would be a rescue. But who else knew to look for me, or where? I peered into the thick brush and got angry at the future: it seemed there was not one good thing left to hope for.

Okay-okay-okay, my mind kept chattering. Why was my mind feasting on the worst pictures? I saw the dredge hung up on rocks and my sister's body inside it, as quiet as a sleeper, her purple skirt draped over the railing. I saw the red Seth floating belly-up on a nameless slough. Every time I heard a stick snap I knew it was the Bird Man. Fear kept making itself inside me. Certain feelings kept making themselves inside me, the way that blood rises to a tiny bead. But if you kept thinking about a fight you'd lost, Mom said, you were programming yourself to lose again.

I did more mental math. I recited primes, which my brother had taught me were the strong, indivisible numbers. *1, 3, 7, 11 . . .* I counted, wrestling off a shoe. I stood on my left leg in the dark water and struggled to pull the soaking shoelace out of its tabs. I was alone, but maybe not for long.

Because the vast floodplain from Okeechobee flows in a southwesterly direction, you can use the swamp water as a compass. I undid the laces from my left sneaker and tied them to a cypress knee. Water in the limestone depression of a dome only appears to be stagnant, you just have to watch it to give the lie to that. After five minutes of storky balancing on one leg, I had my answer. Bingo! The shoelace pointed southwest, toward the Gulf. I relaced. I had a strong itch to run, which would have been a very stupid relief to seek—already I'd found one sinkhole with my stick. A scarlet king snake slithered over a stump, its fantastic licorice colors glowing against the blacky green resurrection ferns.

Although the underworld had been a big hoax, the black raptors continued to map the sky. The buzzards from Ohio had migrated here, too. Turning circles, as docile as party ponies around a mainland carousel. Then they fell, one by one, like little black razors, into the paurotis palms. And it was hard to see this and not to think of carnage. A line of birds falling in a row. Red clouds massed in the southeast and it looked like the sky was getting its stitches out after an operation.

It had been so good for a little bit, to picture my mom out here. To think that I was on my way to meet her, in the blue mists of the underworld. Why had I ever believed the book? Quick as fire on peat, my mists were gone. Now instead of adventuring into an underworld I found myself in the most treacherous part of the swamp.

Seas of saw grass flooded into other, larger seas. No boats and no houses, no smoke rising on the mirror-flat horizon.

I said my little continual prayer that Ossie be alive and dry and far, far, far, far behind me. I tried not to think about the bad possibilities of just where she might be, or who was with her (such thoughts as: *What if the Bird Man has found her?*) and especially to never think about the ending of the Dredgeman's Revelation.

Okay. Okay. I had to move now. There was an orange light thinking its way across the darkness over the swamp and that was the sun.

At the dome's edge, two black branches spooned out of the same wide trunk. They looked like mirror images, these branches, thin and papery and perfectly cupped, blue sky shining behind them, and an egret sat on the scooped air like a pearl earring. I squeezed through the left opening and scraped sooty bark all over my arms. At one point, I went sloshing into an old hole up to my chest; lily pads and mosquito larvae swarmed in front of my eyes. Accidentally I choked more water down. The Chief would have been proud—at last I'd turned the color of a real Indian. My neck and arms and legs were dyed a black-maroon from the tannins and I itched everywhere, as if my whole body was developing a rash. I wrung out my Swamplandia! T-shirt and continued walking. You could barely read the letters on it now. After a while the forest started to change.

CHAPTER TWENTY

Out to Sea

Two days had passed since Kiwi had seen the Chief and he still hadn't made a move to contact him. But he would! Today maybe. He'd mentally scripted the whole encounter—first he would reveal his many mainland accomplishments to his dad. He was a local Loomis hero, surely the Chief had heard something about that? He had saved a girl's life inside the Leviathan, wasn't that something? He'd earned one of four positions in the World of Darkness as an Apocalyptic Pilot; in September he would get his GED.

In Kiwi's fantasy of this meeting, the Chief didn't say much. Really, he didn't say anything—maybe he would be overcome and just sort of paternally beam? Conveniently choked by pride, or joy? Or, failing those ambitious emotions, perhaps they could at least achieve a food truce, the picnic suspension of oedipal feeling that permits the genera- tions to love each other at family reunions? Kiwi prayed that was how it would go down, anyway, because when he tried to imagine having an actual conversation in the English language with his father in that casino: that was the end of the tape.

Okay, new version: the Chief doesn't say anything, but he takes Kiwi upstairs and they eat everything that isn't nailed down in the All U Can Eat Buffet. They shovel it in. At the end of the meal, they plunge their Bigtree fists into the tank and tear apart and eat that final lobster. It would be a moment of savage forgiveness. No words required. It would be barbaric and a little gross, eating that lobster, but it would have the transformative effect of a new ritual on them. After the meal, they would be reconciled. They would make plans to return to Ava and Ossie and Swamplandia! They would bring Grandpa Sawtooth home, possibly they would go downstairs and gamble together, and win.

Kiwi didn't go back to the casino. He didn't look up any bus routes. He didn't call the listed number for Pa-Hay-Okee Gaming and ask for Sam. He didn't ask Vijay for a ride to Pa-Hay-Okee, or thumb up the number in the Loomis Yellow Pages. Kiwi's best conjecture was that the Chief had rented a room at the Bowl-a-Bed hotel, as he always did on his Loomis trips. (THE BOWL-A-BED! WEEKLY RATES. MAJOR CREDIT CARDS ACCEPTED, YOUR PRIVACY=RESPECTED!!)

But he didn't call there.

Instead, he used the bag of change to dial the house at Swamplandia! on his breaks. The phone buzzed and buzzed, a noise that was starting to really frighten him. Were the girls in Loomis County, too?

I have to go back there today, Kiwi thought. *I have to talk to the Chief.* When he picked up the telephone, he fully intended to ask Vijay to drive him back to the casino. On the second ring, the third ring, this remained his intention.

Vijay wanted to know why he was dropping Kiwi off at a fucking *marina.* On Hangover Sunday, no less. Why he was awake at all before dusk—Kiwi had once overheard Vijay having a screaming argument with his mother in which he claimed that getting up before noon made him feel dizzy. Vijay was wearing dark wraparound sunglasses and eating Advil in Halloween fistfuls.

"I'll put the *mace* into your *face,* bitch!" he sang along with the radio.

They pulled into a space between two whiskery palms, both boys shading their eyes from the sun's rays off the white quartzite. Dirty water lapped at a honeycomb of rock; beyond this, the listing masts of all the junker ships at anchor here made the ocean look like a blue pincushion.

"What is this place? Is it a junkyard for boats?"

"And people. Hey, thanks for the ride. I can get the bus back."

"For real? You sure you want to dip into your savings account for that? I think the fare is, like, a whole dollar."

"Shut up."

Vijay's voice brightened theatrically: "Or maybe you want to have your rich *girlfriend* come get you? You can, like, save her from the *ocean* this time?"

"I don't have a girlfriend, V. Emily Barton is not my girlfriend."

"Is that you telling me in your moon language that you're, like, still a virgin?"

"Fuck you."

"Nice, son. You're getting so much quicker at the trigger! Smoother, too," he added generously.

Kiwi thought back to his first weeks, when insults had been impossible for him. One time he'd called Deemer a troglodyte but his delivery had been tentative and way, way too slow, as if the insult were a fork tenderly entering a steak. Now he could tell any man in the World to go fuck himself with a baseball bat. Progress was being made, he guessed.

"Thanks. I try."

Kiwi had arrived at the Out to Sea Retirement Community eleven minutes early. Through the Out to Sea portholes, Kiwi could hear TV laughter and silence.

At four, Kiwi walked the gangplank to his grandfather's boat. A translucent glass-blue crab went skittering behind one of the bolts. Possibly-Robina was sitting there in her civilian clothes—a striped T-shirt with a cartoon cat in a top hat on it, shiny purple leggings. She was watching a soap opera on the boat's biggest television. All around her the elderly residents were involved in their own dramas: smaller televisions glowed and crackled along the rows of portholes.

"Howdy, ma'am . . . okay to visit with Sawtooth Bigtree?"

"Mmh." Robina's chin was sunk behind her big fists. Kiwi bent and scribbled his name on the blank clipboard.

"Good show, huh?"

Possibly-Robina sucked a diet soda through a straw.

Kiwi had to flip back two weeks to find the name he was looking for: Samuel Bigtree. The Chief had last been here two weeks ago. Was the Chief planning to visit today? Kiwi wondered. He thought about erasing his signature from the sheet, then decided to leave it there.

Everyone besides Robina was asleep, or tortoised deeply into their own world; one Russian man with burning cerulean eyes was leaning in to watch an infomercial, his great knuckles bunched like red grape skins on his slacks. On the TV screen, a woman smeared pink jelly on her crow's-feet and became young. "Miracle formula: Mariana diatoms. $69.99 in three payments!" a voiceover announced.

"What she saying?" the Russian man kept repeating. "What she doing? Wheel me closer!"

Soledad, a ninety-something Cuban woman with moist eyes, started screaming at Kiwi in Spanish. She had been Grandpa Sawtooth's friend on the last visit, but maybe Grandpa had bitten her since then.

"Your grandfather is never going to be the prom king of Out to Sea, okay?" Robina had informed them when they'd first moved Sawtooth in. "You guys better give up that dream. He is not a people person."

"Hiya, Soledad. How's my grandpa? What's news?"

Possibly this was an insensitive question. "News" for these retirees no longer meant "events" but instead seemed to describe the lisping voices of the tides. From every corner of the schooner patients blinked down at him, quietly magnetized to the boat's surfaces. Like the swamp's red-toed lizards, they seemed stuck to their bed rails and their chairs' handlebars by the pads of their fingers.

Kiwi walked into the galley. "Hi, Harold."

Harold no longer remembered him. He was sitting on one of a dozen plastic stools, eating a banana very, very slowly in a pair of new pajamas. White ducklings marched up the pant legs on an alarming voyage toward Harold's crotch. A patch was affixed to his chest and he kept scratching at it.

"Do you have a cigarette?" he asked Kiwi. "I could really use a cigarette." When Kiwi did not answer he returned to his contemplation of the banana.

"Harold, have you seen my grandfather?"

"I'm right here, you damn fool!" came a familiar croak from the deck outside the central cabin. Kiwi moved through a blinding square of sun and found his grandfather out on the starboard deck, barefoot in a puddle of the filtered seawater. His feet were bloated and shiny as custard, with curled, wintry toenails.

"Hi, Grandpa."

His face was stubbornly set in its Bigtree crags.

"Grandpa Sawtooth, it's me, Kiwi."

Not a flicker.

"Like a fruit." Grandpa Sawtooth smiled evilly. "That's a damn fool name."

Kiwi moved into the shade of the cabin's roof and took a breath. Behind his grandfather's head, he could see to where the seawall curved and enclosed the entire marina. He didn't know how the residents of Out to Sea could bear to look at it—the future closing its circle on them and the sun dribbling down into the sea behind it.

"So. I saw Dad two days ago."

Kiwi sat down in one of the blue deck chairs and his grandfather followed.

"Grandpa!" Kiwi looked to see if anyone was listening; there were a few dark clouds and one enormous gull leisurely devouring sea bugs on the boom. "Grandpa, the Chief is working at a casino. The one they call the Jesus in the Temple Casino, over by the new penitentiary. Did you know that? I bet you knew that, huh?"

"Look at that big sucker." His grunt sounded satisfied. He was pointing at the feasting gull on the ropes. "Hungry."

"Grandpa, can you tell me, has the Chief been working at the casino for a long time? Has he had other jobs? Did you know about his other jobs?" He paused. "Did Mom know?"

Sawtooth was watching the ocean. Wave after wave covered the sandy bottom of the marina. Jade squiggles alternated with blue and black inky ones wherever the sun hit depth. Something about watching this made Kiwi feel for an instant that he was staring into his grandfather's mind: memories like these bright schools of mullet, abandoning his grandfather in leaps.

"Why did you guys hide it from us, Grandpa? Is the Chief angry that he has to do it? Is it our fault—I mean, the money part?"

Sawtooth was still frowning into the ocean, as if something magnificent were about to occur there. All those small flickers dispersing, unschooling.

"Okay. Fine. Can I please tell you something?" Kiwi's voice tapered to a point. "Can I tell you something? Your daughter-in-law, Hilola?"

At Out to Sea, Sawtooth's lifelong tan had faded to the color of creamed corn. He regarded his grandson warily, as if he were about to lose a privilege. Kiwi imagined that typically if a stranger came to talk to you at Out to Sea, this could portend nothing good.

"I am so sorry to be the one . . ." Kiwi cleared his throat. In a quieter voice, he told Sawtooth what had happened to Hilola Bigtree.

"Dead," Sawtooth croaked. "Hah."

The word had a dull thwack to it, like a fat raindrop hitting tarp. The drop rolled away and vanished. Nothing at all registered on his grandfather's face.

"Mom died a whole year ago, Grandpa. More, now."

For some reason he told him the exact date in a whisper. He could hear Harold coughing up banana inside the cabin; another resident was cycling through her television channels.

"We didn't tell you, I don't know, we didn't want to . . ."

Sawtooth smoothed a finger over his otterish whiskers. He met Kiwi's gaze with bald, staring eyes, the same depth and shape as the Chief's eyes, Kiwi's own eyes. The family had heard from Robina that Sawtooth suffered crying spells, at night—"like a schoolchild!" This was impossible for Kiwi to imagine, his granddad weeping; on Swamplandia! Sawtooth would pry the Mesozoic splinters of an alligator's teeth from his skin with black doll's eyes, unblinking, glassy with pain.

Well, he sure wasn't crying over Mom. His eyes were perfectly calm. Sea light pulsed in them.

"Dead," he repeated. A whisper, conspiratorial. "Huh. Did you tell Robina? Dead is bad, boy. You could get in trouble."

Behind Kiwi's head, a TV audience broke into raucous laughter and applause. Kiwi leaned in until his long nose was almost touching Grandpa Sawtooth. He moved forward, scooting to the edge of the blue-and-white deck chair, until their foreheads *were* touching. He dunked his own dim form into Sawtooth's pupils and waited for a "Hello, Kiwi." Sawtooth held his gaze patiently. Sawtooth Bigtree's hands looked big as lobster claws on his meager thighs; all of the man's ligaments looked to be in some state of bad flux, bulging or withering on the vine. "Normal aging" the textbooks would say, but "normal" seemed an injustice when it described *this*. Sawtooth's wrists were the width of a child's again. Kiwi took a breath.

"After Mom died, we lost most of the tourists . . ."

Kiwi had a sudden urge to topple his grandfather, to dump the elder overboard—maybe that would shake something loose in there or reconnect a wire. What was the point of growing so aged and limp that your mind couldn't make a fist around a name? He wanted Sawtooth Bigtree to hurt, to ache, to mourn, to howl, to push with the cooling poker of his mind into the old ash heap of what he had lost and scrape bottom. He wanted the old man to be depleted to that limit. *Like the rest of us,* Kiwi thought angrily. *Like family.*

"I'm a traitor, Grandpa. Think Benedict Arnold. I'm working at the World of Darkness. You know I've been away from home for months now, Grandpa," he heard himself saying. "Not quite as long as you've been away, but a long time. So I don't have any news to share about your GRANDDAUGHTERS, AVA or OSCEOLA."

"What the Christ are you shouting for, son? People are trying to catch fish out here. You're going to scare all the damn fish away."

Grandpa's jaw muscles sagged and twitched. His eyes were lively, but it was like the empty animation of a fireplace. "I'm hot. I don't like your tone. I'm going inside."

"Mom's dead. Our park is bankrupt. Your son works in a casino now. Ossie went batshit this summer, and I'm pretty sure she thinks she's having sex with ghosts. Ava is alone with her on the island. Do you like that?"

With a look of infantile craftiness, Grandpa Sawtooth reared back and spit in his face.

Sawtooth swung first. Kiwi was still wiping the foamy spittle from his face with his shirt hem when his head snapped back, the old man punching his left cheek. Later, Kiwi would tell Robina and the Loomis EMT that he had provoked his grandfather—which might have even been true. Maybe the pitch of Kiwi's voice tripped an old wire of antagonism in Grandpa Sawtooth's brain, his outburst a limbic accident. Whatever the case, both men threw themselves into the fight. The deck chairs clattered as they fell away from them. Kiwi's eyes widened: *He's choking me.* The moment arrived when he would have killed his grandfather if he could have. He couldn't break the hold, though, and his grandfather tightened his grip around Kiwi's windpipe. With an obscene clarity of mind Kiwi recognized what Sawtooth was doing: this was a Bigtree maneuver, a way to get a Seth to open its jaws.

"You damn fool," he muttered. Kiwi had no air to respond.

They crashed against the railing on the starboard side of the boat; Kiwi's head got swung into the porthole; someone's wrinkled face floated into view there, disappeared. A carousel of faces passed by, deathpale and unfamiliar faces. It was just the other residents. Seniors with no clue what was going on outside the cabin. An anhinga that had been drying its wings on a mile marker shot into the sky. Kiwi was trying to steer his grandfather toward a coil of heavy rope that he hoped the old man might trip on.

"Jaw up," Grandpa Sawtooth used to shout at Kiwi on the Pit stage when he was five, eight, eleven. "Step up. Man up."

Kiwi shut his eyes then. Felt his grandfather's thick hands around his throat. He saw colors and they were slow and round as bubbles: black as bad purpose. Red as purpose (his fists were flailing now, falling down on Sawtooth, he could hear the old man cry out in pain). Blood trickled into his mouth from a cut on his upper lip. Kiwi opened his eyes and he didn't know what he was doing, the whole stereoscopic world having flattened into brilliance. All he knew for certain was that he was fighting back. He could breathe again. He could scream again. He swiped at the old man's wet shirt and closed on a handle of skin. His left hand squeezed down, and Sawtooth screamed with pain. Kiwi banged into a deck chair, howling, and he grabbed at whatever he could and he twisted. Both men looked down at Kiwi's hands around the base of Sawtooth's neck, as if equally surprised to find them there.

"Huh!" gargled his grandfather.

Kiwi could feel the man's birdy veins. His fingers were long enough to stitch a mitt around his grandfather's throat. His grandfather was hissing now, a coarse, inhuman sound. So this was the only answer the old man could give him, the only explanation—a nonsense hiss. *The Seths know more about our family than you do,* Kiwi thought furiously. He squeezed. Instinct drove him forward like a nail and he kept squeezing.

You are squeezing too hard, a small, milk-neutral voice inside Kiwi noted. *You might actually kill him.* The voice didn't have the shrillness of a conscience; it was bored and old, content to let Death happen.

Kiwi let go.

Robina tried to get him to go to the emergency room but he refused; he watched with fascination as welts rose in archipelagos on his skin. Kiwi touched one gingerly and winced, blinked tears back into his eyes. Robina was asking him in a worried hiss if he was going to press charges; she didn't specify who these charges would be pressed against, Sawtooth Bigtree or Out to Sea or her personally, and for a disorienting moment Kiwi thought she was asking him to turn himself in to the police.

"What? Criminal charges? No, I don't think that's necessary, okay? I just want to go. I'm really sorry . . ."

He'd left Grandpa Sawtooth watching *Cheers* reruns with Harold, both men sipping at Vital Light shakes that looked like peed-on snow. The "Heeeere's . . . Cliffy!" episode was on. Grandpa Sawtooth had just two bruises that Kiwi could see—the dark blue-red stain of hemoglobin into bilirubin on his shrunken biceps, and a purpling of ruptured vessels on his cheek. The EMT had given him a clean bill of health.

"You got off *extremely* lucky," the EMT had told him with relish. "He's an old man"—the EMT kept repeating this to Kiwi, as if it were a controversial diagnosis. "An old, old man. You could have suffocated him. How would you like that, huh? How would you like to do jail time for killing your own grandfather?"

Kiwi shook his head, to indicate that he would probably not like that.

"You got off lucky this time, but I wouldn't bet on it again."

Now Kiwi nodded. He was afraid to talk. Two violet thumbprints were darkening at the front of his neck, a tier of ghostly fingerprints at the nape.

When Kiwi returned to the World dormitories, the elevator doors opened on faint sniggering, the TV screen drumming softly with pale light—the lounge was empty, but somebody was inside his dorm room. *The Chief!* Kiwi thought for a crazy moment. Then he heard the phlegmy rocket of Leo's guffaw.

Leo and Vijay were standing in the middle of his room, wearing big shit-eating grins from ear to ear. They both had frozen, red-handed postures.

"What are you dudes doing in here?" Kiwi hated the pitch of his voice.

"Vijay says you're broke, Bigtree," Leo said. "So we decided to get you a little something. Think of it as an early birthday present, like . . ."

He swung the closet door open and Kiwi's heart stopped.

The boys had put up a poster: a shiny centerfold from a porn magazine. Her face was an absolute blank but Kiwi returned the gaze of her enormous brown nipples, which seemed somehow sorrowful and frank, alert to a great sadness behind the pornographer's camera, while the boys smirked.

"Look, he loves it!"

"Ha-ha," Kiwi heard himself say. "Thanks, guys."

Next followed innuendo of the conventionally scatalogical variety and Saturday insults, "cocksuckers" and "pussylickers" raining down on him like blows, and each time Kiwi spoke a word it felt like raising an arm to cover his face: "Fuck you, fuck you, shut *up*."

Kiwi elbowed past them and tried to shut the closet door with a growl of laughter. Then he saw what they had done to the poster of his mother.

"Oh, sorry, bro." Leo let out a buzzy laugh but then changed tone when he saw Kiwi's face, pinching at his earlobe. The mood in the room became cinder-flecked. "That was like an accident? We were trying to get that ugly one off the wall, that's some seventies shit right there . . ."

They had split her down her middle. SWA and MP CENTAUR read two halves of it. Half her face regarded him with its dusk intelligence, and he pushed the scraps of her into his fists. Kiwi wanted to scream at everyone to get out of his room, to die slow and go right to *hell;* out loud he could hear his dull, persistent chuckle.

What he could hear as clearly as if it were still happening was the blare of the Chief's banter through the Pit's loudspeakers:

"Hilola Bigtree has more talent in her pinkie finger than any other wrestler on the planet!

"Hilola Bigtree can tape up a twelve-foot gator in the time it takes you mainlanders to haul your lard asses up to the fridge!"

All day long the Chief's good publicity funneled into the blue sky inside Kiwi, scattering birds.

Patched together the poster would have read HILOLA BIGTREE, SWAMP CENTAUR. Kiwi had always been embarrassed by this particular epithet for her—more of the Chief's lame publicity—but it was a name that his mother was growing into, apparently. Because here she was: a real centaur on the door. The closet wood showed through half a dozen rips in the poster and blanked out one cheek. You could touch the grain of the wood through her torn forehead. A crescent of her smile hung on a little fang of green paper. Death was speeding her evolution into this monster: half woman and half invention. Kiwi couldn't remember the real color of his mother's hair anymore, her nascent wrinkles like the first cracks in an eggshell, her voice, her beautiful scowl, because the poster had papered over her third dimension and now even it was ruined.

"Kiwi? Learn to take a fucking joke, bro . . ."

"No, it's fine."

He touched the paper of her face and shut the door.

CHAPTER TWENTY-ONE

Mama Weeds

Ossie's ribbon was still on my wrist. All it did was remind me that I had a sister somewhere, the way you'd strap a watch to your wrist to keep you in time. If the Bird Man had showed up and tried to take this cloth protection from me then, I really think I might have killed him.

This part of the swamp grew very noisy at night, growls and squelches and the infinitesimal roaring of each mosquito piling into waves. Sticks snapped and once I heard a large animal go crashing through the water; all I saw, though, were the tall gumbo-limbo trees that were like pepper shakers of moths. Probably the Bird Man was miles and miles away from me, I told myself. On his way home, back through the Eye and this phony underworld. In a way, he'd made good on his promise to me, our bargain, because I couldn't imagine a hell that would be worse than this place where he'd left me. Overhead the sky was a fast and swallowing blue.

"Ossie?" I gulped. "Mom?"

I fixed my eyes on two palm trees at the edge of the saw-grass prairie; I was going to use them as goalposts. I started to walk. I could see little oases of thatch-palm and cabbage trees, carpets of gray sea oxeye, of red sea bight, and between these the stalks weaving, endlessly, acres and acres of this.

*   *   *

I walked steadily all morning. By noon I was getting really mixed up. I drank more of the silty groundwater and then threw it back up an hour later.

If I don't find water, I thought, *freshwater, rainwater, potable water, and soon . . .*

Now I didn't always recognize the cries of the animals; whatever adhesion in my brain connected sounds and light to the names of species was breaking down. The leaves that I had easily identified as bay or gumbo-limbo or pop ash gave way to a muted palette of foliage, a glowing russet and gray, much of it alien to me. Fewer and fewer of the plants that I tripped over or pushed through in curling curtains of vines uprooted a name in my mind. I was seeing new geometries of petals and trees, white saplings that pushed through the peat like fantailing spires of coral, big oaky trunks that went wide-arming into the woods (no melaleucas anywhere). A large egretlike bird with true fuchsia eyes and cirrusy plumage went screeching through the canopy. For some reason all the life gurgling in the anonymous hammock made me want to cry. *Some underworld this turned out to be, Ossie.*

I started to think it might not be a terrible thing if the Bird Man found me. A little later I began drafting my apologies to him for leaving. If he had water, I wanted him to find me now. I didn't care at all what happened afterward . . .

Then I pushed through a stand of palms and saw the house. It was a one-room bungalow, the sort of dilapidated structure that swamp rats like Grandpa Sawtooth used for a fish camp or a hunting cabin. A tripod of sticks held a resin pot over a stack of pinewood; a stiller pump stood pondside. My heart leapt—my first thought was that we must have rowed to the Gulf coast, where you could find a few actual towns on the elevated pinelands. I got it in my head that I was walking toward a town. It didn't matter that nothing else I had seen or smelled or heard in the last few hours bore this theory out: I was on the outskirts of some island community, I decided, a place with televisions, telephones, refrigerators filled with sodas and cold cuts and cans of whipped cream, paper towels, pet dogs, telephone wires—I was on a roll now, I was close to blinking back tears—generators! electric light! hot showers! toilet paper! I walked behind the first house.

"Hello?"

This first house appeared to be the only house. A live alligator was sunk into the mud behind the southernmost wall, watching me as I scouted the perimeter. Switchgrass sprayed like a little beard beneath the blue-black apples of its cheeks. Its grin upset me in a way our Seths' musculature never did back home.

"It's not funny," I hissed. "You're the clown, you stupid monster, you don't know anything, you don't love anyone, you can't even imagine . . ."

I looked inside a begrimed window and I thought: *abandoned.* For sure nobody lived here. There was a straw pallet on the needle-covered floor and no furniture that I could see. Dishes on shelves, little cups. Outside its wooden walls had been completely overtaken by weeds and strangler fig, thick vines doing their weird tethered ballet when the wind blew. Water thinned to a brothlike cup between the mangroves. *Oh, yes,* I thought. I was going to drink all of it.

Thirst dragged me by my neck to the bottom creek and I was halfway to water before I noticed the clothesline. Clothes*lines,* I realized— there were half a dozen of them strung like a winking web in the high branches. Clothes were snapping all along both banks of the canal. The blouses nearest to me hung like cutouts against the sun, pinned and flapping. Sunshine turned them mild shades of gold or ghostly whites. The vaguest beiges made me think of photographs waiting to develop.

Some of the clothes looked antique. I found a woman's glove with a star-shaped wine stain over the palm. Each finger was bent against the wire by a clothespin. Many of the items looked burned and stained, moth-eaten. A gingham sundress had holes that I could have put my fist through. I thought again of photographs in the developing solution of the blue-violet air. Only the sky out here seemed like a deteriorating solution—it was erasing them.

A black hat brim—just the brim—hung from two pins like a shocked O.

Oh. I took a step toward the tree line, and for a second the maze of clotheslines looked as if they went on forever and ever. A line of billowing dresses that stretched to infinity, missing their women. All the silhouettes were wrinkling. Then I blinked and the image of an eternally twining line was gone. The clothes just looked like dirty old clothes strung from one branch to another again, mosquitoes shimmering vacantly around them. But where had all this clothing come from, in the middle of the swamp? *Mama.* The name came to me without warning out of the aching blue sky. *Mama Weeds.*

There is a legend in our swamp about a lady, a laundress—or a ghost, or a female monster—named Mama Weeds. She was like an island bogeyman. Her story predated us. The Chief liked to tell it to tourists: he'd ham it up and do all the different drawling voices like a radio play.

Mama Weeds started life as a real woman, Midnight Drouet, a light-skinned black seamstress descended from freed slaves who lived in the Ten Thousand Islands. A beautiful woman, so quiet that strangers assumed she was mute, with no real interest in rearing children or marrying a man. She moved to the deep interior of the swamp and worked there as a seamstress and a laundress; the pioneers could leave their clothing with her and she'd sew up holes and sew on faux gold buttons, a bottomless bucket of which she'd brought with her from the factory that once employed her in Troy, New York. People swore that she could get any stain out in the river by her house. Her few neighbors, moonshiners and gator skinners among them, were incensed by her presence.

"You won't make it," they told her. "You won't last the wet season. You'll howl at all the mosquitoes, the snakes, the scalybacks that dig their holes beneath your floorboards."

But Midnight Drouet didn't howl and she didn't go mad—the way my dad told the story, her composure was like a gun she kept cocked and pointed at her door. Five years later the gator skinners were infuriated to discover that she had, in fact, made it and lasted. Midnight built her own buttonwood shack and never asked for anybody's help. She refused to let her neighbors hunt on her property. One day she mentioned to the bird warden that she'd shot a ten-foot alligator with her .22—he had been going for her dog, she said, a huge smoky mongrel named Luke. No: she had not bothered to skin the alligator for the tanneries. No: she hadn't tried to sell or cure its meat. Word of this failure to profit from slaughter got around and the glade crackers were appalled—the Depression was on and here she'd killed an alligator with a huge dollar value and refused to skin the damn thing? Unforgivable. Selfish. Evil. Any one of them would have been glad to turn the carcass into coins for their own families. Apparently the bull gator's head had languished in the water behind her house until the scales slipped, its hide moon-permeated and worthless.

And then it's said that a man out there, or several men, rowed over to her island at night. "He" or "they" killed Miss Drouet, in cold blood. The decision was cold cognition, explained my brother, who liked to add a pinch of forensics to our gory swamp legends. Most people believe it was the work of several men, owing to the kind of damage that they reputedly did to her. For no other reason than that she'd killed that alligator and let it rot! A cardinal sin in those days, according to the Chief, back when people were killing the last snowy egrets for a buck five . . .

This part always made me dart under the covers, because I couldn't stop seeing poor Miss Drouet in my mind's eye, gagged and dragged down to the water by her murderers, dead already and now drowning, too, her cloth dress opening like a flower on the swamp water in a mixed-up and evil chronology. Her dead body floating. Her dead face, the mask of it, rising and falling on the sea's uneasy breath.

Panthers found and finished her in the cattails. Wind unstitched her skeleton. Weeds sprayed outward from the heart-shaped wreck of her pelvis; a sinkhole opened beneath her and gave way with the suddenness of caved ice, swallowing her bones. Children who had never heard about Luke or Midnight Drouet began to report seeing a shadowy figure along rivers, beneath the dry fingers of palms. "Mama Weeds!" a little glade cracker boy called her: the woman he saw was standing in the Caloosahatchee with a quiet dog by her side, covered in pigweed. The first child who saw her hadn't been frightened: she was doing laundry, he said, beating clothes against rocks, beating the dyes and patterns right out of them until colored oils ran downstream in twining browns and indigos and reds. The name stuck. If ever you saw a woman alone at the edge of the swamp at dusk, that lady was her, that was Mama.

I touched my throat. Personally, I had always considered the story of Mama Weeds a little silly. I had rambled all over the islands and I never once saw a ghost dog or a weedy lady in a lake. Kiwi was always telling me that Chief Bigtree's swamp lore was uniquely stupid and that I didn't have to believe it—if the swamp boomers had killed Midnight, he said, assuming a woman named Midnight Drouet had indeed existed, then she was dead and that was that.

But what if I was looking at an aerial cemetery? What if these clothes were Mama Weeds's collection? In the vacant spots where no clothes were hanging, the line seemed to disappear against the blue sky. Your eyes could pick it up again further down the trees as tines of light. Far down in the west I could see five or six buzzards, spaced out on the clothesline like mainland pigeons on a telephone wire. Below them, some family's checkered tablecloth made half a bubble on the wind.

I nearly jumped out of my skin; I saw a jacket that I recognized. It was one of the articles closest to me, pinned a few feet from where I was standing. A jacket that was so old and sun-faded that it had gone cuticle white—a WPA jacket, Bigtree museum quality, the Chief would have gone berserk for it. The shirt beside it had checks running in a canary net over the fabric; the last time I saw this garment, Osceola had been wearing it in our kitchen. Initials were sewn in cursive on the pocket—L.T.—in fat raspberry thread. Then a brighter purple caught my eye, an amethyst, the same shade as the ribbon around my wrist, and I saw that Ossie's favorite skirt was hanging one line over. It was the clothing she'd been wearing when she left to marry Louis T.

I was pulling Ossie's skirt from the line when a woman appeared around the side of the house. The occupant! I started to open my mouth to call for help, stopped.

She was huge—not fat so much as absolutely solid. She might have seemed ugly in a run-of-the-mill way to me if she'd been a tourist on our boardwalk. I had seen plenty of out-of-the-way women who looked like her before; she wasn't covered in pigweed, there was no panting hound named Luke beside her. She had big dimpled arms, a dizzying profusion of gray-and-black hair. She was wearing a dress that looked ready to burst off her. It was too delicate for her, with its short puffed sleeves and its color, a faded yellow with tiny heart-shaped white flowers. My mother used to wear a dress like that, with a very similar look. No, I thought with a slow and brain-penetrating chill, she used to wear *this* dress. I was certain now that I was staring at Mama Weeds.

"What are you doing here, girl?"

She looked like a woman but I wouldn't be fooled. I saw my mother's dress hanging off her and I knew this creature was a thief, a monster.

"How did you get these things?" I yelled. "What did you do with my sister?"

"Your sister!"

And then her big hand was on my shoulder and I ducked away from her. Her breath felt moist on my cheeks. She grabbed at me and I raked my nails down her arm; she screamed and I twisted away.

"What on God's earth are you talking about? Where's your mother, girl? Are you out here alone? You got a sister with you?"

At the mention of my mother I shuddered out of her grasp. This creature was teasing me. "You can't have her!" I screamed. I tried to wrench the dress off her.

Our eyes met. I looked up, still swaying from my fistfuls of the stolen dress. What I saw inside them was all landscape: no pupil or colored hoop of iris but the great swamp—the islands, the saw-grass prairies. Long grasses seemed to push onward for miles inside the depths of her eyes. Inside each oval I saw a world of saw grass and no people. Believe me—I know how that must sound. But I stood there and I watched as feathery clouds blew from her left eye behind the bridge of her nose and appeared again in her right socket. I saw a nothing that rolled forward forcefully forever. There was nobody in the ether of either white sky.

I heard the wind on the pond all around us, a deep clay smell rising from her skin. When she blinked again, her eyes looked black and oily, ordinary. For years I've wondered if this person I met was only a woman.

"You're a monster," I said quietly. "I wish you'd give me back my mother."

"Girl, you are not making a lick of sense now . . ."

"Get away from me!" I screamed. "You can't have these! My sister is *alive*." I used the Bigtree maneuvers to get away from her, dodging the hand that snaked out for me as quickly as I'd leap away from a Seth's thrashing tail, lunging at a spot above her calf where the dress hung loose. I had to get my family away from her.

"What are you talking about, your sister? You need to calm down. My God, you look like some rabid animal! How old are you, girl? How did you get way out here?"

Her voice made me think of the Bird Man's voice, bright with a false kindness. I held Osceola's and Louis's clothing and began to back away from her, a snarl clawing its way up my throat. I had rescued their clothes and a two-inch triangle of my mother's dress.

"Hey, girl!" the monster shouted. "You need help! Girl, get back here!"

When I got to a small drift slough I drank more of the water. I ate saw-grass buds, peeled sticks between my teeth. No longer did I think that drinking the water was a bad idea—I didn't have any ideas left in my head, I was all clouds. A burning thirst was unraveling my stitching from the inside. I held the clothing to my chest and tried in a fuzzy way to figure out what this jumble of fabrics meant—that my sister was alive out here? That my sister was dead? I clutched what I'd managed to salvage: a small ball. After my battle with Mama Weeds I was tired, tired. Thinking felt like lifting spadefuls of heavy dirt.

As I walked I kept seeing the monster's face: the spheres of grass blown inward and split as easily as bubbles. Her eyes as pure holes. I felt I'd glimpsed then what would happen at the world's end when the stars cracked open. It was not a picture of heaven this Mama Weeds fixed on me like a gaze but something much bigger: a breaking apart, a mindcrush, a red smear pulsing where two black tunnels met; I found I actually couldn't think about it.

I hadn't traveled very far at all when I saw signs of a human presence. Cracked sticks, an empty plastic bottle still dewed with juice. This made sense, I thought, remembering the woman and her nearby shack. But then I saw a black feather, and another. Tiny feathers clinging to a gray net of moss on a trunk.

It's not him, I told myself. There are about a thousand species of birds in our swamp. I didn't run now but pushed forward through the thickets very quickly. I was still hugging what I'd saved from the line. This little yellow triangle of flowers from Mom's old dress. When I looked at it now I wasn't so sure that it had belonged to her dress at all—anyhow, the scrap was so tiny that it just had half a flower on it, the pattern didn't even get a chance to repeat itself. I slid it into one fist and held on to it, punched against the trunks.

In the east the sky throbbed with recurring heat lightning. It was some o'clock. I put on Louis Thanksgiving's jacket, which reached below the crusts of my knees; I unscrolled the old veil that I found in his pocket and tied it around my face. I did this for pragmatic reasons:

an afternoon thundershower was sweeping the prairie and the bugs were all over. I figured the veil would work just as well for me as it had for the early Florida dredgemen to keep the bugs out of my nose and mouth. Out here the mosquitoes were after me for red gallons—you could see clouds of them hanging above the grassland. I'm sure they are still out there hovering like that, like tiny particles of an old, dissolved appetite, something prehistoric and very scary that saturates the air of that swamp. A force that could drain you in sips without ever knowing what you had been, or seeing your face.

Ahead of me, through the tiny squares of the veil, I viewed saw grass for aeons, saw grass with no end in sight. These were the deadlands, the flatlands, I assumed now, the place that the Bird Man had been referring to all along. The plants grew razor-straight, and they were almost twice my height, nine feet tall and fingered with so many tiny knives. Ghost gray or yellowish gray or a dull waspy brown, the colors shifting subtly as clouds passed over them; there was no other variation in any direction on the monotone prairie. The stalks grew out of a calcareous marl, hidden under three feet of water, a soil that crumbles under your weight. My heart sank; my life wasn't going to be long enough to reach the end of this place.

But I walked anyways. I tried not to know that I wasn't going to make it, to undo that knowledge like a knot.

I buttoned Louis Thanksgiving's shirt right up to the collar.

I tightened Ossie's ribbon and I double-knotted the mosquito veil.

I squeezed my mom's scraplet into my fist.

As I walked I told myself a story—I imagined myself as Louis Thanksgiving. I mean I actually pictured myself inside of him. Black hair and swinging elbows. When I closed my eyes I pretended I was Louis, being carried. I could see him rising like a limp balloon into the clouds beneath the birds' beating wings. Through Louis's eyes I saw the dark green tops of the trees, the Argus eyes of the secret lakes and sloughs opening for us as we drifted up. Then Louis Thanksgiving was carried so high that he couldn't see anything besides his own sun-freckled hands. They swung beneath him in two pale green cones of space. The trees vanished. Ice lands whispered up in sulfur curls. The world below him had no rocks, no terrestrial scars, it was fathoms of air and evening blue. The last lakes looked small as stars. Two sets of iron-gray talons dug like prongs into the meat of his shoulders. And I could feel them, under the jacket, eight points of pressure against my sternum.

This wasn't a real possession: I could also feel the mud squeeze into my sneakers, hear thunder. I could fold Louis's thin collar under my fingers and inhale the chalky mosquito wire. I wasn't Ossie, lost in my big trance—I was just myself telling myself a story. But I wouldn't have made it very far without the Dredgeman's Revelation, which distracted me from the pain of sunburn and thirst. If I looked up and saw the buzzards wheeling in the thermals like black motes in a blue eye, I forced myself to relocate my gaze to my sneakers and start again: *The dredgeman had a name, Louis Thanksgiving . . .* My own thoughts were like bad food, so instead I told myself the story of Louis Thanksgiving fishing for bowfin on the deck of the dredge barge, and Louis Thanksgiving lost and happy in the Black Woods, Louis swimming under the wheel with the captain's knife in his mouth, until I became Louis, walking.

Rain began and ended, I don't know how many times. Light faded like water draining into a hole. Through the mosquito veil the endless prairie ordered itself into tiny squares and I kept moving through them. Who knows how long I spent wading through those serrated grasses? I must have recited the Dredgeman's Revelation at least a hundred times forward and backward. I added a new ending: in my version, the dredgeman escaped, and lived. The little hand of a clock sprung back, and Louis Thanksgiving drew breath. The engine room gasped its flames into the wood, and the explosion never happened. Birds shrank away into a fatal yellow moon. Everybody, all the dredgemen, they survived.

At first I didn't understand the scene in front of me: forty-odd yards from where I was standing the line of saw grass ended, and I could see beyond it to maple and bay trees and the brown water of an alligator hole. I was within sight of a sudden elevation—six or seven feet, a spectacular height in this part of the swamp—where the ten-foot-tall stalks sheared away quite suddenly and became dimpled rock. The eternity I'd seen ended as cleanly as if someone had run a scythe through it. I chanced a look at the sky: towering clouds were moving swiftly toward me, as big as white ships. The skies were beautiful here, and empty.

CHAPTER TWENTY-TWO

Kiwi Takes to the Skies

Vijay and Kiwi were ripping Moo Cow creamers for their coffees at the Burger Burger. They kept tossing the crenellated pink containers onto the restaurant table until it looked like a Ken doll had gone on some unmanly daiquiri bender. They'd both ordered the A.M. Delicious! Dollar Breakfast Combo #2: cheddar, sausage, and egg sandwiches. You got what you paid for in this life, said Vijay through a nuclear yellow mouthful of fast-food cheese.

"Sure hope you don't crash today, Bigtree."

"Okay, are you serious? Can we talk about anything else? That is unduly ominous for daybreak."

Kiwi pronounced "ominous" so that it rhymed with "dominoes."

"Huh? *You're* om-in-ohs, bitch. Bro, you're jumping the whole table. Bigtree: is a shark eating you below the waist or something? Calm it down. It's going to be fine."

Kiwi saw that his long legs were indeed bucking the half-moon of their Formica table. The salt and pepper shakers were doing little NBA jumps.

Kiwi was wearing Leo's oxford shirt, even though it was 90 degrees out, to disguise the bruises he'd gotten from his grandfather. He'd thought about trying to pass them off as hickeys from Emily Barton, but he had several on his arms.

Kiwi wished that he could tell Vijay about Grandpa Sawtooth. He kept thinking about the moment when he'd lifted the old man by his frail shoulders and his eyes had widened, full of an animal pain. Even then Kiwi hadn't released him.

They were both sitting on the same side of the booth, as if *they* were copilots of the fast-food rocket ship, Kiwi said, to indigestion and Grade D regret. Kiwi found a crack in the upholstery and started pinching up curly stuffing.

Outside the restaurant window, a bag lady of an advanced, indeterminate age marched forward in front of their window, her face lost in a glassy tangle of curls. Her hair was shockingly white. Red and yellow flags of cloth waved all along her shopping cart like a little parade. She had such an accumulation of crap in there, none of it particularly eye-catching: Kiwi's gaze snagged on a clock radio, a doll with a gouged cheek in a gray and red-ribboned party dress. Enough metal rods to build a really crappy organ. Things so generic that they caused Kiwi a pang; at first he thought he'd recognized them. Bigtree tribal artifacts! he'd thought—really, it was the same junk that every family had.

There was a story that traveled around the islands about a woman named Mama Weeds. A swamp witch. But now Kiwi saw that there were witches everywhere in the world. Witches lining up for free grocery bags of battered tuna cans and half-rotted carrots at the downtown Loomis Army of Mercy. At the bus station, witches telling spells to walls. Only the luckiest ones got to live inside stories. The rest were homeless, pushing carts like this one. They sank out of sight, like the European witches clutching their stones.

"What are you staring at? Are you checking her out?" He peered at the bag lady. "She's a little old for you, Bigtree."

"Bro! No. I'm staring at the, ah. The rods. Sure are a lot of rods in there."

"Rods!" Vijay did his mimicry of a persnickety white man. He started out seriously and then shifted into sniggers, a speech habit of Vijay's where he dropped the mic midsentence and became his own audience. "If you love *rods,* son, you go right ahead. That's your *lifestyle choice . . .*"

"Huh? Oh, right. I forgot. I'm gay. Ha-ha. Very funny."

If you really were gay, Kiwi thought for maybe the thousandth time since he'd arrived at Loomis County, how could you *possibly* live here in

Loomis County? If you were a bookworm, a Mormon, an albino, a virgin; if you were a "reffy" ([n] Loomis slang for a recent immigrant, derivative of "refugee" and used in Loomis night schools as a shorthand for kids with bad clothes, dental afflictions, accents as pure as grain alcohol); if you had any kind of unusual hairstyle, evangelical religion, a gene for altruism or obesity; if you wrestled monsters on an island, like Ava, or conjugated Latin, like he did, or dated the *motherfucking dead,* how could you survive to age eighteen in an LCPS high school?

Ava and Ossie: how would his sisters survive a trip to a high school bathroom, even?

Just that morning Kiwi had found a fanciful lilac Post-it stuck above the faucets of the dormitory john: TO THE ASSHOLE WHO KEEPS BLEEDING IN THE SINK . . .

"You need to have something in your stomach, bro," said Vijay, with the weird brotherly solicitousness that cropped up between them sometimes when nobody else was around. If other dudes were present they stayed gruff and neutral; when girls were in the backseat Vijay treated Kiwi like his mentally challenged ten-year-old cousin, giving him slow, emphatic instructions (Put the *tape* in the *tape deck,* bro . . . *Thank you!*), which Kiwi pretended to hate but somehow didn't exactly mind. *We* are *brothers,* he'd think sometimes in the middle of a volley of "bro"s, pleased that he knew enough about the mainlanders' culture by now to keep this happiness a secret.

"I can't eat," Kiwi said, staring at his thin hands. "I'm going to vomit. What if you do everything right but you vomit your Burger Burger special in the cockpit, do you still pass the test?"

"You'll be fucking fantastic, Bigtree," Vijay said, lying badly and kindly.

"Look, if I go down in flames, turn in my homework for me, okay?"

"Okay." Vijay chewed. "That would suck, though. Who do I give it to?"

"It's under my bed. My night school instructor won't accept late assignments. Miss Voila Arenas—she's kind of a hard-ass. But I bet she will accept it if it's posthumous. Be careful with the toll plaza. I spent, like, sixteen hours on it."

Kiwi had created a scale model of the Golden Gate Bridge out of dry fettuccine. This was a supplement to the actual assignment. The actual assignment had been to describe the Golden Gate Bridge in three paragraphs.

"Good luck up there, Margarita!" Vijay said an hour later when he dropped Kiwi off at the airfield. "Remember you don't got insurance and I'm not going to be the one to spoon-feed you baby food and change your diapers when you shit so *don't crash.*"

"Yeah." Kiwi grinned lamely. "See you."

He would do this, he would get this done. To get a pilot's salary you had to fly a plane. There was no way out but up.

In a Cessna you were soaring, sailing above everything, and a new sense entered the world. All the irregularities retreated into surfaces. Dennis was letting Kiwi do everything this time.

"Okay. Carb heat off, area clear, water rudders up, stick aft.

"Going good. Full power now, watch your nose come up, ease off the back pressure, now you're going to want to accelerate to taxi speed . . . good . . . you ready?"

Kiwi eased the stick forward until it hit 70 and let the plane climb. At 1,000 MSL they hit the cloud bottom. The wind was light and from the north. The sky today was a sea of blues and they flew through cloud wall after cloud wall, bulleting right through the white banks. Tints shifted; the world slid away from them at an angle. The sun made the wings flash tin and gold. Kiwi watched the swell of Coral City, a place he'd never visited. West of Loomis, way out. Rooftops out there made a uniform field of squares as the plane soared higher—brown and mustard and flecks of green quilted the suburbs, while the downtown was mostly eel-flashes of steel and cement white; in the drab center of the city, Kiwi recognized the striking tangerine rooftop of a famous luxury hotel, the Coral Castillo—and everywhere glass flashed, cars moved up the freeway like sluggish blood cells.

His nausea was gone, he realized. His stomach had settled itself somehow, miles above the ground. And then it was happening—Kiwi stared at his two hands moving over the control panel. He was *flying.*

Tailwinds, minor turbulence. The plane sheared gently to the left and clouds veiled the sun; when they emerged the city had vanished. Now they were flying over the saw-grass prairie.

Kiwi was shocked to see how beautiful his home was. This beauty was a secret that the trees had been keeping—the islands looked so different from this altitude. Shining green, shining blue. The sun webbed the mangrove jungle in inky red. Where was Swamplandia!? Kiwi wondered. Distance turned all the tree islands into identical green teardrop shapes—at this altitude you could see how the current's hand had shaped them. You could also see the melaleuca stands, which looked like mildew on bread, gray trees grouped so thickly there was not a breath between them.

They were flying very low—five hundred feet, "dragging the river," Denny called it, to check for sunken logs or boats or other obstructions "that could cause us to swim on a landing, son." Now Kiwi could see the network of Army Corps dams and dikes and levees, which cut up the natural flow of the floodplains from Lake Okeechobee. They looked like Tinkertoys, a small and ambitious child's game—it amazed Kiwi to see the way the river scissored off course or dropped out of sight because of these dikes. He saw hunters' cabins on the banks of remote islands. Kiwi couldn't see any actual alligators, but he sighted dozens of their hairy nests along the bayheads. Now they sheared right and Kiwi saw two Calusa shell middens rising out of the river.

"Look at that." Kiwi touched his forehead to the glass. "What is that thing?"

A woman was standing on the coastline, jumping up and down. Kiwi looked closer, startled: she was waving and waving at them, in some kind of real distress. All he could really make out was the frenzy of her beating arms. Later he'd wonder if something about her movements hadn't seemed familiar to him, even then.

Privately, Kiwi always credited what he did next to Grandpa Sawtooth. If he hadn't won his first fight just yesterday—if he hadn't made a fist and connected with a throat—Kiwi didn't think that the next action he took would ever have occurred to him. But today his body was full of new ideas. Without asking Denny, he began to cut the power.

It was a nerve-jangling ride down—the Cessna came within thirty feet of the treetops, S-turning all the way down to the lake's surface. As the turbulence worsened Kiwi grew steadily calmer. The water he planned to land on was so glassy that he couldn't gauge its depth, but he was going to use the woman as his LVP—the last visual point, the last thing he'd seen to judge his altitude before descending. Incredibly, it seemed like Dennis Pelkis was going to let him do this; Dennis Pelkis was talking him through it: "Seventy mph approach, fifteen hundred rpm—to idle—to LVP, slow to fifty mph, then power to sixteen hundred rpm until touchdown. Power way, way back now . . ." Pull up, pull up, something screamed in Kiwi, wanting to recover the view from the cockpit window—trees were spearing up outside the windows, becoming individual. Slashes of color became streaked and knobbed trunks. There were fish in the lake. Kiwi could see them, individual fish. He turned left just slightly and pulled his nose up when they went gliding onto the water's surface. He straightened out and dropped the bottom rudders. Kiwi heard spray striking the floats, and then it was over: the plane drove hard across the slough, the sun kaleidoscoping through great wheels of water. Kiwi's breathing stopped with the engine.

As soon as he cut the propeller, Kiwi jumped out the cockpit door and waded in front of the seaplane, splashing through water that soaked up to the thighs of his jeans. On the tree island in front of him he saw the wreck—this boat was an antique! It had gone crashing into the black mangroves with enough force to crack several trunks at the knees like scorpion legs; they stood on leafy tiptoe now on the marl. The twenty-foot crane was caught in the canopy, its yellow bucket peering cannily above the fronds. What was the woman screaming at him? It sounded like a foreign language: he heard "C-c-c," and "eee—"

He froze in the water for a moment, trying to understand her. He was still fifty yards away from the shore. *That's my name,* Kiwi realized. The woman was his sister. He went crashing through the mirror of the water toward her, each of them shouting out the other's name like imperfect echoes.

"Terrific landing, son!" Denny was calling behind him. The skin around one eye was puffing tall as bread from where he'd hit the cockpit window while exiting the plane. "One of the best I've seen in my career! Just think of what the papers are going to call you *now.*"

"So let me get this straight—this girl is a relation of yours?"

Osceola was sitting on Denny's cooler lid. A dirty crepe dress frothed over her knees, beneath which long vertical scratches skidded from shin to ankle. She didn't remember how she'd gotten them. She downed half a gallon of water and ate all the candy bars and fruit that Mrs. Pelkis had packed for Denny and she was still hungry, she said, still thirsty.

Kiwi kept hugging her and whispering that everything was okay, wondering if this was true—Ossie looked very sick to him. That thing she had on was their mother's wedding dress, Kiwi noted with a wandering horror. His eyes kept fixing on disturbing new pieces of the picture she made: Ossie's hair was a muddy yellow from the mangrove tannins and her eyes were hollows. Her voice, when it came, was barely a whisper, as if she were afraid the mere act of speech might cause the pilot and her brother to vanish.

"No more water?"

"No, I'm sorry. I'm so sorry, Os. We'll get you more on the mainland."

"I'm going to drink from the faucet. Kiwi, I'm going to drink water for an hour."

"Sure. Come on, get in the shade."

They were on a strip of rocky beach surrounded on all sides by mangroves and thin palms. Dennis "Denny" Pelkis, who seemed somewhat dazed, had waded out to do some kind of make-work maintenance on the plane.

"He left me," she said quietly.

"Who left you? The Chief? What are you doing out here?"

"Louis Thanksgiving. He took me out here and then he left me at the altar."

What she described to Kiwi was the story of a jilted bride: the ghost had proposed to her with a lavish sincerity. He had entered her—forever, she'd thought. When you married a ghost, she explained, you didn't say "till death do us part." Who or what could part you? There was nothing left to part you. No body left to be parted from.

"I'm sorry that didn't work," Kiwi managed to choke out. "But also, I'm not really sorry, you know?"

Kiwi wondered if he could hug Ossie. He was very aware of Dennis Pelkis watching them from the shade of the patchy mangrove saplings, smoking his third or maybe fourth cigarette.

The ghost had taught her how to rig a 5.5-horsepower engine to the back of the dredge scow, how to open the tank vent and move the gearshift lever to neutral, how to set the choke between half and full, adjust the throttle, prime the fuel system by squeezing the flaccid gasline bulb to firmness, how to tie a rope around the engine and pull. The ghost had used her hands to make sure that the dredge barge was firmly attached to the stern of the dredge scow. He had used Osceola's hands to steer.

"You drove that thing by yourself?"

Ossie nodded. "But he was doing the driving through me"—as she spoke she flexed her fingers, her violet eyes squeezed into petals, unreadable—"he possessed my hands on the throttle. At first," she added with the terrible new shyness. "We had an accident. The second day. I lost the bag that had our camp stuff, our food, Louis's old machete, everything went overboard . . . I lost Louis's shirt, the Model Land Company map. Everything, Kiwi. I had to put this dress on, I didn't have anything else."

The dredgeman's ghost had helped her to pilot the boat all the way from Hermit Key to this island—Kiwi had no idea where they were in relation to their home, but Ossie said she'd been following his map toward the Calusa shell mounds. The ghost, she said, was retracing its route. They had been following the canal that the dredge crew had begun digging in 1935 and had failed to complete.

"And then, on our wedding day, Louis left me at the altar. I woke up here alone." She wound what was left of her dress around her fist and shivered a little. "I woke up here so empty, Kiwi. I don't know . . ."

"At the altar . . . ," Kiwi said slowly. He was looking past his sister; his eyes had caught on a frizzled length of rope hanging from the lowest branch of a sweet bay tree. Kiwi watched the rope swaying, almost but not quite sweeping the ground. A fat knot was camouflaged against the trunk, black as a bump on the wood.

Is that how you marry a ghost?

It occurred to him that he was looking at a small noose.

"He was gone and I couldn't finish it . . ."

Ossie stopped talking and gave an angry little shrug, as if refusing to apologize for something she felt terribly about. Waves of wind were moving along the tree line and the rope twisted into complicated shapes, spun out of them.

"Look, I hate to interrupt this . . . this. But you want to tell me exactly what's going on here?"

Denny drew himself up to his full height of five four. He had waded in with a map and a grease-blotched towel that he'd found wedged under the pilot's seat. Outside the cockpit he looked a little like an evicted mole, blinking in the glass glare off the water, and Kiwi wondered what the Philosophy of Denny said about this particular eventuality: a student pilot finding his younger sister in a wedding dress, in the middle of the swamp.

Dennis Pelkis, forty-two-year veteran of the skies around Loomis County, stared at the Bigtrees with a face that flickered between its natural good humor and an uneasiness that was almost fear. Kiwi wondered if it was possible for a man to look less comfortable with a situation. He was wearing his sunglasses, and the swamp grass waved whitely inside them. Sunburn was coloring the lobes of his huge ears.

"My sister was trying to elope with her boyfriend," Kiwi said, staring hard at Denny. "Louis Thanksgiving," he said, because the name seemed to legitimize the scene. Everybody understood a jilting—a soured romance. Everybody liked to hate a pusillanimous groom. "It didn't work out. He's gone now."

"Oh . . . well. Sorry to hear that, young lady. Help is on the way," he mumbled somewhat unconvincingly.

A silence reasserted itself then for a period of seconds, until the air became a still, deepening pool. The rope was twisting and untwisting and whispering something dreadful inside the leaves. Osceola kept staring through the teardrop hoop on the rope into the trees with a vacancy that Kiwi remembered well.

"It's okay," Kiwi said. He kept staring at the rope. He could hear Dennis Pelkis talking in a low voice on his radio. "I promise, Ossie, it's going to be all right. We'll all go home now."

"Kiwi," Ossie said, her voice suddenly tack-sharp. Clouds moved and light caught on a tiny fishhook in her wedding lace. "Have you talked to Ava? Is Ava with the Chief?"

CHAPTER TWENTY-THREE

The End Begins

The alligator's hole was eight feet across. It divided the saw grass prairie that had nearly killed me from the sweet dark shapes of the bay trees. The gap in the grass was the width of an open manhole, a large brown eye of water. A gator had dredged this lake with her claws and was probably swimming invisibly inside it. Flowers like chopped onions covered the surface of the water, which was turbid with mud—a tell that a hole is gator-occupied. I heard a wet swishing in the saw grass behind me and jumped; some warm-blooded, four-legged thing that might have been a bear cub or a wild hog was disappearing into the willow scrub. But I was happy, my heart was bursting with happiness at all the ordinary threats. Pigs and alligators seemed like heaven to me. Creatures of the same mud that we had grown up in, Ossie and Kiwi and I, like our snouty cousins. To my left, a ghostly logger's road looped backward through the mud in the direction I had just come from, a road that I knew better than to walk.

And then I heard my name: "Ava!"

Through the palmetto screen I glimpsed his skin and his hands and his long nose, his shoulder blades, oh I recognized him, dragging our skiff overland. He was wearing the undershirt from the hammock, no coat, and his face looked whiskery and profoundly unmatched to me, indecently arranged, as if his features were floating in jelly. If he was wearing the whistle I couldn't see it. I couldn't get a fix on the gray lights of his eyes, he was still that far away. I ran to the edge of the alligator hole and stopped on my heels. The dark water rippled away from me; the Bird Man was approaching from the treeline, I could hear him; there were no other shadows for miles, nowhere else nearby for me to hide.

"Kid!" he said, and it seemed clear that he had seen me now because he was really *moving*. His long legs flew through the grasses. He was using his machete to hack through the mangle of palmetto scrub. He was—could this be true?—grinning at me. Without thinking I held my nose and jumped.

There have been only eighteen confirmed fatal alligator attacks in Florida since 1948. Nothing to worry about, the Chief tells our tourists. You stay out of a Seth's domain and the Seth leaves you alone. I swam through a brown bloom of mud. I swam hard, my eyes shut against the thick silt, expecting at any moment to graze an alligator's scales with my outstretched hands. I was expecting to hear a splash above me at any minute, the Bird Man diving into the alligator hole. I thought I could hear him calling in a shrunken, watery voice somewhere high above me. This was a true cave in the limestone, nothing that the gator had dug for itself. Now I was maybe six or seven feet below the light pinwheeling on the surface of the hole. I could see a dimmer squint of light at the cave's far end and I swam for it; my reach ended in a wall of mud and decaying plant matter. Long brown grasses swayed in front of me. My hands expected to find the softening carcasses of birds and deer in that mess, or else a sheath of earth—but when I pushed into the decaying weeds, they *yielded*. Grass brushed everywhere against my skin. For a second I felt nothing but slimy green fingers, and then with an ease that shocked me I was clear of them. What I'd thought was a wall was a natural portal, a hole. An aperture in the limestone cave—these holes explain how the largemouth bass and the spade-sized black gambusia can sneak inside an alligator's den. This one was large enough for a small Seth to squiggle into and out of. Weeds and soft rock crumbled around me.

Louis's WPA coat was waterlogged and I couldn't swim well with it on; I ducked my arms out of it, gathered it to my side. I had a new problem now: with the heavy jacket pinned beneath my right arm, I was flailing, kicking frenziedly into the underwater grasses, struggling to find my rhythm. The bundle was becoming so heavy, impossibly heavy, all the drenched clothes dragging at my side like a wing I couldn't beat. And my lungs, my lungs were *bursting.*

The surface was only a few feet above my head, maddeningly close, but still I couldn't reach it. The heavier the bundle got, the more tightly I held on to it, a wrestling instinct. I watched my sister's ribbon flutter up my wrist. Let it drown me, I remember thinking. This cloth was it, I thought, this was the one thing I'd saved. But my arm felt like it was caught in a vise of water and being sucked inexorably down and down and down and then snapped painfully backward. I dove a little myself and tightened my grip on the bundled rags that belonged to my family, to Mom and to Ossie. I couldn't have held on to their real bodies more forcefully. At no point do I remember wanting to let go. When I flipped onto my side, making a panicked grab for my mother's yellow cloth and Louis's sinking coat, I saw the alligator.

The den was rising in front of me again; the thing had gotten ahold of my calf. Dark orange pigment rose everywhere and soon it was too cloudy to see, although I tried—my eyes stung inside a fog that I realized must be plumes of my own blood. Grasses seemed to burst from the rocks, growing feet longer in one blink as I descended. Waving away from me. The alligator was trying to roll me, pulling me backward toward the entrance of the gator hole. I kicked but my calf was still caught—skin tore but I couldn't get loose. Any wrestler knows that once an alligator closes its jaws it's almost impossible to get them open again. Something entered me then and began to swell. My mother, before she died, really was training me to be her understudy, and every Sunday we'd practice the beginning of the Swimming with the Seths act. So I tried to remember what we'd rehearsed in our own Pit, the smooth strokes that carry you to the surface. There is a way to still your body and then slingshot forward in a surprise frog-legged stroke, a Bigtree escape maneuver. Blindly I did this, played possum underwater and then flew forward with a strength that felt far beyond the limits of my small body. I kicked and I was allowed to kick, the pressure vanished, and when I looked the alligator's tail was disappearing into the cave. My calf was freed. Petals of red pain shot through me until my ribs ached, the agonizing pressure expanding in my chest, as round as a sky, and I began to rise like one bubble in a chain. *My skin,* I thought, *is coming apart . . .*

Somehow my body's stitching held. I broke the skin of the water and started breathing again. The deep bright air of our world, I gulped, the scouring air, I kept on gasping. I had never tasted the scattered light in the air before, or pulled it into my mouth with my entire body, even my cycling feet. It felt like the sky had descended to my eye level. Air floated toward me, ghostly and wet, and turned to fire the instant it hit my raw lungs. For a long time the whole world was just oxygen—the lowered heaven of this sky and the explosions of my breath. Then the buoyant and obliterating force inside me began to wane, and my own thoughts crept back in around its edges. I saw that I was bobbing in a gray lake I didn't recognize. Ferns dripped onto its surface. At a certain point I realized that my two hands must be empty, because I was swimming.

The Bird Man, if he'd seen me, didn't follow me through the underwater tunnel. For close to an hour I hid on a mangrove island, hunched next to ibis and anhingas, waiting to see if he'd swim up. After that, I crawled forward on the branches until I found land that would hold my weight.

I checked myself for damage: I had a shallow bite on my calf, that was all. I'd gotten hurt far worse during our staged fights in the Pit. (In fact, the wound looked so relatively puny to me that I didn't treat it; it's a wonder I escaped infection.) It bled a lot at first, but I elevated it on a rock, rested. Adrenaline cured the sting of it. I wasn't scared now; my insides still held the space of the shape my mom had filled. I'd lost everything, all the clothes, even the ribbon on my wrist.

I'd been following a gator haul because I couldn't find any other road out of the slough and the matted brush gave me the easiest passage. Everywhere I felt sore and cruddy, my crotch was burning, the skin on my face came off in white peels when I rubbed at it. When I exited the slough and stood in the grasses I began shivering everywhere, as if my skin were doing its own jolly imitation of the wind-bucked water. Getting my shoes to move on land felt like lifting buckets. Yellowish gray clouds of palmetto scrub wasped away to sticks beneath me. The gator haul petered into water and then I *heard* them, I heard snatches of a human conversation. Someone real on a walkie-talkie. Two wood storks watched incuriously from a high branch as I crashed through a pitch pond of water lilies and hurtled toward what I hoped were real voices. Through the leaves I could see the distinctive dun and olive braid of a ranger's uniform.

Frogs pushed their buffoon throats at me from various heights in the trees in their primordial vaudeville, and I remembered to call back to the voices: "Here! I'm over here!"

As it turned out, I'd been right about one thing: the men I'd seen on the tree island were very much alive. When I'd screamed two days ago on the slough, before the Bird Man got my jaws shut, these men had heard me. The ranger who found me brought me to meet them at the station, my heroes, so that I could thank them: two peckerwood guys sitting on the hard chairs, their cheeks flushed and stubbled. One of them had a haircut like a mushroom cap and nervous snowpea eyes and a cleft chin that made him look a little like Superman, or Superman's sort of squirrelly twin. His friend was about a decade older and balding, with a kind, turkey-wattled face, a shirt so thin and gray it looked like dried sweat to me—not that I was in a position to judge anybody's fashion or hygiene.

"Here she is, boys!" said the ranger (whose name I can't remember now—he was a new recruit, decades younger than Whip). The way he said it, I felt a little like a trophy alligator he had just trussed and dropped onto the blond wood of his desk for these hunters' perusal, a creature routed from its hole. I must have looked like one, too, with my soaked and torn clothing and the reddish mud that had rinsed even my teeth and gums.

The men nodded; the younger one shifted on his tailbone, and the larger, older hunter kept frowning slightly and repeatedly wetting his lips. I crossed my blood- and filth-encrusted arms over my chest and stared back at them. The ranger had offered me a shower on the boat ride over and I'd said no without thinking. He'd seemed surprised, so I'd explained myself—showers were hated chores for me at home, I said, where I had been a kid.

"Who are you?" I said, although I'd meant to say "thank you."

"Trumbull," said the older one.

"Harry," said the younger one.

"Ava," I said, pointing at myself, and the herky rhythms of this exchange felt a little like a show I'd seen on Grandpa's TV about apes who'd learned to fingerpaint the alphabet.

When they weren't hunting Harry and Trumbull worked the grave-yard shift in a prosthetics plant in Ocala. They'd dabbled in greyhound racing, hibiscus farming, migrant strawberry picking, the military, fairground "barbering." Gator hunting was something they'd done together since they were runts. Trumbull was the engine for their two-some, the talker, and his talk kept picking up speed, as if his big voice were on a downhill slope. Harry, who kept glancing at him, seemed to be the brakes.

They had a camp they returned to every July over on the rock glades about a mile before the Calusa shell mounds, and they wouldn't have been out nearly so far if they hadn't found their usual campsite's water pump bent like a hairpin and decided to press on. Not once had they seen another person out that way, not ever in their fifteen years of rambling. We kept exchanging this fact between us until it gleamed gold and I was almost blinded in that tiny room, I felt so lucky.

"It was just the *purest* coincidence . . . ," Harry, the younger one, kept saying. "When Trumbull tells me he thought he seen a little *girl* out there, well . . . !"

Trumbull and Harry started shaking their heads in alternating rhythms. I felt my head beginning to join in, stopped it. I was still shocked by the cool and even feel of tile under my bare feet; the ranger had taken my ruined shoes from me, and was making some quiet arrangement on the telephone in the next room.

"You guys surprised me, too. I thought you guys were ghosts," I offered. I stood on the fault line of the men's laughter and everybody seemed surprised when I started laughing along with them. For a second I had a flutter of the old after-show feeling and I thought, *Oh my God, what if it's really over?*

At that juncture, I wasn't talking about the Bird Man. The ranger didn't ask me any questions about how I'd wound up on the drift slough, and I didn't know what I was supposed to volunteer.

"When you go back to your camp," I asked them, "will you keep an eye out for a red alligator? She's a Seth from my family's alligator-wrestling park. She has this, ah, this special condition, I don't think it's a mutation, exactly, my brother will know . . ."

Harry made a little noise in his throat and looked around the room, like he wished the ranger would come back.

"Now you are not going to believe this . . ." The ranger returned from his desk with two more water bottles for me and a funny expression, a grimace that kept itching up toward a grin and collapsing. It made me think of a bent fishing rod, as if his mood were some monster fish that he couldn't reel in.

"You said your name is Ava Bigtree? Do you by any chance have a relative named Oh-see-oh-la? Because *she* got picked up not five miles from where we found you, kid. They got her just this morning . . ."

He slid a paper toward me: NOTICE JULY 29 SEARCH AND RESCUE UPDATE, BIGTREE, OSCEOLA RECOVERED BY SEAPLANE PILOT . . .

My eyes flew down the column and came to rest on the little ledges of their names: "Bigtree, Osceola" and "Bigtree, Kiwi."

"I would love to hear what you girls thought you were doing out there," the pale ranger said, raising a scabby eyebrow at the gator hunters. Harry stared at Trumbull with a hangdog expression, as if to say that he'd been ready before they even got here to *go,* and Trumbull, who was eating a bag of white potato straws that he'd purchased from the vending machine near the latrine, didn't have a lot to add. He read a few lines and shrugged.

"That's a funny name," said Trumbull, jawing on a potato straw. "Bigtree. What were you all doing way out here? Family vacay-shun, or something?"

Kiwi, Ossie, and an older white couple named Mr. and Mrs. Pelkis were waiting for me at the ferry dock. We talked over one another while the older couple watched from the dock's edge, babbling about Seths and Louis Thanksgiving and the Chief in what must have sounded like a foreign language—behind us, Mrs. Pelkis started sobbing for some reason, her husband loudly shushing her. And I folded into my sister's grief and heat. My brother's wet face. I kept closing my fingers around the secret, enfleshed stones of their wrist bones and breathing in the strange smells of them—Ossie's mangrove dank and Kiwi's hotel scent of aftershave and shampoo—to verify that they were truly alive.

Nobody spoke on the car ride into Loomis. Kiwi had written out directions to the place where our dad was staying, the Bowl-a-Bed hotel, on a card from Mrs. Pelkis's purse. After that brief exchange with us, she'd slammed a cassette of classical music into the tape deck with the attitude of someone turning a door lock. The huband, Dennis Pelkis, was snapping blue gum like he was trying to generate electricity or something. I'd been testing him: every time I asked a question he put another stick of blue gum in his mouth, which meant he had four sticks in there right now. Which was fine by me—nobody seemed capable of speech just then. Ossie and Kiwi watched the rainfall through their respective windows, and because I was squeezed in the middle and I didn't have a window I watched the changes on their faces.

The farms came first. The Seths' country gave way to green and yellow tractors that looked like imperial carriages on their huge tires, and great gusty sprinklers throwing water everywhere. We passed the last gas station before the city began in earnest and Osceola started to cry a little. I leaned over her and pushed the lock down on the car door.

The whole time I was thinking about the buoyancy that saved me. I know that I am a pretty biased interpreter of the events that led to my escape, but I believe I met my mother there, in the final instant. Not her ghost but some vaster portion of her, her self boundlessly recharged beneath the water. Her courage. In the cave I think she must have lent me some of it, because the strength I felt then was as huge as the sun. The yellow inside you that makes you want to live. I believe that she was the pulse and bloom that forced me toward the surface. She was the water that eased the clothes from my fingers. She was the muscular current that rode me through the water away from the den, and she was the victory howl that at last opened my mouth and filled my lungs. I didn't want to tell my sister anything about this in the Pelkises' car—I didn't see how I could manage it with words—but I wished I could at least give Ossie a picture of where I had been, what had been in me. I wished she could bob with me for one second in that air. Black bay trees had lined the sky behind the lake and I was furiously alive around the bubble of our mother.

Was that fullness what Ossie had meant when she talked about her possessions? If so then I had been very wrong, I decided. I was wrong to have laughed at her in our bedroom, in the beginning, back when we'd said that her ghosts weren't real, or her love.

The road spun behind us like something the car was secreting, yards and yards of black filament. I reached over and squeezed my sister's hand.

"Hey," I said. "I believe you."

The bowling lanes at the Bowl-a-Bed hotel stay open until 2:00 a.m. From the lobby, you could hear the belly-growl of the balls hurtling down the lanes and the clatter of the pins. The Bowl-a-Bed's bellhop and concierge was a ghoulish young man wearing orange-and-ruby bowling shoes on his size 13 feet. He was a kid, younger than Kiwi, with braces and thick black eyebrows, eyebrows so muscular and expressive they looked almost prehensile to me. They shot up when he saw us.

Ossie and I stood before him with mud-stiffened hair falling into our burned faces. I was shivering inside the ranger's long T-shirt, and she had on one of Mrs. Pelkis's kitten-printed nightgowns. Our faces in the lanes 1–9 scoreboard glass looked sewn onto our necks with scratches. Kiwi at least was wearing zippered pants.

"No bags?" the bellhop asked us with a practiced little smirk. His big shoes waggled on the desk.

"Fuck you, clown," said my brother with astonishing ease. Ossie and I exchanged glances; he'd lost his accent. "Tell us where Samuel Bigtree is staying."

The Chief was in room 11, just behind the last gutter-ball alley. This would have warranted a joke at some earlier Bigtree epoch but we were BE now, Beyond Exhaustion, and I just wanted to see my dad. The stunned bellhop had given Kiwi a little key, which he turned in the pale blue door to room 11 with a just-audible click.

"Stee-rike!" Kiwi whispered. Then he called out, "Dad. It's us."

On the car ride over, Kiwi had told me in a slow and urgent voice that he was sure the park would go into foreclosure. We would lose our home, the Seths. But it was going to be okay, he kept saying, it would really be okay, because he was almost a pilot and the Chief had a job and we would find an apartment on the mainland . . .

My father's face filled the door frame and his shock was a wonderful thing to behold. The whole hotel was filled with bowlers' thunder at that hour. Pins were falling everywhere around us and I watched my dad's eyes widen to take us in. When my father stepped forward it didn't matter that we were nowhere near our island. All of us, the four of us—the five of us if you counted Mom inside us—we were home. We were a family again, a love that made the roomiest privacy that I have ever occupied.

"Good night, Ossie."

"Good night, Ava."

After a little while I could hear my sister breathing beside me. My father and my brother were snoring in a duel or a duet on the other side of the wall. There had been, as you might imagine, quite a scene between them. Kiwi told us that he'd been working at the World of Darkness for two months and this fact didn't make a dent. The Chief, holding Osceola, had thanked and thanked my brother for finding her until Kiwi grew embarrassed. He pretended to hawk up a wad of phlegm so that he had an excuse to grab tissues for his eyes.

I'd told the Chief about a dream I'd had on Swamplandia!—a great tree had swallowed him, his knuckles sunk into the tree bark—and he listened with such a frightened, pained expression that I stopped talking. So I didn't tell my dad about the Bird Man, or Louis Thanksgiving, or the red Seth, or Mama Weeds. What we did talk about was Mom: "I found her dress out there, Dad. I found it, but I lost it again. I think Mom was with me when I battled the Seth . . ."

The Chief gave me an anguished look. His hand gripped my forearm too tightly, as if he were afraid that any one of us might flash without warning from the room.

"That's okay. That's okay, Ava. They found you, your brother found your sister, that's much better than an old dress, I'm sure."

But that night the Chief wasn't in a talking mood. He looked huge and sad on the horned edge of the hotel bed, which had that goofy look of all "fancy" motel furnishings, cheap wood with stupid designs. The wallpaper nudged its quiet spirals upward toward the ceiling fan. We all looked caged in that hotel room. We watched a sitcom on TV and whenever the canned laughter tumbled into the silence of the room, I wanted to roar. *Turn it off,* I thought, but we were all a little afraid to. We watched the TV family speak their lines to one another as if we were trying to remember how to do it, talk. One on one we probably could have spoken, but the four of us together went mute.

"Did you want to go bowling, girls?" the Chief said at one point, his voice unnaturally loud and cheerful. "Ten free frames. There's a coupon for a game on the desk, comes with the room . . ."

"No thanks," we said in one voice. Ossie didn't have a change of clothes, she said.

"Where's your purple skirt?" I asked, gulping against an icy vision of the clothesline. "Where's Louis's jacket?"

"I don't know." She looked at me strangely. "Back in the swamp, I guess—I lost a bag overboard on the second day." I started to tell her about Mama Weeds, stopped. Now that I was fed and watered and sitting on bedsheets, that whole part of my journey seemed filmy, impossible. Already I'd lost my pet alligator, Louis's jacket, Ossie's ribbon, Mom's dress; I was afraid that if I shared this out loud I'd lose even the story.

The Chief made many weary, angry phone calls about the day's events to "straighten these mainlanders out." News stations were desperate to talk to my brother, Dennis Pelkis said on the telephone— "Hell's Angel strikes again!"—but Dennis reported proudly that he wasn't giving them our number. Then the Chief had to set up a meeting with the ranger who found me and a social worker for Monday, at some foreboding address inside the cold stones of downtown Loomis.

No, it turned out the Chief wasn't angry at me at all. Not for a second, he said, not even when I lowered my voice and explained to him that I had lost Ossie. When I asked him about Swamplandia! and foreclosure and the Seths and his mainland job, he didn't exactly answer. He was very proud of us, was his reply, the tribe of us. "We are going to the island tomorrow," he promised. "We'll put everything in order."

The Chief borrowed forty dollars from Kiwi and rented an adjacent room for me and Ossie, lucky 13, where we were supposed to shower and then sleep, impossibly, in beds. An hour after we turned out the lights, I woke myself up. I stared around the featureless space with my heartbeat stinging me and tried to figure out where I was. I watched a body stand and raise one curtain to half-mast, so that the dark rolled out of the room. The curtains turned the color of weak tea, one droning hallway bulb behind them. My sister! I couldn't quit rubbing at my eyes.

"You okay?" Ossie walked over to my bed. Like me, she was quilted with rashes and burn; she'd showered for close to an hour and her skin had a scoured look. She had lost weight in her arms and her cheeks, which gave her face a crop of new hollows.

"You were laughing in your sleep, Ava."

I reached out and grabbed her warm wrist with Bigtree Wrestling Grip 7. Slowly I remembered that I wasn't in the swamp anymore, that we had made it to the Bowl-a-Bed hotel, a place with color TVs and a confectionery of miniature, jewel-colored soaps and shampoo-plus-conditioners and comforters that smelled reassuringly of ordinary vices: old pepperoni pizza, draft beer, Vaseline, cigarettes.

"It's okay now, Ava. I'm right here, all right?"

"Ossie?" For a second I didn't believe it was really her. She touched my forehead. She touched me as if she were Mom, as if I were a child again back on the island and sick with fever, or even just pretending. Our mom, as stern and all-seeing as she could often seem, would do us this great favor of pretending to be credulous when we faked sick. Mom cooed sincerely over our theatrical moanings and coughs. She would push our hair back from our cool liar's scalps and bring us noodles and icy mainland colas as if happy for an excuse to love us like this.

"Was the ghost real, Ossie?" I asked her sleepily.

"I thought so."

"Okay. Is the ghost back, though?"

"I'm not going anywhere," she told me that night. But until we are old ladies—a cypress age, a Sawtooth age—I will continue to link arms with her, in public, in private, in a panic of love.

I don't believe in ghosts anymore, either. Not the kind from Ossie's book. I think something more mysterious might be happening, less articulable than any of the captioned and numeraled drawings in *The Spiritist's Telegraph*. Mothers burning inside the risen suns of their children.

After my mom died, I used to have these dreams where I arrived to clean out the Pit and found a stadium filled with hissing, booing tourists. Nothing was right about this show: the Seths were gone and the Pit itself had mutated into an opaque, roiling pool. I realized that I had scheduled Mom's show and forgotten to cancel it. Now she was dead and the crowd was enraged. Some people threw bottles. With the irrefutable logic of dreams I knew that I would have to replace Mom on the board. As I climbed the ladder I had the worst case of stage fright because what was I supposed to do after diving? What would happen to me when I followed her down the pickled stars on the green board, and jumped? The next moment was unimaginable. The water bulged beneath me and even in dreams my mind failed to tell my mind what was inside it.

Sometimes I worry that what I did with the Bird Man happened because I really wanted it to. And what if it happens forever, Ossie, I'd ask my sister, the bad laughter of that summer? Like a faucet we left running, a sound we have forgotten we are making. Sometimes I hear the crying of strange birds outside the grates of my apartment window and I wonder. Even deep inland, I still worry that he might be one empty lot over. For our first six months in Loomis County I couldn't sleep.

"It's over," the Chief kept saying when we found each other in the Bowl-a-Bed hotel, his showman's voice partially whited out by the falling pins, "period, the end."

And on a calendar that summer really is over, I guess. Full stop. Ossie and I attended a public school in the fall where they made us wear uniforms in the dull sepias and dark crimsons of fall leaves, these colors that were nothing like the fire of my alligator's skin. But things can be over in horizontal time and just beginning in your body, I'm learning. Sometimes the memory of that summer feels like a spore in me, a seed falling through me. Kiwi is sympathetic, but Ossie is the only one who I can really talk to about this particular descent.

Unlike me, Osceola spent that first year on the mainland sleeping like a paralytic in our new apartment bedroom and going nowhere at night, never entertaining a single ghost. Her "powers" did not interest her anymore, because she was drugged. When we started at Rocklands High, a psychiatrist put Ossie on a variety of helpful, beekeeping-type medications, yellow and root-beer brown tablets that were supposed to thin the ghostly voices in her head to a pleasant drone. "Let's try Osceola on this prescription," he said confidently. "I get great results with patients I try on this medication." And I remember that the verb "to try" in relation to my sister really bothered me, as if the psychiatrist had magical dice that he could keep rolling until we got a saner version of Ossie. I remember her doctor's office as a logged woods of glossy oak end tables, sofas, "antique" chairs. It did not strike me or impress me in the least. Loomis was just like this. Our new apartment was carpeted and wallpapered in rusty browns, a palette that reminded me of dead squirrels. I don't know if those pills helped my sister. Like me, I think that eventually Ossie simply figured out how to occult her own deep weirdness, to shuffle quietly down the chutes of our school hallways.

One regret that I still keep alive is that I never showed anybody the red Seth. Not even Ossie; why didn't I tell Ossie or Kiwi about the miraculous hatchling right away? Sometimes I'll let myself wonder: Where might she be right now, if she survived? In what cave or slough, on what grassless island? It's an unlikely idea but it's not impossible. Alligators in the wild can live for seventy years, and possibly even longer. By now she would have reached her full adult weight and length. Maybe she swam back to the island that we used to call Swamplandia! and is floating her scarlet eyes around our old canals. When I'm awake, I can't seem to draw a stable picture of the red Seth in my mind's eye anymore—it feels like trying to light a candle on a rainy night, your hands cupped and your cheeks puffed and the whole wet world conspiring to snatch the flame away from you. But in a dream I might get to see the part of the swamp where her body washed up, bloated and rippling, or where she escaped to, if the dream was beautiful.

I think the Chief was right about one thing: the show really must go on. Our Seths are still thrashing inside us in an endless loop. I like to think our family is winning. But my brother and my sister and I rarely talk about it anymore—that would be as pointless as making a telephone call to say, "Kiwi, are you there? Listen: my blood is circulating," or, "Howdy, Ossie, it's today, are you breathing?" We used to have this cardboard clock on Swamplandia! and you could move the tiny red hands to whatever time you wanted, NEXT SHOW AT __:__ O'CLOCK!

Acknowledgments

During the years that I spent lost in the swamp, sometimes the only thing that kept me pushing forward was the thought of making it to this acknowledgments page. It's a joy at last to get to thank the following people:

Huge love and gratitude to: Karina Schmid, Alexis Vgeros, Sharon Bowen, Victoria Bourke, Christopher Shannon, Jessica MacDonald, Kate Hasler-Steilen, Laura Storz, Stefan Merrill Block, Lucia Giannetta, Jess Fenn, Scott Snyder, Stu MacDonald, Dan Chaon, J. R. Carpenter, Stephen O'Connor, Bradford Morrow and *Conjunctions,* Karen and Jim Shepard, Andrea Barrett, Barry Goldstein, Larry Raab, François Furstenberg, Sam Swope, Andrea Libin and John High, Rivka Galchen, John Tresch, Putney Student Travel and my Putney kids, Becky Campbell and the staff at Symphony Veterinary Center, and to my teachers, my former classmates, and my students, for being a solar source of inspiration.

To Carey McHugh, Kim Tingley, Lytton Smith, Michael White, Brandon Freeman, Lauren Russell, Kent Russell, Vince Ruiz—thank you to the moon for being my first readers and for the lifeline of your friendship. And thanks to Rob, Carey, New Rob, and Russell Haus for my many fellowship stints on your fine sofas. If I could somehow make this page interactive, I'd give each of you an ovation and a Cadillac.

I'm very grateful to the UCross Foundation, the Corporation of Yaddo, and the Dorothy and Lewis B. Cullman Center for Scholars and Writers at the New York Public Library, Jean Strouse, and my fellow Fellows for the wonderful gift of time and community. Special thanks to Mary Ellen von der Heyden for her friendship and generous support.

ACKNOWLEDGMENTS

Enormous thanks to my incredible agent, Denise Shannon, and to my boundlessly encouraging editor, Jordan Pavlin, for their faith in me and for their tremendous help with revisions. Thanks to the great Leslie Levine and the staff at Knopf. And to the brilliant and indefatigable fiction editor Carin Besser, for parachuting into this novel and helping me to find a way through—*thank you.*

This book is dedicated to my parents, Janice and Bruce Russell, with all my love and with a special thank-you to my dad for helping me with the Florida research; to my bro and my sis; to Alan and Fran Romanchuck; and in loving memory of Alex Romanchuck. The Bigtrees' story owes a huge debt to many authors but especially to Katherine Dunn, George Saunders, and Kelly Link. And a final thank-you to the readers of this book.

A NOTE ABOUT THE AUTHOR

Karen Russell, a native of Miami, has been featured in *The New Yorker*'s debut fiction issue and on *The New Yorker*'s 20 Under 40 list, and was chosen as one of *Granta*'s Best Young American Novelists. In 2009, she received the 5 Under 35 Award from the National Book Foundation for excellence in fiction writing for writers under thirty-five years of age. Her short story collection, *St. Lucy's Home for Girls Raised by Wolves*, was published by Knopf in 2006 and released in paperback in 2007 by Vintage. It was named a best book of the year by the *San Francisco Chronicle, Los Angeles Times,* and *Chicago Tribune.* Her short fiction has appeared in *The New Yorker, Granta, Oxford American, Tin House, Zoetrope: All-Story,* and *Conjunctions.* Three of her short stories have been selected for the *Best American Short Stories* volumes (2007, edited by Stephen King; 2008, edited by Salman Rushdie; and 2010, edited by Richard Russo). She has taught creative writing at Columbia University and Williams College and is currently writer-in-residence at Bard College.

A NOTE ON THE TYPE

The text of this book was set in Garamond No. 3. It is not a true copy of any of the designs of Claude Garamond (ca. 1480–1561), but is an adaptation of his types, which set the European standard for two centuries. It probably owes as much to the designs of Jean Jannon, a Protestant printer working in Sedan in the early seventeenth century, who had worked with Garamond's romans earlier, in Paris, but who was denied their use because of Catholic censorship. Jannon's matrices came into the possession of the Imprimerie nationale, where they were thought to be by Garamond himself, and were so described when the Imprimerie revived the type in 1990. This particular version is based on an adaptation by Morris Fuller Benton.

Composed by Creative Graphics, Allentown, Pennsylvania

Printed and bound by Berryville Graphics, Berryville, Virginia

Designed by Wesley Gott